Suspicion's Gate

Tamara Brigham

Cover Design by: Tamara Brigham; SA-kuva

Published by:
Tamara Brigham
PO Box 151
Clearlake, CA 95422

Printed and bound in the United States of America

First Edition

ISBN # 9781732002449

*ᚹ*ᚹ*
For Kate…
…without whom this would not have been written
*ᚹ*ᚹ*

Chapter 1
July 2, 1943

D arkness.

Darkness and a deafening crunch underfoot.

Labored breathing, echoed back beneath that, and the pounding of blood pushed through constricted veins by desperate exertion, loud enough that surely those fleeing together could hear and bear witness to the wash of terror they were each forced to ignore.

They ran, ran as fast as their legs could propel them through the forest, focused on their own personal fears and the dangers of this night, dangers all around them. There was no time to be concerned, no reason to care, about what the others felt. Self-preservation was what mattered.

The snapping of twigs and branches that clawed and raked as they pushed through the undergrowth, striving to increase the distance between themselves and the baying of dogs and shouts of men on the scent of prey somewhere behind them.

Around them.

On and on, seeming to stretch out towards eternity, as if running through the darkness was the only existence he had ever known, with one thought throbbing beneath the pain behind his eyes.

Someone must have ratted…but who?

Coughing. Newt should not have come. But he was keeping pace, and who could blame him for his choice to come? Was the New Zealander at any greater risk of dying out here than he was in a place where the necessary medical treatment could never be guaranteed, could be withheld for the pettiest reason, or for no reason at all? Where a man might be caught with a bullet in his back just for breathing?

Voices, louder now. Nearer. German voices. The flash and rip of machine gun fire flared through the shadow gaps in the foliage to their right, but the bullets whizzed harmlessly by.

This time.

"Shit, that was close," Newt hissed through another suppressed, wracking cough.

"Too damn close," muttered Paddy under his breath as he kept a grip on Newt's arm and pulled him along. Trickles of sweat were wiped away before it made it into straining eyes. He kept running.

The fingers of summer trees whipped cheeks and temples, causing eyes to tear and skin to burn, but it did not matter. Such a discomfort was infinitely better than taking a bullet. Better than going back.

From the left came a vague change in perception as the spotlight from the southeast corner of Stalag 31 traced a long, smoky arc in its search for the escapees.

Steel fingertips dug into an arm, yanked one man to the ground. "Get down."

Under any other circumstance, Paddy would have flattened any man daring to treat him so roughly and rudely. But not Buck. Never Buck. It did not matter that Buck was no Irishman. Nathaniel Buckman was a leader, their chosen leader. Paddy would never strike a man he had chosen to follow, not without a damn good reason.

Particularly when the act may have just kept him from getting his head blown from his shoulders.

"Bitch did this…"

The hot-headed, chestnut-haired Aussie was probably right, but it was Skip's own fault for not knowing enough to avoid bedding the enemy…or the enemy's wife. If she had tipped off their keepers to their plans, Skip had only himself to blame. Who else could have told her? How else could she have known? How else could the soldiers know? The man needed to learn to think with something other than his dick. One way or another, each man thought as they tried to pinpoint the baying of the dogs, this night should teach Skip a much-needed lesson.

The six lay still upon the ground or crouched tensely until the searching white eye passed its beam over their position. It was tempting to remain there, to rest, to catch their breath in the first moments of freedom any of them had experienced in months. But this was not freedom. Not yet. Their pursuers continued to draw closer, providing impetus to run again.

"Go."

Buck's command was obeyed.

The sounds of pursuit were nearer on their right than elsewhere. "Follow me," called Etienne, his local accent thick with tension. The other five followed without question as he veered away from the closing voices.

A second burst of muzzle flash to the right, close enough to smell. Behind Paddy, Buck gave a single, sharp yelp.

"Colonel!" cried one voice in their midst.

"Keep moving..."

They broke into a clearing.

Newt's voice in the dark. "Too many, Colonel, we'll never..."

"We will," the Frenchman interjected. "Keep..."

Paddy drew up short, stopped by the emergence of a uniformed figure from the bushes directly in front of them. The soldier looked as surprised to see him as Paddy was. With a growl and lunge, Etienne's assurances were cut short. Paddy caught the intruder, causing the man to drop the rifle he carried. With a single, abrupt movement, the Irishman's big hands closed around the soldier's throat. Twisted.

"Idiot."

The body crumpled to the forest floor as the snap ricocheted around the clearing. Behind them, the dogs howled.

"Maybe we should split..." Newt suggested through another stifled gasping cough.

Buck nodded. "Etienne, you and Jamie come with me...we'll buy you three time..."

"Keep going through the trees until you reach the river," the Frenchman directed, pointing. "Follow it north. You're almost there."

"Colonel..."

"Go, Henderson...that's an order."

Skip reluctantly obeyed, knowing that, as the habitual escapee in camp, he could not afford to be caught again. Sooner or later von Hauser would kill him for it. Especially if he learned of the Aussie's affair with his wife.

Paddy disappeared into the trees on the southern edge of the clearing with Newt in tow. Buck led the others, doubling back towards the prison and the sound of approaching soldiers. The hints of the chase were closer now, close enough to smell. Without the risk they were taking, the blood trail Buck was leaving to draw the dogs, the others would never stand a chance.

There was the crack of a single pistol shot. Skip turned as he reached the line of trees, to see Etienne stumble and go down. Jamie instinctively dropped to the man's side, heedless of the dangers to himself. When his balaclava proved inhibitive to his abilities to tend the man, he yanked it from his head and tossed it aside. The bullet had caught the Frenchman's thigh, certainly not life-threatening but something Jamie could not tend under these conditions. Not with the Germans so close. Not if they wanted to keep moving. He ripped a strip of fabric from his shirt and hastily bound the man's wound. The Canadian doctor's blonde hair caught in the glow of the German torches. A soldier raised his gun.

Buckman leaped between the marksman and his intended target. Another flash and crack and Skip watched the Colonel drop to the earth like a sack of wet flour. Jamie's head whipped around, drawn by the sound, and caught sight of the colonel as the man fell.

With Paddy and Newt far ahead of him now, and Jamie about to be recaptured no matter what else happened, the loyal, duty-bound officer instinct forced Skip to return to their fallen leader's side. Etienne tied off the bandaging on his leg and was applying pressure to his wound to stop the bleeding while Jamie scrambled across the damp earth to kneel over Buck.

Outrunning the Germans was no longer an option.

Jamie knew the severity of the injury at once. With blood bubbling at the corners of the man's mouth and from his nose, with the amount of blood staining his grungy gray shirt at both the shoulder and low on his chest, the medic gauged that the second bullet, at least, had shredded its way through the man's lung and possibly out the back of his body. It was a miracle Jamie had not been struck as well. The man's breathing was raspy and thin and slowing with each second that passed.

"Don't…" Buck grasped Jamie's wrist with what little strength he had as the doctor began to rip the colonel's shirt away to view the damage up close.

Crashing down beside them, Skip cuffed Jamie across the head. "What the fuck do you think camouflage is for…?"

Jamie ignored him, his attention instead on witnessing Buck's breath seep from his body. The man twitched, convulsed, and was still.

The pursuing soldiers crashed into the clearing and formed an impenetrable ring around them. Skip was only aware of them on the edges of his perceptions. His anger, at Jamie, at her, at himself, overrode every other instinct. The only thing he noticed was that Renz, the Italian forced to serve in this hell-hole, and Doctor Dengler were leading the search team. That, at least, gave them a better chance of surviving this night.

"Don't move."

The English words spoken by the only Italian soldier in the camp were heavily accented but understandable. The words that followed, however, the Italian-accented German barked to the soldiers and doctor, were less clear. Another order, it seemed, as four of the Germans, those with the dogs, broke away and resumed running towards the river after the other two escapees.

The Aussie and Canadian could only hope that Paddy and Newt had made it to the river and were out of harm's way.

Doctor Dengler stepped closer, eyes scanning the awkwardly sitting villager, the mayor's son, Dengler knew, and then glanced at the other fallen man.

"Keep your bloody butchering hands off…" the Aussie growled, prepared to lunge across Buck's body to tackle the doctor if the man tried to touch their commander.

"Nothing you can do," Jamie said quietly. Nothing anyone could do. Though he was looking at Dengler as he spoke, his words were directed at Skip. The Aussie turned his fury back onto Jamie when he realized what the Canadian had said.

"You bastard!"

One of the German's knocked Skip off balance with the butt of his rifle as the Aussie moved, preventing his attack on Jamie.

"Silence," the handsome Italian ordered as Dengler distanced himself from the fury of Skip's flailing fists and knelt to examine the Frenchman's injury.

"He'll live, but I need to get him inside to treat him properly."

"Get him home," Jamie suggested, knowing, as all of the residents of Stalag 31 did, that if they wanted any consideration and favors at all, Renzo Moretti was their best chance. "He's not part of this; we found him after we got out, made him lead us…"

An argument ensued between the German doctor and Italian Sturmbannfuhrer, words in German that Skip did not understand. Jamie pried Buck's fingers from his wrist, aware of the still seething fury beneath Skip's silent surface. He did not want to be the target of that rage, but when it was released, he knew it was better for him to be the recipient than for Skip to turn his ire on the Germans. To attack any of their captors, or Moretti, could mean instant death. He hoped the Aussie was thinking clearly enough to realize that as well.

Finally, Moretti waved one hand and two soldiers assisted Dengler in getting the Frenchman to his feet to drag him in the direction of Ste Marie sur Canut. Etienne glanced back at Jamie and nodded with a look that offered both reassurance and apology. He was a smart, clever man, whom Jamie trusted, but neither could guess the fate awaiting them this night.

There were more commands in German before the Italian returned his attention to his captives and the dead man between them. Hands bound behind his back, Jamie gave no resistance; it would be a waste of energy to do so. Two soldiers began to manhandle Buck's corpse between them, bringing another roar of outrage as Skip twisted free of those trying to hold him. He dove at the men carrying the colonel's body, causing the one nearest to him to drop Buck's feet.

"You've got no respect for an officer…!"

The sound of guns being primed did not deter Skip's struggles with the German he had latched onto. It took four other men, and a blow to the Aussie's head, to subdue him, leaving him barely conscious, no longer capable of fighting. Jamie shook his head.

Obviously, Skip was not thinking clearly as Jamie had hoped.

"You know what will happen to you for this?"

Jamie kept his gaze straight ahead. Skip glared and snarled.

The Italian issued more commands, including one with the now familiar mention of solitary confinement. The Cooler. Jamie sighed. While not the best predicament they could find themselves in, it was better than the alternative of execution…an end they might still face once camp command learned of the attempted escape.

From the direction of the river, rifle fire split the night. Jamie closed his eyes and stumbled as he bit the inside of his cheek hard enough to draw blood. Again Skip struggled to be free, but the soldiers' grips upon him made the effort futile.

Had Paddy and Newt made it to freedom or had those shots ended their lives?

Moretti watched the two before him as they wove through the forest back towards the Stalag. He felt honest pity for men he grudgingly respected. At the very least, he had bought them a few more hours of life, though not their freedom. He hoped von Hausen would not feel it necessary to make examples of the pair. The death of the American colonel ought to be example enough to the entire camp to discourage further attempts.

Ste Marie sur Canut slept now, basking in ignorance of the night's misadventure. Except for the Arnaud farmhouse to the right, where bedroom lights burned and two silhouettes watched from an upstairs window, and most like the Porteur household where by now Jamie hoped, Etienne was resting comfortably in the care of his wife and daughter. The thought of the graceful Zaline made his stomach tighten, but it was a sensation he closed his eyes against, a sensation he chose to ignore. Who could blame a man for such base thoughts after so many months cut off from the civilizing effects of female company? It was best not to think about another man's wife. Etienne was too important to those in the Camp, a sincerely nice fellow, who did not deserve the thoughts that plagued Jamie at the thought of her.

Better to focus on the barbed wire. Beyond it, glimpses between rows of crude barracks showed the entirety of Camp 1 called to appell. At this late hour, they would all know what such a gathering meant.

A failure to escape.

Surrounded by their captors, they came around the corner of the camp, led towards the main gates which opened only long enough to allow them entry before being securely locked again. The sound of the metal jaws clamping together, imprisoning them once more, made Jamie feel sick.

Through the second gate into the interior of Camp 1, where the rest of the Allied soldiers stood in formation, watching with pensive, troubled faces and hollow eyes sunken with hunger and despair. Upon the top step of the General Service Hut, Sturmbannfuhrer Anton Stetcher was crowing, tapping the end of his walking stick on the wall beside him, proud to have beaten the foreign fools at their game once again.

"By now," he squawked, "you think you would have learned you cannot succeed against the superiority of the Reich. You try, you fail, you are punished…and yet you insist time and again on foolishness. For those who continue to defy me…you know what the following week will bring."

Jamie tuned out the man's thundering drone of punishments to be meted out upon those guilty of nothing more than silence, as well as the single pistol crack that caused a single man, somewhere in the Allied ranks, to fall to the dusty ground. Innocence punished in the place of the guilty. It was always a risk, one that depended on Stetcher's mood, one they could never anticipate. Jamie grimaced and tried not to flinch.

Not all had kept quiet, however. No matter how careful they were with such plans, no matter how secretive, it sometimes happened that word spread. This time, someone had spoken of the plot within earshot of the Germans. The pursuit had been too immediate, too clean and orchestrated to have been random German luck. The punishments Stetcher rattled off were not those he wanted to give, but rather those he was permitted to give; castrated of any real power, the man would wield what he had with brutal force and make those beneath him suffer as dearly as he could.

Undoubtedly there would be harsh words spoken between Stetcher and his commanding officer over the death of that prisoner. But they were only words, and as such, Stetcher did not care.

"Too bad," said the Scotsman, Sparks, clasping Jamie's shoulder as he and Skip were ushered roughly past. One of the soldiers escorting the prisoners pushed the bearded man away with the butt of his rifle; Sparks staggered and would have landed on the hard-packed earth if not for the men behind him who broke his fall. Beside Sparks, the now senior ranking camp officer, Jamie's father as fate would have it, made note of the blood upon his son's shirt.

"James, you alright?" hissed George Campbell.

Though Jamie bristled at the use of his formal name, he did not look at him. He had hoped to be free of the man's shadow in war, and instead, they had both ended up here. The odds against that were so high that Jamie was sure God was having a good laugh at his expense. He ignored his father, kept his eyes ahead, and was thankful when the guards muscled him out of George's reach.

Not a man keen on being ignored, George directed his words to any German within earshot. "This man needs a doctor! He is an officer and deserves reasonable and proper…"

The Germans ignored him.

Ahead of Jamie, the curly-headed American RAF pilot Ronny Zane playfully quipped, "Told you going to the river wouldn't work…"

Skip halfheartedly swung at a man he genuinely liked, but German hands and restraint held him back. It might be easy enough to consider Ronny the rat, the traitor, but Skip knew the man better than that. Or at least he believed he did. Within the barracks, Ronny was rowdy and prone to talking too much and too often, but Skip had never seen him associate with the Germans, or even Moretti, and he stayed away from the gates and fences where he might be overheard.

Besides, Skip knew who the rat truly was. And he would see that the woman responsible for the failure this night got her comeuppance. Dusty Miller's forced chuckle, a sound trying to bring lightness to an otherwise unfortunate situation, made Skip look up from his brooding to meet his friend's gaze.

"Better luck next time, wombat…" the Englishman said sympathetically.

Skip managed to lean near enough to Dusty to make himself heard and hissed, "I'm going to kill her.

"Who?" Dusty asked though he knew well enough who. There was only one woman Skip could possibly mean.

The Germans pushed Skip forward. "Tell her," the Aussie called over his shoulder before he was out of range to say more.

Stetcher had finally stopped talking, allowing the wave of devastated silence to crash over the men of Camp 1 as the body of Colonel Nathaniel Buckman was paraded past and into the GSH. The weight of that silence sucked the air from Jamie's lungs. Stetcher preened and rocked back and forth on his heels.

"Holy Mother of God…" breathed young Corporal Raymond Johnston, voicing the thought of every man present.

Buckman was dead.

Padre 'Bonny' Whyte genuflected and bowed his head. "God help us."

Chapter 2
July 2, 1943

The glossy silver-gray luxury car that whispered up the dusty road towards the Stalag gates drew heads up from prayer, some in fear for the two men yet to be captured, some with the hopes that it might mean a lessening of Stetcher's punishments and a decent, respectful burial for Buckman. The expensive vehicle winding its way along the dark path was one they all recognized by now. It had left earlier in the evening with the Commandant and his family dressed in their finery, an absence the escapees had depended on to make their attempt. Their return was earlier than expected, however, and the premature return supported the notion that the Germans had known about the escape before it was undertaken. While the Commandant frequently left day to day control of the camp in Stetcher's hands, an early return all but guaranteed he would come into Camp 1 and see to this matter himself.

The car passed by, however, and the prisoners were ordered back to their barracks before it stopped near the iron gates of the nearby house he called home. Heads craned to catch a glimpse of the man, hoping to gauge his mood, to determine if he would come to save or punish them further, but all anyone could see was the tall man sliding out of the car to share words and a salute with the guards on duty.

Then the wooden hovels swallowed the residents for the night, blocking anything more from view.

Inside the car, a woman's face hung low, her hand combing through her sleeping daughter's hair as she tried to make out what the guard and her husband were talking about. With his head cocked in listening, she could tell nothing from his pensive, thoughtful expression until he turned to stare at her. She caught the movement of the guard's mouth and hers opened in an O of surprise. Extricating herself from beneath her daughter's weight, she opened the door and rushed to her husband's side.

"Is it true? There was an escape tonight?"

She spoke perfect English, a language the guards were accustomed to hearing in the camp from soldiers and officers alike, yet to hear the language of the enemy spoken by the wife of the Stalag's commanding officer was still off-putting despite von Hausen's year-long appointment to this camp. It was difficult for many to come to terms with the fact that she was British.

Her husband wrapped his arm around her waist, as much for the benefit of the guard with them as it was for himself, and when she attempted to draw away, he pulled her tightly to his side, causing a flash of panic to dart across her face.

"You know there was…" he answered with calculated coolness and a touch of annoyance.

Whether it was his words or the tone, or the implications behind each, Jennifer von Hausen shuddered. Despite the balmy weather of this summer night and the warmth of his body, once she began to shiver, she could not stop.

Her voice a whisper, she asked. "Someone was killed? Who? Who was it?" She did not care that her questions might damn her. Hans had already spoken one truth; now she needed to know the rest.

"Stetcher will tell us soon enough. I do hope…" He paused for effect, his gaze on the guard though his focus, his words, were meant for his wife. "I hope it was that troublesome Australian."

Jennifer stiffened in his arms, a response that did not go unnoticed by either the Commandant or the guard, although the younger man pretended he had not seen it. As if some realization had come over her, she suddenly smiled and touched her husband's face with her fingertips the way she once had, and murmured warmly, "You will tell me when you know?"

It was a touch he had been too long without. Aching with the need for that lost intimacy, his first response was to open up to her, talk to her the way they had once talked, tell her his heart the way he had in the early days of their love. And he might have done it if she had not spoken, her breath heavy with the perfume of brandy. He realized abruptly that she was plying him with wiles that use to work, seeking her own ends with no desire to let him into her heart. Hans scowled. He refused to be used.

"Take Mila inside." He pushed her away gently but she nearly fell on liquor weakened legs. He automatically steadied her with one hand, and when she hesitated and stared at him with wide, innocent eyes, hoping the small kindness represented a shift in mood, he growled, "Do as I say or by God, I will…"

Realizing charm would not work tonight unless she was willing to go to lengths she had not resorted to in too many months, she scurried to the car to retrieve their daughter. A wave of the Commandant's hand sent the car away, leaving Hans to continue conversing with the guard. Hans did not enter the house and had no desire to enter the camp tonight. He was in no mood to face Stetcher but nor was he in any hurry to follow his wife.

❧*❦

Jennifer threw the door open and tumbled into the house, seeking her usual refuge before Hans arrived, trusting that her daughter, would find her way on her own. Bursting into the richly ornate living room, Jennifer headed straight to the liquor cabinet and poured herself a large snifter of brandy with trembling hands. The warming amber liquid was swallowed in a few gulps and another glass quickly poured, the woman ignoring what had spilled upon the mahogany surface of the cabinet. She was standing there still, nursing the drink, staring into the half-empty crystal glass, when her daughter came into the room to embrace her after stopping to hang her wrap in the hallway. A few short minutes later her red-faced husband followed, his expression now promising a tirade where before it had been a less stormy sea. But the diatribe was cut short by the sight of Mila with her arms around her mother. He did not like to fight in front of the girl. He and Jennifer did too much of that already.

Growling, he poured himself a drink as well, took time to mop up the spill with a towel from the cabinet, and then savored the burn of the stronger beverage he had chosen, hoping it would burn away the pain in his chest.

In Mila's short life, the snipping and fighting between her mother and father had become an almost every day occurrence, common enough to cause Mila to wonder if her parents had ever loved one another. There were occasional moments of such tenderness and loving fondness that Mila could only watch them with childish confusion, witnessing their faults, their strengths, loving them both despite the mystery of their disintegrating feelings for one another. Her mother's drinking usually kept Mila at bay, but she feared her father's occasional outburst of temper; it was a force she could feel as he came into the house, a force which had driven her to her mother's side to bury herself in her mother's bosom in the hopes that this episode of anger too would pass.

"It's alright, darling. I'm just a little cold and tired," Jennifer said lightly in an effort to comfort her only child. "Your father knows I hate Wagner...but duty is duty..." There was disdain in her voice at the word duty, but she kissed the girl's dark hair fondly to mask it.

Knowing her mother was lying, Mila raised her head and murmured in agreement, "Duty was very long." She glanced at her father, rather than call out her mother's lie, and asked, "Why must duty be such a boring thing?"

Anger temporarily drained, Hans smiled. "You did not have to attend, Liebchen. You could have remained here with Fraulein Clara." He ignored his wife's expression of disgust as he mentioned the French woman's name. "Only your mother and I needed to suffer the tortures of Tristan." He held out his arms for her to come to him, and though she hesitated, she would not refuse. He no longer seemed angry and she genuinely loved the moments of affection they shared. He was her father and she loved him, even if he sometimes did things that scared her...just as she loved her mother despite the woman's drunken stupors and bouts of disconnected melancholia.

After a quick, loving embrace, Hans let her go. "Time for bed. I have business, and it is already late. Off you go." It was easy to temper his mood around her and he was rarely cross with the child of the love he and Jennifer had lost somewhere along the way. He watched the girl hug and kiss her mother again before dashing towards the stairs.

"Don't I get a kiss too?"

"Yes, Papa."

Jennifer downed her third brandy as Mila gave her father the requisite goodnight kiss. She hated seeing it, as if somehow the girl was being disloyal by adoring her father, but she never spoke of that, not to Hans and not to Mila. Her pained expression, however, did not escape the girl and the embrace she shared with her father grew awkward. Hans frowned as the girl disappeared, having missed the look on his wife's face, and muttered, "What have I done to...?"

Emboldened by the bottle in her hand, and the change in Mila's behavior, as if she had won a victory, Jennifer snorted, "You have become a monster."

His fists clenched as the anger he had shed washed back over him. He snarled in a low voice, not wanting Mila to hear, "And you, my dear, have become a whore," as he began to stalk her across the room. It was an old, familiar argument, one they came back to too often; the accusation should no longer trouble him, perhaps, but despite the distance between them, the knowledge of her infidelities was still enough to provoke him to ire.

The unannounced entry of Stetcher stopped his hunt and made him growl anew. The Gestapo officer was supposed to be his subordinate, yet the little man took more and more liberties around the camp and made more decisions in the running of it than Hans did, always behind his back so that Hans did not know about actions or changes until too late. Try as he had, however, the Commandant had thus far been unable to get rid of the man. Complaints to their superiors in Berlin brought no relief or results. Forced to work with him, Hans endured the situation as best he could. He might have to work with Stetcher, but he did not have to like him. In fact, he loathed the shorter man more than he had ever loathed another person in his life.

Both gave mirroring salutes, but only Stetcher's showed enthusiasm and came with a crisp "Heil Hitler." Well-practiced in the diplomacy of neutrality, the Commandant's face showed no reaction to the words as he motioned to his desk. Han's offer of a drink was rebuffed with a scornful glare as if to remind the Commandant that one should not be under the influence while on duty. Hans shrugged and sat across from him. Stetcher always considered himself on duty it seemed, even when asleep. He never appeared relaxed and never seemed to enjoy life...save for when he was torturing or killing someone. Hans doubted the man knew the meaning of the words fun and relax.

Ignoring the Commandant's inebriated wife after a contemptuous glance, doubting she was sober enough to remember anything he would say, Stetcher began his debriefing in German, but von Hausen stopped him with a wave of his hand after the first five words. "I have asked you before...please, when in my home and my wife's company, you will speak English." He topped off his drink and pushed the bottle to one side. There was no need for Jennifer to know his business, but this night, in this circumstance, Hans wanted Jennifer to hear all everything, wanted her to know the truth her choices had pushed him to.

Stetcher scowled. It was because she spoke so little German, and because she was a weak-seeming woman, that he had begun his debriefing in his native tongue. There was no good reason for her to remain in the room, to overhear what they discussed, but von Hausen was never troubled by her proximity, even when she had proven, through her relations with the men in Stalag 31, that she could not be trusted.

He began telling of the escape details as he knew them, embellishing them as suited his viewpoint, making note that the larger man was paying more attention to his wife as they talked then he seemed to be paying to his subordinate. Two German guards had been killed during the escape, two prisoners had yet to be found, two had been recaptured and one killed during the chase.

"Which one? The Australian?" von Hausen could only hope that was true as he evaluated into his wife's swimmingly drunken gaze. Her fingers were tightly entwined in her string of pearls, twisting them as she listened.

"No...Colonel Buckman. The Australian and Canadian doctor are in holding awaiting determination of further punishment..."

The necklace snapped, sending tiny white beads skittering across the wooden floor as tears spilled down the woman's cheeks, tears Hans knew to be of relief rather than grief. With fury flashing in his eyes, he grunted. "Our subterfuge worked then..." If not quite, he sighed, as he had hoped it would. He had liked and respected Buckman. Perhaps that had been a mistake. "Still...he may not have died, but thanks to my wife's help..." The words hung unfinished in the air for several heartbeats. "The others will turn on him. What of the Frenchman?" Hans wanted to talk to that man himself, learn whatever he could before deciding the man's fate. He did not want to govern the town with fear. He wanted to do his job, nothing more. If there was trouble brewing, if the Resistance had found its way into the heart of Ste Marie sur Canut, it was best to root it out now. The claim of being forced into cooperating with the escapees could be true...or it might not be. Hans wanted to learn of it for himself.

"Your inept Italian sent him home to have his injury tended by his wife," Stetcher snorted in disgust. "He should be made an example of." He closed the notepad he carried to denote he had finished his report and had nothing more to say on the night's matter although his expression suggested a willingness to talk further if it meant he might be given permission to act.

Rubbing his eyes, Hans nodded. "I will question him, and then yes…something will be done. Bring him to my office in the morning." Again watching his wife as she scrambled about in search of the scattered pearls, it was the only order he gave. Stetcher took it as permission to leave; he saluted and marched from the house as unceremoniously as he had come. Hans rose from the stiff padded chair, crossed the room, and brought Jennifer to her feet with his hands upon her elbows. He did not care about the pearls. They would be there in the morning.

"Why?" she asked, her voice rough and slurred.

She might have meant any number of things, but Hans did not ask which. His answer to any of them would have been the same. "Because you are still mine."

He held her body against his for a moment, surprised when she seemed to melt into the embrace with a closed-eyed expression of bliss. Tenderly, he brushed her hair from her face and kissed her mouth, remembering so many other kisses they had shared. When she opened her eyes, however, everything about her changed. Her body stiffened and she struggled to be free of him. He was too strong, however; he lifted her into his arms and carried her up the stairs as she sobbed in defeat against his shoulder.

She knew the truth. Colonel Buckman's death was her fault. Hating herself for it, she allowed the alcohol in her blood to claim her, falling asleep in her husband's arms before they reached the bedroom door.

Chapter 3
July 2, 1943

Her fingers toyed with the wound's dressing as she examined it once more before settling into the bedside chair. Etienne was restless, tossing in his sleep, muttering snatches of words she could not make out. She prayed as she watched over him it was a nightmare and not the result of spreading infection or increasing pain.

Dengler had removed the bullet lodged in her husband's thigh, had cleaned the wound and sutured it closed, before reassuring her that with rest and proper care, Etienne would recover. The German doctor had been posted at Ste Marie sur Canut for more than a year, and despite the villagers' initial misgivings, he had proven himself to be a doctor first and a German second. It was still too easy to distrust him, however, for they knew he had orders to follow, superiors to answer to if he wanted to keep both his job and his life. As for most men, Zaline presumed that position meant a great deal more to Dengler then did the lives of a gaggle of French peasants or Allied prisoners of war.

And Etienne had been playing this dangerous cat and mouse game with the Germans since the day Stalag 31 had been constructed, since the beginning of the German occupation of their country. Even before that, as the rumors of war began to circulate, he had begun making contacts, setting plans into place to help those who might be endangered by the war machines of either a foreign nation or their own. At first, there had been a smattering of German Jews to help, men and women fleeing their country as conditions within Germany continued to deteriorate. Gradually there came to be more people from every corner of the continent until the Resistance had become everything to Etienne. Sometimes even more than his own family.

Zaline respected his choices, had supported what he was doing from the start and was as deeply involved as he was, but not for the first time did she resent what the war and this life of subterfuge had done to their marriage, their family, their lives. Though someday their daughter would respect her parents' stance for the helpless during wartime, Pensee deserved a better upbringing than this.

They all deserved better. Even the soldiers pressed to orders and the men trapped behind barbed wire with the threat of death ever constant over their head. All men deserved peace, freedom, and happiness, except, perhaps, those who had instigated this war. Happiness, peace, and freedom were the cornerstones of what she and Etienne wished for every person they aided.

So they endured the bedlam and did whatever they could to help.

Head drooping upon her chest, she drifted from prayers for the men involved in tonight's attempted escape, to the repose of the dead, to the safety of the two unaccounted for, and for the peace and welfare of those recaptured, into sleep. She prayed especially for Jamie Campbell, who had pressed for tonight's attempt until Buckman had agreed. Neither man would have made the attempt if they had not believed their plan to be foolproof. That they had failed, that the miscalculation had led to Buckman's death, would weigh heavily upon the doctor's shoulders. It would not help that others might blame him as well.

Mostly, however, she prayed for her husband who, because of tonight's catastrophe, would be watched more closely by their German occupiers than he had ever been before.

From troubled prayers into troubled sleep, until the crash of a door smashing against a wall jarred her awake. In the bedroom doorway, Stetcher stood in his Gestapo finery, a wild-eyed wolf on the hunt with his prey down before him.

"Wha...?" Etienne pushed himself up on his elbows, bleary-eyed and confused by the sudden waking and the medication in his bloodstream.

"Take him," the Gestapo officer commanded. Zaline did not need to speak German to know what he said. Nor did she need to wait for the soldiers to act before she understood his intentions.

Flinging herself between the soldiers and her husband, she cried, "Get out of my house!"

One soldier knocked her aside; she fell against the nightstand, knocking the lamp and assorted knickknacks to the floor. The others wrestled Etienne from the bed and dragged him from the room. She lunged, wrapped her arms around her husband's legs as if to keep him with her, and as he yelped in pain, another soldier kicked her shoulder hard enough to cause a scream and make her lose her hold.

"Leave him alone! He's done nothing wrong!"

She did not know if the soldiers spoke French, but she knew Stetcher did. He ignored her, however, and followed his men from the room. Without stopping for a dressing gown, Zaline pursued them. In the corridor outside the bedroom, Pensee stood in the darkness, a doll clutched in one hand, her other hand rubbing her bewildered face. To Zaline, it appeared as though the child had been fortunate enough to miss her father being hauled unceremoniously from his own house.

"Mamman?" the child came to her mother's side and put her hand within the larger one.

Zaline wanted to send Pensee back to her room, but she knew the child would not stay there, not when there was a commotion in the street outside. Pensee was too stubborn for that, and there was no time to fight with her about it as Zaline chased after the soldiers who were now at the bottom of the stairs. "Can't you see he's not well?"

The Gestapo officer turned on his heels, freezing Zaline mid-step in the doorway of her home. "Unwell? Don't you mean injured…whilst aiding an escape attempt?" he asked with a sneer.

"He's a businessman and father, not a martyr," she shot back. She wanted her father beside her. He would know how to handle this; he always seemed to produce a solution for every problem she faced. And if for some reason this time he did not have one, well, surely Clara could use her influence with the camp Commandant to keep further atrocities from happening tonight.

Neither her father nor Clara was here, however, nor was the Commandant. They might not even be aware of what was happening, as the farmhouse was far from the center of the village and Stetcher, as usual, looked to be operating under his own initiative. There was no one to defend Etienne except his wife, and she felt wholly inadequate to the task.

In the dark around them, villagers began to emerge from their homes at the sounds of running engines, shouting Germans, and Zaline's pleas. Those less confident or more fearful peeped through open doors and parted curtains but did not emerge. From the inn next door, Philippe Cuvier had come to stand upon his stoop, his arms crossed, left hand hidden within his overcoat where Zaline knew his pistol to be. No more bloodshed tonight, she thought desperately, willing him to understand and relent. Maybe this was just an arrest and could be sorted out in the morning. Further back in the shadows, Louis Porteur watched his son with a grim expression that could not be easily seen at a distance.

As Philippe reached Zaline's side, Stetcher clucked his tongue and tapped his walking stick on the ground. "He is a traitor, caught in the company of men trying to…"

"He is not part of your Reich," Philippe spat. "He cannot be a traitor…"

"I was returning from the river where I had fallen asleep while fishing…" Etienne started, knowing as well as anyone that no amount of quick thinking would likely unclasp the Gestapo officer's bulldog jaws. His proclamation of innocence was met by the man's wooden walking stick thumping against the back of his skull, knocking him face first into the dusty street. The soldiers around him had their weapons aimed as though he was a beast hunted for sport and cornered for the kill.

Stetcher's stick now waved about wildly as he addressed the villagers, both those he could see and those he could not. "Pay attention; take this lesson to heart." He hooked the stick in the crook of his arm, drew his pistol from his hip, and after having one of his men pull the Frenchman up to his knees, pressed its muzzle to the side of Etienne's head.

"No!" Zaline cried.

Etienne's eyes sought hers, his gaze firm, desperate, but passionate and secure in their knowledge that his life was but a minor sacrifice to the cause he believed in. "I love you bo…"

"Never…" the word was punctuated by the crack of the pistol firing. Etienne toppled sideways, the side of his head oozing red.

"Etienne!" Zaline's voice was barely heard over Pensee's wail of "Papa!"

"…never…" A second unnecessary shot was fired into the man's head.

"Stop it!"

"…anger the Reich."

The third shot echoed and then the streets were silent except for Pensee's wailing and Zaline's ragged, shocked sobs. Philippe's finger was tight upon the trigger of his own gun, but he knew that, even if he succeeded in killing Stetcher, he would be unable to prevent the others from killing him, and possibly Zaline and Pensee, in the process. He had to protect them if he could, as he knew that Zaline could be as impulsive as her husband in thoughts and deeds. Few others stood a chance of keeping her from some rash action. "Bastards," he growled at the Germans.

One of the soldiers aimed at Philippe, but Stetcher waved him down as though swatting a fly. von Hausen had wanted the Frenchman for questioning, but in his opinion, they could neither risk the man being free to support another escape effort or fleeing the village. Stetcher would claim that the man had attacked him or had been shot while trying to escape, even if his bullet wound would have likely prevented either scenario from playing out. His men would support whatever story he put forth, and he knew the villagers would protect their dead. There would never be a body for von Hausen to see and they would not speak the truth to him out of fear. The Commandant would be angry at the disobedience, might not even believe Stetcher's excuse, but there would be nothing to be done about it and the matter would drop.

"Leave them," he chuckled as he put his pistol back in its holster. "We are done. Goodnight, Madam Porteur."

The gall of the man was enough for Philippe to want to strike him down, but his aunt, Sister Isabelle, stood on his other side and now held his wrist as she tended to the crying girl she had scooped out of Zaline's grasp with one arm. The soldiers piled back into their vehicles; there was the clatter of rocks on metal as someone threw stones at the retreating cars, but the smug officer ignored the insult, his bloodlust seemingly sated for the night. With no German's remaining to protect Etienne's corpse, Zaline knelt beside his lifeless body, clutching at him, her face pressed against his chest. His face and head were no longer recognizable, but his hands still felt the same. With Pensee safe in Isabelle's care, Philippe went to Zaline's side and put his hand on her shoulder.

He did not know what to say. He had known Zaline since she was an infant, and he a boy of some years older. Though they had grown up together, he had known that, despite his early intention to marry her, when the charismatic Etienne Porteur had returned from university in Paris and completely captivated Zaline and others ever since, Philippe never stood a chance with her. Now he was her friend, and he wanted to comfort her as a friend would do, but he could think of nothing that would be appropriate. She accepted what little he could offer, however, by collapsing against his leg, Etienne's hand clenched in hers as she wept.

He faced the approaching footsteps as Etienne's father emerged from the shadows. It was the mayor's lot to act as if he knew nothing of his son's illicit activities; it had been a difficult role to play, but never harder than tonight. Now that the Germans were gone, he had no reason to continue with the pretense of ignorance.

Louis put his trembling hand upon his daughter-in-law's shoulder. "Zaline…" he sniffed. "Come away…let us tend him…"

She shook her head but did not pull her face away from Philippe's leg. "You cannot take him…he cannot leave…"

"Tend to your daughter. She needs you. Philippe and I will see to Etienne."

She suddenly looked up, directly into Philippe's eyes. Her grief was still there, but there was something else as well. The impulsive, occasionally fiery woman Philippe had always known had not been defeated yet. "You will see to more than that, Monsieur Cuvier."

Understanding her wishes, Philippe nodded. "I shall, I promise. He will get what he deserves, ma chère…they all will."

Now he freed himself from her grip on his legs and helped Louis carry Etienne to the church. Most of the onlookers had already returned indoors, having fled the sound of gunfire and the gory sight of one of their own lying dead in the street.

Behind him, Zaline remained where he had left her, crying forlornly as her daughter clung to the elderly woman in front of her no longer safe home. Surely, come daylight, everything in Ste Marie sur Canut would be different. After the arrival of war and the Resistance, first blood had been spilled here; it was bound to have an effect on the others. Grinding his teeth and narrowing his gaze, Phillippe made up his mind to be at the heart of those differences. He had slithered along the edges of the Resistance long enough, too long. But now, he would do everything in his power to be certain this carnage would never happen again in the village of his birth.

Chapter 4
July 3, 1943

Von Hausen kicked open his office door with Stetcher hard on his heels, unfazed by the outburst of temper and frustration from the Commandant. von Hausen knew an example had to be made, knew the value of such action, but he had not wanted the Frenchman killed before he had the chance to interrogate him. He did not believe for a moment Stetcher's claim that the injured man had tried to attack him and flee. He also knew he had to make an example of his three top officers. Protocol, and Stetcher's watchful eye scrutinizing everything he did, demanded it. Yet he had no idea what, if any, disciplinary action he would take. Moretti and Dengler had reacted as Hans himself would have in a difficult situation, following the merciful impulses of their souls, unlike Stetcher who acted only out of cruelty. There was middle ground between them, but Hans would be damned if he could find it. At least he knew that Moretti and Dengler had no military combat experience and none in the capturing of prisoners. They would have to learn a hard lesson before the next time, if there was a next time. Dealing with Stetcher in the interim, however, would be trickier.

Both of the accused officers stood to attention in front of his desk. Hans slowly, deliberately, removed the revolver from his waist and placed it upon the desk where they could see it as he circled around it, and the officers, before sitting in the expensive black leather chair. Though both saluted, neither spoke. Stetcher remained near the door, seemingly oblivious that he might be on trial as well, as if to keep one of the others from fleeing. As if, Hans grunted, either of them would. They were not that sort of men.

Unable to hide a smile of absurdity at the thought, he looked at the gun on his desk, and after a long, slow intake and exhale of breath, he began, "Sturmbannfuhrer Moretti, Haupsturmfuhrer Dengler...what am I to do with you? What made you send a suspected Resistance leader home without bringing him to me for interrogation?" His tone rose only a little, as if to suggest outrage, when what he really felt was tired. "Am I missing something or am I cursed with imbeciles for officers?" He considered neither of them to be that; Stetcher was another matter. "Please…enlighten me."

The Italian squared his shoulders and was the first to speak. "The Frenchman was injured and in need of medical attention. Campbell assured us he had no part in the escape attempt, that they found him in the forest and forced him to lead them to the river." He stood by his choices, his actions, and decisions, based on the information he had possessed at the time. Looking back at it, perhaps Campbell had been lying, but he believed the doctor to be honorable and decent and had been willing to trust him. Believing that, as an Italian and not a German, he should be disciplined by his own people rather than by these would-be worldly conquerors, Moretti's voice was colored with indignation. "After examination by both Campbell and Herr Hauptsturmfuhrer Dengler, it was agreed that he should be treated somewhere better equipped than the clearing, and I did not believe it prudent to waste camp supplies on him. It was not as if he could escape…"

Dengler nodded in agreement as Hans got out of the chair again and passed the pair on his way to the opposite window. They were grimy and in need of cleaning, he mused…but everything was grimy here. Nothing was going to clean that away.

He did not speak but instead opened the window and paused to drink in the slightly cooler morning air. Without seeing the two men crouching beneath it at the flower box, he left it open in an effort to allow fresh air into the staleness of the room before returning to his chair once more. This time, however, he did not sit.

"Haupsturmfuhrer Dengler, you know better than to trust the word of a prisoner…an enemy of the Reich…why did you agree to send this man home?"

"Because he was better off there, being cared for by his family. We have better uses for our supplies, and there are better uses for my time than to use either to treat the locals." He did not believe his own words and he often treated any villager's ills who came to him, but he hoped that apparent concern for the Reich's resources would satisfy the Commandant…and maybe even Stetcher. "He was outnumbered by the escapees…with no combat experience or visible weapon. There was no obvious reason to doubt his explanation, or to bring him to the Stalag infirmary for care."

"No obvious reason?" Stetcher spat from the doorway. Before Hans could interrupt him, he added, "Because of your ineptitude, I had to be dispatched to do your work. That man will never aid another escape, and the villagers will think twice before defying the Reich again…"

The subordinate officers looked between Stetcher and von Hausen with dismay. The Gestapo officer was expectedly proud of his actions, but it was unclear how the Commandant felt, or whether he had even known the Frenchman had been killed. Had he given the order, or had Stetcher undertaken the killing on his own? The Commandant failed to show any reaction other than circling the desk once more like a bored, trapped, frustrated animal. This time when he reached the window, he gazed across the camp with his hands gripping the sill. The whiteness of his knuckles was the only clue to his feelings.

Without facing them, his thoughts racing as he fought for the best solution for the three of them, Hans let out a slow, measured breath, eyes squeezed shut, and made a decision. "It should serve as a valuable lesson indeed…" But what sort of lesson? And was it one that would benefit the Reich in the long run. "However…"

He turned, studied the two near his desk, and then stared at Stetcher less than three feet away from them. It was tempting to throttle the little gray-haired man and bash his head through the wall. "As none of you seem prone to act in the best interest of this camp…or to following my orders…" he paused and met Stetcher's gaze, "you all need to learn from this as well. One week confined to barracks, half-rations, normal duties. No fraternizing in the village, no off camp calls and you'll take half pay…"

Though they frowned, Dengler and Moretti successfully kept their expressions largely neutral. As punishment went, a week of confinement, poor food, and docked pay was tolerable. It was better than what each imagined the prisoners in Camp 1 would endure. Stetcher, however, finding himself unexpectedly included in that punishment stared at von Hausen with a mixture of surprise, fury, and…gradually…a small measure of grudging respect. He did not agree that he should be punished and had not expected the Commandant to have the stones for. Maybe he had underestimated von Hausen, at least a small bit.

"Is that understood, gentlemen?"

Heads bobbed and each replied, "Yes, Herr Oberfuhrer."

"Good…now get out."

Moretti and Dengler saluted, turned on their heels, and left without a word, squeezing by Stetcher who refused to move away from the door. Only the small man remained, intending to argue his case and hopefully talk the Commandant out of punishment now that the lesser officers were not here to hear him. But Hans was in no mood to listen. "That includes you," Hans grunted. "I've got work to do." The gray-haired man's scowl deepened, but he decided not to press his luck. Perhaps later the Commandant would be willing to hear him.

With that dismissal, Bonny, the camp clergyman, motioned for his comrade Vic to follow him; they had to get away from the house, the window, before their eavesdropping below the Oberfuhrer's window was discovered. One of the few in camp who spoke fluent German, Bonny had been there with the hopes of learning something about Paddy and Newt, with Vic along as lookout. But instead, all they learned was the fate of the Frenchman who had aided them. He offered a quick prayer for the dead man's soul and family as he and Vic scurried back to the safety of the barracks.

At the doorway of the ramshackle wooden structure that served as home to those of officer rank within Camp 1, Dusty was precariously balancing his chair on the back two legs as he ate his meager lunch. When Bonny and Vic swept passed him, they upset the balance of the chair and only Dusty's quick action kept him from tumbling to the floor and spilling his meal.

"Where's the bloody fire," he growled as he wiped food from the front of his open shirt. When he saw that one of the culprits was the clergyman, he muttered, "Sorry, Padre," though he was still annoyed.

Bonny barely noticed the profanity or the apology as he ran into the dimly lit building. Others were seated around a small table, eating what passed for their noon meal. Curious to hear what had upset the priest so, Dusty followed him in.

"It isn't worth another attempt so soon," George was saying. "The Krauts will be watching…and we don't know yet how they learned of our last plans…so we wait." There were discontent mutterings from the group, but most nodded their heads in agreement. Tempers and German diligence had to relax before they could begin to consider escaping again.

He read the dark expressions on Bonny and Vic's faces and scowled. "News?" Other heads came up and their hushed-tone speech ceased at the interruption.

The Padre shook his head. "Nothing about our men…but Stetcher executed Mr. Porteur…against von Hausen's orders."

Not one man spoke but the grim sets of their mouths said enough as many bowed their head in tribute to the man who had been one of their few reliable links to the outside world. Etienne had risked much for the prisoners in Stalag 31 since the day it had been built, funneling contraband, news, and arranging for the occasional escape. The few who had escaped the Germans' claw-fisted grip…both prisoners and European refugees, owed Etienne Porteur their lives. His efforts had been ultimately rewarded by death, and more than one man in the room thought themselves responsible. Like Etienne and Buckman, death was a price each knew they might have to pay as well if the war did not end before then, but like those two men, that price would not keep them from making a run towards freedom.

"No more attempts until we know more," George said solemnly.

Vic growled, his thin face conveying a menace it often did when he was annoyed. "What's there to know? Skip was a fool to trust that whore…and Buckman was a fool to trust him…we know damn well why things went sideways…"

"Skip won't like it," Dusty mused with an absent smirk, talking over Vic's grumbling. Skip, the habitual discontent, had yet to have a plan, until now, that got him outside of the camp walls. But he continued to try, and this minor success…the getting out, was bound to fuel his hopeful efforts. He would either reach freedom or die trying. It was why the thought of the Aussie spilling their plans to von Hausen's wife made no sense to Dusty, not even as an accident…unless he wanted to die.

Of course, Dusty mused, Skip's death threat against Jennifer von Hausen suggested that he might not know the Aussie's true motivations at all.

"Skip will follow orders."

Dusty doubted that was going to happen. Skip had respected Buckman, but he was never good at following orders. Dusty doubted he would follow new ones now.

Bonny and Vic got their own meals and everyone ate in silence, thinking about those who may have gotten away, those who had died to make the effort possible, and those who were being punished for it. Whether the failure was Skip's fault or not, most in Camp 1 would believe it to be. George suspected the man would be thankful for solitary confinement by the time he confronted the angry Stalag prisoners being punished alongside him.

One of those angry men stopped Campbell as he shuffled towards the door, his lunch finished before the whistle that would summon them back to work. George looked at the hand on his arm and then up into the face of Ray Johnston. He was the youngest officer in Barrack J, a raven-haired idealist sucked into the war because of his medical training. He had been serving as a medic when captured in a small village to the east, a man who did not believe in force or violence against other men but did believe patriotic duty was important. He had carried a gun into battle but rarely used it as he focused on retrieving and tending the wounded. He had been reprimanded for his failures as a soldier more than once. But Ray believed in the power of the Red Cross armband and helmet he wore, trusted they would keep him from harm and lessen any punishments he might receive. He had medals and ribbons to support his bravery, but to many in Camp 1, he was a young, idealistic fool.

George grunted. He had wondered how long it would be before Ray spoke up.

"These escape efforts are promoting further violence," Ray said, scratching his dark head of hair, repeating an oft-spoken sentiment. "Why should the rest of us suffer because a few men want to…?"

Though he normally tried to make time to debate with Ray, today George did not feel up to the task. In the past, Buck had been there with him for such debates and had been occasionally successful in talking Ray around to accepting their point of view. Today, Buck was not there.

"For Christ's sake, Ray," he snarled. "Men have died, good honest men. Some are missing…and you have the balls to complain about extra duty and less sleep? Let us grieve in peace…and if you're not going to join us, take your bullshit somewhere else."

Jaw tight, Clara again scanned the collection of villagers in their mourning finery gathered in the cemetery of Ste Marie's church. The church had stood since some time in the 11th century, a convent that graced the valley with its Norman architecture and protected the peasants who had formed a village around her from the harshness of worldly realities. The villagers were proud of their church and defended it with utmost loyalty from the German invaders, although none had yet to give their lives to do so and the Germans, thankfully, had felt no compulsion to defile or destroy it. Atop the buttresses and stone arches, menacing gargoyles bared their fangs and glowered in the direction of the Stalag erected not far away, their grimaces spitting disapproval at the ugliness built within the shadows of the church's single spire.

As the gargoyles of Ste Marie's watched, so too did Clara. She was not sure what she was looking for, what she expected to see, but it would be better to see it first, to avoid an unwanted surprise than find themselves in a perilous quandary because of distraction. For the most part, there was little to see. Only the lingering Germans and the faces she had long ago become familiar with, faces twisted and painted with varying degrees of grief, shock, fear, and outrage.

Especially outrage.

For even though most of the residents in Ste Marie sur Canut thought they knew the Mayor's only son, few of them knew the true nature, or full extent, of the activities in which Etienne Porteur had been so deeply involved. They considered the manner in which he had been killed heinous and unnecessary, a deep affront to their identity as a village, as a people. That Etienne had been much loved and highly regarded by all only fueled the already festering contempt and hatred for their occupiers. His death had rekindled the Ste Marie's patriotism.

Even here, at an event as personal and private as the funeral of one of the village's own, the Nazi machine made itself known by the presence of four soldiers who loitered at the rear of the assemblage, looking bored and annoyed at having been sent on this detail. Likely, none of them spoke French, a point that Philippe used to his advantage in conducting the burial service. Clara turned her head, tucking her light brown hair behind her ear, to eye the four, knowing that, though they looked bored and inattentive, they were more than prepared to open fire on the villagers if the situation warranted. They were always there at any gathering of more than a handful of people as if to prevent them from taking action, or perhaps to catch wind of some threat against the prison staff if it was being planned. Still, Clara believed that, with the right distraction, it would be simple enough for the villagers to overpower the four, to take their weapons…

…and then what?

The tender squeeze from the arm about her waist drew her focus away from the Germans, away from the thoughts of retribution and revenge for Etienne, for Buckman, for her brother, and for the untold number of innocents the Nazis had butchered. Stasio smiled at her, an adoring look strained with the melancholy of their surroundings and the death of his son-in-law. But it was that adoration and the steady reminder of caution in his eyes that struck her most deeply at that moment, dispelling her immediate desires for action. She smiled gratefully and leaned into the light kiss he placed upon her temple.

To the west, the sun was sinking below the tops of the pines, the burial of another warm, early July day. There had been crops to tend, cows to milk, men who needed water and attention, thus the funeral had not been held earlier in the day. The Nazis would have been infuriated by the absence of the farm's owner, would not have accepted the need to bury family as an excuse from their forced duty, and so the decision had been made to wait. In town, the day had been a series of clandestine meetings between a handful of individuals as the details of the previous night's failure were discussed and new plans were made to take into account the changes Etienne's death forced upon them. But sunset had been Etienne's favorite time of day, and so it was fitting to bury him with the setting sun, as soon as the German expectations on their day had waned. Duty done for the Nazis, the villagers were now free for the night. In the camp, the men would also have the chance to mourn their dead, their daily work behind them as well.

Even bereavement had to be done to the Nazis' schedule.

On Stasio's other side, his youngest daughter Marcella wept, not able to dry her eyes as her hands were occupied with comforting her niece, Pensee, whose mother stood a little further away, physically and emotionally distanced from her family, from the villagers, from the unexpected situation in which she found herself. Clara wanted to reach out to Zaline, comfort her, say anything that would take her pain away, but this was not the time or place to try. Even if she knew the words to say, knew some magic that could ease the grief of losing a loved one, Clara had only recently begun to feel that Stasio's daughters had accepted her relationship with their father. She did not want to be a mother to them; she only wanted to be their friend.

Such bonding over Etienne's grave hardly seemed proper.

Sister Isabelle's voice faded off the final note of the funeral hymn, something by Bach, Clara believed, though she could not be certain. There was the short silence of bowed heads punctuated by dogs barking somewhere in the trees near the river, and then Philippe resumed speaking.

"In closing," he said, opening the Bible he carried, "I will read a selection of passages from the book of Jeremiah, chapter fifty-one. In light of what has brought us here today, these are words that Etienne once asked me to leave with his friends and loved ones, things he wants us to carry with us in his memory. Thus says the Lord..."

❧*❧

The interior wall of his six foot by six-foot cell, the wall that served as the head of his lumpy, filthy, bug infested bed, was the coolest in the room, and it was where Jamie rested his bare back in an effort to find some degree of comfort. Soon enough, the morning sun would return to heat the eastern wall, warming the room, bringing with it the stench of the contents of the bucket in the corner. Not that he had been here before to experience such things, but everyone knew the condition of the Cooler, thanks to the graphic reports of those who spent time here. It was a common subject of talk amongst the men. Jamie knew what to expect and hated the need to endure it himself.

Normally he would not have considered participating in any risky escape attempt. His medical knowledge was needed here, in camp. Dengler was a competent enough doctor, not a sadist or callous monster despite being German, but he would not, or could not, offer aid to all of those men in the Stalag who needed it. Medical supplies were spread thin and often those who required aid here had to do without. It was Jamie's responsibility to make their suffering as bearable as possible, to provide them with the kindest death he could when his other efforts failed.

But this time, he had believed Newt needed him. The man's condition, the sickness in his lungs, had grown steadily worse in the last week, and Jamie had felt strongly that without prompt attention in proper facilities, the man was facing inescapable death. Newt had insisted that, should he get free of the camp, he would fare well enough without a doctor accompanying him, but Buck had overruled them both on the decision. Jamie had been in the camp too long, in his opinion, and Newt needed care. Since Buckman outranked them both and had been the most respected man in the Allied camp, when he instructed Jamie to go, the doctor reluctantly accepted that responsibility. If Buck thought the plan foolproof, if he felt Jamie's presence was best served elsewhere, then Jamie was soldier enough to follow those orders.

And now Buckman was dead.

Perhaps, Jamie mused, leaving his balaclava on his head might have made some difference, as Skip had loudly insisted. But with the Nazis so close behind them, close enough for their gunfire to hit Etienne, Jamie doubted his headwear would have made any difference. By the time he could have tended to that injury with or without it, the Germans would have been upon them regardless. Buck might not have been shot if he had kept running, but looking at the chain of events that night, it was impossible now to say.

In his opinion, Skip had nothing to blame him for. Buck had not needed to stop, and Skip had not needed to turn back for him. He could have continued his run for freedom, joining Paddy and Newt, and been far away from this place by now. And, Jamie thought bitterly, Skip had not needed to cozy up to the Commandant's wife. While he had no proof of betrayal and did not believe Skip would have risked his freedom with foolish loose talk, Jamie did feel that, if Skip had avoided that woman, none of this likely would have happened. Skip was as much to blame for his failure to escape as anyone else, although the arrogant Aussie would never admit to such mistakes. It always seemed to be someone else's fault with him, someone else's failure. From his being pushed into the military, to his capture, to his being brought to this camp, and to every failed escape he had ever made, there was always someone else to blame.

Watching the little trail of fading sunlight poke through the ventilation window and crawl across the opposite wall, Jamie decided he would accept his share of responsibility for Buck's death, accept the repercussions from others within the camp, but he would not accept the blame for Skip's shortcomings.

He focused again on the words carried on the wind, one of the French villagers speaking near the church, and sighed with his head resting on his knees, wondering who they were burying tonight.

"...Behold, I am going to arouse against Babylon and against the inhabitants of Leb-kamai, the spirit of the destroyer. And I shall dispatch foreigners to Babylon that they may winnow her and may devastate her land, for on every side they will be opposed to her in the day of her calamity…"

❧*❧

Vic laid aside the worn bagpipes someone had worked into camp for him and resumed his seat next to Sparks, whose face seemed unusually preoccupied tonight. Actually, his fellow Scot had looked more preoccupied than anyone else since the news of the Frenchman's death had been delivered. No doubt, Sparks was itching to get to the radio, to get any information he could, from whatever sources he had, in the hopes of learning what had become of Paddy and Newt. Sparks, Paddy, Vic, and Bonny had been dubbed the Gaelic Musketeers by others in the camp; now their numbers were down to three. Not knowing what had become of their friends was a constant source of stress and irritation.

Padre Whyte resumed the podium he had constructed himself within a week of his arrival at Stalag 31. Bonny had been in the camp longer than the majority there. It was rumored that he had allowed himself to be captured nearby to be of service to the men behind the wire, but Bonny neither confirmed nor denied the tale. Instead, he continued his clerical duties of support and encouragement as though he were in his native environment back home in Dublin and did his best to remain the voice of hope.

"We've lost someone dear to us, a man we admired and respected…like losing a father…" His voice wavered at the final word as he glanced briefly at George. "Some of us have lost a brother…a friend. But let us not lose faith…"

"What good is fucking faith when Buck's gone?" Dusty quipped, quietly enough to be considered under his breath but loudly enough that Bonny and those nearest to him heard the words clearly.

"Do you have something to say, Captain Miller?"

Dusty shrugged as others looked at him. Another man might have shrunk into his chair. Dusty seemed to grow taller, in spite of his contrite expression. "No, Padre," he grunted. Many were used to his smart-ass remarks, words that frequently held a bite of truth, but today he did not feel like repeating himself in what should have been a respectful ceremony.

"I do," Ray snapped, his youthful features set with determined consternation. "We would not keep losing men if we would stop fighting. The war will end one day and we will be freed…"

"You might be willing to place your odds on the Allies coming out on top…" grumbled Leonard, a large, ebony-skinned man who had served as Buck's second in command within the camp, thus gaining respect from others that his skin color might otherwise have disallowed him.

"Or that the Krauts will let us live either way," interrupted Vic bitingly.

Leonard nodded and continued, "…but I don't want to take that chance. I'd rather gamble on getting out…"

"Nor should we have to," agreed the only Welshman in their camp as he reached for Ray's shoulder. Ray slid away from the touch and Taffy cleared his throat, "Because it may be our efforts, our actions, that determine the outcome of this war…"

Ray crossed his arms indignantly, again faced with the majority united against him. All except Sparks, perhaps, who said nothing, who neither agreed nor disagreed, and whose expression indicated that his thoughts were far away from the room where they sat. It was impossible to tell what he was thinking, but to date, the radio man had not volunteered to join an escape. Sparks always helped with planning but seemed inclined to remain where he was.

"It's a war we should not be in," Ray growled. "Buck would be…we would all be…none of this would have happened if everyone stayed home and tended their own families…"

Spark's face suddenly came alive, showing that he had been listening, even if he appeared not to be. "And what of the French? The Jews…the Russians…the rest of Europe? Don't we have an obligation to stop the Nazis from taking everything…people's homes…their lives? Don't you think they'd come to Britain too…and then who would stop them while we bury our heads in the sand and ignore everyone else?"

No one had the chance to address that sticky question. Outside, the whistle blew, signaling time to return to barracks for lights out. No one might have replied, but from Ray's expression, he was stumped for a good answer. Idealism did not always lend itself to practical solutions in the face of the harsh realities of war.

By default and order of rank, and because Leonard had no desire for the position, George Campbell was now Camp 1 leader. But by the expressions on some of the enlisted men and a few of the officers as they crossed the appell yard it was obvious that the elder Canadian had a tough road ahead to gain the level of respect and trust Buckman had been given. No one believed that any man in Camp 1 had what it took to reach that success. Not even George Campbell.

*

The last wisps of deep purple were fading from the horizon. Philippe continued to read beneath the glow from the light of the lamp Sister Isabelle held.

"…they will fall down slain in the land of the Chaldeans, and pierced through in their streets, for neither Israel, nor Judah, has been forsaken…"

*

Skip was tall enough that, if he stood on his toes on his rickety bed, he could see through the ventilation window. There was little to be seen, only barbed wire and a few of the distant village structures, but looking out, watching the world, gave him the sense of doing something more than waiting to die. He had heard singing not long before, the mixture of women's voices in the sound indicating it was not the camp men gathering to sing for Buckman, and he wondered if today was some holy day he had forgotten.

The thin sheet of plywood supporting his weight cracked and buckled, sending him tumbling backward. He swore, knowing he would now have to sleep on the even filthier, vermin-infested floor rather than the marginally comfortable wooden frame med. He hated this place, hated confinement, and hated Camp 1. Being unable to see outside, or pace in the confined space, made him even angrier.

She would die. Somehow. Yes, he had been warned away from her. Yes, he should have known better than to place faith in a woman who drank as much as she did, a woman married to the enemy. She had given him information, taken from him in return, and steered him to ruin. Him, here in this stench-ridden hole, while somewhere Buckman was being prepared for burial…or had been buried already.

Dead. Better dead, he snarled, then locked up and forgotten like a caged animal in a hole. At least once he was free of the Cooler he would be able to try again…so long as the Commandant or Stetcher did not order him killed. Living meant another chance for freedom. A chance Buck was denied.

He wondered if Paddy and Newt had gotten clear, made it to the river, found the boat that was to take them to freedom. Given half a chance, Skip knew the big Irishman could survive anything. But Newt, with his poor health, was another matter, and Skip knew that the Irishman would stick by the New Zealander until both men were clear of danger. He would make sure they both escaped to freedom, or die trying.

Just as Buck had.

Skip could not remember saying anything that could have given their plan away to the woman, anything she could accidentally have passed on to her husband in a drunken stupor, but it seemed he must have, for how else would the Germans have known their plan? But Jamie Campbell…if that man had kept running, kept his blonde hair hidden from the searching fingers of torchlight, Buckman would not have had reason to go back and the Nazis might not have seen them. It was unlikely they would have remained unseen in that clearing, but Skip had to believe they could have. Anger gave him something to hold on to. Without anger, he would fade, wither, and cease to be.

"You're gonna get yours," Skip yelled through the wooden walls, though whether he was shouting at Jennifer von Hausen, the man in the adjoining cell, or the universe at large, was unclear.

"…for the destroyer is coming against her, against Babylon, and her mighty men will be captured, their bows are shattered, for the Lord is God of recompense. He will fully repay."

Philippe paused for effect, looking over his inherited congregation to see how many of them understood the meaning Etienne had found in those verses. Clearly not the Germans, he could tell, which reinforced Clara's assertion that most of the young men serving under von Hausen could not speak a word of French beyond hello, goodbye, and stop. It was useful to know.

The dogs in the forest bayed again.

The scripture selection appeared to have the desired effect, unifying the villagers against their oppressors, at least for the moment, while simultaneously re-igniting the passion of the other members of the Resistance who had been shaken by this loss. It refueled their need to continue their efforts in spite of the setback. They needed that. Solidarity was all they had left.

He bowed his head. "Amen," he murmured, and the congregation responded in kind.

Louis and three other local men chosen for this task carefully lowered the crude wooden casket into the prepared hole. Most in these times could not afford anything more than a wooden box, and it seemed to Louis that every quality casket in the land had been confiscated by the Germans, just like everything else of value. Many were forced to forego a casket altogether, but for Etienne, a favorite son throughout Ste Marie sur Canut, a box had been deemed respectful, something well deserved. Louis watched Zaline out of the corner of his eye; when the ropes went slack as the casket touched the earth, her shoulders sagged under the weight of inevitability. He rejoined his extended family as one by one, or in small clusters, the villagers trudged past, offering their words of condolences and support and dropping flowers or remembrances into the grave. Zaline, however, did not stand with them. Rather, she stood at the graveside, watching the three men heap spade after spade of warm earth into the hole. Only when most of the villagers had gone and when the hole was filled enough that the box was no longer visible, did she turn and walk square-shouldered towards Philippe.

"Monsieur…"

"Not now, Zaline…"

"You said…" Her protest was cut short as he pulled her head against his chest and stroked her hair as if to comfort her. In the distance, the Germans seemed particularly interested in Zaline and her behavior and Philippe would be damned if he would let her kill herself foolishly.

"They are watching," he whispered. "You must be careful…"

"I do not wish to be careful anymore." She looked up into his face, determination stronger than the grief in her eyes. "I want Etienne's work to continue, and I will do it myself if I must…"

Calloused, gentle fingers pushed her dark hair back from her face. "You won't be able to do anything if they kill you. He wouldn't want that. The work needs you. Pensee needs you. Do not fear, ma chère; I said I would see to matters…"

"You will take up leadership?" she asked, a hopeful glint in her eyes. He had never seemed inclined to lead before, but perhaps Etienne's death had changed him as it had her. She would carry the responsibility of leadership if need be, but she had played a relatively minor role before and would be hard-pressed to lead as efficiently as her husband had done. Philippe, Etienne's primary co-conspirator, knew everything about their cell there was to know.

"It's already been discussed. I can, I will…do what he would have done. He would want that."

Relieved, Zaline kissed him softly on the cheek, once again reminded how close she had come to marrying this man before Etienne had come back into her life. If only Philippe had asked in time, her life might have been much different. "Merci, Philippe…"

For the first time that evening, she looked at Clara, whom she knew had been watching her in return though without seeming to do so. Despite the awkwardness in their relationship, Clara being near Zaline's age while courting her father, Zaline knew that the other woman was one of the staunchest supporters Etienne and the Resistance had. More than once it had been Clara and her radio that had saved them and allowed them to carry on in their efforts against the war. And it was clear to Zaline by the way her father stood behind the young woman and held her against him with both arms that he had found some measure of happiness that Zaline had doubted he would ever find again after the death of his wife. The rest of the family, including Marcella, Pensee, and Louis, had left the gravesite already, but Stasio had stayed, and with him, Clara Beton.

Zaline nodded. As expected, Clara nodded in return, though in a fashion that looked more like a nuzzle against the man's chest behind her than any response to Zaline. But Zaline knew her message had been understood. Ste Marie's Resistance would live on.

Clara tilted her head sideways, speaking to Stasio who had been looking in his eldest daughter's direction in time to catch the exchange between the two women. "London needs to know."

He did not ask what she meant. In the three years Clara had been in his life, he had come to understand every gesture, every nuance because she never hid anything from him. He had made himself part of her self-appointed mission, an indispensable part if her loyalty was any indicator. He turned her around to look eye to eye and brushed back her hair with both hands. "I suppose so. But what of them?" The slight inclination of his head gestured towards the Germans who had apparently witnessed enough and were heading back towards the village, in the direction of the L'Oie de Vol rather than in the direction of the Stalag. Clara sighed as she watched them and he continued. "To go home now…we will be followed, or sought out. They will expect us to be with Zaline and Louis."

"I will have to risk it. Too many hours have passed already. Lives are at stake while London operates under false assumptions about our status here." She closed her eyes as he brushed his lips across her forehead, his beard roughing her skin.

"Can't it wait another thirty minutes? Long enough to put in a polite, expected family appearance, to let them think we're behaving normally? Then we return to the house without drawing suspicion…"

Clara shook her head. "You don't have to…"

Expression sternly affectionate, he scowled. "You will not go about alone tonight. Stetcher is likely stalking our streets for victims, and I will not risk losing another member of my family."

He let the argument stand and she chose not to fight him. Instead, she kissed the palm of his hand that was still pressed against her cheek. Part of his family. Not officially, perhaps, but just as surely family as were his daughters, his granddaughter, or his late son-in-law. Perhaps even more strongly a part than that, if the fire in his eyes meant anything. He wiped away tears from the corner of her eyes with his thumbs.

"Your concern for my welfare wins once more, mon aimé."

He chuckled. "My concern, and the patience of my experience win over your impetuous desire for action?"

"Perhaps," she chuckled as well.

The echo of barking dogs that had moved within the confines of the forest broke into the clearing at the edge of the graveyard. There were three of them, with the lead dog carrying something in its mouth that the others were trying to take from him. One of the men filling the grave called the dogs to him; surprisingly they responded. It took the fellow effort to coax the lead animal to give up its treasure, but it was enough time for those remaining in the area to gather around him.

Clara quickly identified the scrap as a large portion of torn jacket, one of military origin. She did not have to hold it to know. Louis took the fabric from the man who held it, noting the clink of metal as he did so. He turned it around in his hands, searching, noticing the stains of blood, until he found the source of the sound.

"Whose…?" Zaline whispered, afraid to learn the answer, afraid that it would belong to someone they had known.

Philippe cleared his throat and placed the small metal tags in Clara's outstretched palm. "O'Callaghan's…"

"Merde," Stasio muttered, clasping Clara's free hand in his. She had been particularly fond of the four Celts, having had extensive dealings with them in the relay of radio intelligence. Her hand felt disturbingly cold in his.

"Do you think he was…they were…wouldn't they have been brought back if the German's had found them?" asked Louis.

"Not if they fell into the river. In the dark, the current is swift enough that a wounded man might not swim it." Stasio wanted to take Clara back to the house. Now. Take her away from Ste Marie sur Canut. Forget everything else in the world. But he already knew what she was thinking.

"They might still be alive. This might have torn off on a branch. He might have left the tags on purpose to avoid being identified. Philippe, tell the others; ask Isabelle to get the word out. There might be wounded men out there. They have to be found and taken to safety if they're still…"

"We'll organize a search at once…if you can manage the inn?" Philippe looked at Zaline and waited for an answer, not sure if she was up to the task but hoping she was.

Having a mission of importance now, something that Etienne would have been neck deep in, the task enabled the grieving woman to shift focus away from his death. "I will, of course."

"Good." Clara pocketed the tags. "I will let London know tonight…and I will let the men know tomorrow…if I can. They deserve that much." Perhaps the prayers of their fellow soldiers would be enough to get Paddy and Newt safely home.

Chapter 5
July 3-9, 1943

From her vantage point as a relative outsider, Clara witnessed the passing of another week, the routine of it no different than any other week save for the extended work hours heaped upon the Stalag prisoners in retaliation for allowing the escape effort to be made. She worked around the farmhouse, tutored von Hausen's daughter in history, reading, mathematics, and grammar as she had been hired to do, all while continuing her efforts, as small as they were, on behalf of the inmates of Stalag 31. Buckman's death had not brought an end to the war, and so long as the German machine pushed across Europe, there was work to be done against them. She was instrumental in directing Philippe and his newly inherited cell to the successful bombing of a portion of the nearby railway line, a fete Etienne had orchestrated long before his death and one that he and Clara had organized in detail with very little help from her London contacts. That Philippe so easily assumed Etienne's role as cell leader, had eagerly undertaken such a bold action as his first solo project, and had carried it out without a hitch, was a boost to his credibility amongst the warier Resistance members and a boost to their shaken confidence. It proved the sort of dedicated, determined, and successful leader Philippe Cuvier could be.

Clara wished she had been there to see it, wished she could have had a more direct hand in the bombing, but her place was behind the radio, the ears and mouth of Ste Marie sur Canut. Make the arrangements, help with supplying the cell with what was needed, but never actually participate. It was a mission she had given herself long ago, a position she had struggled to create and carefully cultivated as the war progressed. She needed to remain careful, to stay inconspicuous. But often of late she felt a strong desire to do more. It was only Stasio and the men in Stalag 31 that kept her in this relatively sheltered village, that kept her from the hub of things in Paris or somewhere nearer the frontline of the fight.

But Stasio was reason enough. As long as he lived, she could not imagine leaving Ste Marie. He had been there for her, her rock and support, for the three years she had been here, saving her in the beginning from her self-destructive pursuit against the Germans, sheltering her as she healed the loss of her brother, showering her with gifts and warmth and affection as she built a life once again. Her success here, her success with London and Paris were surely as much Stasio's as her own, for without him, she knew she might long ago have been found out and executed. He was not in a position of action within the Resistance, but protecting Clara and her radio, while giving her reign to do as duty demanded were as much of a risk as anything his daughters or his son-in-law had done.

Over the past three years, she had played her part well, gaining access not only to the Resistance, but also to the camp inmates, and, upon his arrival, von Hausen himself. Why the camp Commandant gave her any ear, any trust, was still a mystery, but it was a risk she took advantage of and played as carefully as she could. A dangerous game, where the wolf lurked not far behind von Hausen's usual kindness to her, waiting to snap its jaws around her shadow and snuff out her life. The blonde, blue-eyed Aryan wolf named Hans, with whom she waltzed ever nearer the edge of blackness, could devour her in a single moment should she make a misstep or show any morsel of fear.

Despite reaching out to all of her normally profitable links, she failed to learn anything about the two missing men from Stalag 31. It was as if they had vanished into the air. In the single brief dialogue with Hans allowed to her that week, she learned only that he was as ignorant of their whereabouts, their fates, as she was. Even when she was fortunate enough to intercept a radio communiqué between Stetcher and Berlin, there had been no mention of Paddy or Newt.

She presumed that meant that either the men were dead and thus not worth mentioning, or else the Gestapo officer knew nothing of their fates and did not dare admit his failure to capture them to his superiors.

Either way, it was not news she anticipated sharing with Sparks and the other Stalag residents. Already she could see the effects of recent events in the faces of the men she saw on Stasio's small farm on a daily basis. Tension, anger, remorse, but most pervasive was a blankness, a sense of despair in the belief that they were one step nearer to death now that Buckman was gone. Too many wore a look of defeat and hopelessness as they teetered on the edge of giving up. A successful escape, even if it was only by two men, would give them something to cling to. Instead, their chosen leader was dead and the other four had been broken or scattered. The men needed hope, something positive, and Clara had nothing to offer.

It was of little help that, for the week of Skip and Jamie's incarceration, Stetcher assumed a more direct role in the lives of the men of Camp 1 than he normally did. Angry at being punished by von Hausen, he used the week to torment the Italian officer, denigrating him in front of the prisoners whenever he could, cursing him for stupidity and ineptitude. Moretti was a decent man in Clara's opinion, a man caught in a war, in a German army, and in a role he had no interest in. His presence in France was not his choice. Whenever his back was turned, and von Hausen was not around, Stetcher found some excuse to strike prisoners, particularly those officers in Barrack's J where Buckman had once bunked. By the week's end, not one of the officers was without some bruise or scar or scabbed over wound left by the Gestapo officer. They could not complain, there was no one to complain to, for the other German soldiers and officers turned a blind eye to Stetcher's actions and, with Sturmbannfuhrer Moretti and Doctor Dengler in disfavor with the Commandant, there was no one willing to listen.

Well, thought Clara, Hans would listen to her. He might not act, but he would listen. If she got the chance, she would plead the men's case because no one else would…or could.

It was not until Thursday morning that the Scottish radioman, Sparks, was assigned to milking duty at the farmhouse. He and Paddy had been the men she normally interfaced with, the two men with knowledge of radios and covert communications. Now that Paddy was gone, Sparks was her only contact, at least for now, and as the only one of the men she knew well enough to fully trust, he had to be the one she revealed the truth to.

She crept into the barn where he greeted her with his typical enthusiastic boyish smile, as though he had anticipated her arrival. His jaw beneath his beard was bruised and swollen from his ear to his chin, the effect of Stetcher's walking stick she presumed, but he only shrugged away her concern when she traced her fingertips over the purpling skin as though it embarrassed him to be fussed over. He thankfully, without a word, accepted the bits of wire and packet of flour she gave him, offerings that would help ease men's' hunger as well as keep his makeshift radio receiver functioning. These things, and her friendly smile as the cow he was milking struggled to avoid his hands, spoke to her of a comfort in her company that she imagined he rarely felt behind the barbed wire. Without Paddy as the usual buffer between them, the man who normally undertook the exchanges and dialogue, it was up to the two of them to make this new relationship work.

Sparks updated her on the conditions in the camp, as Paddy normally would have, and they discussed the latest news of the war that they had both been able to obtain, thankful that the Germans rarely chose to closely guard the milking barn. With only one entrance and exit, no one who went in was going to escape, and surrounded as the farm was by fencing, the village, and the camp, anyone who considered digging their way out from here would only endanger themselves and the farms' owners. The Germans, or at least von Hausen, saw a benefit to cultivating a friendly relationship with Stasio, Clara, and Marcella. If the prisoners felt compelled to keep the family safe for the foodstuffs they provided, they would, von Hausen expected, be more inclined to behave themselves.

It meant a constant close eye kept on the residents of the farmhouse, but the relationship had worked thus far because none of them sought to cause trouble. They cooperated, they worked, and the Germans, more or less, turned a blind eye to their interactions with the Stalag residents.

In those moments when they could speak inside that barn, Sparks seemed so innocent, untouched by the war, by the grueling life in the Stalag; it was easy to forget there was a war outside. And it seemed that the brief touch of the outside world she offered him through conversation, a smile, a bit of laughter, was enough to revitalize him, giving him back some of the hope that had gone out of the men since Buckman's death.

His buoyant air melted quickly, however, when she revealed what little she knew about his missing friends. When she placed O'Callaghan's dog tags into his hand, his expression became so grief-stricken that she wanted to embrace him, reassure him, as he wept, that if any man could survive the wilds of the French countryside it would be Patrick O'Callaghan. Her words of comfort had little effect, however, and by now one of the soldiers outside had decided that the milking was taking too long; he barked at the Scot to hurry up and Clara was forced to abandon Sparks and leave the barn. She tried to catch his eye as she retreated, but he was slipping the tags around his neck and returned his attention to the task of milking again. She suspected he would see or hear very little until he processed the news she had given.

From him, she had learned that after a brief, touching ceremony held for Colonel Buckman, there had been further discussion about the wisdom or futility of further escape attempts. No consensus or agreement had been reached, but at least the men were still talking. They could not agree on Colonel Campbell's leadership, nor agree to disagree. Daily life for the prisoners swung between apathy and a barrage of flaring tempers.

And it was Spark's guess that the atmosphere would continue to grow more strained until Skip and Jamie were released from the Cooler and either returned to the barracks or executed for their part in the escape attempt. Whichever end they faced, tempers would again come to a head. Given the chance, the Scot would rather move into any other barracks to be clear of the fighting when the implosion came than to be present when it happened.

Life after Buckman's death was no less troubled in the von Hausen household when Clara went there on Friday morning to fetch Mila for a horseback outing with Stasio and the mandatory entourage of German soldiers. She had just arrived, sliding down from the gray nag typically used for plowing, when the Commandant blustered down the front steps and pushed past without seeing her, or at least without acknowledging her in some fashion, something that was most unusual these days. He got into the rumbling silver car that had been waiting and stared straight ahead with a sour, stiff expression as his driver put the car into gear and the car pulled away.

In the doorway, Frau von Hausen watched dispassionately, the only tension visible in her body was the tremor in her hand as she drank from the ever-present glass of brandy. She looked at Clara coldly, turned, and went inside, closing the door without speaking or asking why she was there. Clara waited, presuming that the woman remembered the agreed upon outing and would send Mila to the door. It was nearly ten minutes later before she heard the clatter of the drapes pulling back; Mila's young face peered out at her with a sad look of disappointment and a shake of her head.

With a regretful sigh, Clara returned to her horse. She disliked being between Hans and his wife and even more deeply disliked that the child was so often caught between her warring parents, caught in the effects of a war she had no business being in. What the Commandant and his wife had fought about this time was unimportant; it was likely nothing new, the rehashing of old arguments Clara imagined she would hear about later from the frustrated and lonely Hans.

At least Mila's absence meant a day-long ride with Stasio without the inconvenience of German guards. It was something she eagerly anticipated as she hurried back to the farmhouse. Such moments alone with Stasio were too rare with the Germans ever-present in their lives. She treasured those moments when they came. She would accept no excuses from Stasio today. The farm and the Germans could wait and get along without him. She could not.

Chapter 6
July 9, 1943

I n the open area that served as both recreation yard and parade grounds, beneath the dusty heat of the setting sun, the work-weary men of Camp 1 gathered for evening appell, stoop-shouldered and ready for a night's rest. Long shadows cast by the barracks, the watchtowers, and the posts which stretched the sharp wire were the only shade to be had, but at least there was a breeze, blowing tonight through the trees on the river side of the camp, evaporating the sweat of the day from skin and clothing, blowing away the stale stench that seemed to cling to the men no matter what effort they made to be free of it.

The stench of slow death. There was no other explanation for it.

As always, their keepers were punctual, 1800 hours precisely. During the colder months, appell came earlier, before it was too dark for the soldiers to keep an eye on their wards within the perimeter of camp without the glare of spotlights from the towers. In the warmer months, however, even with the later hour, the men still found they had sufficient daylight hours to amuse themselves...

...as long as their enjoyment did not upset the soldiers.

The men congregated, six units in all, lined up four by four where they could. Those from Barracks J did likewise, but their queues were less orderly. Three, two, two and one, with Leonard having assumed Buck's place at the head of the third row. Every day that week, Stetcher took a perverse pleasure in making George count and recount his men, driving home the fact that his comrades had disobeyed orders and were paying the price for it.

Not that J barrack had ever been full. Stalag 31 was far enough from the frontline and secluded enough in locale that new intakes were rare. There were fewer men housed here now than when the camp had opened early in 1941. The prisoners were mostly pilots shot down in the region, or soldiers suspected of being spies and saboteurs kept for periodic interrogation. Some were navy men captured off the Brittany coast or foot soldiers who had been in Western France for some purpose not necessarily connected to combat. The majority were enlisted men, and so the captured officers were pooled into a single barracks where they were easier to keep watch over. Death, the rare escapes, and the occasional weeding out of troublemakers by sending them elsewhere, kept the numbers in Barracks J relatively small.

Trying to keep the dissention to a minimum, Sparks mused as he fell into his usual place behind Vic. He cast a quick glance over his shoulder out of habit, still expecting to see Paddy's lumbering frame behind him. Of course, the man was not there, and Spark put his hand on his chest, over the extra set of I.D. tags that hung there, in salute to his missing friend. To his left, Taffy, Bonny, and Ray stood silently at attention as always, as none of those three were given to causing trouble.

Beyond them, Leonard, a frequent enough agitator in the past, stared at the ground. The Alabama tailor had been hardest hit by Buckman's death. He looked to have lost his will to survive as well as his friend. These days, he only seemed alive when he stood at the fence talking with the residents of Camp 2, a collection of Jews, Gypsies, and French insurgents the Germans felt too potentially useful to kill outright. Without something meaningful to latch on to, Leonard's body would soon waste and follow his already dying soul.

Sparks had seen it before during his time in Stalag 31. He had no desire to see it again.

The fourth row of men, Dusty and Ronny, were the last to fall in as usual. Dusty took his position behind the American barnstormer, slapping him on the back of his head as he did so. Ronny turned and punched the smaller man squarely on the shoulder. It was a playful act, but one with enough force behind it to cause Dusty to wince and step out of Ronny's reach before gesturing rudely. Ronny tried a second playful swing but missed, and with one of the German guards now passing by, he surrendered his pursuit.

A painful jab in the chest drew Spark's attention forward. Vic tipped his head to the right, towards the GSH, where Moretti and five soldiers were escorting Jamie and Skip into their midst. Both men squinted and stumbled as they were pushed along. Jamie looked weary, shell-shocked and demoralized, but Sparks imagined he would snap out of it after a shower, a meal, and a decent night's sleep. There would be the inevitable questions, but for the most part, Sparks believed the officers would let Jamie be.

Because it was Skip whom most blamed for the failed escape. Skip who had gotten involved with the Commandant's wife. Skip who, intentionally or not, had the opportunity to give away their plans and provide information from the Englishwoman that proved to be false. Of course, Buckman must have known the risk in believing that intel, must have known her words could have been misleading, but he had taken the chance anyhow. Skip could not be faulted for a decision that had ultimately been Buck's. Perhaps if Newt's condition had not been so dire, the plan, the timing, would have been different. Perhaps they would have succeeded.

Sparks, being the pragmatist he was, believed that in this instance, there was enough blame to go around. The blame should, rightly, be on the commanding officer's shoulder, for it had been, in the end, his choice, but as admired as Buckman was, the majority of men would choose a more immediate, more troublesome target to blame, whether guilty or not. Skip Henderson was that target.

That particular man walked quietly enough, not fighting his escorts as he usually would, but it was the coiled silence of a man wound too tight by anger. His gaze remained low, front of his trudging feet, but to Sparks, who thrived on perception and communication, Skip's attention was focused on the soldiers around them and how near Jamie was.

Vic snickered. "Wager we'll have a brawl before lights out."

That was a wager Sparks knew better than to take.

George threw Vic a scathing, silencing look, but his attention, too, was on Jamie. There were no obvious signs of injury, abuse, or mistreatment beyond what had been obtained during the escape effort, but there was a visible lack of food and sleep. The new camp leader sighed with relief and focus his eyes forward. The two men were deposited at the rear of the group from Barrack J. Jamie stepped into place behind Leonard, and Skip took his place behind Dusty. Their escorts assumed their positions with the perimeter guard as Stetcher arrived and began putting the men through their calls.

Too much tension. Sparks knew he was not the only one to feel it. Dusty fidgeted, ready to wrestle Skip to the ground on a moment's notice if he needed to, though he was smaller and wirier than the Australian. Even Bonny, Taffy and Leonard were ready to pounce, though Sparks figured that in Leonard's case, it would be to teach

Skip a lesson rather than to break up any fights. Would Leonard get to Skip, Sparks wondered, before Skip reached Jamie?

Stetcher did not torment the officers with multiple recounts of their ranks today as he sometimes did; he seemed in a hurry, eager to get out of Camp 1 now that his week of punishment was over as well. He passed each cluster, counting the men himself by fours, each time writing down numbers in a notebook he carried. Sparks felt several sets of eyes upon him, as if he was supposed to know what the Gestapo officer was up to. This was a different routine than normal, this cataloging of their numbers, by his guess for some sort of report requested by the German high command.

If he was lucky, Sparks would have the radio up and running soon enough to intercept any pertinent radio information that might explain the count, but so far he had not found a way to tap into any of the officers' phone lines.

In front of J, Stetcher counted twice more and lingered long enough to glower at Skip and Jamie with a bird of prey stare. Then, with a gesture that looked like a wave of dismissal but might have been something else, he walked to the next unit of men and paid no further attention to the officers.

Finished with the census taking, Stetcher stopped at the camp gateway, writing notes, speaking to Moretti in a manner that seemed more the style of command-giving than an actual conversation. The Italian officer begrudgingly waited for him to finish whatever he was writing, saluted, and then watched him leave with a clenched jaw before turning to the prisoners long enough to bark "Ecarté," in an unusually angry tone before he followed the Gestapo officer towards the Stalag office building.

"What do you think that was about?" Vic asked as the ben began to fall out of rank and drift towards their usual hangouts.

Sparks shrugged. "Dunno." He had not been any closer to hear the conversation than Vic had been.

"Maybe I'll have a chat with Wagner…"

Vic's words were cut short by an unintelligible angry shout.

As anticipated, Skip had waited until the German officers' backs were turned and the prisoners no longer standing at attention before pouncing on Jamie and knocking him to the ground with a single blow. Now he was atop him, his hands around the smaller man's throat, with George, Ray, and Dusty trying to pull him away. They eventually succeeded, helped by Leonard pulling Jamie out of the fray from the other direction and helping him to his feet, but as soon as Jamie was steady, Skip broke away from the arms that held him and charged again.

This time, however, Jamie was ready and held his ground as Skip's larger, broader shoulders caught him across the chest.

"You killed him, you mother…"

Jamie did not reply but instead shoved Skip away before catching him across the jaw with a well-aimed punch. This was not the time for words, not while Skip's emotions ran hot and speaking took too much effort from the fight for dominance. Ray found himself in the middle of the scuffle as he tried to separate the men again, and ended up with Skip's fist catching him squarely in the ribs. Unable to breathe through the pain, Ray dropped to his knees, and Sparks, now near enough, pulled the British medic away from the continuing brawl.

There was cheering now, from both the men of Camps 1 and 2 and from German guards who never failed to enjoy the spectacle of their prisoners beating one another. Few knew the particulars of the fight, but they did not need to when there were friendly wagers to be made on the winner. Somewhere far back in the crowd, however, beyond the men crowded around the combatants, the metal gates clanged open again and Moretti's voice could barely be heard demanding, "Nein! Halt! No!"

If either Skip or Jamie heard him, neither responded.

Vic, ever one for a brawl, took it upon himself to express how unhappy some of the men in camp were with the Australian's presumed breach of propriety. He was faster than the Aussie, able to slide in, crack his fist across the side of the man's face, and dance away before Skip realized who had struck the blow. Rage temporarily turned from Jamie, he rushed at the retreating assailant, only to be caught unexpectedly by a punch in the back. Skip snapped backward, clutching the small of his back as he spun around to be met by Jamie's fist in his nose.

"Stop this at once," Moretti demanded when he broke through to the front of the throng with three other soldiers at his heels, stopping with his revolver aimed at Jamie's chest. The man knew it was unlikely that the Canadian had started the fight, but it did not matter. Moretti and the guards who had yanked Skip back, were ending it. Jamie took a step back, hands raised in surrender. More furious now, Skip tried to lunge again, but as he slipped out of the Germans' grips,

Vic stuck his foot out and brought Skip crashing to the ground. Skip landed, rolled, but when he struggled to his feet, it was to find Moretti's revolver and the three soldiers' guns now aimed at him instead of Jamie.

"Cara Dio, Captain Henderson. Are you so fond of confinement that you had to start a fight to ensure another stay? What is the meaning of this?"

Skip said nothing, only growled, and Jamie just shrugged, neither interested in explaining what had happened. Moretti studied the faces of the other gathered about, ringed by guards with drawn weapons, annoyed that his question was unanswered but grudgingly the men chose solidarity even when embroiled in disagreement. He needed that answer, however, in order to mete out punishment, and without those answers, Stetcher would demand the entire barracks, perhaps the entire camp, be punished.

"Signori, please…must I punish everyone?" His gaze lingered on Ray, knowing that man was the most likely to talk to avoid group punishment. The young man, with a sheepish look of panic at Skip, at Jamie, and lastly at George, sighed and lowered his gaze.

"Captain Henderson struck Captain Campbell…" was what he finally said, true words that were enough to garner glares from many around him.

Moretti barely resisted shaking his head. True or not, Jamie had clearly taken the brunt of the fight and the Italian feared there were broken bones. "Obersturmfuhrer Wagner, summon Herr Dengler; tell him we are in need of his skills. The rest of you, take Campbell to his bunk and make him comfortable. Henderson…if you will promise not to do this again, I will ensure you only have to endure tonight and tomorrow in confinement. Agreed?"

Glowering at Ray now instead of Jamie, wiping blood from his nose and upper lip, Skip snarled, "Sure…" It was an easy enough promise to make to avoid extended punishment, although no one, not even the Italian, expected him to adhere to that promise.

Two soldiers took the Australian away. Though Skip had come out ahead in the fight, even he walked with stiffness and obvious pain…and his sagging shoulders suggested that he understood his standing in the camp and was wrestling with his recent actions. He would be the outcast, the one no one trusted, for a very long time.

With Ray's constant interference and efforts to appease the Germans, however, Skip would not be the only pariah.

Sparks remained where he was, staring at the darkening sky as the others dispersed and Dengler arrived at Barrack J to tend Jamie. He would rather not go inside while the doctor was there, while the tension inside the barracks was so high. He, like everyone else, wanted to know what had happened to Paddy, to Newt, wanted to know where the blame actually fell. He wanted his radio.

He would have to wait, however, until Dengler departed.

Chapter 7
July 10, 1943

"Don't start," Jamie muttered to the docile-looking cow as he peeled off his ragged shirt and hung it over the wall of the stall. "You'd feel like shit too if you'd been through what I have, so go easy on me." He paused and patted the animal's side. "Yeah, you're right...I shoulda kept my distance..."

As he sat upon the bale of hay to examine his wounds, the cow nudged him, reminding him of the reason he was there. "Ouch!" he protested, pushing her head away, but she ignored his pain and continued pushing against his bruised stomach, showing no signs of letting up her assault. "Okay, okay...just a minute...let me find the bloody stool..."

"Do you make a habit of talking to animals, James?"

His heart skipped a beat and he hid the warmth that spread across his cheeks by keeping his head turned away from the woman who had come in behind him. Without turning or seeing her, he knew who it was. He would know Zaline's voice anywhere. Gingerly, when he thought he could look at her without giving away his immediate response to her company, he rose to greet her, his brow wrinkled in consternation at the way she used his formal name, even if it had been in jest. It was a minor annoyance, easily forgiven since this was the first time she had ever addressed him as something other than Captain Campbell.

He started to answer her but she cut him off with alarm in her voice. "Mon Dieu, monsieur, you are bleeding. Did the Germans...?"

"No. I'm fine..." He tried to brush off the aide she offered. No matter how much he wanted her to touch him, it would be a very bad idea if she did. Very bad for him at least.

A fight in the Stalag then. Zaline did not need to know which men had been involved, or what the fight had been over, to understand it was what Jamie meant, what he was not saying. "What is wrong with men? Don't you get enough fighting with the Germans? Do you need to fight amongst yourselves?" She tore a length of cloth from her underskirt and began to dab away the blood from a gash over his left eye.

"Hey!" he swore with a wince, unable to back away from her attention due to the bale of hay behind him and the wall behind that.

"Sorry." She dabbed more carefully, the contrite sweetness in her voice burdened with a note of remorse that seemed from a deeper well than such a minor pain should have warranted.

Jamie watched her eyes as she worked, mesmerizing eyes that had haunted his dreams for many months, erotic dreams that always ended the same way. He imagined himself even now stroking her cheek, brushing her dark hair from her face, leaning to kiss her and being met with a fierce, all-consuming passion. There was no need for words in that place of dreams, only a yearning that had waited too long to be fulfilled. His fantasy had just shifted to laying her down into the fresh straw, lowering himself over her with her arms and legs entangled with his, when she cleared her throat and murmured, "There...that's better."

He blinked, startled back to the present, startled into noticing the tears in her eyes. He knew her husband's fate, understood the grief he had forgotten she bore, and now felt like a cad for his fantasy when she had recently endured such a loss.

A loss that was, in part at least, his fault.

"I am sorry about Etienne..." he murmured, an apology for the inappropriate daydream as well as for the part he had played in her husband's death.

She stood with a shrug. "You did nothing, Captain. He knew the dangers...the risks. As did I. We all know..."

"Maybe...but that doesn't prepare us for things like this. It's a little different than watching someone die slowly, knowing what's coming but being unable to stop it...and when it does..." His voice quavered. When she offered her hand to help him to his feet, he stared at it for a moment before taking it. The touch made the ache in his center a little more bearable.

It seemed to Jamie, the contact between them had a similar effect on her.

"Your mother?" He had told her shortly after his arrival at the camp of his mother's illness and death when he had been quite young, a death he carried with him despite the protracted passage of years, and she guessed now that was whom he spoke of.

Jamie shrugged the question away. The subject of lost mothers had come up in that long ago conversation, but it was not something Jamie liked to talk about. "Some things we never get over...we learn to live with them and move on...but I'll tell you this...Etienne was a helluva brave man to do the things he did. We're all grateful, regardless of the way things went down....so...thank you."

The tears that rimmed her eyes broke free and she impulsively kissed his cheek. Such gratitude coming from this particular man struck her more deeply than expected.

Lingering there for a moment, her face against his, she whispered, "Thank you...James..."

The shrill wail of the lunch break whistle intruded on what Jamie irrationally hoped would become the kiss of his dreams. Zaline jerked back and hissed, "Go...I'll finish here..."

Jamie scrambled out of the barn, knowing he would not be allowed to eat if he was not in the line in time, embarrassed that it had taken him so long to even start his job as well as by the thoughts that refused to give him peace. She was right to push him away. She was still married in her heart, her husband not long dead, and he was likely a dead man walking himself...the same as every other man in Stalag 31. He was the very last thing she needed.

But despite the guilt, he felt unexpected hope, for she had once again called him by name.

❧*❧

The barracks of Stalag 31 had been hastily erected as soon as German forces arrived in the village of Ste Marie sur Canut, constructed largely from lumber gleaned from the nearby forest and slapped together as quickly as possible by the villagers who had been pressed into labor. The cleared stretch of trees had been added onto the Arnauds' farmable land and pressed into service to feed the newcomers as prisoners began to appear behind the barbed wire almost immediately. The untreated lumber already showed signs of wear and weather, the wood gray now, cracked and splintered and warped, creating gaps that allowed daylight and air to push inside and allowed light and sound to seep out. In the winter months, that ventilation was a curse, as there was no way to keep warm before the drafty chill. In the summer months as now, however, the cooling breezed reduced the stuffiness and the stench of sweat that might otherwise suffocate them all.

Sparks fiddled with his hand-built radio, trying to hear the only bit of British broadcasting he had been able to find. The attempt to hear was proving futile, however, because Vic, Taffy, Dusty and Ronny were gathered around the stained wooden table engaged in a raucous game of poker with a deck of playing cards Taffy had acquired in his last parcel from his wife in Cardiff. Ray was outside leaning against the edge of the barrack, alone, watching without knowing for what, Bonny sat upon the stoop preparing tomorrow's sermon and keeping a lookout for the Germans, while Jamie lay on his bunk trying to will away the pain of his injuries enough to find solace in sleep. Leonard sat on his bunk too, but from this angle, with Sparks in the upper bunk and Leonard in the lower one, the Scot did not know what the man was doing.

George stood beside the bunk, leaning against the frame as he too tried to listen for whatever news the radio might share tonight. News from London, news about the Allied progress in the war, those things were what gave the men in Stalag 31 hope. That commodity made Sparks and his radio invaluable, and the men did their best to protect both. It was worth every bit of scrounging for materials they had to do in order to keep the radio functioning.

When Sparks cast an irritated glare in the direction of the game, the elder Campbell looked over his shoulder and growled, "Would you keep it down?" Some noise was required in order to mask the radio voices from the Germans, but too much noise meant not only that they could not hear the radio, but they might also attract their keepers to come in and discipline them.

"George," Taffy grinned at him, flipping the Canadian a cigar that had been in his pocket most of the day, "no need to be cranky."

"We're trying to..."

"Krauts on deck," hissed Bonny from the doorway.

Sparks scrambled to disassemble the radio and hide it, some pieces in the loose boards of the ceiling, some beneath the rotted sill of the nearest window, some within the flabby pillow of cloth that passed as his mattress, and some in George's shoe. Fortunately, they had once again been given enough warning to have the pieces obscured by the time Moretti, the guard named Conrad Wagner, and another too-young German soldier pushed Skip up the stairs into the barracks. Not far behind, Ray followed, in a rush to witness the Aussie's return to 'civilization'.

"Good evening, gentlemen," the Italian said as the Australian shuffled towards his bunk. Though his anger was palpable, Skip did not appear as if he intended to misbehave. His nose was swollen, one eye was dark, and he moved as if favoring his ribs. There were a few murmurs in the room from those who felt he deserved the beating he had gotten, but Jamie chose not to acknowledge him, not even cracking his eyes to see who had come in.

He knew who it was by the sound of the man's shambling footsteps.

"Evening, Renz," Dusty called. "Wanna join?" He waved his cards at the major.

Ignoring the nickname used in place of his title, Moretti shook his head. "No, no…it is too late for that…and you know that fraternizing with the pris…with you, is forbidden."

Taffy did not look at him as he pushed his wager to the center of the table. "Is that a Berlin rule or a Stetcher one?"

Moretti began to say something, skewed his face, and shrugged. "It does not matter. Rules are meant to be obeyed…

"And you do such a good job of that," snorted Vic. Others in the room laughed, his tone as biting as it was teasing. "Your respect for the Krauts is so damn touching."

"Lieutenant Burns," Moretti said, straightening his posture as if offended. "I may not be one of them, but you are expected to show me the same respect and…"

"They don't get my respect or courtesy," Vic snorted, his expression sour as he folded his cards and laid them on the table, surrendering the hand. "And neither would you if it weren't so bloody obvious that you want out of here as badly as we do."

"Come," the Italian barked at the soldiers with him. He did not know why he let these men goad him, teasing or not. But he did not have to listen to it, and it was not worth knocking Vic across the head. Wagner went out first, followed by the other soldier. Moretti paused in the doorway. "Five minutes until lights out."

"Aw, Renz," Taffy chuckled, "Can't we finish the game? I'm winning!"

"Five minutes."

Barracks J remained still until well after the Germans were out of visual range of the building. Some looked from one another to

Skip, who had sunk into his bunk with a groan and stared at the bunk above him with his hands laced behind his head. Sparks caught the look that passed between Vic and Ronny as Vic pushed slowly back from the table and the game he had been losing.

George saw it too. "Lieutenant," he hissed. The one-time Olympic hopeful appeared not to hear, or chose not to listen to, the Barracks highest-ranking officer. His eyes never left Skip, even when the Australian returned the stare as if waiting. In a fair fight, his size and strength meant Skip would win against Alistair Victor Burns, but in his condition, he was not likely to win anything. Any fight was going to be far from fair.

Vic took a step towards the bunk.

George raised his voice as the whistle wailed for lights out. "Lieutenant."

Sill ignoring the man who should be his leader, Vic took a second step and was snapped in the back of the head with the twisted shirt Jamie had been using as a pillow.

"Leave it, Vic."

Skip's brow arched as he glanced at the man he currently considered the enemy.

"Yeah," Bonny added, his soothing tone a sharp contrast to the tension simmering in the room. "Not worth a night in the Cooler. Lights out." He pulled the string on the single bulb in the room that served as their primary lighting as Taffy put out the small oil lamp used during their card game.

Vic, not yet convinced to back down, turned from Jamie's interference to find Leonard's towering frame between him and his target. "Turn in. 'nough for tonight, don't ya think?"

Vic's fists balled at his side; he muttered something demeaning at the dark, mountainous man, and then went to his own bunk. "Suit yourself," he grunted, thumping the bunk above him in annoyance.

Bonny, already settling down to sleep in that bunk, ignored him.

The men quickly took to their beds. Most did not want to risk attracting attention to the barracks should any German guards be passing outside. George's gate and the slump of his shoulders suggested defeat and frustration. He knew it took time for men to come around to a change of command at the best of times, but whether or not George Campbell had the patience to wait long enough for it to happen within Barracks J, whether the prisoners in Stalag 31 could afford to wait, remained to be seen.

⁊*↩

The sun was approaching the horizon again, another day closing, but there was still time before the German-imposed curfew for her to make her way home. Her detour had drawn her across town, to where she knelt now beside her husband's grave marker, running her hand over its treated wood, confused, embarrassed, and mortified by her feelings, and angry with Etienne for dying and leaving her in such a position. Before his death, the thought of being unfaithful had never crossed her mind. She had noticed handsome James Campbell, but noticing was all there was. She had adored her husband from the depths of her soul, still did, so what was the meaning of this weakness now?

Barely a week after his death, she had felt herself on the brink of kissing another man, of wanting more than a kiss. Was this part of the grieving process, she wondered? Did it stem from weakness, from loneliness, from the stinging loss and a need for reassurance that she was still beautiful and desirable and that her life had not ended with Etienne's death? Were her feelings only those of pity for a man she liked, whom she knew was equally alone? Was her fragile heart seeking to take advantage of a lonely man's obvious attraction to assuage her own desperate needs? Were they rooted in the fear of facing the remainder of this war alone?

She would need time, time to think about her feelings, to grieve and heal without taking advantage of Jamie Campbell. It would be best to keep distance between them. No one, not even James, could help her get over the loss of Etienne. She had to do that on her own. James deserved better than being used as her survival crutch.

Hopefully, she sighed, he would understand. Hopefully, wherever Etienne was, he understood too.

❧Suspicion's Gate❦

Chapter 8
July 11, 1943

T hose fortunate enough to find favor with their captors, or who were able to bribe or buy the privilege from either the Germans or the other men in Camp 1 were allowed just enough water to shave and bathe each week. It was a rare luxury, instituted when von Hausen came to Stalag 31 as a means of managing the captives' behavior and reducing the instances of disease and infestation that were so common in squalid conditions. It was an unusual measure, or so the prisoners surmised by the amount of complaining Stetcher did about it, but on average, the desire for an occasional shower motivated the Stalag residents to just the sort of obedience the Commandant intended. After the near-escape, however, showers and shaving had not been allowed for the duration of their punishment period, thus those given the privilege today were doubly grateful for it. As the warmest water ran out quickly, the sticky, wet room was packed with men in various stages of undress.

When Dusty elbowed his way into the hut with Skip in tow, the cacophony of voices ceased. All eyes turned to look at the quiet, downcast Aussie who still bore the wounds of his personal war with the Germans. His normally mischievous eyes were devoid of emotion and did little more than stare at the dingy cement floor as he undressed. The responses to his arrival last night, and then this morning over breakfast as he faced the entire camp population, had left their marks upon him as surely as any beating would have. If there was any anger there for the woman he blamed, it was hidden deep inside now.

More than one man muttered under their breath as they discussed how Skip had gained the privilege of a shower after his recent conduct. Dusty was ready for them, should they ask, as it had been his efforts, and the loss of a few of his own privileges, that had gotten Skip in here, and as he watched his friend undress out of the corner of his eye, he saw the full extent of the man's injuries. It was going to take more than a warm shower to ease his friend's suffering, but giving up a few cigarettes and privileges would be worth it. From head to toe, the Aussie was covered in angry bruises in various stages of healing, reminding the Brit of a badly beaten prizefighter after a losing match. On top of those injuries he had sustained from Jamie, the Germans had made sure Skip paid for his errors.

If he had suffered worse than James Campbell, it was because Skip fought back…and because of the Commandant's wife, whether the soldiers were aware of that or not.

Eyes closed, Dusty let the water play over his head and shoulders, forgetting everything that had happened in the past week for a few moments, but his revelry in the lukewarm water was cut short by nearby voices that brought him immediately to attention.

"Just had to see what's so special about your dick that you had to betray Buck for it," snarled Vic.

"Hope it was worth it," Leonard muttered.

Under other circumstances, Skip would have challenged them, naked or not, pushed them towards a fight that none likely wanted. But the fire had gone out of him; he shrugged, turned his back to the spray of water, and reached for the tiny bar of harsh soap that rested on the nearby ledge.

Before his hand could close around it, Vic snatched it away and threw it towards the water house door. He had enough of an arm that the tiny morsel landed in the courtyard dust. "Traitor," he snapped before taking off at a run to avoid the multitude of other protesting men who were now without soap. He grabbed Skip's clothes on the way and dropped them outside as he ran.

Some men took off after Vic, some playfully, some in annoyance, but those who did not watched to see how Skip would take this affront. For a moment, Dusty thought Skip was going to give chase as well, but the anger in his eyes gave way to something else. On another man, Dusty might have called it defeat, On Skip, the unusual expression went far deeper than that, but Dusty did not know what to call it.

Near the door, in the process of dressing, George cleared his throat and spoke loudly enough for everyone in the water house to hear. "Blame won't bring Buck back. He wasn't a fool…don't make him look like one for second-guessing his commands. Let's not cheapen his sacrifices with this bullshit."

There were a few mutters, some of agreement, and a few sneers, but no one spoke again as Stetcher appeared in the doorway with disdain on his face, his walking stick in one hand and a clipboard in the other. His icy glare traveled the room as if seeking someone in particular, and then he spoke. "Herr Oberfuhrer has issued work orders for today…"

"It's Sunday," someone complained. The walking stick hit the door frame with a loud crack.

"There is work to be done. The world doesn't stop because it is Sunday." He did not glance at the clipboard again as he began assigning duties, perhaps at random, perhaps by memory. "Milking…Corporal Ellis, Private Jenkins…" That meant that the Commandant or one of his officers perhaps required extra milk, possibly for entertaining guests. Usually, the farm owners were allowed to keep Sunday's milk for themselves.

"Mail…Captain Campbell…" Jamie was not in the water house to hear it, having been the one to give up the shower pass he had procured from Wagner for Dusty to share with Skip. He would be told of his day's duties soon enough. Mail deliveries were sporadic, and since all men looked forward to the possibility of something from home, that was one responsibility no one complained about.

"Latrines, same as yesterday; Commandant's gardens…Captains Miller and…" Stetcher paused for deliberate effect before adding, "Henderson."

Skip was the last person anyone expected to be given a work detail near the Commandant's house, given what had recently happened. It was likely a trap concocted by Stetcher, von Hausen, or both, to get Skip into close proximity to the man's wife to see what would happen. There was no way von Hausen could not know about his wife's various affairs, particularly the one with Skip Henderson. If the prisoners all knew, the Germans must as well. It was also possible that Jennifer von Hausen had requested that Skip be there, but allowing even that had to make this appointment a trap.

The malevolent gleam that sparked in Skip's previously vacant eyes was too far away for Stetcher to notice.

Hoping to avoid an incident he anticipated, even if no one else did, George took a cautious step forward, while staying well away from Stetcher's walking stick, and said, "As his C.O., Henderson is not fit for heavy labor and I respectfully request to be sent in his stead until he is well enough to work…" Hopefully, he thought, by the time the man healed, whatever he felt for the von Hausen's wife would have cooled.

"Doctor Dengler has deemed Henderson fit enough. The rota is final. Auf Wiedersehen." the Gestapo officer clicked the heels of his boots together and marched out of the sweltering water house, his expression smug and pleased.

Dusty sighed and closed his hand on Skip's shoulder, possibly in sympathy, possibly as a reminder to stay out of trouble, but the Aussie shrugged the touch away. Whatever happened today was on Stetcher's head, Dusty mused, hoping he could keep Skip from making a horrible mistake.

❧*❧

The first time she found herself alone in the presence of Hans von Hausen, Clara had been terrified. Stetcher had arrived on Stasio's doorstep and demanded that she accompany him, indicating only that Stalag 31's new commandant had requested her attendance in his office. Having never met the man, nor seen him, she had logically assumed that her radio subterfuge had finally been discovered and that the German officer intended to address the crime personally. She had shared one sweet, tender, terrified kiss with Stasio, feeling his fear for her in the way he held her, in the touch of his trembling fingers against her face. And then he let her go.

The imposing blonde figure with the piercing blue eyes had been seated behind his desk with his back to her when she and Stetcher entered his compound office. He had not moved as Stetcher introduced her as the most likely candidate to tutor Mila, the commandant's young daughter. Though she did not know how she had come by that recommendation, the hot, hard knot of fear in Clara's stomach unraveled a little at that moment, though not completely. After all, an offer of tutoring could be a ploy to keep an eye on her, catch her in an act of betrayal, or maneuver her into revealing information she swore never to share.

She had decided at once that that would never happen.

With a tired gesture, Hans dismissed Stetcher without turning his chair. The older man lingered, apparently thinking it unwise to leave his superior alone with her, but Hans barked something derisive in German that caused Stetcher to blanch. Clara had stared at Stetcher with as much confusion as she could muster, hoping that neither man knew how much German she could speak and understand. Stetcher looked as if he had swallowed something sharp and painful, as if he wanted to say something hateful, but all he did was salute and depart with a warning glance at the woman he had brought into the room.

She had found it amusing that the small man with the gun and attitude though her to be a threat.

Only after the door slammed shut, leaving the room silent for too many nervous minutes, did the man in the leather chair turn slowly around to face her.

Even now, so many months after that meeting, Clara could still see that expression when she closed her eyes, recall his demeanor, the sound of his breathing as he stood, extended his hand across the desk to her, and bid her sit in nearly flawless French. He had expected to give her the full force of his military training and it was the face she had expected to see. Something brusque, demanding, and impersonal. But that mask had slipped off, the ice melting in his eyes in those first few moments before their hands touched.

And she had experienced a lifting of the fear and hatred she had expected to feel for any German officer sent to Ste Marie.

They had talked of music, of history, and of architecture in that interview that stretched out for the better part of the afternoon. They had talked of her father's years as an architect in Brest before age had taken the man away. They spoke of Marseille, where they had both spent a great deal of time and to where both longed to return. They spoke of their mutual love of the sea.

And they spoke of Mila, his only child, whose love of horses had been sadly neglected as life in Berlin had ruled out pursuing such a passion. That Clara rode and had access to horses, and was willing to indulge the girl as well as tutor her in book studies, pleased Hans tremendously.

Clara seemed so fearless in his company, willing to look beyond the uniform to the man beneath it, that it made Hans eager to trust her. It had not been until several weeks later that she came to understand this perplexity. His wife, the beautiful British former opera singer Jennifer spurned him, seemingly because of the uniform he wore; it was both understandable to Clara and appalling at the same time. How hard must it be to have married a man whose people now attacked her homeland? Yet as she had surely known the growing state of affairs in Germany, how could she not have known the man she had chosen to marry, the requirements of his station, the responsibilities of the military service he had already been in tied to when they met? In time, Clara learned that the von Hausen's relationship was much more complicated than that, but still, she wondered. Hans was a smart, introspective, gentleman, well-learned and cultured. Wasn't the man Jennifer had married there behind the uniform his nationality required him to wear? Had the advent of war changed him so much?

Perhaps a better question, she sometimes mused, was why Clara could so easily see a side of the man that others seemed not to see. Even though his face bore the twisted responsibilities of his position and duty, his eyes always spoke of something else. There were little nuances of gesture that told Clara this man was more complex than appearances revealed.

It had not taken her long to graduate from being Mila's tutor to also being the girl's caretaker when it was necessary for her parents to be away. Clara liked to think of herself as Mila's friend, thought that rapport became more difficult to foster and maintain as she and Hans moved beyond business-type interactions towards something different. Something more personal than either had expected.

If Hans von Hausen had any friends in Ste Marie, Clara Beton was surely the first of them. The truth of it, she told herself again as she went up the steps and rang the bell, was that she was his only friend. The only person in the village and surrounding regions that the man trusted. That made the game she played, always hoping to gain intelligence from him, harder and harder to carry out.

Never get too close to your sources, her brother, Robert, had warned her.

As the door opened and the squat little woman who served as the von Hausens' only servant admitted her into the house, Clara wondered again how she possibly could have avoided getting too close to Hans.

"This way, Miss Clara," the woman said, indicating the study to their right. It was the room Clara was most often in when in the von Hausens' home, often brightly lit by the sun shining through the window glass to pool on the hardwood floor, but she still felt uncomfortable here. Jennifer did not like her; she seemed to believe Clara was sleeping with her husband, which to Clara seemed a sad absurdity coming from a woman who had known more affairs in her months in Ste Marie then young Mila had known years of life.

The servant opened the door to the study after a single knock, telling Clara she was expected. She was ushered into the room and the door was closed behind her, leaving her alone with Hans.

He was at his desk, as usual, his elbows resting upon its mahogany surface, his head buried in his hands as if he might be weeping. But his shoulders were still, his breathing measured, calm and strong. The drapes were still drawn, shrouding the room in near darkness, so Clara considered that perhaps he was suffering a headache. She placed her purse on the small table beside the door and crossed the room, her heels clacking upon the polished wood. He knew she was there though he did not move or speak, even when she stopped to draw back the drapes. The morning sun spilled across Han's hair so that it glittered silver and gold in the light.

She watched him, feeling no particular urgency to move or speak, but rather, finding an unusual peacefulness in this room and his quiet company. Sounds outside, the car being brought up and the driver Hans sometimes used getting out to tend to some last minute polishing, broke the mood as Hans stiffened at the sound.

Wanting to ease his troubles briefly, Clara stepped behind him and put her hands upon his shoulders. His uniform jacket hung upon the coat rack near the door, a dark ominous hell-ghost hovering on the periphery. There was only the crispness of black linen between her hands and his skin. The muscles there were too taut as she anticipated. He flinched, as though not having anticipated such an intimate, gentle contact. Her thumbs and fingers moved across muscles, kneading the tension until they began to unknot and relax.

Hans sighed and leaned his head back against her breasts before covering her hands with his.

"Thank you," he murmured. She could not see his face as he kissed the back of one hand, but she did not need to. That such a small act of kindness could touch the lonely man so deeply made her heart ache. How long had his life been so emotionally empty?

"It is nothing," she whispered, not trusting her voice to speak any louder.

He looked at her then, his eyes expressing thoughts and feelings he dared not voice. "You look lovely today."

"It is Sunday, Hans…or did you forget?" The arrangement to allow Mila to attend church with Clara and Stasio had been in place since Clara had first begun to work for him, but sometimes Hans seemed to lose track of the days of the week.

"Of course I didn't…she needs such rituals." He kissed her other hand before squeezing them both and releasing her. "You do not object to the inconvenience of escorts, do you…?" Sensing her coming retort, he shook his head and continued, "Of course I trust you…but them…" He gestured towards the window that faced the direction of Ste Marie. "I doubt they would harm her…but Stetcher expects nothing less after recent events…and Jennifer is afraid she will be…I would be remiss in my duties to allow my daughter to continue to travel unescorted amongst non-Germans."

"Just once," Clara muttered as she stepped away from him, "I would like such rules not to affect our lives."

"Yes…I would like that too."

"You will be home late?" She regretted changing the subject when he seemed willing to talk, but she could not afford to get into a discussion of wishes and plans for the future. It was a topic both avoided whenever it arose, because each knew what the future held. Regardless of the outcome of the war, his life was with Jennifer, either Berlin or elsewhere, and hers was with Stasio here in Ste Marie. Circumstances had thrown them together, but they had no more of each other than what the present offered. No future either of them could have would involve the other. That was the reality of it, and they knew it.

"Seven or eight, I imagine. This luncheon to entertain dignitaries should be over long before then, but there will be other business…dreadfully dreary and unnecessary…"

"You don't want to bring Jennifer…?" She did not need to ask. She could already hear it in his voice.

"She will hate it more than I will, but she must attend. It is expected. She will invariably drink too much…and then…God knows…I do not even know how I will manage the drive with her. We have barely spoken since that…"

He stopped short of giving away any part he might have had in feeding the prisoners false information or in receiving information about their plans from some other source. "And when we have spoken," he continued, rising from his chair to retrieve the shadow hanging near the door, "it has been nothing but angry words and insults. She asks about nothing but that damned Australian. It is enough of a burden that she'll sleep with any man who asks…and asks just as many…but must she…?"

"They are men, Hans, just as you are…" She could not excuse the behavior, but she could, at least, sympathize with their position and how they might find the offering too tempting to resist.

"That does not make it right."

"None of this is right; none of this should be happening. Them, you, Jennifer…the war. None of it. Perhaps if you try to talk…"

It was tired ground, a discussion they had shared before, weary words heavy from overuse. "You know I have tried, but she will not listen. She is too full of drink to hear what I say…and I am afraid my words are inadequate to tell her…"

"You are eloquent with words when you choose to be." Clara's smile was sincere and reassuring. There was no intent to flatter, only genuine appreciation of his gifts. "No one can save your marriage but you, Hans. You and Jennifer."

"Can I save what she has obviously given up on?" Now he donned his jacket and watched for the shadow to pass over her that always came over his wife.

Clara, however, still smiled softly and said, "You can try."

Hans put on his hat, the image of the monster complete. He took a step towards Clara and then hesitated, expecting her to shrink away. But it was a monster she did not fear in him, and as she stepped closer to accept the embrace he was looking to give, he released a long, shuddering sigh. It was a simple gesture of affection, something he wished he could get from his wife but that Jennifer no longer wished to give. An embrace that was more than an act of fear or apathy. He held Clara, and though his grip never tightened and his breathing remained steady, she could feel the increasing tension in every muscle of his body. Into her hair, with a voice thick with a multitude of emotions, he asked, "Can a man keep trying when he himself has given up?"

Clara's instinct was to stiffen, to pull away, or to flee what she believed would come next. But when she did not speak, he let her go and she was relieved to see on his face that it was a question with none of the obvious meaning behind it she had believed. If it was there, he had not yet admitted it to himself. Despite his feelings of hopelessness and despair, she knew Hans was not yet ready to give up on his troubled, wayward wife.

Even if, as he said, she had long ago given up on him.

The car horn blared. "Come. Mila is waiting and I must go."

"Hans?" Clara caught his hand as he reached for the door handle. He opened it before she could release him, and in the hall beyond Jennifer greeted them with an unsettling look of horror. Clara quickly let go of his hand, but it was too late. It was the only act of intimacy Jennifer had ever witnessed between them, and she had no way of knowing who had initiated it or what it meant, but knowing what Clara did of Jennifer, it was likely confirmation enough of her fears about her husband's loyalties, hypocritical though it was in comparison to her flagrant affairs with men from the prison camp. Hans seemed not notice Jennifer's expression as he crossed towards the bottom of the staircase. If he noticed anything at all, it was her haste to get out the door, which in his eyes was as much an attempt to escape him and the uniform as it was anything else.

"Mila? Miss Beton is here for you…and your mother and I are leaving." His voice echoed up the stairwell.

"Coming, father."

Hans glanced back at Clara, noticed her unhappy expression, and frowned. "You were about to say something?"

"Talk to her, Hans; tell her the truth, before it is too late."

He nodded his head, expression grim. "I will try."

❧*❧

The nearer they got to the von Hausen house, the more visible Skip's anger became. The rage that had bubbled in his veins for nearly a week had been temporarily beaten down, but now it was back, and soon he hoped it would be fed and extinguished. Nothing less than the death of the woman he believed had betrayed him to her husband would satiate his wrath. He knew too well that risking such revenge would likely come at the sacrifice of his life, but he did not care. He wanted her to suffer as he suffered. It was the only thing that had kept him going during those long days in confinement.

As he marched beside Dusty, two guards before and aft, he recalled happier times, when he and Jennifer had laughed and reveled in each other's company.

At first, she had been someone to talk to, to share memories of home with, to tell about his family and the girl waiting for his return. Even Dusty, on the occasions when the three had talked together, had chimed in with his usual wit and banter and seemed to like the woman well enough, despite her propensity to drink too much. They would sit on the steps and chat, much to the annoyance of the duty guards who knew that the men had come to the house to work and not talk. But the soldiers were under strict orders to indulge the Commandant's wife, and so if she wanted the company of scrawny, dirty prisoners, who were they to rebuke her? Doing so would have meant ill favor with the Commandant, so they turned a blind eye, just as the Commandant did when all knew her to be sleeping with some of the Stalag prisoners.

One day, things had changed.

On that morning, Skip had been sitting upon the step, reading a letter from home when Jennifer brought him and Dusty a well-earned drink of tea. She could tell something was wrong at first glance. Somehow, the brandy she brought for herself ended up spilled on his trousers and she had pulled him into the house to clean them, in spite of Dusty's warning look.

Given that his pants were dirty already, as dirty as the rest of their unwashed clothes, he tried to protest preferential treatment. But he discovered that Jennifer could be both persistent and persuasive; soon she had him inside with the door closed behind them and had pulled the letter from between his fingers. His girl back home had left him for a college professor, a man too gutless, in Skip's opinion, to fight in this war and thus not worthy of such a woman.

When Jennifer had finished reading it, she folded it, gave it back to him, and offered him a sympathetic, comforting hug which, despite Skip's intentions, quickly gave way to her efforts to kiss his pain away. It had been so very long since a woman had held him that close, had kissed him, and in his desperate place, he returned those kisses with unexpected hunger. He had not been truly surprised when she met his passion in kind, given her rumored history with the men in Stalag 31. Before Skip realized what was happening, they had consummated their desires there in the laundry room.

They had become lovers.

He did not care about the number of men she was rumored to be intimate with. He did not care that she was married to the commandant or that she might still be seeing other men from the camp. Being with her broke the monotony and loneliness of prison life and offered a bright spot in his routine that had not existed before. He saw now that he should have realized her actions were a ploy meant to gain information. If von Hausen was not putting his wife up to her affairs, pimping her out to the camp as a spy, why else would the man tolerate his wife bedding so many others?

Now she had betrayed Skip in a way worse than his girlfriend, used him against his comrades and, in Skip's eyes, proven herself to be a traitor to her country. Her betrayal had come at a high price, resulting in the execution of a local man and that of a fine, honorable officer. Skip's heart had been broken for the last time.

Now she would pay for her treason in the way all traitors paid.

With images of revenge and scenario after scenario playing in his head, he watched his feet follow through with one step after another, determined to remain strong. Yes, she had to die, and he had to pay the price for ending her life, but in spite of that decision, his heart clung to the hope that she loved him. He was unaware of reaching the house until a slamming door jerked his head up, the sound passing through him with a jolt. One hand involuntarily lifted to shield his eyes from the sun in time to note a figure running towards him with outstretched arms.

"Tom!" Jennifer cried as she threw her arms around his neck, oblivious to the German guards or Dusty at Skip's side. "Thank God you're alive."

Skip did not react at first, blinded as he was by the feel of her head against his shoulder, her body pressed against his as she sobbed with hysterical relief. The heady smell of her perfume evoked memories of their last meeting, when he had foolishly confessed that he thought he loved her. For a moment it once again felt as if no one else existed, that nothing else mattered, and he found himself asking, "What has happened?" without thinking and then planted a kiss hotly upon her mouth as if nothing had ever changed between them.

"What the bloody...?" Dusty started.

But Skip had not forgotten his vow of vengeance, had not forgotten her betrayal. With her body pliant against his, he stiffened. The hand against her cheek slid lower to tighten around her throat.

Dusty had not expected that, neither the kiss nor the attack, though he knew perhaps he should have. He had not believed Skip stupid enough to do either in front of the Germans soldiers, in front of the house where she lived, in the open air of morning before the world. He rushed in, hoping to pull his friend away before real damage was done. "For fuck sake, Skip...she ain't worth it..."

Dusty's efforts came too late. The first German guard had reached them and struck Skip's arm hard with the butt of his rifle but it was not enough to break his grip. More soldiers entered the fray as the woman began to go limp in his grasp and Skip sank with her as if to escape the blows of his assailants. Her face was beginning to redden by the time a blow to Skip's temple forced him to fall backward. His grip broke and both he and Jennifer collapsed, falling in different directions.

Dusty dropped to his knees near enough to Jennifer to pat her face and tilt her head to allow her unimpeded breathing. One of the guards took exception to his efforts and struck him, but as he fell back on his ass, he saw that his efforts were helpful. Jennifer gasped, choked, and coughed her way to consciousness. Relieved that Skip had not killed her, but knowing the attempt itself could guarantee his death, Dusty rubbed his aching shoulder and watched the guards wrestle with Skip as they tried to tie his hands behind him.

Though the blow dazed him, Skip continued to struggle to reach the woman, his fury blinding him to the steep price he would pay, despite his failure to kill her. "Whore!" he screamed. Unable to get closer, unable to get free of the guards who held him, or those who gathered around Jennifer, he spat at her in frustration and rage.

Dusty's head turned when the door opened again and a second set of footsteps, heavier than Jennifer's, barreled down the wooden steps. von Hausen's revolver was drawn and cocked and Dusty expected him to use it. Intending to throw himself in harm's way, to protect Skip, Dusty struggled to his feet. One shot did ring out, and though the gun was pointed in Skip's direction, the bullet passed harmlessly over his head, hitting no one. A warning shot only. Next time, Skip would not be so lucky.

"No...Hans...please...it is my fault..." croaked Jennifer as she realized through the haze what had happened and why.

Hans reached the foot of the steps and stopped, his pistol still aimed at the Australian. The guards had cleared away and he now had a clear shot if he chose to take it, a shot he could not miss. His finger trembled upon the trigger.

"Please, Hans. If you ever felt anything for me, I beg you. Hansy...please!"

He paused, hesitated, his resolve softened when he heard her use his pet name for the first time in months. He could not remember the last time she had used it. In his heart, however, he knew the usage was a trick, a way to manipulate him into giving her what she wanted, regardless of the effect to their marriage. His jaw clenched and the gun, which had begun to lower, came back up, this time turning ever so slightly in Jennifer's direction. Then, unexpectedly, he relaxed at the noises behind him, the sound of two other sets of footfalls on the wooden veranda. Clara and Mila.

"Hans!" Clara shouted, not considering at that moment that perhaps she should use his rank or title or something other than his name in front of his wife and the soldiers. Lives were at stake and she had to do her part to save them. All of them. He looked at her. Oblivious to anything then except her hypnotic green eyes, and then lower, to the protective arms she had wrapped around his child.

Hans squeezed the trigger. A cloud of dust hovered in the air above where the bullet was now embedded in the earth. His desire not to subject his child to the gruesome execution of a prisoner, and possibly her mother, stayed him from action more than anything else. There was a collective sigh of relief when he replaced his pistol in its fine leather holster and went to his wife's side. He bent down to see if she was well. Despite that he had just spared, her life, and for the moment Skip's, all Jennifer could see was the gun pointed at her by that man in that uniform and she recoiled from his touch. She believed it had been Clara who had prevented the killing, not her own efforts or some personal decision of her husband's; in truth, it had been Mila's presence that had stopped him. Her fury at Clara's interference in her life only fueled her desire to escape Hans' touch.

Hans saw it all in her eyes. Every fear, every rejection, every touch of blame. Glaring at Jennifer, he hissed in frustration, "This is your doing. Are you happy now?" Snarling with hurt, he resisted striking her and instead struck Skip hard across the face with the back of his hand, a blow that would have knocked Skip to the ground if the soldiers had not been holding him. "Take him to my office. I will deal with him there."

He looked again at his wife, who still lay upon the ground and was now being hugged by their child, both reassuring one another that everything would be alright. Jennifer was murmuring that she had tripped and fallen, nothing more, a likelihood due to her drinking, though she had not had much to drink yet this morning. Hans wanted to kneel with them, offer his own words of love and comfort as he hugged them both...

...and then he saw Clara.

He growled and turned on to follow Skip and the guards to his office to mete out Skip's punishment and hopefully still make it to the required luncheon on time. He was full of anger, resentment, and passion. But passion for who, he could not say.

Chapter 9
July 11, 1943

Obersturmfuhrer Wagner crossed the parade yard at a quick pace, though not at a run as he thought that would seem undignified or at least cowardly. He could almost feel Stetcher's walking stick beating upon the ground as the Gestapo officer supervised Haupsturmfuhrer Hirsch's work. Hirsch, like Stetcher, reveled in such tasks, and thus was taking great pleasure in lashing Henderson to the electric pole outside of Barrack's A. Those men from Camp 1 not at the Sunday morning worship had already begun gathering to witness whatever punishment lay in store for the Australian. At the front of the gathering, Stetcher bounced with nervous energy, his fingers dug deep into Jennifer von Hausen's arm.

Wagner was not sure why she was there, or what this incident had to do with her. He did not know why the Aussie was facing further punishment, or if there was even a good reason. He had seen the angry exchange between the Commandant and his wife as von Hausen had gotten into his car, and thus presumed she was here at the Commandant's order. As the car took von Hausen away, and Henderson and Miller were brought back into the confines of Camp 1, Stetcher ordered Wagner to pick replacements for duty in the garden and to present them to him at once.

"Be merciful, just as your Father is merciful," Bonny read, trying to regain his congregation's attention. The sound of a pair of gunshots some time before had distracted them, making men squirm and try to see what had happened through the GSH windows. It was difficult to preach forgiveness and compassion, a sermon meant to draw their ire away from Skip and the unproven accusations made against him, when the Germans were once more working hard to undermine the sincerity of the Padre's message.

Wagner opened the door to the GSH but did not otherwise interrupt. Instead, he paused to listen to the Padre's fading words, his hat in his hands, ignoring as best he could the glances that turned on him with anger and inquiry. Bonny, however, knew better than to put off a German soldier, and knew he would not recapture the men's attention so long as Wagner was in the room. He stopped speaking and was met with a squaring of the soldier's shoulders.

"Apologies for interrupting, Father," he said in stilted English. Wagner was one of the few soldiers in the camp who made an effort to speak the language of the men he attended. "Lieutenant Burns, Corporal Johnston, come with me."

Expression wary, George got to his feet. "Where are you taking them?" He could not stop the Germans from whatever they intended, but he could at least show his concern for the men beneath his leadership.

Wagner did not have to answer; he did not owe them an explanation, especially when they would learn the truth soon enough. But he respected them as men and so replied, "They are summoned to work in the garden in place of Captains Miller and Henderson…"

Men in the room looked at one another, now making the assumption that the two earlier gunshots had killed both Skip and Dusty. Through the open doorway, the gathering in the appell yard could be seen and heard, but what was happening at the front of the gathering was hidden from view. George shot Sam and Vic a warning look to behave and Wagner escorted them out.

No one moved to close the door. Bonny hesitated, wondering if he should go out to investigate, but opted to begin reading again. "And do not judge and you will not be judged, and do not condemn and you will not be condemned; pardon and you will be pardoned."

Leonard got out of his chair and went to the window. "Looks like Henderson's gotten himself into trouble," he muttered. The men behind were listening more to him and to the noises outside than they were to Bonny, and a handful of them now joined Leonard at the window. George was about to protest, to order them back to their seats so that Bonny could finish the service, but Ronny had gone out onto the steps and others followed. Sparks was one of the few to remain seated. No one else may have thought to pray for Skip and Dusty, or whoever had been the recipient of the gunfire, so he figured he might as well. Someone had to.

Sighing, George got to his feet at last and left to investigate the commotion. Wagner and his charges had stopped near the gate, looking back towards the front of the crowd. It was difficult to see

Skip through the gathering but no one needed to. The crack of leather against skin, and the agonizing howl that followed, were clear enough to give the only explanation anyone needed.

Near the pole, though not bound or even held at gunpoint, Dusty gritted his teeth and tightened his jaw as the whip snaked out of Hirsch's gnarled hand and bit into Skip's bare flesh again and again. Not far away, the Commandant's wife tried to turn away from the spectacle, but Stetcher roughly pointed her face forward and hissed something into her ear. Whatever he said had the effect he desired, for she stared with wide, terrified eyes and did not look away again. She was directly in Skip's line of sight and he did not move his glare from her face except when the crack of the whip caused his head to jerk involuntarily or when he squeezed his eyes shut against the pain.

Dusty balled his fists, wanting to hit someone but not daring to. Exactly whose bloody idea was it to bring the woman here? Skip had, in Dusty's opinion, every right to be furious with her. Whether she had gotten the plans from him to give to her husband or had, unknowingly or otherwise, provided the false intel on which Buckman had based his plan, it was still betrayal, and throwing herself at Skip the way she had, in front of her husband, she was just as responsible for this punishment as Skip was. Trying to kill her in front of her home, her family had been an idiotic act, but if Jennifer had kept to herself, said nothing, steered clear of Skip, he would not have been able to touch her.

Dusty needed to find a better way to temper the Aussie's rage.

It was not possible to tell by her hysterical responses if she had intended to betray them or not, if she had been aware of the consequences of her choices or whether she was merely foolish. As much as she usually drank, no doubt her judgment was severely impaired. But both she and Skip should have known better than to have become involved with one another. With all of the rumors about her in camp, Skip especially should have been smarter.

Lord knew, if the man survived this beating, his opinion of the woman was not likely to change.

ᴥ*ᴥ

"Give and it will be given to you; good measure pressed down, shaken together, running over, they will pour into your lap. For by your standard of measure, it will be measured to you in return."

In the GSH, Bonny's voice continued softly, mostly speaking to himself in the quest for comfort from the sound of the whip that cracked a second time. A third. A fourth. He wondered if there would be thirty-nine and realized he did not believe Skip could survive that long. Nor did he believe he could tolerate it either. Another crack and a chair materialized behind him as his knees buckled. He looked up into Sparks' face.

"And by his stripes, we are healed," the Scot murmured, hoping it was so, but doubting it could be.

"Dear God, I pray it is so."

❧*❦

Clara held the girl's head against her shoulder, not standing for the closing hymn as the rest of the congregation did. And while Stasio did stand, he kept Clara's hand clasped tightly in his, indicating that his attention was more upon her and the girl than upon the service or the song he was mouthing. He did not know what had happened at the von Hausen's home, only that there had been some incident between one of the prisoners and the Commandant's family, something traumatic enough that their daughter, who had witnessed some of it, had been in tears ever since.

It worried him as Clara became more deeply enmeshed in that troubled relationship and in the triangle between the Commandant and his work, between him and his subordinates. Stasio would not stop her, as he believed in her efforts and cared too deeply about her cause, but with each incident that came to pass, he feared more and more for her safety and her life.

And he scolded himself daily for being the one that kept her in Ste Marie.

Clara kissed his knuckles and he looked down at her. She understood his thoughts without him voicing them. She always had.

His heart twisted within his chest as his voice faltered and failed.

❧*❦

By the time Dengler pushed through the crowd of prisoners and saw what Stetcher was doing, Skip's back was bloody and raw. The man was near unrecoverable collapse, only the pain of each snap of the whip kept him from losing consciousness. The doctor got into a heated, though quiet, verbal exchange with the Gestapo officer, with wild gestures pointing in Skip's direction punctuating whatever was being said. Or rather, the Doctor's half of the dialogue seemed heated; Stetcher might have been watching a newsreel of flowers blooming for all of the attention he was paying.

The arrival of Jamie Campbell, the Canadian doctor escorted by one of the guards, made Stetcher sneer. No matter where the relationship stood, Dengler knew Jamie would never wish this sort of brutality on another man. Jamie and Skip had gotten on well enough before Jennifer von Hausen came into the picture and Campbell was a doctor. He would want to help Skip now.

That friendship was one more thing she had ruined.

After twenty torturous lashes, Stetcher barked, "Das ist genug! Hört auf!" his tone bored and sullen.

The whip arm dropped to Hirsch's side and he wiped his sweating brow with the other; he looked disappointed that he was not allowed to continue. Dengler motioned Jamie to join him and together they approached the sagging man. Dusty was already there, having pushed forward the moment Stetcher's command was given, trying to untie the ropes that bound his friend to the pole If his actions were out of line, Stetcher did not say so. The Gestapo officer ignored him.

Instead, Stetcher climbed the steps of Barracks A to be in a position to be seen and heard by the entire yard. As usual, he smacked his cane against the wall as though to draw attention to himself even though most men's attention was already on him.

"Let this be a lesson to those who think an attack on upstanding Reich citizens is a profitable choice." His gaze swept over them and ended on von Hausen's wife, though the disdain in his eyes showed he considered her neither upstanding nor a Reich citizen. Jamie noticed this as he bore Skip's weight while Dusty untied him. The Canadian took Stetcher's words to mean that Skip had indeed made some effort to harm her, but Stetcher's cold gaze could just as easily have been a warning to the woman in case she was considering retaliation against her husband.

"The next time any of you decides to be so blatantly stupid, it will mean instant death. I promise you that."

Wagner had seen enough. He and the men he was escorting passed through the outer gates as Skip fell into Jamie's waiting arms.

❧•*•❧

Stasio stopped the old worn truck in front of the von Hausen home, allowing the engine to idle rough and loud as Clara slid out and held her hand to Mila. As the vehicle approached the house, they had each seen Jennifer disappear through the front door as if fleeing for her life. In Camp 1, many of its residents could be seen gathered in the parade yard. Stasio's expression was grim, Clara's attentive and curious. No doubt there had been repercussions for Skip's earlier actions. She wondered what his punishment had been.

In the flowerbed near the porch, Ray and Vic now worked, pausing only to identify the arriving vehicle. Ray went back to weeding while Vic straightened his shoulders and leaned upon the handle of his hoe, watching Clara emerge from the truck.

At first, Mila did not move, only stared past Clara in the direction of the front door.

"Would you like me to find out if your father is home?" Clara guessed that it was he whom Mila was afraid of because, for all of her faults, Jennifer had never been seen to raise her voice or hand in the company of her daughter. The gun in Hans' hand that morning would have instilled fear into almost anyone. Hans should be off to his meeting, assuming he had not chosen to let duty keep him away. As angry as he had been at Jennifer, Clara knew he would go to that meeting just to escape his wife, no matter how boring, uncomfortable, and unnecessary he thought such luncheons were.

After a pause, Mila shook her head as if she had willed her fear to pass. "I…thank you…but no. Mother is home. I must go."

"You could spend the day with us," Stasio volunteered. "The horses would appreciate a good run."

Mila's face brightened, but then she sighed and her mood deflated just as quickly. "I must do as expected…or you will get into trouble."

Refusing to let his cheerful expression fade, Stasio tousled her hair. "Well then, we shall ride another time. And we will have to sit down at the piano, you and me."

"I would like that, monsieur." The corners of her mouth and eyes crinkled a little into the beginnings of a smile.

As she climbed from the truck and took Clara's hand, Clara said, "I will see her to the door."

Stasio's gaze flicked to the two gardeners and three German soldiers who stood watch nearby. Clara had come and gone often enough from the von Hausen home, as well as from the German section of the camp itself, that they troubled her no longer. In fact, they rarely even searched her now, as Hans had long ago discouraged them from doing so. And they knew better than to harass the Commandant's daughter, so the two passed unhindered and stopped at the top of the steps near the door.

Clara adjusted her purse precariously upon her arm. "Do you want me to come in?"

"No, it will only make mother more upset…" Her tremulous voice nearly broke.

"It's okay, Mila. I'm here if you need me." She gave the girl a one-armed hug and kissed the top of her head.

"Thank you." Mila returned the embrace before going indoors, closing the door quietly to avoid being heard by her mother. Clara waited upon the porch until the girl waved through the open curtain, and then she started down the steps.

Before reaching the bottom, however, her unsteadily perched purse fell, spilling its contents upon the ground. The Germans did no more than glance at her to see what had happened. Vic, however, moved to help her retrieve the scatter of personal items.

"Let me help," he said with a grin, fumbling for a tube of lipstick that had rolled beneath a cluster of flowers. When he found it, he handed it back to her, meeting her gaze when he did so.

"Merci, Lieutenant," she replied, pressing the cigarette package she had just picked up into the outstretched hand after taking back her lipstick. "Take these, and share them with Lieutenant McKenzie, please."

"Will do," he replied, making a show of removing a cigarette from the pack and then patting the breast pocket of his shirt. "You got a light?"

From her purse, amongst the items she had picked up, she produced a book of matches and gave them to him as well. Sometimes the Germans discouraged the gift of matches, as if the prisoners might be tempted to burn down their barracks or use them against their captors. But matches, like soap and cigarettes, were rare and precious commodities and not something the men were likely to waste on such a futile effort. "Keep them," she said as he helped her to her feet. The soldiers ignored the exchange.

"Appreciate it." He grinned and winked, which to the guards and to Ray was nothing more than Vic's usual flirtation with the woman.

"Least I can do."

She heard Ray ask for a cigarette as she reached the still open truck door, and heard Vic reply, "They're for Sparks," as he shoved the pack into his pocket and resumed work. Ray grumbled something in response but Clara did not hear it as she got into the truck and closed the door.

Stasio glanced at her before pointing the vehicle towards home. "I wish the risks weren't necessary," he muttered.

In the rearview mirror, Clara watched the house and the men in the garden recede from view and then slid closer to the man at her side. "So do I."

∽*∽

Jennifer downed another gulp of the ochre liquor as she nervously paced the length of the room. Occasionally she sat on the edge of the piano stool and tinkered with the ivory keys, playing no recognizable tune. She did it only to stop her hands from trembling.

But the effort was futile. She could not stop thinking about Skip's attack, how he might believe this was all her fault but not understanding why he had lashed out at her here. She thought about the ensuing argument with Hans and the terrible punishment she had witnessed within Camp 1. Normally she was kept away from all of that; life within the Stalag only crossed hers when she interacted with those who worked her gardens and when Stetcher or one of the others came to the house to discuss business with Hans. Was it her fault that Skip had been beaten? Had she caused that?

She desperately wanted to understand what had happened and why, and she wanted to drown the images and sounds in her head with the brandy, but her efforts were not working. Even Mila's return from church failed to pull her thoughts away from the darkness Stetcher and her husband had forced her to endure. Her daughter gave her a sympathetic hug, but when Jennifer failed to speak or otherwise respond, Mila retreated upstairs, leaving Jennifer alone.

Tears dropped onto the keys and she stroked them away with her free hand. Setting the drink aside, the note blossomed into a recognizable tune, the first phrase of "Waltzing Matilda," which Skip had often whistled when working. Once, in a happier moment, he had sung it for her, and then laughed when she had joined in. The memory brought a faint smile, but then the image of his whip-streaked back blasted across her thoughts and she smacked the keys in a loud note of discord.

"Mother?" called Mila from upstairs.

"It is nothing, darling..." Her reassurance, whether believed or not, kept her daughter from coming down.

Jennifer stared at her trembling hands upon the keys and in frustration reached for another mouthful of calming brandy, hoping it would soothe her nerves and erase the image from her mind.

A libretto lay open upon the music stand; she had forgotten when she had left it there and hoped Hans had not noticed it. If he had, he would think she was singing again. For the last year or more she had gone to great pains to hide her singing from him, only flexing her vocal muscles when she knew he was out of earshot. She even hid from him the fact that she had been teaching Mila more advanced musical theory than the French whore ever could, and was trying to give their daughter singing lessons. Hans must not know. As far as he was concerned, she had not sung a note since...

The memory was too painful.

She thumbed through the worn pages of the libretto, wistfully recalling when and where the penciled notations on each page had been added. Notes about intonation, pronunciation, high notes, everything she had one considered important for singing well. Now, the ever-present brandy had robbed her of the best of her voice, but she pretended not to notice that.

What she did notice, however, was something written in one of the margins, not in her hand but someone else's. It was the sweeping form of her husband's handwriting, affectionate words written in German. The color drained from her face as she read them, not for the words themselves but because, in writing there, he had invaded even that bit of pleasant memory as well. She dropped the document and it landed title up. Un Ballo in Maschera.

"No..." She gasped and hid her face in her hands. Why was he everywhere she turned?

Eventually, when she was calm again, she retrieved the libretto from where it had landed, replaced it upon the stand, turned to a familiar, dog-eared page, and began to play. The tremulous music washed over her, bringing with it the memories of the first time she had sung in this opera. She had met Hans that night, so long ago, and had loved him from the first, as he had loved her. He had loved her so much that he had trailed Europe to be with her, to woo her, proving he had no desire to be apart from her, that he desired nothing else in the world.

There was no terror now, only melancholy as she wondered what had happened to the devotion and love they had once shared.

Aglow in those memories, she began to sing, her shaky, rough soprano expressing more feeling in the words this day then she had ever felt upon the stage. "Morro, ma prima in grazia…"

☙*❧

The music wafted into the garden where Ray and Vic worked. It was not the first time she had been heard; the rumor was that she was a trained singer, but any training had been muted by too much drink. It did not keep the woman from humming, from playing the piano, or occasionally undertaking vocal exercises when her husband was not home. Few in the Camp knew her name, few believed her claim, but Ray had heard her upon the stage at Covent Garden, and he relished each time he heard her sing, though he mourned the loss of the beauty of sound she had once been capable of. He paused his work and lifted his head towards the window.

Vic saw him, rolled his eyes, and snorted. "Cat dying in there if you ask me. Makes no sense at all." He struggled with a particularly stubborn weed and tried to ignore the singing.

"It's Italian," Ray explained as though Vic should know that. "The character has been told by her husband that he is going to kill her for her infidelity and she wants to see her children before she dies."

"Sounds about right…'cept Skip's gonna be the one doing the killing if he gets at her again." He did not look up.

Throwing him a sour look, Ray dropped his tools and headed up the steps. "Cover me…"

"Keep clear of the bitch…"

But his warning came too late. Ray was already disappearing into the house, and the guards, knowing the men were allowed to use the downstairs toilet, did not stop him.

☙*❧

Jennifer did not notice Ray in the doorway as she continued to sing. When the memories, the emotions struggling within her, and the events of the day grew too much, she gave up on finishing the song, opting instead to throw the brandy glass across the room when it failed to yield up further drink. When Ray jumped to one side to avoid being struck by the flying glass and the shards of it as it shattered against the wall, she realized she was no longer alone.

After a briefly horrified look, she muttered, "I am sorry…I did not see you there. I hope you are not hurt." She fumbled with the piano lid and it clattered closed as it slipped out of her grasp.

"No, ma'am, I'm fine." The words barely came out of his throat. He had spoken to her in passing, but that had been before the latest disaster, and he had never been alone with her.

"Would you care for water?" She assumed, because he had worked in her gardens before, he knew where the toilet was. She and her family never used that room, leaving it for the serving staff, for soldiers who came to the house, and occasionally for the prisoners.

"No…I…just wanted to say…that was lovely." Voice quavering, he looked at his filthy hands sheepishly.

It had not been lovely to Jennifer's ears, so rather than thank him for a compliment she did not believe, she asked, "You know opera?"

"I've been to Convent Gardens…before the war…that was from 'Ballo' wasn't it? You're Jenny Carter…or were…the Manchester Nightingale…before the war?" Standing before her now, he knew it was true, though it felt awkward to say it to her.

Jennifer stared at the young man in amazement. It had been a long time since anyone had used her stage nickname, or had used her professional name, and it sounded good to hear both. Hans had once called her his Jenny Wren, but any more, he most often used her formal name. No pet names, no terms of endearment, not even on the most intimate occasions…of which there were so few. She could not blame anyone for that but herself.

"I was…but I gave all of that up for this…" She motioned around them, the trail of her arm stopping to point at the family portrait upon the wall as her voice caught in a sob.

"Don't cry," Ray mumbled, feeling more awkward now. "You couldn't predict this war…brother against brother…guilty and innocent suffering alike…people acting like brutes to survive." He did not know the details of her marriage, only that she seemed unhappy in it. He knew her reputation for sleeping with other men, and it was obvious she drank too much. But he could see she was sad, and enemy or not, he did not like to see people miserable.

He believed his words, believed in the futility of war. How much he reminded her of Hans in the days when they had first met. There had been a time when Hans had abhorred the thought of war and unnecessary death; now he wore the uniform of tyranny and oppression and it made her sick and scared.

"Have you read Schiller?" she asked, changing the subject to force her thoughts off the dark path they had again begun to follow.

"You mean Ode to Joy?"

Jennifer almost smiled. "I sang Beethoven's Ninth in Albert Hall…Hans cajoled me into it…it's his favorite piece." She sank heavily onto the sofa. "He once talked like you do…now I don't even know him. Fine line…love and hate…"

Ray did not know why she was telling him these things, why she was discussing her husband with him, and he knew he should not stay to hear it. He had only come in to listen to the music. But like a siren, she beckoned until he was sitting nervously on the sofa beside her. "I…don't know…" he stammered, his gaze traveling from her eyes, down the long line of her throat, across the swell of her breasts, and finally down to her fingers that seemed to be absently stroking circles upon his thigh. His brain screamed at him to leave, but before he could stop her she was leaning forward to kiss him…

…and then the doorbell rang.

Both bolted upright, Ray with enough force to knock himself from the sofa while Jennifer casually smoothed her clothes and rose to her feet, stepping easily away as if nothing had almost happened between them. Moments later the housekeeper entered the music room, followed by Dr. Dengler who looked oddly at the young man upon the floor before looking at the woman who greeted him. Jennifer appeared as calm as her drunken state would allow; he could not decide if there was anything suspicious here or not. He did know, however, that it was none of his business either way.

"Frau von Hausen. I came to check on you after that attack. How are you feeling?" He took her wrist in his hand to check her pulse; it was elevated, but that might also have been from drink or an effect of the uniform she hated.

"I am fine, Josef," she assured him in a friendly fashion, ignoring Ray as if his being on her floor was normal. Ray, in an effort to appear as if he belonged there, made a show of shaking the end table and examining the leg nearest him as if it had been loose and he had been repairing it…without tools. "My throat is a little raw, but it will heal. Thank you." She glanced at Ray and smiled. "It appears you have fixed it, Corporal. Thank you."

"Ma'am," he said, head bowed as he scurried to his feet and shuffled hastily outside. He was reluctant to leave and yet eager for it. More than once, after seeing her on stage, he had fantasized about possessing her, and now, for whatever reason, she had been…at least momentarily…interested in him. As he resumed work in the garden beneath Vic's sour stare, he decided he would do whatever it took to redeem her in the eyes of the men of Camp 1, whatever it took to rescue her from her unhappy life and make her his.

Skip lay face down on his bunk, trying with difficulty to block the pain radiating throughout his body. Dengler had left him in Jamie's care as soon as the gashes on his back were cleaned and those that needed it were stitched and bandaged. There were no medications available to dull the pain, only a bottle of some stout whiskey the German doctor had provided unbeknownst to Stetcher or Hirsch. It was strong enough to dull his senses; he had been aware of the prick of the needle in his skin, but the worst of the pain had been washed away and Skip endured what remained in stoic silence.

What had not grown numb, however, was his mind, as his thoughts stumbled over themselves in their quest to explain the Canadian's willingness to help. He had little doubt that, in their earlier fight, he might have killed Jamie if he had been given the chance. He had been too out of control for anything else. Jamie knew it too. Thus it made little sense for Jamie to continue to defend and care for him, to protect him and tend his injuries. The man was either acting out of his usual selflessness or he intended to ask for some favor in return.

Grating his teeth in irritation, he decided that whatever Jamie would ask for in recompense, would not be given. At least not easily.

He heard the distorted clicking that meant Sparks was tinkering with the radio. Skip had seen the delivery earlier, when Vic had given Sparks the cigarette pack; Sparks had been at the radio ever since. Skip wanted to warn them against trusting Clara; hell they should not trust anyone, but he knew that warning would be disregarded. Clara had been too helpful, too unwavering in her support, for too long, for Sparks to heed warnings now. Just as Skip had failed to heed Buckman's warnings about Jennifer von Hausen.

And this was different. Sparks was not bedding the woman, at least not as far as Skip knew. It also made a difference that she was not married, not to von Hausen, not even to the Frenchman with whom she lived.

While Leonard sat alone on his bunk, mending socks and other torn clothing for men in Camp 1, many of the others were gathered around the table engaged in another card game. It was often the only entertainment available to them. Even George was playing this time, something he rarely did, but he was making a concerted effort to fit in and win the men to his leadership. Once again Vic appeared to be winning. It was a common belief that the Scot cheated, but no one had caught him at it yet. As he slammed down another winning hand with a whoop of victory and began scooping up the cigarettes that had been used as wagers, Skip mumbled, "Prick..."

"Ssh..." Jamie scolded as he set the container of salve on the floor and wiped his hands upon his trousers. "Rest."

"Like I'm bloody all going to do anything else..."

The Aussie's voice was so slurred that Jamie knew Skip was not going to be moving from that bed, and even Vic blamed his words on the drink and chose not to take offense. If Skip was lucky, he would be left alone come morning, as he would still be in no condition to move or work. He had already been excused from evening appell because he could not stand, but it was unlikely that Stetcher or Hirsch would show leniency for long. Ray brought in Skip's portion of the Red Cross deliveries and sat with Skip while Jamie tended his mail duties. There had been no mail for the Aussie this week, indeed there had been none for several weeks, and Jamie, at least, had noticed it. Nothing from his siblings, nothing from his parents, nothing from his girl back home in Perth.

Was it any wonder the man had foolishly reached out for a sympathetic shoulder when it had been offered?

The guilty manner in which the corporal attended to Skip, and now watched him from across the room, made Jamie wonder if the young medic was finally beginning to understand the nature of this place, this war, and the enemy they faced every day.

He looked across Dusty's empty bunk to where Sparks sat cross-legged with his ear tuned to the radio. "Anything?"

"Airwaves are quiet." It frequently seemed that such an occurrence suggested some big event waging somewhere, so hopefully, there would be news soon enough.

Jamie was about to say more as he leaned closer to the window, intending to open it, when movement outside caught his eye. "Shit! Krauts at the door!" he hissed.

Sparks shoved the radio into the hole in his mattress as Jamie yanked down the bit of wire strung from the radio to the metal frame of the window as an antenna. In an effort to keep the Germans' attention away from that half of the room while the radio was hastily hidden, and to express his annoyance with losing much of his weekly ration of cigarettes to Vic yet again, Dusty lurched up as the door opened. He shoved the table so that it toppled over to one side and swung at Vic, hitting him hard enough to knock him backward.

"Cheatin' son of a bitch!"

While the scuffle drew attention away from him and Sparks, Jamie shoved the length of wire into the front of his trousers while Sparks fluffed his mattress as casually as he could to make the lump there less conspicuous. Vic tried to push himself up from the floor with the help of Ronny's rough grip on his arm and a yanking pull. "Cheating?" he cried, angry less by the distraction they were creating than by the painful slug to his jaw. "How the hell can I cheat? I don't have any sleeves!"

"Check his trousers!" demanded Dusty as Bonny jumped into the fray.

"Gentlemen, please."

The men froze where they were in that blossoming dog pile and looked at Sturmbannfuhrer Moretti as though they had been unaware of his arrival.   With him were Obersturmfuhrer Wagner and two other men, a British soldier and an American, judging by the scraps of filthy uniforms they wore. The intake of new prisoners was always noteworthy, and so their attention left the game and shifted entirely to the newcomers as they extracted themselves from the heap they were in, glad they had been able to protect Sparks and the radio one more time.

"This is Lieutenant Collins...Lieutenant Gray. I expect you to see that they are properly briefed and supplied. Any failings on their parts will be blamed on the rest of you."

"No surprise there," muttered Taffy.

Morretti's eyes narrowed in annoyance at being interrupted, although his voice, when he continued talking, carried little of that annoyance. "Since their arrival has come after the Red Cross delivery, you will need to share all rations...make due..."

Taffy spoke again, standing now to pull a couple of empty stools from the corners. "There's a choice? You'd rather us starve to death than provide what we need...even though we're officers..."

"We deserve more than that from you Krauts," Dusty grunted

The Italian straightened his shoulders. "I am not German..."

"But you work like a dog serving its master..."

Moretti glared at Vic. "Are you calling me a dog?"

Vic righted his chair to get comfortable. "I said you obey their orders like one for whatever scraps they throw from their tables."

"You're better fed than we are," Bonny said quietly. Across the room, George nodded his head in agreement before getting up from his chair. It was to be expected of course; no captor would feed their captives as well as themselves, but most of the men felt they deserved better. "Can't you make allowances for newcomers just once? There must be some provision in the Geneva Convention..."

"This is not Geneva." Feeling pressed into a corner, into a position where he must either betray his commission or his personal ethics, Moretti growled, grunted, and muttered, "Goodnight, gentlemen," before withdrawing with Wagner on his heels.

"Padre..." George waited for the two to be far enough from the barracks so that he would not easily be overheard. "Watch the door. We want no more surprises tonight."

"Yes, sir," the clergyman said. He scooped up the papers scattered across his mattress, the upcoming sermon most likely, and sat with his back against one side of the doorframe and his feet propped against the other. In his alcoholic haze, on the cusp of sleep, Skip noted, as did Jamie and others, that the Padre, at least, had given his allegiance to George Campbell. It would not be long, he imagined, before others did likewise.

"That was...interesting..." said the older of the two newcomers, an American naval man.

"Stick around," Leonard muttered, his darning set aside in favor of investigating another American.

Ronny laughed, "Yeah...it only gets more entertaining."

"Michael Gray," the American said as he offered his hand to George, the man he deemed to be in charge. "Most of my men call me Farmer."

"Is that what you are then?" asked Ray.

"Family's got about forty acres back near Jasper, Indiana."

"Krauts will love it. We all get time on the neighboring farm…keeps our hands busy and keeps the Germans fat and happy. Sometimes we get a few benefits for ourselves," explained Jamie, "but mostly we work so they don't have to." He thought of one particular benefit, which brought a flush to his cheeks, but Sparks was fretting over his radio and Skip's eyes were closed; no one else was near enough to notice.

Though it seemed that Sparks was absorbed in his radio, he did add, "Monsieur Arnaud will be pleased that at least one of us has a bloody clue what we're doing…"

"And you?" George asked the second, shorter man.

The British officer accepted George's hand. "Lieutenant Kevin Collins, Royal Engineers."

"We don't put much stock in rank here, gentlemen…"

Taffy's burst of laughter cut George off. "No one has rank except him," the Welshman said with a grin. "Call me Taffy."

Both men clasped the Welshman's hand. "A pleasure, all things considered."

"As for the rest of these renegades…that's Leonard, Dusty, Ray, our Bonny Padre there at the door. Ronny and Vic over there; Sparks back there on the bunk…" George paused his introductions long enough to note the Scot's disheartened expression. "How's it look?"

"Connection's busted. Plate's scratched…gonna need new parts before it'll work again."

"I'm sure our little pigeon will be happy to help," Vic teased, although he, like the others, realized the seriousness of their lack of radio reception. Sparks flipped him off but did not say anything. Though the two newcomers did not know what they were speaking of, no one saw fit to enlighten them. That would wait until they knew each other better.

George resumed the introductions. "My son, James…"

"Jamie," he corrected, not bothering to look at his father.

"…and that is Skip…"

Farmer bent for a closer look at the prone man covered with stitches and gauze and grimaced. "What the hell happened?"

"Long story," Dusty said, putting his arm around the American's shoulder and ushering him to the table that had been righted in the meantime.

"Let's just say," Bonny added, "that's what happens when you get on the wrong side of Sturmbannfuhrer Stetcher…"

"The commandant?" asked Collins.

"Stetcher only think's he's in charge," snarled Vic.

"The Gestapo thinks it runs everything," Taffy finished as he pushed Farmer gently down onto a stool.

Vic offered each of them a cigarette from the stash he had won.

"Just stay away from von Hausen's wife," warned Dusty. "She'll eat you alive and spit out your bones for fun."

The new Brit's eyes grew wide as George pointed to the other empty seat. "Sit down, KC. Have a cigarette…play a little poker…tell us about things outside."

"And make yourselves at home," added Bonny. "You're gonna be here for quite a while."

None of them noticed Ray's awkward glance away.

Chapter 10
July 12, 1943

T hough Louis' voice rattled on beside her, Clara's attention was riveted on the two men at the counter with whom Zaline was speaking. Zaline was setting breakfast for them, and Clara knew, from the way she set their napkins next to their plates, that within those bits of cloth were those men's futures. Credentials they would need to travel safely within France and then out of the country, as long as they followed the instructions Philippe had laid out for them the night before. If successful, those two would make it to whatever pickup point Sister Isabelle had arranged, and from there they would make it out of France to safety. Neither looked to be soldiers; one was too old for fighting and the other too small and mousy behind his thick-rimmed glasses to last a day in combat.

A father and son, she decided, possibly Jews but more likely gypsies, although most of the gypsies she encountered were not inclined to flee the continent.

L'Oie de Vol was empty this morning, a frequent case on Mondays as the work week began. To the Germans, Philippe had long ago explained that Monday's were his slow day. Other than those rooming in the inn, there were rarely breakfast customers anyhow. Since the start of the war, overnight patrons had become fewer, thus the earlier morning quiet of a Monday made an ideal time for the six to meet, and the fact that they were, in one way or another, related to each other, made their gathering less suspect. Sometimes the other four members were in attendance as well, and once Etienne had been part of this gathering, but the others were occupied elsewhere, and Etienne would never again sit at the head of the table. That place was now Philippe's.

"The shipment of wood from Guichen has arrived," Louis was telling Philippe.

"Marked?"

"Yes, I inspected it myself."

"Where is it now?"

"In the truck, in the warehouse."

"Good." Philippe looked through the ledger he kept for the L'Oie de Vol, which also contained notations pertaining to work the Germans knew nothing about, coded into the books so that only someone who knew what they were looking for might find it. "Delivery is expected this afternoon, so your man's timing is excellent. Relay my thanks."

"I think he just wants to be done with it and that will be thanks enough. He's not military...and he's scared about getting too close."

"Would he rather one of us deliver it?" Marcella asked, leaning her elbows on the table to better watch her sister behind the bar.

Philippe shook his head. "Not possible. They'll recognize any of us...and the moment that stuff goes, Stetcher will want the head of whoever is responsible. By that time, your man will be out of their reach if he's taken other precautions."

Louis nodded. "Yes, it's settled. He has what he needs to destroy the truck when he's far enough away...and the body to leave in it in his place. Everything else is ready. When do you want him there?"

"Noon. Clara, find out who will be unloading the trucks and make sure they know what they're looking for."

Clara nodded, accepting the duty without question or reluctance. Of everyone in Ste Marie, she had the most unquestioned access to the camp and its men. It put her in a dangerous position, but it was one she had initiated and carried out willingly. Any messages in or out of the Camp normally traveled through her.

She watched the older woman beside her spread fruit preserves upon her bread. "Has there been any news about Commander Newton and Sergeant O'Callaghan?" Clara asked hopefully.

Sister Isabelle set down her knife and shook her head. The elderly woman was the only one of her order left in Ste Marie; the rest had been massacred along with the priest when the Germans had arrived in town. She had only survived because she had not been with them that day. Since then, she had taken on the guise of village postmistress and school teacher to avoid the same fate whilst helping others escape the horrors of war. As mail functions had once been her nephew Philippe's duty, since what little mail that came to the village was routed through L'Oie de Vol, being here was a natural place for her. And it put her right in the middle of the Resistance where she wanted to be.

"They never made it to their contacts on the coast. None of the cells between here and St Malo have seen them. I think we must assume…"

"No," Clara grunted. "I will not believe it. They are alive. They have to be."

Philippe put his hand firmly but tenderly over hers. "We cannot allow personal feelings…"

"Why not?" she asked bitterly. "Isn't that the nature of what we're doing? Allowing our feelings to…"

She was cut off as the front door of the inn opened. Stetcher and Hirsch entered, both stopping long enough to cast cold stares about the murky waters of the room's atmosphere, taking in the faces, familiar and unfamiliar alike. Clara could almost feel the sweat forming upon the brows of the two men at the counter. Stetcher waved Hirsch off to find a table near the front window where they frequently sat while he strode to the bar and stopped directly beside the two strangers.

Philippe's hand on hers held Clara back, but he himself was only moments away from rising. To draw attention to themselves, however, might put the entire operation in Ste Marie at risk. They could only hope that the two men at the bar did nothing to endanger themselves or anyone else. From the way his hand rested in his coat pocket, Clara knew Philippe's pistol was ready. He would protect any of them if he could, but it might well be the last thing he did.

"Good morning, Miss Beton," Hirsch said with a leering smile.

"Good morning, Herr Hirsch," Clara replied, only because she knew it was expected, though the stocky young German officer had continued past towards the lavatory at the rear of the room and did not respond to her reply.

At the bar, Stetcher planted his arms upon the counter. "The usual, Madam Porteur, and one for Haupsturmfuhrer Hirsch."

"Certainly, sir," Zaline replied. She poured both drinks, marveling that any man could drink such strong liquor at this early hour. Considering how much of a stickler Stetcher was for rules and protocol, it was odd for the Gestapo officer to be drinking anything other than water while in uniform. Perhaps he felt he had something to celebrate. Though it was tempting to throw both glasses in his face as she felt his eyes devouring her every move and curve, she maintained her composure long enough to set the glasses before him. The very thought of him touching her filled her with disgust. "Will there be anything else?"

"Yes." He drained one of the two glasses quickly and slid it towards her. "Another."

"Something to celebrate, Herr Stetcher?" she asked casually, hoping for any tidbit of information he might let slip, though doubting he would reveal anything useful.

"Very good news," he replied before turning to stare at the men seated beside him. "Very good news indeed." Zaline gave him the second glass and waited to see if he would want another refill, but he did not appear to notice the glass was there. He seemed to notice nothing except the two men he was glaring at.

"You are not locals. I know the faces around here..."

His French was not good, but it was understandable to those in the room. The elder of the two men at the bar, though speaking with a nervous stutter, replied in flawless, unaccented French. "No, sir. We are merchants from Laille, stopped to do business on our way to Saint-Senoux..."

Stetcher looked them up and down skeptically. "Merchants. Bah. What are you selling? Let me see. Where are your wares?"

"In the wine cellar, Herr Stetcher," Philippe interjected, getting up at last and taking his hand from his pocket. "I bought the last six bottles of wine they were carrying."

"Yes," said the man with the spectacles. "We are to pick up a wagon-load in Saint Senoux and bring it back to Laille."

"I can show you the purchase if you wish," started Philippe, staying carefully out of the reach of Stetcher's walking stick.

Stetcher ignored him. "Where is your money? Your bill of sales? Your order for purchase? Your citizenship papers?"

"Here." No one knew why the two looked suspicious to Stetcher, beyond not being residents of Ste Marie, but it might have been nothing more than a mood on the German's part. The younger man pushed a satchel across the bar. "It is all here...except the money...the purchases were already paid for you see. We are only supposed to pick it up and deliver it."

There was a tense pause as Stetcher opened the satchel and looked each document he found over, one at a time, with great thoroughness. Hirsch had, by now, rejoined him and stood on the other side of the two men with his hand resting on his pistol. Clara was watching Hirsch's face, hoping to read Stetcher's reaction early enough to respond to it, since she could not see Stetcher's expression from where she sat. Zaline made an effort to look busy behind the bar, hoping it would lead credence to business as usual in L'Oie de Vol. Louis intentionally clinked his coffee cup as he sat down and Sister Isabelle continued to nibble at her toast as she made small-talk of gossip with Marcella.

Finally, the Gestapo officer shoved the papers into the satchel and pushed it back across the counter. He did not speak at first, but picked up his drink and emptied it in a single gulp. "Monsieur Cuvier...the bill of sale...and bring me a bottle of this wine."

"Now?" Philippe asked.

"Now."

"Zaline, will you...?"

"I said you, Monsieur." Philippe had made the claim, and it was his establishment.

"Of course." Philippe picked up the open ledger, flipped through the pages, and from it produced a slip of paper which he in turned handed to Stetcher before hurrying to the back room. He unlocked the door with a key from his waist pocket and disappeared down the stairs. Within the time it took Stetcher to complete his perusal of the sales bill, Philippe returned with all six bottles of wine he claimed to have bought. He set the basket he carried them in on the counter, confident in his actions. Stetcher lay the bill aside, took one of the bottles from the basket, and read the label as he held the bottle up to the morning light.

"You don't mind my taking this..." Stetcher stepped away from the bar, wine bottle in hand.

Hoping to appear accommodating, Philippe said, "If you would care for more..."

"One is enough. We will take our celebration back to the office." He tapped his walking stick on the counter next to the still full glass. "Drink up, Eugen. No point in letting a paid for drink go to waste."

"Of course not, sir," said Hirsch with a grin, knowing as well as everyone in the room that, like the bottle of wine in Stetcher's hand, the drinks had been paid for with nothing but the fear Stetcher instilled. But at least the man appeared satisfied that the two strangers were who they claimed to be.

Hirsch drank loudly and followed his superior out.

As soon as the door closed, Clara rushed to the window and watched until the German officers were out of sight. "They're gone."

"You two," Philippe pointed to the men at the bar. "Lie low for a few hours. Zaline, Isabelle, keep an eye on them and watch for the Germans. Isabelle, you may need to adjust the papers. We can't send them on the south road; Stetcher may have men waiting. We change the route…supply their needs…and have them on the road by eleven, as planned. Clara…Marcella…you are already overdue. You'll have Stasio worried beyond belief if you do not hurry. Louis…"

"I know what to do. You take care of business here and leave mine to me."

Rather than exit all at once, Louis left first, turning west towards his home and the warehouse in question. Clara and Marcella waited for the promised basket of baked goods being delivered to the Germans at the farm today and then they left as well, turning south in the direction of the farmhouse.

"Thank you," said the older man at the bar, whose brow still shown with nervous sweat.

"You can thank us by making it safely to England, that will be enough." Zaline smiled in agreement with Philippe's words.

Isabelle took each of the men by one arm and escorted them to the third door at the back of the room where the laundry equipment was kept. "Come along. Let us see about your papers."

Alone at last, Zaline picked up the glasses the Germans had used and set them in the wash pail after sharing a look with Philippe that expressed her worries about whether Stetcher believed their ruse and her hope for a day's worth of successes. They were thoughts and fears Philippe shared as well.

The day's work detail of fifteen men was already toiling in the fields when Clara and Marcella returned to the farmhouse. The standard allotment of five German soldiers with machine guns at the ready walked amongst the hunched figures, encouraging slackers to work harder while one was stationed near the barn. A quick glance over the working men revealed that none of the officers were in the field today, though as usual, Stasio was there, his bare back and shoulders as dirty and sweaty as those of the Allied prisoners. They had brought in the first harvest of hay and potatoes and had already replanted those portions of the fields. The grapes would be next, but for now, it was the fallow quarter that was being tilled and fertilized and readied for planting.

Clara skewed her face, wondering if the Germans had decided that something needed to be planted on ground that should be left alone for a season.

Stasio's small flock of twenty-six sheep had been herded out of the fallow field, rounded into a pen at the far side to keep them out of the workers' way. The neighboring farm which had been abandoned when the Germans arrived, had been annexed onto Stasio's farm by German command and while Stasio enjoyed the extra expanse of land to work, he would never have been able to manage it without the help of the men forced to work in the fields each day.

Before von Hausen's arrival in Ste Marie, his predecessors had taken an average of eighty-five to ninety percent of the harvested goods. Of the animals that were slaughtered each year, two or three cows per year and up to five sheep, as well as a dozen or more chickens, the share they demanded had been the same. The increase in the amount of workable land had allowed for more harvestable product and larger herd sizes, thus, in the end, Stasio managed to come out a little ahead. The excess food he produced frequently found its way into parcels for those the Resistance helped to flee, or else was provided to the residents of Ste Marie whom the Germans had somehow or other deprived of livelihood and resources.

The generosity had kept Stasio in good community standing, otherwise his tolerance of the Germans on his property would have been suspect. Not that he had a choice, but some felt he should stand up to them more than he did. Still, his donations and his willingness to house and protect Clara and her radio had won him the undying respect, acceptance, and gratitude of the Resistance. It turned out that his family's daily interaction with the Germans was to their benefit, and they made use of it every chance they got.

When von Hausen had come to Ste Marie, he had met with Stasio to discuss the farm's productivity. It was the first time the Commandant had seen Clara, although she had not seen him and did not know of it until sometime later. It had been Hans' decision, unsolicited by Stasio, to limit the camp's share of the farm's production to seventy-five percent. In return, he doubled the number of prisoners who worked there each day, extended their hours, and thus increased overall output. The result was that the amount of food going to the Germans and the prisoners changed very little, whereas Stasio's personal gain increased dramatically.

That this might be due to the von Hausen's fascination with Clara did not escape Stasio. But he trusted her and told her often that he had no hold over her. What he gave came with no strings attached. In exchange, she gave him loyalty, and, he believed, love. The concept of being unfaithful to him never crossed her mind.

Clara prepared to go into the house with the baked goods they had brought when she realized that at least one officer had been sent to the farm today after all. Skip Henderson sat at the grindstone, sharpening the workmen's tools, moving gingerly about his task as if in great pain. Clara had not yet learned of the punishment the Australian received for his attack on Jennifer von Hausen, though she had known punishment was inevitable. It had obviously been brutal, though not fatal. Marcella noticed him too, took several steps towards him, and then stopped and stared, at a loss for words as his head came up and their gazes met. The way the two looked at one another brought a flush to Clara's face, as if she had stumbled across something too private, and to mask her notice of them, she made a quick search for Stetcher or whichever member of the German command was overseeing them today. Thankfully, there was no sign of the man, nor of Hirsch, so Clara presumed they had taken their bottle of wine to his office as Stetcher had claimed. There were no Germans within earshot of Skip and Marcella.

It was not the first time Clara had noticed their shared looks of undisguised longing. But Marcella was not confident enough to pursue a man who seemed beyond her reach. She was helpful to the Resistance, but only when her contributions presented no immediate threat to her own life. She was too timid a soul for risky duty or to approach a man, particularly after what the Germans had done to her.

Eyeing a batch of kindling near the barn door, Clara set the basket of baked goods upon the wooden table near the back door and walked past Marcella, pausing long enough to whisper, "Tell him about the wood." Marcella jumped, startled, and Clara continued past. "Bonjour, Captain."

Skip grunted, barely looking at her, though to Clara's eyes he seemed pleased to have someone acknowledge him in a way that did not include scorn, ridicule, anger or punishment. She could only imagine how his fellow prisoners were treating him, given his rumored involvement with Frau von Hausen. Traitors, proven or not, were rarely treated well. From her pocket, she produced one of the last two packs of cigarettes she had stashed for the men and held it out to him. Now he did look at her, his gaze suspicious and tormented. His eyes shifted from the pack, to her face, and to the guard not far away; she decided to address the guard directly.

"May I give this to him?"

"What is it?" the guard asked in stilted French.

"Cigarettes." She opened the pack so that he could see inside.

The soldier looked about to refuse. Clara knew that if anyone else had made that offer to Skip, the soldier would have already done so. But the fellow did not want to risk the wrath of the Commandant, should the man hear that he had denied Clara anything, and so he replied with an eventual grunt, "Go ahead."

"Merci." Skip still hesitated to take them when Clara again made the offer, and so she put the pack directly in his hand and clasped his between hers. "Dieu vous bénissent, monsieur."

He grunted again, though whether because he did not understand her or did not agree with the sentiment, Clara could not tell. He stuffed the pack into the waistband of his pants and returned to work.

Behind her, Marcella was motionless. Clara gestured with her head and moved to the bundle of kindling. Perhaps she could occupy the guard long enough to give Marcella a chance to speak. "Monsieur, can you help me carry this kindling into the house. I am not feeling well this morning and do not believe I can manage…"

The soldier scowled at her and then at the badly beaten man sharpening tools. He shook his head. "I cannot. Sturmbannfuhrer Stetcher's orders were to guard this man at all times…"

"Oh, very well," Clara sighed with exasperation, realizing they were wasting valuable time. Someone had to be told about the wood delivery soon. And words alone were not going to persuade the soldier to leave Skip unattended long enough for Marcella to speak to him. There was one other possibility, however, so she made a show of trying to lift the hefty bunch of kindling and dropping it on her foot. The twine that bound the sticks together snapped and the kindling scattered.

"Merde…" she swore as she stooped to gather it into a bundle once more.

The soldier looked torn. Assisting would mean leaving Henderson unattended and thus angering Stetcher. But if he did nothing to assist this woman, he had few doubts that the

Commandant would learn of it and he would be just as severely punished. Henderson was unlikely to run; he was too weak and injured for that, thus the soldier finally growled before calling into the barn. "McKenzie. Come here."

Sparks? Here? That information made Clara's chest tighten, and though it was not an uncomfortable sensation, it was unexpected.

The Scot emerged from the barn, wiping his hands upon his shirt as he appeared. "Yeah?" he asked, and then yelped, "Shite!" as he nearly tripped over Clara's kneeling form.

"Gather the kindling and take it into the house for Mademoiselle Beton."

The Scot seemed uncharacteristically nervous as he gathered the scattered twigs and branches, and he avoided looking at Clara when she helped arrange the bundle so it could be carried without dropping. She wondered where his usual smile was, but as they passed Skip, the Aussie glared at Sparks with a resentful warning. Perhaps Spark's reticence had something to do with Henderson.

She realized then, however, that Sparks' brightest smiles were only shared with her when no one else was around to see them. She had never considered him to be shy, he had never seemed that way around Vic, Paddy, and Bonny, so maybe his shyness came from being alone with a woman…or perhaps he was concerned about how the men in Stalag 31 might view his friendship with her. Clara had always taken their alliance for granted, as though he was no prisoner at all. Maybe the men were concerned that she would betray them as Jennifer von Hausen had.

At the house, she opened the door for him to enter, noticing how the breeze ruffled his unkempt hair. It occurred to her that she was noticing too many details about him today.

"Here…by the stove." She held open the large wooden box where the kindling and firewood were stored.

He scowled. "It's almost full," he started, dropping his load into it and arranging it so that the lid of the box would almost close.

"I needed to occupy the guard. I need to know who will be on duty to unload delivery trucks today. The firewood from Guichen is arriving at noon. I did not know you were here, so intended for Marcella to relay the information to Captain Henderson."

"The explosive wood?" His face grew animated and excited though he still seemed nervous in her company. Or maybe it was this place, for it had been quite some time since he had been in anything resembling a home. And who knew when one of the Germans would come in and either punish him for being here or force him to leave.

"Yes."

Now he understood her need to be alone with him. "The milking is done, though it needs to be bottled. If you can see to that, I can make sure the others know what to look for…what to do when it arrives."

"You can do that without…?"

"Aye…I'm due to return to camp after the milking. Others drag it out to avoid the barracks, but I can't bear letting the ladies suffer that long," he chuckled, making Clara grin.

"I am sure they appreciate someone who knows what they're doing and is considerate of their feelings."

"Won't just be me now…at least I don't think so. Got a couple of new guys last night, including an American farm boy. I told him to make sure to ask for you or Monsieur Arnaud when he gets his first rotation."

"I'll watch for new faces. Did the Oberfuhrer make it back to camp last night?"

"von Hausen?" The name was said with distaste and a hint of something else. "He hadn't by the time we were put out this morning. You should be careful around him."

Her head cocked as she studied him with unexpected surprise at his concern. "I always am. I do what I have to…to survive and help all of you…"

"I suppose…believe me, we appreciate it…seems to be a lot of that going around these days…"

"Are you comparing me to Frau von Hausen?" she asked with a touch of offense. She should not be surprised that some of the men might think of her in those terms, but she was hurt that Sparks might.

"You?" His expression went from awkward to apologetic. "Good God, no. You're nothing like her; any fool can see that." His cheeks flushed. "I mean…it's just…we all seem to be doing things we wouldn't normally do…to stay alive…."

"Yes…I suppose that is true." His flush made her feel embarrassed, so she turned towards the sink to give them both a chance to regain composure and asked. "Would you care for a drink before going back?"

He was grateful she had broken the awkward moment between them. "Aye, if it is no imposition…"

"Of course it isn't." She filled a tumbler with water and offered it; when he took it, his hand touched hers and lingered long enough for her to take note of his fingers. Strong, slender, a musician's fingers, she knew. Not a soldier's hands at all. Unlike some of the men, his nails were relatively clean and neatly trimmed. She realized how little she knew about him, what his life had been before the war, who he had been…who he was now. Their eyes met; she swallowed and tried to form words to ask, but he quickly finished the water and put the cup on the sink board so as not to risk contact again."

"I gotta go…"

"Yes," she whispered, marveling over the sudden sinking feeling in her stomach as he hurried to the door. He paused after opening it and her heart skipped a bit.

"Shite…I almost forgot…" He took a slip of paper from his sock and handed it to her. Safer that he did not speak of the parts he needed and why, in case any Germans were outside the door.

Without looking at it, knowing it was a request for some bit or bob that could only come from the outside, she nodded and tucked it into her blouse next to her heart. "It will take time."

His voice low, he murmured, "Got a foxhole, for now…pencils, razor blades…but it's not as good…whatever you can do…"

She nodded and then he was gone, down the back steps, stopping long enough to inform the guard that he was done with the milking and ready to return to camp. The guard did not bother to check as that would require leaving his post. If Sparks was lying, it was his ass on the line. The soldier whistled and waved one of the others in from the field. Clara decided she should finish the bottling before someone noticed it had not been done, but by the time she made it out the back door and started towards the barn, Sparks was already on his way back to camp.

And Marcella, who was now preparing the low table with a sparse noon meal for the workers, was still playing eye games with Skip, though it seemed unlikely she had yet to speak to him.

The intimacy of those glances brought to mind those few moments of silence with Sparks. Clara had never imagined that he might feel anything for her; he had always been the model of propriety and politeness. Beyond the jokes and harmless pranks he and Paddy sometimes pulled, she had seen nothing but good humor and fun, things that perhaps he had been hiding behind. For his feelings had been clear today, and it had been equally clear to her that this was no new development for him. For some reason, the thought of it did not trouble her as much as she thought it should. If anything, it was the excitement that coursed through her veins that she found troubling.

Best to help Marcella with lunch and forget such nonsense. Marcella was right to keep her feelings hidden. Keep a healthy distance between the men in Stalag 31 and themselves. Do not let them get to close, for who knew how long any of them had to live.

After all, surely Sparks knew where Clara's loyalties lay.

With the man who was coming in from the fields with a pleased grin on his face at a morning's work well met. She waved at Stasio and smiled.

❧Suspicion's Gate❧

Chapter 11
July 12, 1943

G rinding his teeth, Jamie tried to concentrate on the pan he was scrubbing, aware that behind him, his father had tried several times to engage him in conversation. Each time, however, the older man stopped himself and went back to lunch preparations. Jamie hated working with his father, particularly when there was no one to serve as a buffer between them. If he was lucky, they would continue to work in brittle silence.

If he was unlucky, they invariably fell into a well-worn circle of arguments that neither of them won.

Sparks had come in with an armload of firewood for the stove, deposited it in its usual place as he notified them of today's special delivery, and then he went out again as quietly as he had come. Jamie assumed the Scot's agitation was connected to that delivery or the broken radio, but he did not ask. His cushioning company was not there long enough for that.

The clang of the stove door disrupted his thoughts; George jumped back. "You're paranoid," he said mildly, both hoping his father would hear him and hoping he would not.

"Always a chance that firewood ends up in the wrong place…"

"Ronny may be crazy and reckless with his own safety, but he's not going to risk anyone else…shit!" He yelped and shoved his knuckle into his mouth, pretending he had cut himself rather than admit he had left himself open for some sort of scathing remark.

Fortunately, George missed the cue. "There's always a chance that the Germans…"

"Don't give them too much credit…"

"You give them too little," George grunted, annoyed with being second-guessed by his own son. Deciding that he had been harsher than necessary, he continued, "Who knows what they might know."

"You think there's another rat?"

"I didn't say that." Another grunt. "But Henderson's smarter than that…"

"Mrs. von Hausen…"

The elder Campbell cut him off. "I'm not foolish or blind. Everyone knows there was something between those two…but no matter how good the sex may have been, it's not like him to lay out plans…and she's usually too drunk to remember anything well enough to pass on. But we also know he's not the only one she's been with…and to have been so prepared …the details would have had to be specific…written down even…and he's not…"

George did not finish. He did not need to. Jamie had been thinking about little else since that unfortunate night and for once he and his father agreed. He had gone over the events in his head, trying to figure out what had gone wrong, how much fault for the failure, and Buck's death, had been his. Their captors had not only known there would be an attempt, but seemed to have known the day, the hour, the direction they intended to run, and likely even the number of men involved judging by the number of soldiers and dogs that had pursued them. The Germans had lain in wait along the path. Their knowledge had been too exact.

It seemed possible, looking at it now, that the Oberfuhrer's wife had fed Skip information to influence their choice of date and time. They had chosen the night von Hausen was to be away…only to have him return earlier than expected. That had been no coincidence. And it seemed likely that Skip had said his goodbyes to the woman, giving away their intent to take advantage of that opportunity. Anyone else could have tipped off the Germans to their path, accidentally or otherwise. But who?

Someone they trusted?

Again Jamie's thoughts scrambled. Had Sparks, Paddy, or Bonny misspoken to Clara and she to von Hausen? Had Leonard let something slip to the men in Camp 2 during one of their talks at the dividing fence? Had Ronny been too loud or loose with the common rank men he frequently associated with? Had Ray decided the plan was too detrimental to the stability of the Stalag and turned to the Germans when his own prison mates refused to listen? Had Vic, the most volatile and outspoken man about the failure and the man who had been the hardest on Skip afterward, let something slip and was now covering his own guilt? Had he or anyone of them been careless about who they had spoken to and who might have been close enough to overhear?

It was inconceivable that any man in Barracks J would have intentionally endangered the lives of the others, of Buckman, but it did seem unlikely that Skip had been the sole leak of information, that he was the only man to blame.

"If you hadn't stopped to play doctor…"

"I AM a doctor. The sooner you accept that, the happier we'll both be."

"Your grandfathers must be…"

"Let them roll. Good for them. I'm not here to take lives if I can help it, I'm here to save them,"

"Soft like your mother…"

"You'd rather have her be a heartless bastard like you? I'm surprised you remember her well enough to…"

"I loved you…"

"…enough to give her two children to care for alone while you were off playing big shot soldier…"

"I had a duty…"

"Your family was your duty…and you left us alone…"

"I am sorry you feel I failed you…"

"We did well enough without you. Mama did her best to teach us to follow our own paths. You have no right to complain." He hurled the now clean soup pot at his father and headed towards the door, guessing that George had caught it since it did not clatter to the floor.

"James, we're on KP duty. Get back here…"

"It's Jamie," he snarled. "What are you going to do…spank me?" He stormed out of the room, leaving George to complete the preparations alone.

❧*❧

"And there was Stetcher, that damn stick flailing like it was looking for a woman…"

Ronny strutted back and forth across the small room, his gait and the way he gestured with the stick he had found serving up a surprisingly accurate portrayal of the despised Gestapo officer. So accurate that, while only one of the three French prisoners working in the leather shop understood his words, they all understood who he was ridiculing. The third Frenchman, the one who served as leader in

Camp 2, translated Ronny's words for his comrades. The youngest said something that caused the oldest to laugh harder.

"Wha'd he say?" asked Ronny.

Wiping his eyes, the leader replied, "He thinks Stetcher is uptight because he's been without a woman longer than we have."

In stilted English, between guffaws of laughter, the oldest man said, "I think he not know what to do with a woman if he had one."

Ronny joined in the laughter. "Probably can't get it up…"

"Why else would he wave that thing around?" asked the translator, wiping his teary eyes. "It's the only erection he can get…"

"The way he ogles Mrs. von Hausen…"

"Any woman…"

"Or even Hirsch," Ronny added with a mock expression of horror and disgust.

The oldest man asked, "Maybe he prefer men…no?"

The American pilot groaned, clutching his side. "Damn, I hope not…" With one hand to his forehead in a simulated swoon, waving the stick suggestively, he crooned, "Oh Hirschy dahlink…I can wait no longer…"

"I don't want to think it," snorted the translator.

The topic of conversation seemed to have run its course as the laughter dwindled and serious work resumed. Before the war, the elder Frenchman had been a cobbler and thus had been put to work making and repairing shoes for the Germans. The youngest had once made coats and hats, but other than an occasional request from the Stalag staff, he was now relegated to gun belts, rifle harnesses and the like. They held two of the three permanent job assignments in Stalag 31, though occasionally Hirsch or Stetcher decided to employ them elsewhere for amusement, just because they could.

And though Ronny knew nothing about leatherworking, he had been assigned here this morning while waiting for the delivery trucks to arrive. As he tended to be in the way more than he helped…he wanted to assist but had neither the skill nor the patience to be of practical use…he stayed to the side, passing tools and cleaning up as the work progressed. Plus, he was a talker and kept his co-workers entertained with wild stories and joke, and thus they were willing to forgive any slackness in exchange for making their day a little more enjoyable, so long as the Germans did not intervene to punish them all for slacking.

He had just taken hold of one side section of leather, preparing to help the older Frenchman stretch it flat, when the door opened and one of the Germans entered with a bored scowl upon his face. Beyond him, the sound of a large truck rumbled steadily.

"Major Zane, come. You are to help Lieutenant McKenzie and Privates Solomon and Davis unload the wood."

"It's almost lunchtime," he grumbled, though he was already heading for the door.

"Then you had better work quickly because you will not eat until you are finished…and if you take too long…"

"Yeah…yeah…I know."

Before following Ronny, the soldier paused long enough to cuff the youngest Frenchman roughly on one side of the head. "Get back to work.

The door closed. Over the rumble of the truck's engine, the soldier did not hear the sound of a boot sole hitting the closed door between them.

❧*❧

"Delivery went as planned?" asked George, directing his question at Ronny who was removing splinters from his arms as the weekly Flight Meeting commenced. The meetings had little to do with flight, but since many of the original participants had been pilots or flight crew, the name for the meetings had continued as the high residential turnover ground on. Flight Meetings, conducted by pilots and air personnel, sounded less suspicious to the Germans than did 'escape meetings' as these frequently turned out to be, and thus far they had made no effort to disband the gatherings. On the occasions when one or another of the German staff did come into the barracks, the conversation was quickly skewed to involve flight technology, techniques, and strategy. Thus far it had kept the Germans from being suspicious.

"Yep," Ronny replied, "right under their noses, to their mess as planned. It's towards the bottom, mixed in with the wood from previous deliveries. May be awhile before the Krauts get to it in this heat, but when they do…"

"Boom!" cried Ollie Randal, the Florida flight engineer who was a friend of Ronny's. He was at the meeting that night as a representative of Barracks C. Each of the barracks took turns sending men to these meetings. Those delegates were responsible for keeping the enlisted men informed of decisions and the details of the discussion as well as serving them by speaking up on matters that would affect the entirety of Camp 1. Such liaisons were deemed necessary to support the normal military chain of command in this place and to keep the possibility of information leaks to a minimum, something that now seemed more important than ever.

Unfortunately, the fiasco of the last escape attempt had damaged the power hierarchy in the Camp, the enlisted men's willingness to trust the officers and vice versa. No one knew yet how to undo that damage, especially since most were too busy trying to find someone, anyone, to blame.

At Ollie's exclamation, Ronny tipped the man's chair backward, knocking the flight engineer onto the floor. Many laughed, Ollie's laughter being the loudest of all.

KC took a long drag of the cigarette he had bummed off of Vic and exhaled slowly. He glanced around the room, expecting someone to voice the thoughts that were on his mind. Ronny and Ollie were too busy wrestling. In the doorway, keeping watch for the Germans, Vic was whittling something out of a small bit of wood with a sliver of metal he had fashioned into a blade. Sparks seemed more interested in whatever he was writing in his journal, and no one else seemed to be thinking the same as he was.

Maybe they were, but they did not voice their thoughts.

"Am I the only one that thinks such a blast would be an ideal cover to get the hell out of here?" KC finally asked, though he did not know the details of how much explosives had been planted.

"No…you're not…" muttered Leonard who, even in the middle of a meeting, felt compelled to mend clothing. "Came up the first time this wood idea was brought up. Those intended to use it already know who they are and are seeing to their own preparations."

From the expression on Taffy's face, KC assumed the Welshman was one of those involved, or that they might not be planning an escape for everyone. "Oh…" he murmured with disappointment.

"I know the last attempt failed…" George started, clapping KC's shoulder in a friendly fashion.

"I'd call it more than a failure," grunted Vic.

George shot him a measured, cool look. "Don't start…"

"Besides," Sparks said without looking up from his journal, "There's still a chance Paddy and Newt made it."

From his bunk where he lay upon his stomach, Skip mumbled in a voice heavy with guilt, "Face it, Sparky…they're history…"

Vic was on his feet and yanking Skip off of the bunk before anyone could stop him. "Whose fault is that you goddamn bloody…"

"Stop it," George ordered as Dusty and Sparks pulled the two apart, an easier task than usual since Skip was not in fighting form.

Dusty snapped, "It was a bad spot of information, that's all. Couldn't know they were playing us; could've happened to anyone."

"But it didn't happen to anyone," said Bonny from his place beside George. "It happened to us…to Buckman. We'll never know for sure how it happened…we just have to make sure it doesn't happen again."

"It won't," Skip snarled, wresting free of Dusty's grasp and settling painfully onto his bunk again. Sparks continued to hold Vic back since the taller Scot seemed determined to lunge at Skip instead of backing away from the fight.

"If nothing else," Ronny said, his own wrestling match with Ollie abandoned, "it served to prove whose side she's on."

Bonny sighed. "I would've thought that was obvious. With the practiced measure of his religious calling, he kept his voice neutral, but his words carried enough weight to have the desired effect.

"Yeah," growled Vic as Sparks reluctantly released him. He did not look at Skip as he resumed his place in the doorway.

Sparks straddled the chair next to Ray who looked as though he wanted to shrink and disappear into his own skin. Knowing how the young man felt about this topic, it was no wonder. Sooner or later he would voice his pacifistic dogma and another argument would ensue.

From Ray's other side, Jamie spoke at last. "I vote for a change of subject." If that disastrous escape continued to be discussed, nothing productive was going to be accomplished.

"I second that," Taffy agreed with his elbows on the table.

"So who's next out?" Sparks asked.

"That will depend on what sort of plan we decide to undertake," replied George as he read the written roster before him "but it looks like Leonard and Ronny…"

"Scratch my name," Ronny said, propping his feet on the table. Leonard pushed them back onto the floor, scowling at the barnstormer's disrespect.

Across the circle, Farmer asked, "Why the hell would you pass?"

Ronny shrugged. "I'm needed here…"

"Needed?" Ray snorted.

Several pairs of eyes rolled. "Who else is gonna come up with ideas to get your sorry asses out of here?" Ronny asked.

"I'm not going anywhere, and neither should you," challenged Ray with his arms crossed over his chest as Dusty simultaneously asked, "You mean like the lame idea to use gliders off the watchtower?"

"It should work," Ronny protested, ignoring Ray as everyone else was doing.

Jamie interjected, "Yeah, if we could get gliders…and you could get the guards out of there and get your skinny butt up there without being shot…"

"And keep from being shot in the backside on the way down," added Leonard.

"If he's not going, I want his place."

Most of the men's eyes turned to KC. As often happened with newcomers, KC was having a difficult time adjusting to life in Stalag 31. He was just shy of being a slacker, continually striving to see how little he could get away with, and the Germans did not tolerate laziness. It was a wonder, thought George, the man had succeeded as he had in the military to date.

Maybe his slacker attitude was purely to rankle their captors.

George shook his head. "We have an order of…"

"Oh, Georgie," Ronny quipped, "What will it hurt? Let him have my slot; I don't care."

After another glance at the roster, George said, "Maybe you don't, but Sparks might. He's next up…"

Ronny flicked a playing card at Sparks so that it landed on the open journal pages. "Whaddya say, Sparky? Up to you."

Sparks bit the inside of his lip without looking up. As much as he wanted out of this place, he knew his radio expertise was needed. And after that interlude with Clara that morning, an unexpected but long hoped for turn of events he hoped to capitalize on, Sparks was not prepared to leave yet.

"Let him go. You'll need another radio tech before I bug out."

"Thanks!" KC's grin lit up his entire face.

Scowling at Sparks' selflessness, George looked at Leonard. "You up for it?"

"Yeah," replied the big man.

"Then it's settled. Once planning gets underway, you and Taffy will be responsible for the others."

"Whatever you do," Bonny warned, "don't go towards the river. That's where they expect us to go…"

"After the last time, they'll probably expect us to avoid the river…could be the safest route," countered Taffy.

"I'm not willing to take that risk," Leonard huffed.

"Any attempt is a risk," Ray started, hoping he would be listened to by the two fresh sets of ears. "Would be a lot wiser to stay…"

Ronny talked over top of Ray's words. "We could burn down E Barracks and use the confusion to cover…"

"You're fucking nuts," snapped Vic, "a fire in an empty barracks would…"

"…then how about D or F…"

"…then we can all go up in flames!"

Dusty grumbled, "Do the German's work for them…they'll probably applaud…"

"And we'd all end up sleeping in the parade yard," Jamie added.

"Besides," interrupted Bonnie, "You think we can burn down a barracks with a single book of matches…"

"Maybe with a little well-distributed spirits…" Taffy mused.

Ronny shrugged, already having abandoned that idea under the barrage of negativity. "Who said anything about matches?" The remark earned him several puzzled or disbelieving looks, but no one asked him to elaborate.

"How about a tunnel?" asked Farmer. Ronny bristled, not liking having his position as idea-man challenged by a newcomer.

"A lengthy and difficult undertaking," Jamie mused. "Would be hard to hide all that dirt…"

"Already begun," Ollie started; Ronny slugged him in the shoulder but Ollie pushed him back. "D Barracks has been working on one for quite a while. Expect it to come up on the far side of the shrubs between Arnaud's fields and the Stalag. Should be about three weeks…if all goes well…"

"If the Germans don't find it first," hissed Ray with narrowed eyes.

The potential for a workable escape brought Skip up on one elbow and he stared at Ollie with interest. "How in hell are you…?"

"Never mind that," George interrupted. Something in Ray's expression made the hairs on the back of his neck stand on end. "Doesn't matter tonight…"

The shriek of the night whistle ended their dialogue. "Next week." The men began to get up from the table. "We'll discuss options then." His hand caught Ray's shoulder with a firm grip as the young man tried to get up as well. No one else noticed as he bent down and hissed near Ray's ear. "Be careful.

Ray froze, the sweat on his brow having nothing to do with the July heat. He looked around. Most of the Barrack's J men were already in their bunks. Sparks was closing the tattered box where he kept his treasures and Jamie stood with his hand on the light chord waiting to put out the bulb when the men were settled. No one, other than George, paid the young medic any mind. He was not sure what George was implying, but he did not dare ask.

"Yes, sir…" he answered in a trembling voice. Only when the creak of the elder Canadian's bunk registered in his ears, did Ray make his way to his bed.

Jamie pulled the chord as the night gave birth to the second lights out whistle.

Chapter 12
July 13, 1943

Jennifer stood by the tall bay window staring at Hans' uniform hanging from the coat rack as he rummaged through the papers on his desk and placed the ones he needed into his leather briefcase that sat open on his chair.

The hour was too early for this, she thought with a sigh. He was in a hurry, so was eating breakfast on the move, a croissant half-eaten and his second steaming cup of black coffee sat to one side of the desk out of the way of his paper-finding expedition. As was more frequently the case, Jennifer's breakfast consisted of the glass of brandy in her hand. Perhaps she would eat when Hans was gone. She would feel calmer by then at least.

"Must you drink at this hour?" he groused, knowing she would not answer or heed his concerns. Sighing, he arranged the papers neatly in the briefcase and muttered, "I'm late; pass my coat."

She hesitated long enough for him to close and latch the case and straighten. Once his eyes were on her, she found she could not resist though she wanted to. While he tucked his shirt into his pants, she crept to the coat rack and gingerly picked up the coat as if it would bite her. Her sapphire eyes were wrinkled nearly shut in disgust and he watched as she held the article at arm's length, using only her fingertips to carry it to him.

"It won't hurt you," he grunted, snatching it from her in annoyance and began to put it on. "It's the man in it you should be wary of…that's the truth of any uniform. It's just a coat."

Preferring not to think about being afraid of him for more reasons than she already was, she tried to change the subject. "Will you be late?"

"We should return in time for dinner. God knows why we've been summoned to Chartes. I seem to spend more and more time at HQ of late…"

"Maybe they are considering promoting you…"

"No." It was not the first time she had spoken of being away from Ste Marie, though it was the first time her eagerness was colored by a tint of distress. "That's the furthest thing from their minds, I'm afraid. It was hinted that Oberstgruppenfuhrer Volheim may be coming on a flying visit…"

The color drained from the woman's face and her knees buckled. She was near enough that Hans caught her before she hit the floor. "Are you alright? Shall I send for Josef?"

"No…I'm fine…just a little dizzy," she said in a shaky voice that did not mask her lie.

Hans grunted, annoyed both with the lie and with the fact that she was hiding something. "No doubt from drinking so early," he grunted, gazing at her and running his thumb across her brandy kissed lips. When her lids fluttered at the touch, he shivered and bent impulsively to kiss her. For a moment she returned his kiss, and though it tasted too strongly of brandy for so early in the day, he reveled in her surrender. It had been so long since she had given him even this much and the sudden longing that flared within made him ache in unimaginable ways.

Feeling it, however, she stiffened and pushed against his chest with one hand, turning her face to the side as she attempted to escape. The brandy snifter tumbled to the floor, spilling its contents upon his polished shoes. Still caught in his desire, needing her to be his wife again in ways beyond name only, he barely noticed the spillage or her attempts to be free and continued kissing her face.

"No." she gasped. "No…no…" With one last effort, she managed to unbalance him, forcing him to lose his grip on her waist. Without a word, only hysterical sobbing, she fled the room, not looking back at the apparition of the man she had once adored.

Aching inside, his body tight and uncomfortable with need, Hans methodically straightened his clothes in an effort to calm himself. Briefcase in hand, he stared at the stairs, trying to understand what could have changed his wife so drastically, how she could go from passionate to revolted in a few short moments. Had he changed so much with the donning of this uniform? Had the war changed him? Her rejection, the sound of a door slamming, twisted his hurt into anger, drawing a huff as he started for the front door.

He would leave the choice of dinner to her. He did not care at that moment if he ate dinner with her tonight or not.

❧*❦

Stooping to pick up the tools that had been tossed at his feet, Skip grimaced. He should have allowed Jamie or Ray to change his dressings, but his obduracy had won out. He regretted it now, since some of the old bandages had worked loose, allowing the shirt Dusty had helped him put on to stick to the oozing wounds. The day was hot and humid and his clothes were soaked with sweat, causing additional stinging in the freshly reopened gashes. A stab of agony made him twitch and he dropped the hoe on his foot.

"Fucking hell..." he swore, gingerly trying to straighten and unstick the cloth from his back. Without fresh bandaging, he did not think it wise to expose his injuries to the sun and flies.

"Monsieur?" asked Zaline, lightly resting one hand on his shoulder. She had come out of the barn to find him at the grinding wheel where he had been the day before.

"Goddamn..." he yelped, wrenching away from her touch, an act which caused more pain than the gentle contact had created.

"Pardon...I did not think..."

"No, you bloody well didn't!" Seeing contrition in her eyes and the heavy pail of fresh milk in her other hand, he sighed gruffly. He wondered if he should apologize but she was already moving off towards the German sergeant in charge of the farm workers today. He scowled, watching her, wondering what she intended. Seeking punishment for his rudeness, no doubt. After a brief exchange with the guard, the man motioned for Skip to follow, which Skip did reluctantly, noting Zaline's neutral but somehow proud expression as he did so. His scowl deepened. Punishment for sure.

The sergeant looked him over as if assessing a wounded animal. "Captain, you are in no condition to be here."

"Stetcher doesn't give a rat's ass..."

"I will see to Herr Sturmbannfuhrer Stetcher," the German barked, annoyed at the interruption. Productivity was von Hausen's primary concern, and to the soldier's view, Henderson was useless in his condition. It was the overseer's prerogative to send men back to the camp if there seemed good cause, but too many days of being deemed useless could end a man's life.

"Sturmman Klein!"

Maybe, thought Skip, that was what the Germans were aiming for with him.

The soldier nearest them came running at the summons.

"Take Henderson to the repair shed." It would get the man out of the sun and keep him on the day's duty roster. To Skip, he said, "You will work there…and be more productive…" The threat of punishment if he did not meet expectations went unspoken.

"Yeah…sure…"

Before shuffling after Klein, Skip glanced at Zaline, who nodded with a hidden smile. He presumed he should thank her for being influential in sparing him a day of laborious pain beneath the sun, but the sergeant pushed him along and Skip kept his words to himself. Marcella was picking her way across the fields from the annexed farmhouse she had called home since Clara's arrival in Ste Marie; she smiled when she saw him but was too far away to speak. Skip suppressed the shiver in his stomach and looked away from her.

Jamie emerged from the barn as Skip passed, wondering where Zaline, who had come for the first pail of milk and left without a word, had gone. He wondered if she felt as awkward and embarrassed today as he did. He saw her watching Skip being led away and wondered as well, before returning to the milking, what Skip had done this time.

"Why should we be ashamed?" he muttered under his breath to the next cow as he adjusted the stool and empty pail.

He knew why. Her husband was barely gone when they had shared that moment, brief and innocent as it had been. Jamie should know better, should have shown respectful restraint. Loneliness was no excuse. If he was in her shoes, he would keep his distance as well. There was no future to be had in Ste Marie, not while the Germans held sway and the world was at war. No future while she mourned the loss of her husband.

It was easy to berate himself and see nothing but darkness and death in the world when he was alone, but when Zaline returned for the next bucket, their eyes met again, saying words with a smile that could not be spoken, that perhaps he only imagined. Well, he thought, things might not be perfect here, might not be the way he wanted them, but there was her smile, the fantasy of her, and that was enough to sustain him during the long nights in Stalag 31.

"Campbell, you are needed at the von Hausen house," Wagner spoke as he rushed into the barn past Zaline without noticing her.

She took the opportunity to withdraw towards the door, hiding her worries and any thoughts the summons brought to mind. Fearing for Jamie's safety, she listened as Wagner continued, "von Hausen's daughter is ill...you must come."

Not entirely hidden in shadow, Zaline's gaze met Jamie's as he pushed to his feet. "I will finish here," she offered as the two men marched past her. Jamie brushed his fingers against the back of her hand in gratitude, and then had to run to keep up with Wagner who had neither seen nor heard the exchange.

❧*❧

Hans found Stetcher's grunts to every bit of dialogue between the Commandant and the camp doctor to be annoying. If only the man had something intelligent and productive to say, his company might be tolerable. It would have been better if the Gestapo officer had remained at the Stalag. Anything would have been better than those grunts, or Stetcher's penchant for bringing up how the various medical practices in discussion might be used experimentally or as torture. It was the sort of distasteful topic Hans could not tune out, no matter how he tried, and it did little to help his already low appetite.

Thankfully the man had spoken little since their arrival at the café where they had been instructed to meet Oberstgruppenfuhrer Volheim; his continual grunting suggested he was monitoring every word the other two men said rather than expressing any desire to join the small talk about family, of which it was known Stetcher had none. Mila, Hans would have gladly discussed, as he was proud of his daughter and her accomplishments, but knowing he would not be able to keep such a discussion from drifting onto his wife, he avoided talking about his family whenever possible and left that topic to Dengler. One small opening would be all Stetcher needed to start with the pointed questions, the accusations, and the snide comments intended to rile the Commandant and provoke a reaction. Fortunately, Dengler noticed and understood this as well, and kept the commandant's family out of their discussion.

Now, however, dessert had been brought and the conversation had melted into largely awkward silence with no sign of Volheim. It took every bit of willpower for Hans to refrain from making a visual sweep of the room. Maybe this was a trap, a set up to make any or all of them easy to watch. If they were targets, or being observed, Hans had learned long ago that it was wiser to feign ignorance of the fact.

He would rather know and fake it than be caught unaware.

It was a great relief, therefore, when another uniformed officer entered the establishment and headed for their table as soon as he spotted them. Hans was further relieved to recognize Sturmbannfuhrer Ulrich, an easier man to stomach than Volheim would ever be.

"Herr Sturmbannfuher," he said cordially, standing from the table and offering his hand.

"Herr Oberfuhrer. It is good to see you. You look fit and well."

"Well enough, at any rate. Have you met Sturmbannfuhrer Stetcher and Doctor Dengler?"

The younger officer shook hands with each of them. "I have not had the pleasure. Gentlemen, I apologize for my tardiness. The Oberstgruppenfuhrer is delayed in Paris and sent me in his stead. Between train delays and the most horrid road conditions…I dare say it is a wonder these French get anywhere on time."

Each man laughed, though in a different way. Stetcher's was harsh and raucous, Dengler's was polite and soft, while Hans' was uncomfortable as he found such a slur to be directed at Clara and the people of Ste Marie, of whom he had to confess to a level of unexpected fondness that he could admit only to himself.

"Will you join us, Sturmbannfuhrer?" Hans asked as he pulled back the empty chair.

"Only briefly. I am late for all of my appointments as you can imagine. How long has it been, Herr Oberfuhrer? Over a year since we last met?" Ulrich accepted the chair and placed his briefcase upon the space on the table Stetcher had just cleared. He waved away the waiter's offer of coffee and kept his attention on Hans.

"I believe so; shortly after my return to Berlin I believe…"

"Ah, yes, that unfortunate dinner at the Oberstgruppenfuhrer's home, when your wife had quite the upset. Is she well?" With his handkerchief, he mopped his brow and then lay the fabric square on the table.

"Fine," Hans said a touch too curtly, bristling at the memories Ulrich brought up. Clearly, the man's memory was better than his; Hans had managed to forget that particular party, one of his wife's worst episodes. Or at least, he had tried to forget it. Such memories never seemed to settle very far below the surface.

"And your daughter?"

"Excellent, a brilliant child, an asset to the Reich." Despite his belief in the sentiment, the final words were uncomfortable and he did his best to hide that discomfort from the others.

"That is good to hear. Did you bring the reports Herr Oberstgruppenfuhrer asked for?"

"Yes. Here." Hans produced the requested documents from his briefcase while Dengler and Stetcher produced theirs as well. All documents were placed in Ulrich's hands without knowing what the others had written. Ulrich glanced quickly through the files before putting them in his case.

"Good. Excellent. Having the required documentation will make matters so much simpler."

Feeling the hairs stand up on the back of his neck, Hans asked, "What matters?"

Ulrich chuckled. "You still worry too much, don't you, Herr Oberfuhrer? No matters, only that of pleasing the boys in Berlin. You know how bureaucrats can be. One missing piece of paperwork, one missing signature, and it sends them into fits of fury."

"Indeed," Dengler agreed. "Medical bureaucracy is no better, I'm afraid."

Again Ulrich laughed. "How are things in Ste Marie?"

If he was fishing for details to use against them, Hans was not about to take the bait, nor let Stetcher do so. "We have had our difficulties, but what camp doesn't?" he replied offhandedly.

Dengler nodded. "Particularly when you send us all of the troublemakers who are considered too valuable to kill...but do not see fit to equip us with the necessary manpower and supplies." He cast a sidelong glance at Stetcher. Even if the prisoners did not realize it, their potential individual value to the Reich was why they were still alive, why they had not been butchered after so many escape attempts, why they fared better than prisoners in other camps. He, like von Hausen, presumed that was the only reason Stetcher had resisted killing more of them.

"All of that will change soon, I suspect, Doctor," Ulrich said evasively as he snapped his briefcase closed.

"Are we to receive additional staff? Better equipment? More supplies?" Hans asked, suspecting that was not what the man meant.

"Let's say that SS Command is looking into your needs and will address them accordingly. You will not have to be concerned with such things much longer, Herr Oberfuhrer. You have Herr Oberstgruppenfuhrer's personal assurance of that."

Hans bristled at words he perceived to be a threat but did not speak.

"About time," Stetcher muttered with a guttural sound deep in his throat that sounded like a growl. It did not appear that he, or Dengler, heard the words to be a threat as Hans did. Maybe he was wrong. Stetcher crossed his arms and began to lean back in his chair with a smug expression, but Ulrich was already pushing his chair away from the table.

"Now, I am sorry to cut our meeting short since you have traveled all of this way, but I must go. Herr Oberfuhrer, Herr Oberstgruppenfuhrer will be in touch soon. He will be pleased that you were so forthcoming with these reports."

Hans and his officers stood as well, the Commandant hiding his feelings as he did so. "Let me see you to your car…"

Ulrich shook his head. "That will not be necessary but I thank you for the offer. It was a pleasure to see you again, Herr Oberfuhrer…and to meet you, Herr Dengler, Herr Stetcher. When you are next in Berlin, look me up and we shall dine properly."

Dengler nodded, "Of course, Herr Sturmbannfuhrer.

"Certainly," said Stetcher.

Relieved that the meeting had gone more smoothly than anticipated, though more troubled by what Ulrich had not said than what he had, Hans asked for the bill, noting that the Sturmbannfuhrer had left his handkerchief on the table. He picked it up, prepared to summon the man back, but Ulrich was already out the door.

Stetcher held out his hand. "I will see if I can catch him."

Without consideration, Hans placed the napkin into Stetcher's hand. The Gestapo officer hurried out the door. Dengler loitered in his chair while Hans paid for the meal, and then the two of them left the building together.

Across the street near an expensive looking car, Stetcher was shaking Ulrich's hand. When his officer turned his head to look at him, as Ulrich got into the car, Hans felt a cold sliver pierce his temples. The handshake, to him, appeared to be one of familiarity. Of agreement. Of sealing a deal.

Stetcher's air briefly looked to be one of malice and warning.

Hans wished he did not have to return to Ste Marie with the man. He wanted a strong drink.

And a visit with Clara.

∂*∞

Jamie wiped his hands on his trousers as he followed Jennifer out of the girl's room and back down the stairs without speaking. The summons to the house had brought him to Mila in the midst of a severe asthma attack. Though Dengler had treated her for such attacks before, with the German doctor attending whatever duty the three camp officers had been pressed into that day, the matter could not await his return. Fortunately, Jamie knew what to do. He had worked in the shadow of Jennifer's anxious, intoxicated presence but she, at least, had agreed to stand away and let him work rather than hovering too closely at the bedside as she longed to do.

Despite his promise that Mila was out of danger, however, Jennifer was no less calm than she had been when Jamie arrived.

They entered a room with a piano, a room decorated differently than the others Jamie had passed through on his way upstairs. This room had more of a feminine touch and from Skip's description of the house, Jamie presumed it was the woman's private haven. He felt uncomfortable, wondered why he had been led into this place now that his medical mission was complete. He presumed it was because the woman wanted him near, in case Mila relapsed, despite every reassurance Jamie had made to the contrary. Though it was a nice change of pace from the drabness of the barracks, Wagner and the other soldier who had come with them were disallowed to enter this room, and Jamie was reluctant to leave on his own.

Someone was likely to shoot him for trying to escape.

Jennifer's first stop was the table where she poured two glasses of brandy, one which she offered to him with a trembling hand.

"I can't…" he started.

"Nonsense…it is the least I can do. Take it. No one will know."

No one but me, he thought warily. He reluctantly took the glass but did not drink from it. "Thank you."

"No…thank you…you have no idea." Her voice quavered. "I am forever in your debt, Dr. Campbell." Draining the glass and refilling it, she added, "Mila is the world to me…if anything happens…"

She collapsed onto the sofa with a defeated sag of her shoulders, giving into tears she had forced away upon his arrival. His humanitarian nature brought him to sit beside her, though he kept a respectable distance between them. "She'll be fine; she needed a little help to breathe, but she's okay now."

Jennifer clutched his hand tightly, an act which seemed to fulfill whatever need she had for reassurance as she gradually grew calmer and wiped her face. They sat that way in silence for several minutes until the sound of a car door slamming caused Jennifer to jump and tense like an animal caught in the headlights of an oncoming car. Jamie released her hand, fearful that the Commandant, or anyone else, might find him here, but no door opened, no doorbell sounded, and when Jamie looked out the window, he saw only the guards changing post outside and Ray tending the shrubs, looking at the window until he saw Jamie there. Ray went quickly back to work as though embarrassed to have been caught spying. Jamie tried to relax, but Jennifer did not.

Second glass of brandy now drained, she got up and paced to the next window as if to reassure herself there was no one there. "He wasn't always the way he is, you know," she murmured. "He was kind...gentle...romantic...the first time I saw him...when we met...I knew...do you believe in love at first sight, Captain?"

"I don't know..." he murmured with a shrug. He had been drawn to Zaline at first sight, but love? In this place, he was afraid to label anything he felt as love.

"Mila completed everything...everything was perfect...and then...him." She spat the last word as she glanced at the portrait of the Fuhrer upon the wall, the only item out of place with the rest of the very British décor. "Thirty-nine...Hans had to go to Berlin...fell under his spell..." She shivered. "He was sent east, to fight..." She had never bothered to learn the details of his time away; she only knew that he had been injured in battle and brought home. "He came back a different person...he recovered and served in Berlin for a time, then we were sent here. It was too late then...to undo any of it...and if I tried to leave...to take Mila...I would be placed in detention or..."

"He wouldn't..." Jamie did not know that; for all he knew the choice to arrest her might be out of von Hausen's hands.

"Wouldn't he? He has the means...motive...now even Tom hates me...thinks I betrayed him...but it wasn't me...it was them...I'm so alone here..." With each word, her pitch inched higher, her tone more hysterical, so that Jamie, afraid she would draw Wagner's attention and believe he was hurting her, joined her at the window and put a calming arm around her shoulders. "You must convince Tom I didn't know," she squeaked. "You must…"

Convince Skip? Jamie had no intention of doing any such thing. The woman had used Skip and other men from the camp as an emotional crutch, a tool against her husband and their crumbling marriage. Never the men from town, never the soldiers under von Hausen's command, only the prisoners in Camp 1 who she knew, on some level, were mostly protected from death by the value of their knowledge to the Reich. She might want Tom back in her sway, but Jamie was going to do everything he could to put distance between her, Henderson, and every other man in the Stalag.

Without warning, though Jamie realized he should have seen it coming, Jennifer lifted her head and kissed him on the mouth. For a moment he did not react, tempted, as any lonely man would be by a beautiful woman, to seize the opportunity. But reason prevailed and he pushed her gently away. Risking punishment for leaving without being dismissed, risking a bullet in the back, he made it through the door as the brandy glass came crashing after him.

"He said you weren't man enough!" she cried.

Jamie refused to look back or acknowledge those words with a response.

❧*❧

Ray leaned on the spade, wiping his brow whilst gazing longingly at the partially open screen door. It had been nearly an hour since Jamie had left the von Hausens' home, red-faced and indignant, knowing that the guards outside and Ray too had heard that final hurled accusation and the breaking of glass. Jamie had paused only long enough to ask Ray to check on the girl's condition regularly until Dengler returned, for as long as his day's duties kept him stationed in the garden.

Now he guessed an hour had passed. That seemed long enough to wait.

He dropped the spade and started up the steps. Aware of Campbell's medical orders and that the welfare of the Commandant's daughter was on their heads if they did not allow Ray to pass, the guards stood aside to allow him entry. With men also stationed at the rear door, Ray would not be able to escape, and from experience, they knew that pacifistic Ray was as unlikely to harm the woman inside as the sun was to fall from the sky.

Ray's heart thundered as the screen door bumped closed; the thought of being in Jennifer's company again made him feel light-headed and giddy. He had little hope of resuming the kiss where they had left it when Dengler had interrupted, but just seeing her, being with her, would be enough. He could think of no one he would rather spend time with. He passed the music room, hoping to see her, but she was no longer there and the broken glass she had hurled at Jamie had been cleared away. His heart sank as he moved slowly from room to room, finding neither servants nor the woman he hoped to see. Confused, thinking she must have left through the back door, he could not imagine her leaving her ailing daughter alone. No car had left. She had nowhere to go.

It occurred to him that she was likely with Mila, and he felt foolish for his worries. Mila's room was the first place he should have gone, as Jamie had instructed, but with no one to escort him, and no idea where that room was, a room to room search for the servant, or for Jennifer, had seemed the wisest course. It was crazy to be walking through the house unescorted, but he knew he would be searched when he left, so he could not get away with theft or murder or any other crime against the Commandant's family. He snorted as he mounted the stairs and did his best to ignore the increasingly louder thump of his heart. He listened for movement as he passed each open door until he reached the very last one on the upper floor.

The child slept, her breathing soft and even, telling Ray everything he needed to know about her condition. At first, he thought her to be alone, but there was a rustling on the other side of the bed and the woman sat up from where she had been resting her head upon the girl's pillow. Ray's heart fluttered at the sight of her; she was every bit as lovely as she had been upon the stage of Covent Garden in spite of eyes swollen from crying and hair unkempt from where it had been upon the pillow.

"Frau von Hausen?"

"Yes?" At first, he thought she did not recognize him, and that hurt, but he realized quickly that the light in the corridor behind him probably showed her only the silhouette of a man. He stepped into the dim room where she might see him better.

"It's Ray...Captain Campbell asked me to check on your daughter. There was no one downstairs so I came up...I hope you don't object..."

"Ray...oh...yes...come in." She stood up and made a vain attempt to straighten her hair, her clothes, and to wipe her face of tears. "Is she alright?"

He took the girl's wrist in his hand, felt for her pulse, and pressed his ear to her chest. Jennifer came around the bed to stand beside him. "Yes...everything sounds good..."

"Thank god..." Her shoulders began to shake as she started to weep again. "I'm sorry...I must look dreadful...but I was so afraid I would lose her..."

It seemed to Ray she was always afraid. He quickly, without a thought, enfolded her in his arms, rocking her gently in time to the thundering in his chest. "No...you look beautiful..." he murmured, wishing he could tell her how he had loved and admired her from the first moment he had heard her sing. How he had dreamt of her often in those distant days, and how he dreamed now of rescuing her from her Nazi husband and taking her far away from this war where it would never touch either of them again. She may not have noticed him before, not when compared with the likes of charismatic Skip Henderson, but she noticed him now, and he believed with all of his heart that he could make things right for her if given the chance. "She'll be alright. I swear it..."

"You think so?" she whispered, gazing into his eyes.

"Yes." Maybe she had been asking about Mila. Maybe sought reassurance that she was still beautiful. Either way, the answer was the same. Her body, soft and warm, felt right in his arms, and her perfume was intoxicating. It was a perfect moment, one to cherish, for in it she belonged to him and no one else. But the moment could not last; as she calmed, she drew away and he reluctantly let her go.

"Thank you," she whispered, leaning in for a grateful kiss. "You are very kind. How can you...when your friends hate me so...?"

"Friends?" His fingers traced his mouth as if they could still feel her lips there. He would not consider any man in Stalag 31 to be his friend. They were strangers confined to the same place.

"They blame..." She caught his face between her hands. "Do you blame me?"

Logically, there was no doubt that some or all of the information about the escape had reached von Hausen through his wife. But at this moment, Ray shook his head and replied, "No…you would never…you are too…" His voice faltered as he realized she was steering him out of her daughter's room. Of course, they would not want their talk to wake the girl.

"Too what, Ray?" she asked in a breathy whisper that sucked all resistance out of him.

"Perfect."

She chuckled softly, a melancholy noise that made him weak. "I'm not perfect, Ray…you don't even know me…" They made it as far as the room across the corridor and now both doors were closed behind them without Ray realizing what was happening.

"To me…you are…"

They were the words Jennifer needed to hear…that no matter what she had done, someone safe still found her desirable. Her arms wound around his neck and she pulled him into a kiss he had no desire to break. She did not resist when he picked her up and stumbled towards the huge bed covered with a brightly colored patchwork quilt. He was beyond noticing the pink-shaded flower motif in the room or the prints from a variety of her shows that adorned the walls. He was aware only of her body against his and how badly he wanted her. She did not seem to notice that he was dirty, smelled of sweat and earth, and was too thin from inappropriate nutrition. The fact that she might want him at all flooded him with even stronger longing.

When her hands found their way to his hips, to push his pants down, he lifted his head out of the kiss and gasped, "Are you…?"

"I've never been more sure of anything."

Whether the words were true, Ray did not care. He heard them as though they were gospel to his ears and fell into kissing her more fervently than before. Without considering the wisdom of his words, they tumbled from his mouth as he found his way home within her.

"Jenny…I love you…"

Chapter 13
July 13, 1943

Of all the possible work details in Stalag 31, repairing broken tools was better than most. It was a rare assignment, as there was a gaggle of French prisoners in Camp 2 who had done such work as tradesmen before the war and were most often given those duties now. The Germans, particularly Hirsch and Stetcher, had less respect and patience with the people in Camp 2 and delighted in finding ways to degrade and torment them, often assigning them unfamiliar duties and allowing officers from Camp 1, with whom they could barely communicate, to assist them. Any failure in productivity was entertaining to their captors. The Camp 2 prisoners worked seven days a week and were frequently fed only one or two meals a day. Supplementing their work ranks with Camp 1 soldiers was wise because it kept those, the brains, contained inside the wire walls where they could cause less trouble. Outside the wire, the potential for an attempted escape was too high.

For reasons best left un-probed, there were no other men from Camp 2 assigned to repair work today, only Dusty and Skip, a fact for which Skip felt incredibly grateful. If Stetcher had his way, Skip would be in the field, or he would have been saddled with Ray, Vic, Leonard or Jamie as work partners. He imagined he could have kept his mouth shut around Jamie or Leonard, so long as they had likewise remained quiet, because he knew neither of those men was itching for a fight. A day working in close quarters with Ray or Vic, however, would have started off uncomfortable and progressed to impossible quickly, and with Vic, one or both of them would have ended up in the Cooler, the infirmary, or dead.

Fortunately, Stetcher had not been around when Skip was escorted into camp and Kaufman, the next in the chain of command below Stetcher, was not stupid or sadistic enough to assign Skip someplace where there would be trouble. von Hausen would blame

Skip, no matter who was actually at fault and that blame might splash back onto Kaufman. He wanted to oversee a quiet, uneventful day in order to supply the Commandant with a positive report of his leadership upon the man's return.

Staying out of trouble mattered to Skip now, though it had not only days before. Until recently he had been prepared to die simply for the sake of revenge on Jennifer. But during and after that flogging, he had begun to reconsider his choices. Perhaps he could still have his revenge, but he had to stay alive if he wanted the chance. He had decided that the best revenge was to live. To live, to be happy, to be free, things that Jennifer von Hausen had not been in a very long time.

Living...and freedom, those were things Skip believed he could attain. He was less certain he would ever be happy again.

To accomplish freedom, he had to be far away from Stalag 31. He was treading on thinning ice with the Germans, and he knew that every day he was here, the chance of their learning who he really was increased. Once they learned of his Special Forces background, he imagined his torture for information, or his execution, would be swift. He had come close to death many times already, but thus far luck had been on his side. That flogging, however, had taught him that he had no interest in dying...and reminded him that sooner or later his luck would run out.

Something else had driven home the desire to live. Realizing that the lovely Marcella Arnaud was staring at him, realizing that he, in turn, had begun watching her, had been an unexpected turn of events. He had noticed her before, a man would have to be dead to not notice her honey-eyed almost innocence. She moved with a child-like grace that seemed out of place in this setting of war and horror, but her eyes carried a haunting weight, a woman-child touched by darkness. Though before they had exchanged glances and occasional greetings in passing, she had seemed as unattainable to him as the Virgin Mother on a church altar...until yesterday. Despite having sworn off women after Jennifer's betrayal, the look Marcella had given him, and the smile she had flashed today, colored not with merely compassion but also longing, suggested she might not be beyond his reach...if only he was not locked up here.

Though it ignited a burning in his belly, the possibility of her also frightened him. He had little doubt that she and her sister, wife of the late Etienne, were involved in the Resistance movement that had helped with escape efforts in the past. She seemed too young, too innocent, to be part of that dangerous world. And though she seemed trustworthy, so too had the Oberfuhrer's wife. She was a woman, after all, and women, in his experience, betrayed the men who trusted them. The possibility that Marcella might do likewise was strong.

He could not allow that to happen. Before he got too close, before he found himself in a position where she could betray him, he needed to get far away from Ste Marie. He needed to escape the Stalag, Jennifer von Hausen, and Marcella Arnaud. One of those three would surely be the death of him.

He dropped the broken hammer he had picked up for repair and stood with a careful stretch. His back was less painful than earlier in the morning, but it would be a long time before those lashes healed. A long time before the pain and memory left him. Stopping at the window, he glared at the back of the guard posted outside the door.

"We gotta find a way out of here, mate."

Dusty looked up from his attempts to reattach a hoe head to its shaft. "Tell me something I don't know."

"I don't mean eventually…I mean now. As soon as possible. You and me."

"Our own escape?" Dusty arched one brow as he contemplated the suggestion but continued working.

"There's gotta be a way."

"George won't like it."

"Fuck George; this has nothing to do with him. They're gonna kill me if I stay much longer."

"Maybe you shouldn't encourage them, mate," Dusty grunted. "You'd live longer…be in less pain." He turned on his stool. "Got something in mind?" He might be discouraging his best friend from foolhardy actions, but he knew his words would not be a deterrent. If the Aussie decided to go, he would go regardless, and Dusty was loyal enough to stick by his side.

Skip shook his head. "Not yet, but going under the wire, heading for the river…still seems feasible. They're not expecting any of us to be stupid enough to try that again."

"Which is precisely why we would. Maybe we should wait a spell and see what comes up at the next meeting. What they decide to do…and when…maybe we can work with it. Think talking to Miss Beton would be…"

"No bloody way in hell!"

Dusty smirked, well aware of the buttons he was pushing. "She's our best link to the resources…we'll need papers, clothing…help…"

"We don't need help."

"She can get the things we need…because we sure as hell can't get them from Leonard or others in here and keep this under wraps," Dusty pressed. "They'll know we're up to something. We either get help or count me out. I'm not sticking my neck out for some half-assed plan. If I wanted that, I'd take Ronny up on his glider proposition."

For several minutes, Skip neither moved nor spoke, and since Dusty could not see his face, he was uncertain of his proposals reception. "If you want, I'll talk to her next time I'm farmside…"

"I'll do it," the Aussie growled low and dangerous. Clara seemed friendly enough and sympathetic, and she had successfully helped them in the past. He was not sure he trusted her, but better her than anyone else. At least he would better be able to gauge her trustworthiness if he discussed the plan face to face.

Dusty shrugged his shoulders, reached across the work table, and picked up the headless hammer Skip had discarded. "Whatever works." He threw a bit of wood so that it struck the back of Skip's leg. "Now get back to work, Roo, or we'll never get this stuff done. Stetcher'll be all over you again and you won't have to worry about getting' out."

"Wanker," Skip grumbled without malice and returned to the table, pulled his stool closer, and set about the repairs once more.

❧*❧

With a trembling hand, Clara set the dirty teacups in the sink, imagining she could still hear the sound of Sister Isabelle's footsteps upon the front stoop. That was not possible, of course, because the front door was too far away from where she stood, and at the moment she did not believe she would hear anything over the pounding of the blood in her ears.

It could not be. It was not possible.

She shook her head as if to clear it of the thoughts and fears trying to root there. When that seemed not to work, she tried to concentrate on the few dishes that cluttered the sink and countertop.

Isabelle would not lie to her. She had experience in these things. And it explained the last several days all too well. Clara did not need a doctor's confirmation to know the Sister was right.

She already knew it in her soul

Thank God Stasio had not been home for that visit and conversation. He would have to know, have to be told, but Clara felt infinitely better that the truth had come to her when he was not home to fret. He would be soon enough, she presumed, as he had only driven to Guichen to buy farming supplies and foodstuffs that could not be easily gotten in Ste Marie, as well as pick up some of the items she needed to pass along to Sparks for his radio. Stasio had been gone too long as it was, long enough for Clara to worry, long enough for her to consider going to Hans and asking him to undertake a search. Long enough for her to consider saddling a horse and looking for him herself, if he did not return soon.

She would already have done so if Sister Isabelle had not stopped for lunch with the weekly news to send to London, and with a letter arrived from Clara's sister-in-law in Paris.

Hands trembling again, it dawned on her that this added significant complication to her duties. How was she going to carry on, continue putting her life at risk, now that there was someone else to consider? The good sister had introduced too many questions into Clara's head and no answers.

The soapy saucer she had been scrubbing too roughly slipped from her hand. It shattered as it hit the sink, masking the sound of the firm but tentative knock on the back door. Swearing softly, she hung her head and tried not to weep.

"Clara? May I…?"

Startled, she looked up to see Hans standing with the back screen door pushed open enough that he was part way through it into the kitchen. He rarely came to her home, except to bring Mila for riding lessons. He had never come to the back door where the workers would see him, and he had never come here alone. Given his appearance, his disheveled uniform and bleary eyes, she presumed he had just arrived from wherever he, Stetcher, and Dengler had gone early that morning. He did not look as if he had slept well recently. In fact, he rather looked as if he had not slept for some time.

She scowled a little through her unshed tears, wondering how he had gotten away from Stetcher to come here, why he was here alone, and if he had even been home yet. She wagered he had not.

Wiping her face on her wrist, careful not to get suds in her eyes, she tried to regain her composure. "Good afternoon, Herr…"

Hans, taking his cue from her formality while noticing the tears lingering on her lashes, glanced toward the passageway into the main room of the house. "Have I come at a bad time?"

"Stasio is in Guichen," was all she said.

He took her words as an invitation and stepped into the kitchen, closing the door behind him. He did not seem concerned about any of the men outside having seen him come in. "What is wrong?"

"I broke a saucer…"

With a soft chuckle, he stopped at the sink, pushed up his sleeve, and stuck his hand into the heated water. "It is only broken china. No cause for tears."

"I know." His nearness was unsettling, as it led her to thoughts she did not dare ponder, but she did not move away. At the moment, she felt in desperate need of strength, of arms around her, and if no one else was available to provide it, Hans would suffice.

She watched him fish several pieces of the plate from the sink and then he let the water drain. When he removed his hand to dry it, she noticed blood on his fingers. "You cut yourself. Sit. I'll tend it."

Comfortable and trusting in her presence, Hans pulled out one of the chairs at the kitchen table and waited as she found the various medical supplies kept in the kitchen to tend farm injuries. She sat beside him, her knee pressed against his innocently, and cleaned the small cut before bandaging it. He was torn between closing his eyes and reveling in her touch or watching her movements. He could not recall the last time Jennifer had been so gentle and attentive, and it made him wonder again why he stayed in a marriage that, to all appearances, had ended several years ago.

Clara's fingers played across his hand, the touch sending little shivers throughout his body. It took great effort to ignore the sudden surge of jealousy. How very lucky Stasio was to have a woman so loving and loyal. Hans missed that aspect the most. And though he knew the possibility was beyond his grasp, he could not help but think that Clara might fill that void in his life.

"There." She smoothed the bandages and kissed it tenderly as one might a small child's injuries. She had always liked his hands. "Leave that on overnight if you can." Beneath her fingers, she could tell that hers were not the only ones trembling. As he reached for her face, she stood to put the medical supplies away. The place where her knee had touched his felt suddenly cold.

"Clara..." He caught her free hand but she did not turn to face him. She shook her head in denial. First Sparks, now Hans. Perhaps she could blame it on her condition. Either way, the swirl of emotions burning within felt wrong.

From the sounds of it, she was close to crying again and Hans let her go, flustered by the reaction he had not intended. He had never seen her cry and he was afraid that he had somehow hurt or upset her. Causing Jennifer to cry these days was too easy, but he never meant to, any more than he had meant this now. And unlike Jennifer, who most often cried out of fear of him, Clara was not afraid. Her fear of him had vanished after the first few tense moments of their initial meeting. The meeting with Ulrich now seemed unimportant. He pushed weakly to his feet, wondering if he should leave, watching her put the supplies back into the cupboards. She froze and uttered one long sob as the cupboard door closed.

"Geliebte," he whispered, shaken and hurt by her state. Though he had never done so before because she discouraged intimacy, he put his arms around her hesitantly. For a moment she did not move, but eventually, she turned to face him, and though she did not return his embrace, she did not fight when he pulled her to his chest. "What is wrong? What has happened? Is it Monsieur Arnaud?"

He regretted speaking the man's name for as soon as he did, Clara stiffened. She did not pull free, but she did not need to. Use to Jennifer reacting thus, the moment Clara tensed, Hans let her go.

Clara wiped her face and eyes. She could not, would not, tell him the truth. Not now. If he learned of it, it might well endanger any relationship she had with him and she could not afford that. Besides, the news belonged to Stasio first. Hans would learn of it soon enough. But there was the letter in her apron pocket that she could mention, the other reason for her upset. The primary reason, she decided stubbornly. "No...my brother...in Paris. He is missing."

"Missing..." Hans started to ask what she meant but knew such a question was mute. In a state of war, in a city occupied by foreigners, anything could have happened to her brother. He could be hiding, arrested, dead, or he could have successfully fled the continent without telling his sister. Though Hans knew little about her family, as he had thought it too crass to ask for details that might seem like a

German soldier fishing for information on the enemy, he knew her well enough to understand how much family meant to her.

"Is there anything I can do?" I will do my best to find him...if you want me to."

She shook her head. The thought was tempting, but it was too dangerous. "I think it would only place him, and you, at too great risk. He will return home in time." Her voice did not carry the assurance of her words, but Hans recognized the stubborn set of her jaw. She had made up her mind that her brother would be safe and nothing would sway her from that belief except for the occasional doubts that had brought her tears. "Did you come to let me know you are back?" she asked, seeking a change of subjects.

He chuckled grimly, pretending not to notice, or be troubled by, the loss of momentary intimacy. "I knew you would worry until you knew I was safely returned...but no...I want to discuss Mila..."

"Has there been trouble? Is she okay?" She did not know about Jamie's visit to the von Hausen home that day, that Mila had been ill.

"Yes, Gott sei Dank ...she is well...obedient, well-mannered, even-tempered...even if she hates me as much as her mother does..." He shook his head with a forlorn expression on his face.

Clara put her hand upon his arm. "She does not hate you...she merely doesn't understand...and she's afraid...of tempers...of the future." A child caught in the throes of war, how could she not be? When he said nothing else, she asked, "Did you talk to Jennifer?"

Leaving his hands upon the countertop, Hans stared out the window and replied with a snort, "It is not like I've had the opportunity. Three days in a row I've been away on business; by the time I get home, she is either too drunk to hold coherent conversation or else she's asleep. And after what Henderson..."

"Thank you...for not killing him..." She covered his hand with hers. It would be inappropriate to speak against his choice of punishments for Skip's offenses, but she could at least express appreciation for what kindness he did permit. If it helped encouraged further acts of kindness, it would be worth the effort.

"I hope I don't regret it. That man has been nothing but trouble since the day I arrived. He has interfered in my marriage and..."

"And I do not?"

Hans bit his lip. "This is not the same. Whatever else this might be, not once have I been unfaithful to my..."

"Only in thought, if not in deed...but is that really different, Hans? You saw her face. No matter how chaste our friendship, she believes otherwise. I am sure that belief must fuel her infidelities..."

"I know...but she isn't...I can't...I need this, Clara. I need you. I need someone to talk to I can trust. Someone honest, not afraid of me...who listens. There is no one else. That is all this..."

"A confidante," she finished with a nod, uncomfortable with his trust in her. He only knew what she showed him, but he believed she kept no important secrets from him. Knowing that she might one day have to betray that trust publically made her uneasy in his company. Both knew his words were a lie, that their relationship was not as simple as being confidantes, but for their own purposes, the lie had to suffice. "What about Mila then...?" she encouraged.

Accepting the shift back on topic, Hans straightened his posture and uniform. "Yes...Mila...I think, perhaps, until Jennifer has regained some perspective on my relationship with you, it would be best if you did not come to the house. I will bring Mila here thrice a week, for riding and schooling, but I think it necessary to reduce your contact with Jennifer. Perhaps she will feel less threatened then. Maybe her behavior and attitude will change."

He did not sound as if he believed that would happen, but it pleased Clara that he was taking steps to strengthen his marriage. At the same time, she found the thought that she might see him less frequently to be a melancholy one. As if reading her thoughts, he tried to smile as he kissed the side of her head.

"You will, of course, continue to be welcome in my office. Jennifer never comes there and I..."

"Yes..." It felt wiser not to allow him to voice whatever he had been about to say. "What of Herr Stetcher?"

His suspicions of the day crept back and he scowled. "Leave him to me. He is not your concern."

"You can't protect me from him forever. He sees me as a threat..."

"Because he's a fool."

Is he, Clara thought with a sigh, weary of everything and wanting to be alone. "You should go; Stasio will be home soon and you should take advantage of an early arrival home to talk to Jennifer."

Hans grimaced but nodded. "Of course...you are right. Will you be okay?"

There were so many layers to that question, more layers than Clara wanted to address or think about now, so she smiled and said, "Of course," and followed him to the door, holding it open for him after he opened it. "I always am."

"Yes…you are." He brushed a stray wisp of hair from her face and tucked it behind her ear. "Good day, Clara. I will let you know when I will bring Mila next."

"I look forward to it. Take care, Hans."

He went out the way he came, though with more spring in his step and confidence in the set of his shoulders than there had been when he had arrived. Clara did not move from where she stood but did not watch him leave. Hormones or not, she refused to give in to further indulgences today. Particularly when there were others who would be her witnesses. It was bad enough that Hans had been seen coming into her home. She wondered what Stasio…and Sparks…would think when they learned of it.

Scolding herself for the way her thoughts betrayed her, she pushed her focus into housework and mental preparation for contact with London. Most of her attention, however, swirled around the puzzle of how best to inform Stasio that he would be a father again.

❧*❧

"Fuck you."

Evening appell had ended, but George had not moved. He stood where he had been, the place in the yard where he stood every time the Germans called the men together, watching the others in Camp 1 scatter across the parade yard towards whatever evening activity they had planned or towards their barracks. From some of the clusters, angry words erupted like bursts of machine-gun fire. Small squabbles here and there, frustration, boredom, and loneliness expressed at inanimate objects, each other, or at their German captors, annoyance that the heat and flies and the living conditions they found themselves in brought bubbling to the surface.

He wondered how much of the blooming tension was due to those things and how much might be to his struggling effectiveness to lead. He had never had command problems before, had been a damned fine leader before his capture, but this place, and the circumstances the men found themselves in, was significantly different from anything he had faced before.

It did not help that his son refused to respect him. Jamie had avoided him since yesterday's altercation in the KP. George had tried to speak to him when appell had been dismissed last night, had tried several times today, but his efforts were soundly rebuffed. Jamie's last harsh words still echoed in the older man's ears.

"It would be easier if you treat him as a soldier and a doctor rather than as a child in need of scolding and guidance," said Taffy as he and Ronny came to stand with George.

"He's my boy…"

The Welshman nodded. "He's your son, but he's a grown man, George, and a damn fine one at that."

"And a helluva doctor," Ronny added. "I don't think he's been a boy in a long time."

"I know," George said with a sigh. He had shared this discussion with Taffy before. This was nothing new. Someday he might even be able to take the advice to heart.

"Have you told him that lately?"

Ronny chuckled, "And without calling him James?"

George's reply was cut off by an outburst of voices behind them.

"Son of a bitch!" Vic was shouting at newcomer KC whom he had pushed out the front doors of Barrack's J. Sparks was right behind his fellow Scot, grabbing his arm to hold him back as Jamie pushed past to aid the man on the ground. "Do you know how many hours I spent on that? You've ruined it, you bloody tosser!"

"He didn't know…" Sparks was saying, trying to calm his friend.

"It shouldn't have been left on…"

Jamie clapped his hand over KC's mouth and hissed, "Shut up or he'll kill you."

"My own goddamn bunk!" Vic cried. He would have been down the steps if Leonard had not come from the barracks to help Sparks hold him back.

By now, Ray was helping Jamie get KC to his feet and together they steered him away from the barracks to give Vic time to calm down. Sparks and Leonard pulled Vic back inside.

George shook his head. "They won't have to kill us. At this rate, we'll kill each other first."

"You noticed," replied Ronny evenly.

"How can I not, with displays like that…"

He gestured towards the barracks as Vic reappeared in the doorway. "Wanker!" the Scot shouted after KC, throwing something angrily out the door. Ronny went to retrieve whatever it had been.

"...are becoming more frequent and pronounced?" George finished.

"Ronny and I have been talking...about ways to boost morale, lessen the tension, ease the boredom..."

"And?" Ronny was an idea man, and though most of the time he had good ones, George was a little worried about what they might suggest. Ronny returned and placed two items in George's hand. They were two halves of the little wooden soldier Vic had been carving. It had been a clean break; with a little adhesive from the tool shop, perhaps it could be repaired. George was willing to try.

Ronny grinned. "I think we need a party."

The Canadian was slightly taken aback by such a relatively rational suggestion. He had half expected Ronny to suggest they all storm the gates and escape together or something else just as unrealistic.

Taffy chortled. "When was the last time any of us had a good time? That Christmas carol fest Bonny put together? Nothing but work since...too many deaths...people are hot and cranky. I think celebrating that we're still alive is in order..."

"But why...?"

Ronny slugged the older man's shoulder playfully. "Do we need a reason? Midsummer? Celebrating everyone's birthdays at once? A welcome for the new chaps...or hell, like Taffy said, a 'Thank God We're Still Breathing' party. Doesn't really matter. I doubt anyone will care about the reason as long as it's a party..."

"Get all the musicians in the ranks...damn fine voices..."

"Oh shit," Ronny snorted with a laugh, "not Vic and those silly bagpipes."

Taffy ignored him. "We've got a dozen or so records...if we can rig a chord we can set the player near an open window...get men to decorate...pool camp rations to make something festive..."

"Maybe even get the Krauts to give us a little extra...maybe alcohol even..."

George shook his head, "They would never allow..."

"Maybe not," Ronny concurred, "but they might allow us a little extra rations in exchange for good behavior and some extra work hours…and the higher we aim, the more likely they'll be to fall somewhere in the middle."

"It's worth a try. Maybe we could get them to extend lights out for a day…or dismiss the workers from duty early."

Considering the notion, George looked across the parade yard at the clusters and faces of men he could see. Ronny's idea had merit, and with a little creativity, they could fashion some sort of party out of whatever leeway the Germans allowed. His gaze lingered on Dusty and Skip who looked to be playing dice near the corner of one of the barracks. Jamie, Ray, and KC were just passing them. Some sort of look was exchanged between Jamie and Skip but George was too far away to read it and guess what it meant. At least this time there was no violence.

"I'll talk to Moretti. Worst they can do is say no…leave us the supplies and hours we have…and if that's the case, we make due and make our own party on our own time. Let's keep this to ourselves until we hear what the Krauts have to say.

"Of course," said Taffy as he lit a cigarette. "If we get their hopes up for nothing we'll have a riot on our hands…"

"It'll be worse than it is," Ronny agreed. "Wouldn't want that."

Taffy inclined his head towards the barracks. "Cards?"

With a shrug and a quick look around to see if Moretti was anywhere near, George replied, "Why not?"

"We should invite Vic in," Ronny suggested. "I wager he'll get over this other business after he wins a few hands."

Shifting the bits of wood within his closed fist, George chuckled. "I wager you are right.

❧*❧

The fading sun illuminated the music room with beams of amber and pink as Hans watched it slowly sink beyond the horizon, pulling darkness down over Ste Marie again. When he returned to the house, all had been quiet, a blessing for which he felt great relief. He had not wanted a confrontation until he had a chance to sort out what he wanted to say, and just as importantly he wanted to sort out his feelings for Clara.

He knew his wife and daughter were asleep upstairs, as those had been the first places he had gone upon returning to what sounded like an empty house. Instead of reading, his daughter had been curled up asleep. As he gazed at the sleeping child, her hair cascading across her pillow, he marveled again at how much she looked like her mother. Perhaps all of the time spent enduring his wife's drinking and hatred had been worth it to create and protect this beautiful creature from the evils of the world.

He kissed her forehead and left the room; the girl's only response was to move slightly towards him in her slumber. Then she was still again.

Hans stopped in the hall to listen at the door of the room he shared with his wife, and then decided he did not want to wake her for conversation. Now, though he had paced his wife's music room for a while, he stopped to watch the fiery sunset while pondering the course his life had taken.

Darkness won its daily battle as he drained the last dregs of whiskey from the glass in his hand. He looked at his uniform jacket that lay across the piano bench and wondered if he should move it. Since his return from the Eastern front, Jennifer had cringed violently away any time he wore it. He did not understand why; it was nothing more than fabric and silver buttons, nothing to fear, and he did not think he had ever given her cause to be afraid of him. If he could understand her fear, he felt he might be able to work through their problems and recover some of the love, the caring, the passion they had once shared.

He snorted wryly, sat long enough to remove his leather boots and then carried both them and his coat out of the music room. The coat was hung in its usual place in the study, his boots placed at the foot of the stairs where he would find them again in the morning, polished by the housekeeper, and started upstairs. It had been too much to expect his wife to come down to greet him, to share a dinner he was not even hungry for. Now it was time for bed.

In their room, Jennifer was lying on her back, arms outstretched above her head, her hair tangled and fanned beneath her head, and she was obviously nude beneath the single sheet. For all the world, she looked to Hans as if she were some classical sculpture draped with a dust sheet, waiting to be admired by her owner. He wanted her so much, wanted to admire, to love, to adore her as he once had if only she would let him. He entered the dark room, the light spilling in from the corridor, and stared as he began loosening his shirt.

Then he saw it. A hollow in the pillow on his side of the bed.

He did not need to ask. Jennifer had betrayed him again. His hand tightened around the metal clasp of his belt so that it cut into his palm. Anger and resentment fought for control. It was bad enough that she was unfaithful on a regular basis, but to be confronted with the proof in their bed was enough to break his heart.

"Why?" he shouted, lunging at the bed to shake her shoulders. "Why in our bed? Who was it this time? The Australian? The Canadian? Tell me who!"

Jennifer, dazed and half asleep, was not sure what was happening. When she had fallen asleep, she had been in Ray's arms and now she was awakened by her husband's rage. She worried that he had found Ray with her, but she saw that it was quite dark and she was alone...but perhaps Ray had already been dragged out of the house.

"No one!" she gasped sleepily. "Mila had a bad asthma attack...I fell asleep listening for her...no one has been here..."

"Do you think I'm an idiot? The bed is rumpled...damp..."

Struggling for words that might reassure him, she countered, "It is hot! You know I don't sleep well." It was an easy lie as she pulled from his grasp and escaped off the other side of the bed to don her silken robe.

Her excuse was plausible, enough so that Hans held onto the tiny sliver of doubt about his own perceptions. He wanted to believe her, though his head, and deep within his heart and soul, knew she was lying. With the bed between them, he could not reach her, and so he collapsed onto the edge of the mattress with frustration and hurt. "How did we come to this Jen...?"

"You weren't there when I needed you..." She wiped away the tears the memories brought with them.

"I was in my office...I swear it. I would never lie about that...yet still you blame me..." He looked over his shoulder, seeking some sign in her face, some indication that she believed him.

"Blame you? I don't blame anyone but myself. I should not have gone to Ingrid's...but I had to convince her to leave before..."

"I told you I would see to her safety...would get her on the train...with the papers...but you wouldn't..."

"You sent your thugs to arrest her...sent her God knows where!" Jennifer sobbed.

Exasperated, Hans threw up his hands. "I didn't send anyone! I was not at the blockade; you know it! Eight months pregnant…running into oncoming traffic…"

"You DO blame me! If you'd been at the office when the hospital called, Feilin would be…"

"I WAS in my office! I was not with Dorene! I've told you…ask Oberstgruppenfuhrer Volheim…he'll tell you where I…"

Jennifer froze and stared, trying to find something in Hans' expression that held answers about the night their son had been born…and died.

"I did ask him."

Hans stared back. "When? When was this?" If she had asked the one man who could clear him of this blame, why did she continue to accuse him of wrongs he had never committed?

"When you were in Russia," she admitted with a shudder of disgust.

"Then you know he and I were looking over plans for an attack at that time. You have to believe me…"

"No, Hans," she shook her head, her expression grim. "He told me you had left for lunch with your secretary…the same as he told me that day…"

Hans gawked in disbelief. Volheim had lied? Why would the man do such a thing? Hans remembered that day well; he had gone to the office early, had been there the entire day without a single break except to use the toilet. Volheim had been with him during much of that time, except when he had gone out to make or take phone calls. Hans had not gotten a call from the hospital until too late, and by the time he reached the hospital, Jennifer had already been taken into surgery, with the doctors having to make the agonizing decision on whether mother, child, or both would die. She was hemorrhaging and needed surgery to stem the flow of blood. The baby had already been removed, but due to difficulty breathing, he had died after a few short minutes. One of the nurses had suggested that perhaps if Hans had arrived sooner, the child might have survived, and if his wife did not it might well be because they postponed the surgery too long while trying to contact him. His blood, and a timelier surgery, might have saved them both.

Since that day, Hans blamed Feilin's death, and Jennifer's inability to conceive again, on himself, although he still questioned why she had been careless enough to run into oncoming traffic, putting them both at risk.

But none of that explained why Volheim might have lied to him, or to Jennifer.

"It was a choice...you or the child..." he said weakly, unable to convince her that he was guiltless of any affair with his secretary.

"You should have let me die," she snipped with a cold edge to her voice. "None of this would...and you could have your pregnant French whore..."

Bristling, Hans lurched to his feet and rounded the bed so that he could grasp Jennifer's shoulders and make her look at him. "I have never been unfaithful to you, so I assure you, everything you say about me is wrong. Miss Beton is not pregnant..."

"I assure you she is. I'm not blind to the way you look at her...and I know she visits your office..."

His disbelief was slowly morphing back into rage. "That's rich coming from someone who will fuck anyone who...all they have to do is look at you. Waters...Michaels...Fitzgerald...Henderson. Who else? Campbell? Hirsch? Stetcher? Tell me!"

"I would never..."

"Why them and not me?"

"You don't love me anymore! You get as much satisfaction with your hand as..."

A slap across her face caused her to lose her balance and land on the bed.

"You want to be fucked?" He fell on top of her and groped between her legs, fury at too many betrayals driving away rational thought. Jennifer clawed at his arms to push him away as he opened his trousers. He was planning to take her whether she wanted it or not, in a way he never had before, making her realize she may have pushed him too far.

"No...Hans...not like...don't...not like him..." She begged, sobbing hysterically as memories swarmed over her like a flight of angry bees. "Mila's..."

As suddenly as the attack had begun, it was aborted. Hans yanked to his feet, stomped to the dresser, and leaned against it with his arms outstretched and his head hanging between them. The reminder that their daughter might hear them was sobering, but it was something else Jennifer had said that forced the reassessment of his actions.

"He who?" he asked between panted breaths.

"Who what?" whimpered Jennifer, lying the way he had left her.

"Who raped you? When?"

Wanting only to forget those memories, having vowed never to speak of them to anyone, she shook her head, curled onto her side, and replied, "No one...I swear...I just wanted you to stop..."

He looked at her in the mirror, her expression too stricken to cry, and he knew she was lying again. Her lip bled from the slap he had given. He might have believed her, that she had said them only to make him stop, if not for the expression that belied her words. Was this why he hated her? Because something had happened when he was stationed in the east and she blamed him for it? Had it been another soldier or officer...was that why she hated the uniform? What had they both suffered during those months apart that they had never told one another?

"Tell me who it was."

"I can't." She whispered it with another shake of her head, no longer denying what had happened, only resisting talking about it. "It was my fault...I couldn't stop him...he threatened us...me and Mila...with detention...and you weren't there to stop it..."

"I left you in good hands...you should have been safe..." He had trusted every man he had set to watch over his family while he had been gone. If one of them had betrayed him, he wanted to know.

"You left us in a city of vipers...and I was bitten by the most poisonous of all...too many times...to protect Mila..."

Her life had been hell...and he had never known. He had fought for his country, served with distinction, and all of that time one of his trusted comrades had taken advantage of his wife. She had paid the price for his ignorance and apparent naiveté and had not been the same since.

Or perhaps she was lying again to save herself. He honestly could not tell any longer.

"It will never happen again. I promise. Tell me who...and I swear I will..."

"No...leave it. I don't want to...and he will hurt you. Forget this, Hans..." The angles of her body changed, beckoning him to her, a hint of the old heat in her eyes suggesting that revealing even this much of her secret might have been enough to free her to love him again. "Let us start over, Hans...and forget all of that."

He watched her for a few quiet moments and proceeded to undress with a flutter of hope in his belly. All too quickly, however, before he made it to the bed, she drifted back into a deep, alcohol-induced slumber. Her breathing became less labored as the stress of fighting left her, but she was restless there upon the bed, as if her demons plagued her still from the depths of her dreams.

In one respect, he believed she was right. They should start again. And he decided in that moment when that new start would begin.

He would give her a birthday party.

He shifted her to a more comfortable position and covered her with the blankets, deciding to sleep in his office. Several kisses were spread over her soft blonde hair before he stood to leave.

"We can try, Jenny," he promised. "We can try."

≈Suspicion's Gate≈

Chapter 14
July 14, 1943

"Ms. Porteur…?"

Zaline had come to the farmhouse early to share breakfast with her father and sister, knowing that Clara had gone out even earlier. She missed spending time with them, but since her marriage, times alone with father and sister were very rare. Usually, she had to make do with gatherings that included a great portion of Ste Marie's population.

But now breakfast was over, her father and sister hard at work, he to get his mind off of Clara's absence, and Zaline had remained to clear away the remnants of the meal. She had stepped onto the porch to watch her father struggle with a broken wagon wheel and was drying her hands upon her apron when Skip found the nerve to approach her. He never had before, they barely spoke, so she assumed this was a request for water unless the Germans had sent him to fetch something from her.

"I see that Herr Stetcher insists on assigning you to hard labor in spite of…" she started.

"I'm fine."

She looked him over skeptically then nodded. "You look better than yesterday."

He shuffled his feet and looked away from her, though he had yet to look her in the eye. "Yeah…thanks for that…"

"No need to thank me." He warily glanced over his shoulder at the field workers and she presumed he was concerned about a reprimand for speaking to her. "How can I help you, Captain?"

"Dusty and I…" He paused, the asking of this favor more difficult than he imagined. "We need your help."

"Help?"

Voice low, barely heard, he muttered, "Maps, supplies, papers." He had never concerned himself with such things during previous escape attempts. He did not know if Buckman had arranged for them during their last effort or not, though he guessed he had.

"I was wondering when…"

"Just me and Dusty. No one else…"

"Captain…"

"Yes or no. Can you get us what we need…?"

"When do you…?"

"Soon as we can…soon as things are arranged."

"It would take at least a week…"

"We may not have a week."

Zaline crossed her arms and gauged the distance to the nearest German guard. He could not hear them from where he stood, not with Stasio pounding the rim of the wheel into place with loud thwacks of the mallet.

"Look," Skip growled at the negativity he perceived in her words. "Are you going to help or not…?"

"I need more information, Captain…I can't just…"

"I'll take that as a no." He snarled, having met the resistance he expected from people he never fully trusted, and strode away, his steps still marred by the pain in his back.

"Captain."

But Skip was not listening. Zaline wondered, as she went back through the house and out the front door towards her home and her daughter, if the Australian had actually wanted her help or had only meant to inform the cell of his impending plans. He certainly had not given her the opportunity to be of assistance. This was a matter to present to Philippe. He would know how best to proceed.

On edge, wary and nervous, Clara turned the wagon away from the river and headed in the direction of the farmhouse. Communication with London had gone as scheduled, with no news on Paddy or Newt forthcoming. There were the usual instructions for supply drop-offs and the relay of details for the next refugee transports, but none of the good news she had hoped for. She had wanted good news to give to Sparks, in addition to the parts obtained for his radio, but it seemed that would not happen today.

Transmission complete, she had disassembled her radio and hidden the parts carefully amongst the wagon's contents. She had seen no one all morning, no merchants or travelers, not since leaving the farm well before sun up. Relieved that the most difficult part of her day was over, she looked forward to getting home…and dreaded the conversation with Stasio that had not come to pass the night before as she had intended. There had been opportunity enough, but she had lacked the courage. Never before had she been afraid to tell him anything. But this was different. After all, he was already a grandfather; would he welcome the chance to be a parent again. Would he think she was trying to trap him into a more permanent relationship than he seemed to want? Would he believe it was his, or would he accuse her of infidelity with Hans and send her away? Not knowing, or at least being uncertain of the reception the news would receive, had kept her silent until both fell asleep.

But it had to be done. Soon, before Isabelle or someone else told him. Before it became physically obvious and unable to be hidden.

After her unusual silence last night, he already knew something was on her mind.

The wagon bounced across the rutted, bumpy meadow, the shortest route home, and back onto the main road, her thoughts on the subject of children and duty. She was so preoccupied that, by the time she noticed she was no longer alone on the road, she could not guess how long the other vehicle might have been there far behind.

It was a small vehicle, but as it crested the hillock behind her, its form silhouetted by the mid-morning sun, it was a shape she recognized, one that made her grow cold.

That truck had swept through Ste Marie more than once in her time here. Every month or so it came, a persistent hunter determined to corner its prey. Looking, listening, seeking the rebel radio that had not yet been found.

If the vehicle caught up to her, passed her, or turned away onto one of the various side roads, she would feel calmer. But the predator moved slowly enough that she knew it was conducting a signal sweep, intentionally keeping its distance from her. Maybe they had detected her signals earlier and already suspected her. Maybe they were paying her no heed out of the assumption of her innocence. The driver stopped the truck more than once, for no discernible reason she could tell, and then resumed its forward motion, always remaining far enough back that she could just make out its ominous silhouette without hearing the rumble of its motor.

That the Germans might purposely tail her to learn where she went did not escape her. Unable to reveal her destination, out of deference to Stasio, to the working men, and even to Hans, she traveled past the farmhouse road and turned instead into the center of the village, where she stopped outside of the inn. Perhaps, she mused, she had lost the truck by coming into the village, but she could not take that chance. Philippe was out on daily town business, but with Isabelle's help, she left a crate containing cheese, milk, and fish, and some bits of the dismantled radio as though she were making a scheduled delivery to guests lodging there. In return, she loaded several baskets of baked goods into the wagon. After a cordial exchange, a slightly stilted but hopefully not exaggerated one in case she was being watched, she walked briskly next door, to the seamstress' shop and, along with a bouquet of wildflowers and box of sewing supplies and a few bolts of cloth, left a smaller portion of the radio there as well. Zaline, on her way back to the farmhouse now to aid in serving lunch to the horde of prisoners, offered to travel with Clara, hoping the ruse would pay off in distracting the persistent Germans, if that truck was still in the area.

It left only the largest part of the radio to be hidden, but Clara would not leave that with anyone else. The other parts could be used for anything, repair of machinery, sewing, cooking…whatever an enterprising individual might fabricate during a wartime shortage of goods. The main body of the radio, however, had but a single use and Clara would endanger no one else with it. If it was found, it was her burden to accept full responsibility for its existence and use.

No one else would ever be accused or punished for her actions.

The wagon was driven back through the bustling village streets with no evidence of the truck to be seen. Zaline sighed with relief, but it was relief Clara did not yet share. If nothing else, the Germans were persistent. They would either search until they found what they were looking for, or until they decided it was not going to be found today and they opted to move on to the next village or town.

Once more aiming for the road that would take her to Stasio, Clara held her breath and watched the road before and behind for danger more closely than before. They had just made the turn onto the farmhouse road when the German truck came into view from the east. She guessed they had stopped to recalibrate their equipment, hoping to pick up either the receiving or transmitting signal that might have precipitated the day's search. There would be no signal here unless someone else in Ste Marie, unbeknownst to her, also possessed a transmitter. But the men in the truck were determined to follow her now, supporting the idea that they had detected her pre-dawn radio usage. For the second time that day, Clara felt sick. If she was lucky, this was a routine sweep and they had no specific suspicions in mind, only the desire to find someone to pin blame on for wrongs committed or suspected. Not that it mattered. If they found what she carried, there was going to be trouble.

Focus. Don't look back.

They had already seen her turn towards the farmhouse. There were no side roads, nowhere else to go along this path unless she drove across the more recently cut paths worn by the Germans to and from the Stalag. She could not turn around without appearing suspect, and a turn towards the Stalag was not likely to buy her much time. If they were determined to follow her they would likely do so until they caught up with her. Hans would not be able to protect her. There was nowhere else to run. At least she could pray for the time to hide the radio if she reached the barn far enough ahead of the truck's arrival.

"Merde," she swore under her breath. Her options had dwindled to a meager few, and some were not options at all.

"What do we do?" Zaline squeaked anxiously.

"Pray."

She scanned the area, hoping for an idea as the wagon came to a halt outside of the barn. Sparks sat at the grinding wheel. Stasio and Skip were heading into the barn with fresh hay for the cows.

"Hey," she called to Stasio with a wave, a specific gesture he recognized from many discussions shared in preparation for just such a day. He glanced towards the main road and the truck in the distance.

"Captain…a hand with the wagon." The bales were dropped and Stasio grabbed the nearest horse's head when Clara's wagon was within reach. "Lieutenant…"

The soldier standing guard outside the barn scowled but did not interfere; he had not yet seen the approaching vehicle and had no reason to think this was anything other than routine farm business.

Clara struggled to pull the radio from beneath the seat as she climbed from the wagon. Stasio was unloading the crates of goods from the back, crates he had brought home yesterday but had left in the wagon to offer cover for Clara's early morning outing. Sparks, noting the looming shadow on the road, offered his empty hand to help her down. In the commotion of her intentionally awkward dismount, the radio was slipped into the bundle Sparks carried beneath his other arm. Then he too sauntered off to the barn as Clara picked up a coil of new rope from the floorboards and followed.

Skip, meanwhile, uncoupled the horses from the wagon as Stasio indicated, when he too noticed the small truck now ambling down the dusty packed dirt road towards them.

"Shit," he growled with a glance into the barn. He understood the sudden tension the wagon's arrival had brought with it. It was easy to imagine what was going on in that barn and what would happen if Clara and Sparks were discovered. He did not personally trust the woman, but she had supplied them with radio intelligence and parts for their own wireless, and had, so far, not betrayed them as far as anyone knew. Those were necessary things, and Skip did not want to witness, or suffer, the consequences, should the Germans find any radio here.

Some sort of distraction to draw the Germans' attention long enough for the radio to be hidden was in order. Seeing Jamie approaching with tools to be sharpened, the Aussie latched on to the first plan that came to mind and hoped Jamie was intuitive enough to quickly catch on to his intentions. In a single effort, the movement painful due to the still healing stripes across his back and shoulders, Skip swung onto the back of the nearest draft horse, scooped Zaline up onto the animal's back with him, and called, "Come and get her if you want her, Canadian wanker!"

Zaline uttered an unexpected squawk, not realizing immediately what was happening or why. Jamie turned, caught the glint of sunlight off the windshield of the approaching vehicle, and dropped the tools where he stood. He grabbed the bridle of the other horse, barely freed from the wagon, and jumped up on its back to dash after the Aussie. The German soldier stationed there tried to grab the animal to end the pursuit before it began, but his hand only brushed across the animal's body and he stumbled into the muck as Jamie and the horse lurched away.

With the truck now obvious to everyone, and the men in the fallow quarter of the field aware of the disturbance, they began to cheer the impromptu race, adding to the distraction the mounted men had initiated. They did not know what the truck's presence meant, but the Nazi emblem on the side and the radio antenna mounted on it made its mission a fairly obvious one. Some of the Germans scattered across the field ran to catch the horses, some ran towards the barn, and a few others cheered with their prisoners and exchanged bets as to the outcome of the race. The horses had now headed away from the arriving truck and were charging along the western perimeter of the farm.

Stasio emerged from the barn in response to the commotion. "Mon Dieu!" he swore, torn between worry for his horses, the men and his daughter upon them, those within the barn and the two men emerging from the now stopped radio truck. The newcomers' attention was also on the horses, and Stasio breathed with nervous appreciation for what the two captains were doing on Clara's behalf, even if the gesture did seem foolhardy.

One of the two unfamiliar men raised a rifle, aiming at the fleeing horses, his assumption being that an escape was in process. "Don't you dare shoot my horses or my daughter…" Stasio bellowed in stilted, broken German. They might be radio techs, but he could not assume that they spoke French, or English, just as he made no assumptions that they would heed his plea and spare his daughter and his horses.

There was a loud crack.

Jamie winced at the sound, his body dropping nearer the frightened horse's back, the animal now galloping faster to escape the startling sound. A quick glance towards Skip showed that the shot had missed them both, though he could not be certain they were the targets. With the lighter, smaller horse, Jamie was closing the gap between him and Skip and as they whipped around the southeast corner and continued along the southern edge of the field, he wondered what he would do when he caught up to the other man.

The soldiers pursuing them had given up trying to run down the horses and were now demanding that the two men return at once. They had begun corralling the prisoners into a group on the north side of the fields near the house and the barn, perhaps trying to form a blockade or prevent others from getting any similarly foolish notions of escape. Skip was aware that Jamie was catching up to him, but he was less concerned with winning than he was with giving Clara time to complete her task and come safely out of the barn.

"Think she's good enough for you?" he taunted Jamie.

"Bastard," Jamie shouted.

Skip laughed, a forced sound that carried less mirth then he hoped for. As far as he was from the Germans or any other farm hands, he did not think they would hear anything other than a laugh.

Inside the barn, Clara scrambled into the loft and found the hidden hatch in the wall she and Stasio had built just after her arrival. Sparks charged up after her, radio in hand, and thrust the unit it into the empty, well-insulated space. When it was closed, hidden behind old, moldering hay with nothing appearing obviously amiss, the hay was spread about to cover their being there and they started down again. At the sound of the gunshot, however, coming as it had at the tail end of Stasio's demand, Clara jumped from the loft ladder, fearing she would find the worst at the other end of that sound. Sparks was right behind her, snatching up a partially full pail of milk as he followed.

Jamie's horse had come alongside Skip's. He did not reach for Zaline; the risk of her falling if he tried to grab her, of being trampled beneath the draft animals' hooves, was too great. And they were coming to the end of their circuit, with several of the Germans scowling in front of them with raised guns. Jamie pulled his horse up short, causing the animal to shriek in frustration. Skip, aware that Jamie had slowed, glanced ahead to see why. He had been so focused on Jamie's approach that he had not realized how close they were to the carefully aimed guns. He stopped laughing and tugged on the reins. By the time his horse skittered into that forced stopped, Jamie had dismounted and a German guard with pistol drawn grabbed the bridle of his horse. Another pulled Zaline roughly out of Skip's hold, dragging her roughly off of the horse. It pulled Skip down as well; unprepared, he landed face first in the dust and caught the butt of the rifle into his side as he tried to roll to his feet. He expected more blows but a honking car horn stopped the soldiers before they could beat him further.

"What is going on?" Moretti shouted, climbing out of the Jeep, mentally cursing for having left the fields and not returning sooner.

One of the two men from the truck saluted him with a sneer. "Heil Hitler," he replied, recognizing Moretti as a higher ranking officer…but a non-German nonetheless.

To the man's words, Moretti muttered under his breath. "Hitler my ass." In a louder voice, now near enough to be heard in normal conversation as he assessed the dwindling commotion he could see, he barked, "Well? Answer me?"

"A bit of fun," Jamie said. The German guard who had taken over his horse was now near enough to the gathered group for Stasio to grab the reins with enough visible annoyance to be convincing. Jamie spoke before any of the Germans could reply, and oddly they seemed content to let the prisoner speak and dig his own grave. Stasio took hold of both horses now and began to draw them away towards the barn.

"Stay, Monsieur Arnaud," Moretti grunted. "No one moves until I have the truth."

Stasio stopped. Clara moved to his side as if she could protect him.

"Like Campbell said," Skip groaned, nursing his aching side as he pushed to his feet. "I was asked to unhook the horses…haven't ridden since I was home…thought a race sounded fun. Wasn't hurtin' anyone."

"Not like they were going anywhere," grunted Sparks.

Jamie nodded, his tone when speaking sounding meeker than either Skip or Sparks'. "We were not intending to steal Monsieur's horses…or his daughter…"

"We're not that fucking stupid," Skip snorted.

The language drew a sharp cuff of a pistol butt across the side of his head.

Moretti studied the two men and then the flushed face of the woman Zaline who appeared no worse for the adventure. There was no evidence that anyone had been hurt, other than Henderson's wincing. If the two men had intended escape, they would not have ridden back to the barn where the soldiers waited. Maybe Henderson had finally learned not to attempt escape at every foolish opportunity. Other than several minutes of lost work, it appeared no harm had been caused by this diversion and he could certainly understand a man's desire for a break from routine, even if Hirsch and Stetcher might not.

The two strangers standing beside the unfamiliar truck looked to be as equally unforgiving as Stetcher.

"Henderson… Campbell, return to camp…now. Perhaps you meant no harm, intended no escape, but such disruptive disobedience must be punished. A week's latrine duty for both of you." Both grimaced at the thought of such an ugly job in the heat of summer, but it was better that than the punishment Stetcher would have meted out if he had been here. "Sturmann Gerde, use my car and take them back. The rest of you, get back to work…and because you have been lax in your duties, there will be no lunch today."

Men groaned and grumbled, but as punishments went, it was, at least, bearable.

Moretti waited as the guards shooed the men back to their work and Gerde took Jamie and Skip to the car. He had not yet dismissed Stasio or Clara, but he had a feeling these visiting Germans and their radio truck had not come here by chance. Whatever their intentions, it likely involved the farm owner and the woman at his side.

"As for you, gentlemen, who are you and what is your business here?"

Skip glanced over his shoulder at Clara and Stasio, and at Sparks who had moved back to the grinding wheel not far away and was staring at Clara with barely hidden concern. To Jamie, he said, "This is gonna be the talk of the camp tonight."

One of the two strangers, the man who had taken the shot at the racing animals, drew back his shoulders and answered, "We have reason to believe there is a radio transmitter on these premises."

"Here?" Moretti laughed heartily. "Sir, prisoners from Stalag 31 work this farm six days a week and our staff oversees them. They are on the perimeter of the Stalag." He pointed towards the tall walls of barbed wire in the distance. "With the Reich's presence, there is no way a radio could operate from here without us knowing. And that one," he pointed to Clara, "you will have to take up with Oberfuhrer von Hausen. He will not be pleased with such idle accusations against her without proof…"

The two men looked at one another, not sure what the Italian was inferring, but the spokesman replied, "Then he may have to be displeased. We have our orders; these premises are to be searched, top to bottom, inside and out…"

"No one goes into my house," Stasio started, releasing the horses and stepping towards the intruders. Sparks grabbed the animals' reins.

"You have no choice…"

"Like hell I don't!"

Clara knew Stasio was trying to draw attention to the house and away from the barn by leading the Germans to believe there was something in the house to hide. His vehemence and menacing tone, however, caused the lead German to strike him hard enough to knock him to the ground and draw blood from his mouth and nose. The other aimed his rifle at the fallen man, his expression one of nervous fear as if he had never shot a man before and yet was eager for the opportunity. Clara gave only a fleeting thought to that gun as she charged, knocking the barrel aside so that, when the trigger was pulled, it fired harmlessly into the ground. His companion lifted his arm to strike her, but Moretti caught the man's closed fist as Clara dropped to her knees beside the farmer and wiped the blood from his lip with the muslin cloth of her floral dress.

It took every ounce of willpower for Sparks not to erupt to his feet and charge into the fray to protect her…protect them both.

"I wouldn't if I were you," the Italian growled. "You may have your orders, but Oberfuhrer von Hausen is the authority here, and no one harms Mademoiselle Beton without answering to him. Your authority stretches only to your search for a transmitter that I guarantee is not here. But if you must confirm that yourselves, please do. Obersturmfuhrer Wagner?" Moretti gestured to the young man who had been left at the barn post when Gerde was sent to camp with the car and the misbehaving captains. "Accompany these men and make a full accounting of everything they destroy or damage. I will stay with these two to prevent them from interfering in the search."

"Yes, sir," replied Wagner with a salute.

After the two grouchy Germans marched into the house with Wagner and were no longer within hearing distance, Moretti offered Stasio his hand. The Frenchman glared at him with venom, angry that the Italian had allowed those men to defile his home with their intrusion. Moretti sighed and lowered his hand.

"I will see that the Oberfuhrer gets full notice of anything they damage," he promised.

"Including my dignity and the sanctity of my home and this?" He pointed to his bleeding face.

Moretti cleared his throat. "I apologize, Monsieur, but there are no options. To deny them would reflect badly not only on the Oberfuhrer, but also on you, and they would likely destroy everything out of spiteful punishment. We can't afford for the crops and animals to go to waste. Their authority is different. They will satisfy themselves that there is no transmitter and they will leave you be. It must be this way."

Clara cradled Stasio's head against her bosom, stroking his hair, kissing his forehead, soothing both herself and him. He glanced into her eyes but saw no trace of the fear that was fueling her anxious touch. She hid her feelings well. With one hand, he touched hers and she managed to smile.

"It'll be alright," she whispered, not caring if Moretti heard. He would interpret her words as he wished. "Everything will be alright."

Stasio clung to that belief, though he knew well enough that it was not the whole truth. If the Germans suspected her now, or suspected him, they would be watched more carefully. And after her assault on one soldier to knock the gun away, her reputation in the eyes of the Germans might suffer. He doubted that even Oberfuhrer von Hausen's authority would keep her safe much longer.

No. Nothing would ever be alright again.

≈*≈

Skip was the first one out of the Jeep when it rolled to a stop within the camp perimeter. "Halt," yelled the soldier Gerde who had brought them back. Though Skip's first impulse was to ignore the command, common sense prevailed and he reluctantly obeyed, waiting where he stood until Jamie was beside him. The soldier left the car idling while the camp gates were closed behind them. Beyond that, on the stoop of the GSH, Bonny, Ray, and Farmer looked up from their conversation to watch.

No doubt the men in Stalag 31 had heard the cheering and the commotion from the fields, though he did not know if they had witnessed any of it. Either way, he knew those three, and every other set of eyes in the Camp who followed them, wondered what had happened and what the results would be.

Nearer the fence, a group of men began to cheer when they were escorted into Camp 1. It brought a ghost of a smile to Skip's face, the first one anyone had seen there in many days. Jamie presumed Skip was basking in what little adulation the men who had recently scorned him were now offering. Feeling no need to revel in it or call Skip out, Jamie kept walking. It had been duty, nothing more. Jamie certainly had not done it for praise.

"Campbell."

Jamie stopped and looked back. Some of the bruises on the Aussie's face were fading, but he still looked like hell. This was the first time Skip had addressed him since their fight after Buckman's death.

Without any other display or expression, Skip nodded his head and said, "Thanks," before trudging past without another word.

Though Jamie was not certain what Skip was thanking him for, he understood that such thanks from Tom Henderson meant a lot.

Rather than follow Skip into the barracks, which would have been awkward for both of them, Jamie turned towards the GSH, whistling softly as he went.

Chapter 15
July 14, 1943

"**D**on't go."

Stasio did not turn from the window to look at Clara as she set the phone receiver back into its cradle. His lip was split and swollen, his jaw and cheek darkening from the blow he had received, but those were small discomforts in comparison to what he feared Clara faced now.

He was thankful Marcella possessed the wisdom to stay across the field in her own house and that the Germans had not thought to search her home as well. It had kept his youngest child out of harm's way. Once Zaline had been off the horse and dismissed, she had the good sense to go about her business, giving the German bloodhounds no reason to follow her or suspect her involvement in anything covert. Neither of his daughters had been here as the soldiers had pilfered his home, only he and Clara and the prisoners working the farm outside. If he had been forced to protect all three women at once, he was not certain what he would have done.

As Moretti predicted, the German patrollers found no radio, nor any trace of the components to make one. They had left the farmhouse half an hour before, after spending nearly two hours scouring each room and surrounding buildings. Although they apologized to the Italian for the intrusion, they ignored Stasio and Clara except to glare at them with suspicion. It confirmed his fears that they would be watched more closely now, if not by von Hausen and his men, then by other agents passing through Ste Marie. He had expressed his concern but Clara continued to cling to her belief that the matter was now behind them until the phone had rung...

...and von Hausen summoned her to his Stalag office.

Stasio did not know what the man had said. He only surmised from Clara's responses that the Oberfuhrer's words had been curt and commanding.

"I must." She stood behind him and put her hand upon his arm.

Though it was a reluctant gesture, he shrugged free and inched away from her. "If you go, you will not come back."

Clara looked at the phone, hurt by his actions though she understood them. She was not used to him withdrawing from her. "I will come back…I prom…"

"Don't. Do not promise something you have no control over."

"It's only Hans…"

"Yes…Hans…the Commandant. Don't you think he has been told what happened? Don't you think there will be penalties for…"

"If there's a penalty for saving your life, I'll gladly pay it," she whispered, taking her handbag from the hook upon which it hung. Surely he knew how much he meant to her.

Her words brought tears and he could not speak past the knot in his throat. All he could do was close his eyes and shut out the strongest effects of the wave of emotion when it hit. If not for him, she would have gone to her brother in Paris, as she had intended, and would be far away from von Hausen and his disastrous marriage.

The blare of the car horn pierced his thoughts. The Oberfuhrer must have sent the car before picking up the phone to summon her. The click of the door latch sounded loud and foreboding, but he did not turn, even though he was aware that Clara had not yet gone out.

"He wants to make new arrangements for Mila, that is all." At least, that was what he had said to her over the phone. It could be more than that. They both knew it. Her denial did not make the danger any less real. She paused. Stasio could almost hear her anxious breath but he could not look at her. "I will be home soon."

The tone of her voice, however, betrayed her assurances.

The door closed.

Stasio opened his eyes, at last, to watch her cross the porch, go down the steps, and approach the car where von Hausen's driver held the door open for her. When she reached it, she looked back. He raised his hand to the glass as if to touch her, and though she made no gesture in return, he knew she had seen and understood.

Just as he understood the things she had not said.

The car passed through the main gate without incident or fanfare. Why should it not? It was the Commandant's car, and this was not the first time he had sent it to bring Clara to him. Neither the driver nor the guards at the gate seemed to think this summons was different from any other, behaved no differently towards her than they ever had. But they likely knew little about the morning's incident at the farmhouse, or at least knew nothing but gossip based on unreliable accountings from distant witnesses. None of these men had been present, and whatever Hans had been told, he had little reason to discuss the events with anyone else.

And given how little he trusted the men who worked for, or with, him, he would be disinclined to say anything more to them than necessary to have his orders carried out. Especially if he meant for their ignorance to appear as reassurances for her.

But she did not regret what she had done. Not the months of radio dialog conducted with London, not the work done with the Resistance, not saving Stasio's life.

If she regretted anything, it was that she had not yet told Stasio about the baby. Now she might not have the chance, which might be for the best if she was coming to the commandant's office to die.

The car stopped in front of the administrative center of Stalag 31. As usual, the driver came around, assisted her from the car, and escorted her as far as the building's front door. He opened it and then closed it again once she was inside. For a few anxious moments, she did not move. Thus far, she had maintained the façade of business as usual. That was more difficult to do here, knowing that Stetcher was likely nearby, lurking around a corner, waiting. Whatever the official report may have been about the charges of harboring a radio, the Gestapo officer would continue to suspect her.

In this particular instance, his suspicions would be accurate.

A few more steps and she reached the Commandant's door. Swallowing her fear, wanting to appear as casual as she could, given the circumstances, she knocked on the door and was mildly startled when Doctor Dengler opened it.

"Mademoiselle Beton," he said politely with a bow of his head and a gesture meant to invite her into the room.

"Clara...please come in." Hans extended a hand to her from behind his desk. His smile was warm and sincere, the sort she had grown to expect of him. But behind it flickered aggravation, frustration, and a look of betrayal and defeat. She began to speak but was saved the embarrassment of a quavering voice as he added, "Thank you, doctor."

They were words of dismissal, not angry in any way. Clara cast a wary glance from Hans to the doctor and back while appearing to be preoccupied with removing her hat and settling into the chair she often sat in when here. Dengler saluted and left the room, closing the door behind him.

Feeling no need to avoid what was now inevitable, Clara started, "Hans…"

"I'm glad you came. I was not sure you would. Today has been hell. I needed to see you. Do you want a drink?"

"No."

"Do you mind if I…?"

"Certainly not, but should you…?"

Hans growled. "I don't care what Anton thinks. Not today anyways. And he's not here. He gets called away far too frequently for my liking. I don't trust him."

Nor should you, Clara wanted to say, but instead kept her opinion to herself. Without rising, Hans took the carafe from the table and poured a drink.

"Stasio made it safely home yesterday?"

It was not a question, despite the undertones. "Hans, before you ask about what happened…"

"Ask about…oh, you mean the fiasco with the radio hounds? Don't fret about that. It has already been taken care of."

"Taken care of?" Clara felt as if her stomach had risen into her chest, forcing her heart into her throat in a way that caused her windpipe to wrap around her esophagus and cut off the flow of air.

"I told the bastards, the next time they feel compelled to harass you and violate your privacy, they are to come to me first. It is utterly ridiculous to suspect you, of all people…"

"Stasio…"

"I apologize for his treatment as well; it was uncalled for. I have read Sturmbannfuhrer Moretti's report; Stasio was acting completely within his rights as far as I'm concerned, protecting you and your home. Does he require medical attention? I will send Dengler, and personally reimburse…"

"He does not want your money."

"Would you accept…?"

"You know better than to…"

Hans sighed with a defeated shrug. "I'm sorry…I had to try. I feel the need to make recompense, even though I had nothing to do with what happened…"

"This is your need, not mine. Not Stasio's. You owe us nothing."

"Ah, there you are so wrong, geliebte." He drained his glass and filled it once more.

Letting out a long sigh of relief that, as she had believed, Hans had no intention of punishing either her or Stasio, she allowed herself to relax. "Thank you though." She paused, watching his trembling hand, and asked, "You have spoken to Jennifer?" His wife was usually the cause of such upset and discussing her offered a change of topic.

"I tried," he admitted. "Unsuccessfully. She was in a state when I got home. Mila took ill yesterday, and since Dengler was not there, Campbell tended her..." Remembering what he had seen upon entering the bedroom, his hand began to shake more, his grip on the glass so tight that his knuckles turned white. "She probably slept with him too..."

"Captain Campbell is not so foolish," she assured him, placing her hand on his wrist and coaxing him to put the glass down. Slowly he lowered his arm as her fingers caressed the back of his hand, but it was several more minutes before he was calm enough to speak.

"You're probably right...he seems to have a good head on his shoulders. It's just...she told me he was there...and the state of the bed led me to think..." He shook his head. "And then there were the nightmares..."

"She still has them?

"Always...since the baby...since my return from..."

He shuddered, and this time, when he lifted the glass to drink, Clara did not stop him. She did not know what had happened during his months fighting in the east, in the earliest days of the war—he had never told her and she had never asked—but whatever had occurred had left deep, lasting scars, scars which had not been helped by the state of his wife upon his return. He appeared tough and foreboding, but sometimes the chinks in his armor revealed his soul. At least they revealed it to her.

His wife's continuing infidelities certainly did not help him heal.

"Henderson said..." He poured a third drink and stared at the glass in his hand. "I know he was not the first. I have long known...and she rarely denies it outright. Leaving for the war was the hardest thing...she had to cope with Feilin's loss alone...but I provided for her as best I could, made sure she would be safe and taken care of. When I returned...the drinking, the manipulating...the avoidance…it was all new, and when the others looked at me, it was with disdain and pity…as if they knew…"

"Perhaps they felt for your loss…"

"Perhaps…or perhaps they knew what she was doing. Lord knows she's got Eugene, and Anton, sniffing around like tomcats."

His voice had grown angrier, more hurt as he talked, until the sound caught in his throat and stuck there. He set down the still full glass, rose from the chair, and stood at the window with his back to her. "And with all of this…her infidelities and indiscretions…she has the gall to accuse me of being unfaithful. To accuse me of fathering your child…"

Clara was grateful that his back was to her as she felt the color drain from her face. "Hans…"

"I told her it was ridiculous, that you are no more with child than she is…that it is just as impossible for you to be carrying my child as it is for her." He stopped upon hearing Clara's sharp intake of air. "Insensitive and uncalled for, I know…and I tried to apologize…but she refuses to accept the truth…continues to hold me responsible…so, of course, she believes she is childless because of you. She says she can see it in your face."

"She sees what she wants to see," Clara murmured, watching as he turned to stare at her. She stared back, struggling to keep her expression as calm and neutral as possible. Though her breathing quickened when he moved behind her, she refused to move. She swallowed hard as his fingers wound in her hair, though whether the reaction was out of fear or a flash of desire, she was not certain. Gently, his fingers fluttered down the side of her neck and then lingered upon her shoulder.

"You would tell me if you were?"

Pressing her cheek against his hand, she replied, "Would you really want to know? Would it make a difference?"

He was trembling, emotions dredged and brought to the surface by Clara's reaction to his touch. All of his anger, frustration, fear, longing…everything that was going through his mind was exposed. She did not need to see his face to know it; she could feel it in his touch. Briefly, he rested his other hand on her opposite shoulder and let it slide forwards to her throat, down over her collarbone.

"Hans…"

He paused, his libido warring with what his ears heard. She might be physically responsive, as he could feel her heart fluttering beneath his hand, but her tone said stop and he knew why.

In a husky voice, he said, "Jennifer once responded as you do...now she only pushes me away...with far less reason than you have." Though he sighed and resisted exploring further, his hands remained upon her. "She seems to have forgotten she is mine..."

"Perhaps if you approached her more as a woman and less like property...prove to her that you love her still, not just want to possess her..."

He froze. Clara could feel his tension through his hands and wondered for a moment if he would hurt her. "I can't," he rumbled. "She no longer believes anything I do or say." He abruptly released her and returned to his chair.

"I will bring Mila to you tomorrow morning," he said tersely, changing the subject again. "It may be late before I can come for her, however. I will be busy placating Anton as he will demand an accounting of today and will likely force me to reprimand Sturmbannfuhrer Moretti, though I see no need to do so."

"Captains Henderson and Campbell?"

"They've already been dealt with...though likely not to Stetcher's liking. Now I must go home...where I am unwelcome, but I need...won't you...can...?"

He uttered a sound that was halfway between a groan and a growl as he fought his own frustration. "Thank you for coming, Clara. It has done me good to see you. Please...relay my apologies to Stasio, and tell him if there is anything I can do..."

Clara sat still for a few more moments, knowing she had been dismissed by his efforts to avoid further temptation. But she did not want to go, did not want to leave him. There was some irrational fear that he would do something regrettable if she left him now.

But there was no other option short of giving in to temptation. That would only make things worse. She positioned her hat upon her head, stood, and made it as far as the door before glancing at him. He seemed to have immersed himself in writing some sort of document, but from the odd movement of his hand, Clara knew it was only meant to make her believe he was too busy to notice her departure.

This time she went out and did not look back.

৯৹*৹৯

George Campbell scanned the parade yard from the steps of the GSH, hoping to find Sturmbannfuhrer Moretti but willing to settle for Doctor Dengler if he had to.

As usual, Taffy had made his point. Because of Buck's death, the unknown fates of Newt and Paddy, and Skip's recent episodes of borderline insanity, the morale of Camp 1 was the lowest it had been in the more than eight months the elder Canadian had been here. He understood, from his talk with Sparks over dinner, that Skip's madness today had not been madness at all, but intended to protect the all-important Resistance radio and the people who housed it, but it was also another indicator of how uptight the men were. Any sort of revelry, while held captive by the enemy, was a temporary salve at best, but it would be better than doing nothing. If George could arrange it, and get approval from their captors, his own standing in the eyes of the men he guided might be strengthened. They needed leadership, and so far George did not feel successful in providing it.

Despite the insanity of that horse race, he had to admit he was proud of Skip, and his son, for taking the risk to protect the Resistance fighters, though he had not yet expressed that praise to either of them. He did not know how, particularly with Jamie.

As usual, his son was standing at the fence that separated Camps 1 and 2, trying to converse with the captive French on the other side. Honing his language skills, George presumed, another thing George was proud of. Jamie's gift for languages kept communication open with Camp 2 and between Jamie, Bonnie, and Sparks, the mastery of languages allowed the prisoners to know what the Germans were doing. Fewer surprises meant more relaxed men.

Along the back fence, Dusty and Skip were seated on the ground, smoking and avoiding the rest of the camp residents. It appeared the worst of the animosity towards Skip had boiled down to annoyance and evasion, that the worst of it had blown over with the advent of the day's race. Cool stares and a wide berth were better than the confrontations of days before. For a man who had once been near the center of attention, however, admired, respected and liked by most, Skip was undoubtedly finding the role of outcast a distasteful one. It seemed he daily withdrew further from the company of everyone but Dusty.

George hoped that, in time, Skip would be brought back into the camaraderie. The men needed his experience, intelligence, and drive to survive this place. He also hoped the man had learned his lesson and would refrain from further dalliances with the Commandant's wife and stay out of von Hausen's path.

Outside of Camp 1, in the German section of the compound, George finally saw Dengler, Moretti, and von Hausen leaving the infirmary so he sauntered in their direction. The three stopped to share words, but by the time George was near enough to the fence to get their attention, the Commandant was already gone. That was preferable, as pitching the idea of a camp celebration to Moretti would be infinitely easier than selling it to von Hausen.

"Sturmbannfuhrer," he called. "A word please."

Parting words were spoken between the doctor and Italian before Moretti came to the fence. "What can I do for you, Campbell?" The men did not often speak directly to their captors unless spoken to first, so he anticipated a request.

"Sir," George bowed his head as a show of respect before continuing. "I am asking that the men be allowed to conduct a welcome party for the new intakes…"

"A welcome party?" Moretti scowled. He did not think there had ever been such a thing in Stalag 31.

"You have seen for yourself…today and recently…how restless they are…too eager for a change in routine if you ask me. Their eagerness has resulted in too much breaking protocol, in disobedience and fighting…simply to have something different. I've discussed this with my officers and we've agreed something needs to be done. It was suggested that an evening party would be least disruptive to routine and would require the least amount of preparation or worry on your part…"

Moretti looked past George from one cluster of men to the next. For the most part, he could agree that George's assessment of the men was accurate. The majority wore either the void of despair or apathy or the simmering glower of frustration looking for the nearest outlet. And though he claimed no knowledge of human psychology, it seemed reasonable to deduce that boredom, tension, fatigue, and despair were behind the recent rash of misbehaviors. They either needed to break the men completely, as Hirsch and Stetcher sought to do at every opportunity, or they needed to provide some positive motivation for good behavior. Some incentive other than the ever-looming, and less than successful, threat of punishment.

"Go on, Colonel," he urged.

"Nothing elaborate mind you," George continued, pleased the Italian was willing to hear him at least. "A late night of music…a bit of extra food…perhaps a touch of alcohol…"

"I don't know…"

"Perhaps not the alcohol then," George shrugged, hoping to appear willing to concede a point though he had known it would likely be denied. "One event…a few extra hours of sleep the following morning to allow for the late night and the cleanup time. I believe it will do wonders for the men's' morale…and should reduce these negative incidents significantly. I think everyone, German and otherwise, will be happier with that outcome."

Moretti nodded absently. "I will discuss the proposal with Oberfuhrer von Hausen. But I can say this…any more occurrences like today and he will never permit it. We need assurances of good behavior before…"

"I will talk to them, make them understand that obedience may be rewarded…"

"Good. Then I will speak to the Commandant on your behalf. Good night, Colonel."

"Thank you, sir…goodnight."

Moretti departed after a nod and George turned, barely taking a step before Ronny and Taffy flanked him with eager gazes and bated breath. He wondered if they had been near enough to overhear any of that discussion, but when Ronny asked, "Any luck?" he presumed they had not been.

"He's willing to bring the idea up to von Hausen, champion our cause provided we can assure good behavior in the meantime…and afterward."

"And of course during. With Vic still hot to blast Skip…" Ronny began.

"Then we do our best to keep them apart," Taffy said, "and run interference when Stetcher insists on assigning them work together."

Nodding as they returned to the barracks, George said, "Taffy, talk to Skip and Dusty…especially Dusty. If anyone can influence Skip's temper, it'll be him. Tell them what we're up against if they want a little legal fun. Ronny, find Ray and Ollie and the three of you talk to the men. I'll have a talk with Sparks, Bonny, and Jamie and see if we can't keep Vic under control."

"Sure," grinned Ronny. "I think the promise of a good time ought to keep most everyone in line…for a few weeks anyhow."

"It had better," George grunted, "or else we can forget ever being allowed such liberties again."

❧*❦

Dusty watched Skip as the Welshman withdrew towards the barracks. The Australian had been offended at first, thinking that he had been singled out for warnings, despite Taffy's assurances that others were receiving equally stern admonitions. By the time Taffy left them, however, the offense on Skip's face had morphed into a purposeful glint in his blue-green eyes. The whistle sounded, calling the men indoors for the night, but when Dusty stood and brushed off his trousers, Skip did not move.

"Come on, Roo…"

Skip gave a grunt of playful malice but accepted the offered hand. His back still hurt enough that such simple movements were difficult, but he knew Dusty's offered assistance had nothing to do with perceived weakness. It was only a friendly gesture."

"What?" He could tell his friend was plotting now, and he was worried about what sort of plot that might be.

"This could be our ticket outta here." Skip glanced into the forest beyond the camp, at the guard towers on either side of his position, and then at the far end of the enclosure where the GSH was. "Yeah; I think we just might have enough cover."

That told Dusty enough. "It'll piss the others off. You said you didn't think the Resistance will…"

Skip shrugged. "I don't know if they will…but there's one other possibility, otherwise we wing it."

"Without papers…clothing…food? I dunno, Roo…that's a helluva risk…"

"Then stay here…"

"Hey," Dusty raised his hands in a gesture of surrender. "I never said I wasn't with you…just saying I'd prefer less unknowns before we take flight."

"Living is an unknown," Skip muttered with a touch of vehemence.

"Yeah…but I don't think we should keep adding trouble to it."

Chapter 16
July 15, 1943

"**I**s Zaline here?" asked Louis as he closed the door.
Philippe looked up from behind the bar where he was counting bottles, taking inventory of his dwindling supplies. "Good morning, Monsieur Porteur."

The mayor bristled at the formality of the greeting. Although Louis did not recognize any of the seven individuals scattered about L'Oie de Vol, he could only presume that the innkeeper knew of a threat he had not noticed.

"She is in the kitchen, preparing breakfast for our guests. Shall I fetch her?"

"No, I can wait." He sat at the counter, accepted the coffee Philippe offered, and toyed with the envelope he carried in his hands.

After making the rounds of the room with the coffee pot, Philippe returned to the counter, noting the man was still fondling the envelope nervously. "You got one too."

"Too...What? Oh...this. Did you...?

"Yes, but I am not going."

"Is refusal wise?"

Philippe snorted. "It would be more unwise to go, I fear. I cannot risk being in a position to say something that might undo everything we've worked for. This place," he gestured around them, "is reason enough for my refusal. Besides..." He paused as two of the patrons, young men plainly dressed but with an air of military service about them, got up, placed a handful of money upon the counter, and went into the street. "Zaline has been asked to take Pensee to the house that night...someone to keep the Oberfuhrer's daughter entertained I suppose. Zaline will go in my stead...but at least she can offer my apologies..." He was not happy about the woman and her daughter exposing themselves to such risk, but to refuse might present even more danger. It was a difficult position to be in.

"I was going to ask her to accompany me, but if she is attending on her own..."

"I would prefer she goes with you...if she must go at all." Philippe snorted and squinted in distaste for the whole idea. "If she insists on attending, it would be better for her to be in male company, make her less vulnerable. She is too valuable...and if Pensee is there and something goes wrong..."

Louis frowned. "Yes...I agree. This is damn peculiar. You think it is a trap?"

"That is difficult to say. It is his wife's birthday...I confirmed that...but I don't know them well enough to guess their intentions. It isn't like they have friends to invite...and if we all snub the invitation, I suspect there will be trouble. But I advise caution..."

"I will speak to Clara, see what she knows. If the motive seems suspicious to her, we will find some reason not to go and pray to God the Germans don't retaliate. Tell Zaline I shall come for her in the evening, 7:30..."

"And I will have something for you when you arrive..."

It was not difficult to guess what the young man had in mind. "Philippe..."

Philippe shook his head. "I insist...for protection. It is in your best interest...and theirs."

Louis scowled but chose not to argue. He was not a violent man. Matters of self-defense were as foreign to him as was offensive aggression. But he would abide by Philippe's wishes. His son had already died for the cause. Louis did not feel compelled to join him just yet, but he'd be damned if he would allow Zaline or Pensee to be taken too.

❧*❧

"You think more punishment is in order over yesterday's incident?" Hans remarked, staring at the two men across the well-polished desk but speaking only to Stetcher, who again accused Moretti of gross misconduct.

So urgent was Stetcher's need to have the Italian punished that he had frog marched Moretti to the Commandant's house, even though von Hausen had repeatedly made it clear he should not be disturbed at home except for matters of extreme urgency. It irked Hans that Stetcher thought this matter so important that it could not wait until he went to the camp office. Hans felt that Moretti had acted admirably and with more restraint than he himself might have. If Hans had been there, his selfish motive to protect Clara might have produced quite different results. Moretti's actions and choices had been about keeping peace with the locals they were forced to live amongst and preserving as many lives as possible.

He studied Stetcher and his lap-dog Hirsch as they stood at attention awaiting an answer from their leader on the matter posed to him. Both were their uniforms with pride and were immaculately turned out. In contrast, Hans was off duty and wore only his uniform trousers with his shirt still unbuttoned. Following Clara's advice, Hans never donned his complete uniform before breakfast unless necessary, in an effort to ease Jennifer's fears, and since officers had come to his home while he was dressing and he had not wanted to leave them unattended, it was not his fault they had caught him in less than full dress.

He did not know if his efforts to placate his wife's fears was working.

It seemed to Hans that thoughts of his wife and Clara invaded every part of his day. Now, while confronted with administrative duties, his thoughts still drifted towards them when they should, perhaps, be strictly focused on business. In the hopes of pushing his tumultuous personal life aside, he began to reach for the glass in front of him, decided against it, and then turned to gaze out the window so that he would not have to test his own resolve by meeting Stetcher's steely stare. He inhaled, steepled his fingers beneath his chin, and cleared his throat.

"Sturmbannfuhrer…you should not have left your post unattended, allowing the chaos to erupt as it did, do you agree?" He spoke in the sternest voice he could muster, though his face, if they could have seen it, read differently. He and Moretti had not yet discussed the incident, though perhaps they should have.

"Yes, Herr Oberfuhrer," the Italian replied. That had been his first thought when returning to the farm yesterday, towards the end of the race, so agreeing was a simple truth.

"This is the second time in as many weeks that I have had cause to discipline you."

"Yes, sir. I am sure I will learn German ways eventually…"

"Eventually is not good enough. Herr Sturmbannfuhrer Stetcher demands that an example be made. I have no alternative but to confine you to quarters for a week, starting the day after tomorrow."

Stetcher growled. "I object. The punishment is too lenient…and should begin at once…"

Hans turned abruptly, anger in his eyes at the Sturmbannfuhrer's interruption.

"You question my judgment? He was not there to prevent what happened, but his return saw a quick and peaceful resolution to the matter. He is reprimanded for leaving his post, nothing more. And I have errands for him today that cannot wait. His punishment will begin when I say…"

"Oberfuhrer…"

"You barge into my home before breakfast, upset my wife, to deal with a matter that could have waited. You contradict my verdict and try to tell me how to do my duty." He came around the desk to stare down at the other man, more threat in his stance and expression then he felt. "You are not in command here…"

"Yes…Oberfuhrer…" It was the nearest Stetcher had ever come to an apology.

Hans stood where he was for several more moments then walked back around his desk, patting the Italian's arm in reassurance though he made sure Stetcher could not see the gesture. "You will, Sturmbannfuhrer, see to the men on duty yesterday who should have acted faster to halt the nonsense. After that, I do not want to hear any more about it. The matter is resolved and I will not speak of it again. You are…"

Before he could finish, Jennifer stuck her head into the room, only to recoil when she saw the collection of officers around Hans' desk. All men turned in her direction.

"Jenny…please…come in." Hans said in the warmest voice he could manage and held his hand out to her. He knew she would be uncomfortable in the room, surrounded by so many uniforms, but he wanted to reassure her that there was no danger here. "I was about to call you."

Hesitantly, clearly nervous, she crept closer. "I am sorry to interrupt. I came to announce breakfast." Her voice trailed off, leaving the smell of fear in its wake. Needing a drink to cope with the request, she hurried to the cupboard for the day's first glass of liquid courage.

Jennifer opened the cupboard door and searched frantically for the brandy, but all she found was an empty bottle. The new bottles on the upper shelf were beyond her reach.

Hirsch, seeing her plight, was more than happy to assist. He had admired the Oberfuhrer's wife from afar for a long time. Now he was in touching distance, and having witnessed alleged 'availability' in the past, assuming von Hausen would not mind as he had never put a stop to Jennifer's affairs, he was determined not to miss the opportunity to let his interest be known.

She felt the presence of the odious man behind her as she reached for a bottle. He was close, pressed against her in a way that would likely appear innocent to her husband, and grabbed the nearest bottle over her shoulder.

"You want it, don't you," he whispered into her ear. "I know how you like to serve the Reich..."

She felt sick. Her knees began to buckle and as she feared Hans would be angry if she insulted one of his men, she jerked away, her elbow catching Hirsch in the stomach, and ran straight to Hans.

Feeling her fear, Hans side-eyed his wife and glared at Hirsch with distaste as the man brought the brandy bottle to his desk. He had not seen anything unusual from his angle of vision, but he was no fonder of Hirsch than he was of Stetcher, and imagined his wife was simply striving to keep distance between herself and the other man. It pleased Hans, however, that she came to him for security rather than flee the room. "Are you alright, little wren?"

She shook her head no, noting with surprise the term of endearment he had not used in a long time. Perhaps it was for the benefit of his officers, but it was still unexpected to hear. "You wanted to see me? Are we going back to Berlin?" It was her greatest fear, a conclusion she often jumped to when Hans said he wanted to speak with her in the presence of his underling officers.

"No...nothing like that." He continued to glower at Hirsch's feigned innocence. "Tomorrow is your birthday." He smiled at her expression of surprise. "See, I have not forgotten. I have decided we shall have a party. I have missed the last two, I know, so I am hoping you will let me make it up to you this year. Will that please you?"

Jennifer could hardly believe his words. Never did she think that there could be another celebration of her birthday, let alone a public acknowledgment. She had stopped expecting him to remember. She recalled the grand occasions they had shared when they were first married, living in Bavaria, the balls with dancing, singing, and expensive food and drink. No expense had ever been spared. In this time of war, she doubted they could enjoy anything of that scale, but to celebrate with her family would be a priceless gift, no matter how meager the affair.

"Yes…oh yes! Thank you! Please. Everyone is invited! Bring a date." In her exuberance, she even included Stetcher and the offender Hirsch, though later she would likely regret her own impulsiveness. "That is alright, isn't it Hans?" She flung her arms around his neck and kissed him happily.

Elated with her response, Hans returned the kiss before replying. "You can invite whomever you wish. I have already sent a few invitations in anticipation, but the rest I will leave to you. It is your day, and no one will spoil it. If they do, they shall answer to me," he said, though his gaze never wavered from Hirsch and Stetcher.

Stetcher ignored the stare as he so often ignored anything his commanding officer did or said. "Does this mean the French shall be here? I must point out that it will compromise security…"

"Anton…relax. For two years, I have either served as general staff or fought in the east. I missed birthdays, holidays…everything. This is but a small thing. Security at the house can be doubled, especially as the men in Camp 1 will be too busy with their own party to cause trouble…"

"What?" The Gestapo officer's face turned red. "Why was I not informed or consulted in this? Whatever possessed you…?"

"A contented prisoner is less likely to cause trouble or risk escape. Your efforts to beat and torture them into submission and obedience have failed, so I decided to try something different." He gazed briefly at the Italian before continuing. "They will be allowed a celebration in Jennifer's honor and that is that. We will discuss security matters once I come to the office, understood?"

Stetcher felt inclined to protest, but he could tell von Hausen's resolve would not be budged, at least not with his wife in his arms. He wondered when that decision had been made, and if it had anything to do with the delay in Moretti's lax punishment. He could prove nothing, and so with a grunt, he stormed out of the house, Hirsch following at the same pace after a sneer at Jennifer.

A gesture from Hans, however, kept Moretti in place while Hans pressed his mouth against the side of Jennifer's head. "Now…little wren…go to breakfast. I shall be there shortly and we will discuss the details of the party."

"Yes, Hans, thank you," she bubbled, more relaxed now that the other two officers were gone.

Hans waited until he and the Italian were alone in the room before speaking of a matter he had not wanted to mention in his wife's company. "I need a favor," he murmured. 'When you bring Mila home this afternoon, ask Ms. Beton to accompany you to our party. She should be here…for Mila," he hastily added, "but I cannot invite her myself…" His voice trailed off. An invitation from him would be inappropriate, would anger his wife, but he wanted Clara here, even if it was only to see her. Coming as the guest of another seemed to be the only way. "Will you do this for me?"

Moretti frowned. "I do not believe she will come without the Frenchman…but I will ask." It was either that, he suspected, or begin his week of confinement now. He did not consider himself a fool.

"Thank you." He did not believe the Frenchman would deign to set foot into the von Hausen home, but Hans was hopeful that Clara would find some reason, some excuse, to attend, however briefly, despite the Frenchman's protests. As he escorted Moretti to the door and proceeded to the kitchen where his wife waited, Hans breathed a sigh of relief. He trusted the Italian not to speak of this request to anyone. Especially not to Hans' wife.

☙*☙

For several moments after the echo of the closing door had faded, Moretti stood upon the porch, staring in the direction of the farmhouse but not actually seeing it. Hirsch and Stetcher were already out of view, on their way back to camp he imagined, and now that von Hausen had dismissed him, Moretti was alone. He could not, however, will his feet to move.

Why had he been asked to bring Mademoiselle Beton to Frau von Hausen's party?

He scolded himself for that question. He knew why. The Commandant could not invite her, and if she came alone, or even came with Arnaud, it would likely appear that it had been Hans' request. If she was to come, it would have to be as someone else's guest. Even with Frau von Hausen's request that they bring dates, Moretti knew Dengler would bring no one; he would be faithful to his wife and son in Germany and would never consider an innocent occasion spent in the company of another woman. Given von Hausen's dislike and distrust of Stetcher and Hirsch, the man would never entrust Clara's life to an evening spent in their company, or in the company of some lesser soldier who could be bullied. Moretti also knew, as well as von Hausen would, that if either man was to invite her, she would be disinclined to accept.

That left the task in the hands of the very single, and handsome, Italian officer. Moretti realized that any date he brought would put him under suspicion with Stetcher, as he was known not to be seeing anyone, but at least bringing Mademoiselle Beton to the party would not be a shock. It would come with some measure of protection because Hans would never allow her death.

That was, if she accepted. For it would not only be Stetcher who would question her attendance. Surely she, and Jennifer von Hausen, would see her attendance for what it truly was...

Hans' efforts to be in the company of his almost-mistress.

Squinting into the sun, Moretti realized he was being stared at; he expected to find the Scot, who was tending von Hausen's garden, to look away when discovered. Instead, when he was sure he had the Italian's attention, he stood and leaned the rake against the bottom step. Behind him, the stocky private he was working with continued without more than a glance in their direction.

"You gonna do it?" Sparks asked. "You gonna ask her?" The Scot was almost bouncing on his toes.

"I..." Moretti wondered if the Commandant was aware, or cared, that their dialogue had been overheard and understood by one of their prisoners. The Italian had long ago concluded that at least a few of the prisoners understood German. He shrugged at the confirmation of his suspicions. "It is not a request; I will do as commanded but I do not believe she will accept."

"I think she will." Seeing Moretti's expression of confusion, Sparks reconsidered his words. He knew she would want to go, simply for the potential of gathering intelligence. But none of these men, not even Moretti, must know that. "Like you...she doesn't have a choice, does she? Whether you mention him or not, she'll guess he put you up to it, and I doubt she'll risk defying him."

Exhaling as his confusion dissipated, Moretti nodded. "I suppose you are right...she wouldn't...not if she wishes to protect her..."

When his voice faded, leaving out words that Sparks was just as happy not to hear, the Scot asked, "Are you going to see her now?"

It occurred to the Italian that Sparks was not curious, he was smitten. With a pang of melancholy in his breast for the futility of it all, he replied, "Not until I retrieve the Commandant's daughter later."

"Tell her hello for me..." Sparks bit his tongue, embarrassed for uttering those words without planning to. Clara was already aware of his interest, and he knew her devotion lay with the Frenchman. He was trying unsuccessfully to keep that knowledge in mind, keep their friendship platonic. It would not do to spoil things, but it would be harder to restrain himself now that he had witnessed a bud, however small, of interest in him as well.

"I will...now get to work before I am forced to provide incentive. As my duties may deter me, please relay to Colonel Campbell that permission has been granted for his requested celebration. Tomorrow night, after appell."

The Italian came down from the porch and strode away. Sparks, smiling with delight, took a moment to twirl around the rake in a dance of exuberance. They were going to have a party.

The only thing that would make it more perfect would be the attendance of Clara Beton.

As breakfast went on, Jennifer chatted eagerly about her ideas for the first party they had held since coming to France. With so short notice, there was much to be done if guests were to be in her home the next evening. Hans sipped his coffee, delighted by her excitement, as it had been a long time since he had been able to do something that made her happy. He enjoyed the feeling it gave him.

Jennifer pushed her empty plate back and looked long at her husband. "Hansy...I heard you mention prisoners being allowed their own party...on my behalf. I know it's not normally done...but would it be possible to give the men a barrel of ale to toast my birthday?"

She trailed off as he stared into his cup, pondering her idea carefully. It was an unusual request, but if it would make her happy...and perhaps ease the men's' troublesome moods, it might be worth the expense. Moretti had mentioned the same thing as part of Campbell's request, with much the same thinking. A reward for positive behavior in place of punishing the bad. More than one makeshift still had been confiscated from the barracks over the months Hans had been in Ste Marie, but he had never felt particularly strong about that practice either way. If the men wanted to use their meager rations to create some foul tasting, foul-smelling brew, then let them go hungry.

So long as there were no resultant fires or explosions from it, Hans had not cared. Only Stetcher had seen fit to erase all traces of pleasure from the inmates' lives.

Permitting his wife's request to irritate Stetcher made the idea all the more appealing.

Finally, decision made, he nodded, "On this one occasion...to please you...half a barrel, no more." He looked forward to waving that decision under Stetcher's nose, though how he would defend the choice, he did not yet know.

"Hansy!" Again Jennifer threw her arms around him, drawing his face near enough to kiss him. That kiss, and the use of his pet name, were reward enough for choosing to do as she requested. "Thank you!"

"Mmm...just remember the things I'm willing to do for you when I am in front of a firing squad for obeying my wife," he joked, adjusting himself to pull her onto his lap. It had been a long time since she had sat there willingly.

But the happy moment crashed quickly due to his poor taste in humor. "Don't joke about such things, Hans...it frightens me. I know I have not been the...but there are reasons..."

"What reasons, little wren?" he prodded gently. "If something happened when I was away...something you could not tell the Oberstgruppenfuhrer...you should tell me, so the perpetrators can be punished. Trust me...please."

"I...can't..." she whispered, her posture once more stiff. "Just know that...I never stopped loving you..." She buried her face against his neck.

"Then why do you give yourself to them...and not to me? Why?" he choked.

She shook her head where it was. "I am not fit to be your wife. I've tried...but I can't..."

He tried to reassure her by holding her close and rocking her with a sigh. Yes, he wanted her to be happy. He wanted to give her one night of frivolity in the turmoil that life had thrown upon them. And yet, he realized, he had invited Clara to his wife's party.

He could not take back that invitation now. Besides, what harm could there be, having her there just to see her smile? He would have to hope that Moretti could convince Jennifer that Clara's attendance as his guest had nothing to do with Hans.

Murmuring into her hair, he whispered, "God knows I worried every day I was away...I did not want to go...never want to leave you...I only want to protect you and keep you safe and happy." He might not be able to save their marriage, but he meant every word he said. He would never leave her. He knew doing so in the midst of war would mean certain death for his wife and child. He could not live with himself if he did that. Not even for Clara.

❧*❦

Though latrine duty was not something Skip enjoyed, as a punishment it was better than many the Germans could have meted out. No inflicting fresh physical pain, no immediately impending death, and no ridicule from others in the camp. And oddly enough, though he and Jamie had not spoken during their morning's work, the time had not been as uncomfortable as Skip had anticipated it would be.

Maybe, just maybe, there might be a chance to rekindle that friendship before it was too late. Before he and Dusty were gone.

At the moment, however, Skip was working alone.

But the news filtering through the ranks of Camp 1 prisoners now, courtesy of Sparks, was that the rumored party would indeed come to pass. Tomorrow evening, in fact, which meant that, come the following morning, Ste Marie was destined to be a distant memory. His closest friend would come with him, but the rest Skip would leave behind. He wanted no ties to this place, no connections other than those that might cling to his nightmares for years to come.

Dusty had brought the news shortly before, when he and one of the other workers were brought back to camp to exchange broken tools for repaired ones. Dusty had heard the news from Sparks, who had come to the repair shed to make his own tool exchange. The blonde Brit offered to speak to Zaline when he returned to the farm, certain they would be safer if their attempt was aided by the Resistance. But whether that came into play or not meant little. Skip would leave tomorrow night with or without their aid.

Now it was nearing time for the mid-day meal. A shadow loomed in the door of the latrine again.

"You still in here, Roo?" Dusty called. Skip rocked back off his hands and knees and peered around the corner.

"Where else would I be?"

"Stetcher sent me to replace Jamie; I'd say that he did it so you don't have to do this by yourself, but this is Stetcher we're talking about."

"How thoughtful." Skip snorted and returned to his scrubbing. As Dusty had not been gone long, Skip assumed he had only just delivered the tools to the farmhouse when Jamie had been called away, likely to assist Dengler with some medical matter.

Medical emergencies often got Jamie out of unpleasant duties.

Dusty knelt where Jamie had left his cleaning bucket, wiped his brow on the back of his arm and said, "Madame Porteur…"

"Is not going to help us, I know," Skip growled, recalling that previous discussion.

"Can't a man finish what he was going to say?" Skip's grunt was the only apology Dusty got. "She says there's not enough time to get the papers, but Mademoiselle Arnaud has agreed to…?"

"What?" Skip leaned back on his heels again and stared at his friend, feeling unexpectedly annoyed and afraid that Marcella should get involved.

"Says she'll have bikes and packs waiting in the woods…hidden where the Krauts won't find them…all fueled to get us a good way down the road. She'll tell us where they'll be…"

"Bloody hell…" He wondered how the girl was going to accomplish that. He had not expected help from her, or anyone; he had not thought the girl would risk being caught and angering her kin to help him. If he had any inkling that she was willing to do this, he wondered if he would have asked her before. "Bikes?"

Dusty nodded. "She has access to two…"

"…and if they're not where she says they will be, we make it to the river and follow it as planned."

"Once it gets dark and the party is in full stream…"

"We slip the back fence and regain our freedom."

"I've netted us some cutters…stowed them in the barracks."

So we wait, Skip thought. There was nothing else to do.

One of the enlisted men came into the water house, bringing an end to the conversation. But there was little more to say. Both knew what had to be done. It was now a matter of biding time and remaining calm so as not to arouse suspicions.

For Skip, there was another matter of importance to fret over. Was Marcella Arnaud reliable and would she keep her word? He also wondered if, in the course of escape, he might be able to get revenge on Jennifer von Hausen…and whether it was worth the risk to try.

Chapter 17
July 15, 1943

J amie stopped in the doorway of the Camp 2 mess, looking at the bloody pile of towels and the large kitchen knife that lay at Doctor Dengler's feet as the German checked his handiwork. On the table, one of the French prisoners lay unmoving, watching the Canadian depart though his eyes were so glazed with the residue of pain and alcohol that it was questionable he saw anything.

Exactly how the man had ended up with that knife embedded in his thigh, Jamie did not know. He would likely never know. From the tale the Camp 2 leader told, it was possible the injury had been self-inflicted, the intent being either to find an artery and bleed out or else to inflict some injury serious enough to keep the man off of his feet for several days and inhibit his mobility for a long time to come. With whispers abounding that the men of Camp 2 were planning their own escape, Jamie guessed that this poor fellow had chosen to be no part of it, or had been left out and was thus seeking his own way out. Jamie pitied him either way.

"Come, Captain," Wagner said, already at the bottom of the steps waiting for Jamie to follow.

Since Dengler had dismissed him and there was nothing more to do that the German doctor could not do alone, Jamie patted his pocket, withdrew a cigarette, and grunted, "I'm coming."

He looked at his hands, red with blood. The front of his shirt and trousers were stained as well. He frowned as he returned to Camp 1, hoping the Frenchman could convince his fellow prisoners to postpone their efforts long enough for Jamie to speak to his father and gain the Resistance's help.

If those men were to have any chance of succeeding, they needed the aid that the Ste Marie cell had to offer…and a lot of luck."

"Sturmbannfuhrer Moretti…"

Clara was more than a little surprised to find the Italian officer at her front door. Wiping her hands on the stained and tattered apron she wore, she glanced past him expecting to see a car and at least one German soldier. Not only was he alone, it appeared he had walked to the farmhouse as there was no car within view. He was also out of uniform, a sight she had never seen before. If his casual air was meant to reassure her, it failed to do so. Something was amiss.

"Pardon my intrusion, mademoiselle…may I…?"

"Yes…of course." She stepped back to allow him to enter, ever more puzzled by his polite request when he could have demanded entry. He came in only far enough so that the door could be closed and he seemed uncomfortable to be there. He took off the cap he wore and twisted it nervously in his hands.

"May I offer you a drink, Sturmbannfuhrer? Something else perhaps?"

"No, I cannot stay long. I came to fetch Miss von Hausen. Is Monsieur Arnaud here?"

"No," she bristled, concerned that Moretti had come to summon Stasio to Hans' office, to arrest him or worse. As he was out of uniform, none of those possibilities seemed likely, but after the incident with the radio sniffers, it was a fear she still carried.

He picked up on her suspicions quickly. "Pardon, mademoiselle; I do not mean you harm…or worry. Rather, I have come to ask a favor of you."

"A favor?" Relieved that Stasio was not in danger, her shoulders relaxed. What sort of favor could she possibly do for this man?

He could not blame her for being skeptical. The notion of his wanting or needing a favor seemed absurd now that he had voiced it that way. He cleared his throat. "Tomorrow evening is Frau von Hausen's birthday. The Commandant is giving a party, to which I am invited and instructed to bring a date…"

He needed to say no more. She could see in his face that Hans had done that instructing and she understood that she was to be his date at the Oberfuhrer's request. He watched her frown as she absently pretended to swipe dust from the mantel with her fingertips, a mantle that held photos of Monsieur Arnaud, his daughters, his granddaughter, and most recently, Clara.

"I do not know if that would be wise…"

"I don't know that it is either," he agreed. When she looked at him, he flushed with embarrassment. If she did not attend, they both knew he would have to deal with von Hausen's displeasure, and if she did accept the invitation, he would find himself in an awkward position between her, the Commandant, and the other man's wife.

"If I refuse?"

There was no indication that he expected her question, but nor did he seem caught off guard by it. "I will not force you of course; I have no desire to do that." Clara could almost hear him thinking that he would be relieved if she chose to refuse. "I can think of no other woman who would not arouse Herr Stetcher's suspicions so I will attend on my own. The choice is yours…but I cannot say what he will do, however."

He. Hans. Clara paused long enough to appear to consider the request. She already knew about the party, having spoken with Louis earlier. The awkwardness of being in the von Hausen home as the date of one of his officers, for his wife's birthday, would be stressful, but it would be an opportunity too good to pass up. The Resistance could use her there. She had offered to go as Louis' date if he wished, simply to gain access to the officers who might fall under the influence of too much alcohol at such a party and might let some tidbit of useful information slip. Louis was intending to attend with Zaline on his arm, however, and Clara had not expected her own invitation.

Perhaps she should have.

And if, as Louis and Philippe feared, this was some sort of trap to get the founding members of the Ste Marie Resistance cell in one place, she might be able to see the trap coming in time to warn the others or have some influence over Hans.

"I must speak with Stasio before I can give an answer. I would not want to do this without his consent."

"His…?" Moretti seemed baffled to hear that this woman's association with Commandant von Hausen came with the Frenchman's consent. The relationship between Clara and these two men was more complicated than he realized. "Yes, of course…"

"I will speak with him tonight when he returns. How shall I…?"

"You may get a message to me at any time. I will notify the sentries to expect you; they will bring any message directly to me. If I have not heard from you…I shall wait briefly for you at the door and assume you are not attending if you do not appear."

He was relieved to retreat to the front door, to open it and back onto the stoop. "I shall do my best to see that, whatever your decision, Oberfuhrer von Hausen will not hold you accountable."

"That is hardly necessary," Clara assured him, believing she knew Hans well enough to anticipate that, while he would be disappointed if she failed to attend, he would not blame Moretti, or be angry with her, at least not for long. "I shall fetch Mila."

She left him alone in the open doorway and went to the study where Stasio kept his piano and all of his books. "Mila, Sturmbannfuhrer Moretti has come to escort you home."

He heard the girl's polite reply, the shuffling of papers and the closing of the keyboard cover before woman and child came into the entrance hall, Mila with two books clutched to her chest.

"I am sorry I have not brought the car," Moretti said to the girl. "There were none available..." He was the only officer to apologize to her, to treat her like something other than a duty, and it was clear by her expression that she was more comfortable with him than with any of the German soldiers.

"I like to walk," Mila said in a tone that made both adults believe she preferred to walk because it would delay her return home.

Moretti stepped aside and gestured. "Shall we?"

"Good day, Miss Beton. Thank you for the books. I will bring them back."

"Take your time, Mila. I shall see you soon."

Mila smiled and bounded down the steps. Moretti followed, but stopped before descending and looked back. "Oh, I was asked to relay a message..."

Expecting it to be a message from Hans, given his even more awkward expression, Clara sighed and asked, "Yes?" in a weary tone. She anticipated it to be a message designed to influence her attendance.

"Lieutenant McKenzie bid me tell you hello. Good day, mademoiselle."

As he joined Mila at the bottom of the stairs and Clara let the door close, she was thankful neither could see the flush on her cheeks or the tremor in her hands.

༈*࿆

"I know it's early," KC started, pulling a chair to the table where the evening card game was in full swing. The usual players were gathered, while the rest of the Barrack J residents were discussing party plans. Ronny had not yet returned to the barracks. "But I was thinking this little party might be the perfect opportunity to…"

From the open doorway where he stood smoking his first cigarette since the whipping, Skip shot Dusty a quick glance. Dusty intended to shoot down KC's idea so as to prevent interference in his and Skip's plan, but Leonard spoke first.

"I've considered the same thing…" the large man said over his mending.

"I think it would be suicide," Skip muttered, the words gaining him several peculiar glances. Skip was normally one of the first to throw in with any escape plan.

"Not like you to shoot an idea down so hastily…" commented Taffy while placing his bet. He did not sound suspicious. "Unless it's one of Ronny's…"

"Bloody hell," Dusty growled, "think! Every floodlight in the place will be focused here…"

"Not to mention, the guards will be paying close attention to us, making sure our party does not get out of control," added Bonny.

"It's not like we'll be taking up the whole sodding parade yard," KC snorted. "There should be dark spots along the perimeter…"

George laid down his cards, conceding the hand to Taffy. "No, they have a point. We don't know where those dark spots will be, and even if we can anticipate them, they'll likely be guarded heavily.

On his bunk, Sparks was working to piece together his makeshift radio with scraps of things he had found around camp. His efforts were proving futile and he was not in the mood to listen to the arguing. "That's just the sort of thing they will be expecting…give us enough rope to hang ourselves and they're sure we will…and for those who don't try…there would never be another party again."

"We'd be lucky to remain alive. Best to give up the notion of escape and accept…" began Ray.

Jamie, emerging from the night latrine, grunted, "We're not the only ones considering escape."

Skip and Dusty stared at him, both wondering if Jamie had uncovered their intentions through Zaline or Marcella or if someone else had overheard them and passed the information on. Skip snuffed out his cigarette on the doorframe; no one noticed their tension or staring, as they too were gawking at Jamie expectantly.

"Some of the French in Camp 2 are planning a run…"

"Now that is suicide," scoffed Vic as he lay his cards down. Taffy did likewise. "They're more heavily guarded than we are."

"Bollocks," grunted the Welshman, watching Vic gather up another game's winnings.

George leaned his elbows on the table. "When?"

"I don't think that's been decided. I told them to wait, to talk to you about setting up papers before…"

"No."

Jamie narrowed his eyes. "They'll never make it without…"

"Most of them can't speak English…"

"I can translate…"

"They wouldn't make it five miles."

"This is their country…their language. Hell, they have a better chance of surviving out there than any of us at this point. We have no right to decide their…"

George pushed away from the table as Jamie drew nearer. Everyone in the barracks backed away from the two, whom Vic was tempted to place bets on coming to blows. Sparks laid aside his radio efforts when he saw what was transpiring and sat up on his bunk.

"I am the ranking…"

"Not in Camp 2, you're not," Dusty reminded him before ducking out of the way of a swung fist.

"You would rather let them fail, let them die, than…" spat Jamie.

"I did not say that. They are simply better off not…"

Ray cleared his throat, drawing attention from the fight so that the men's moods were momentarily tempered. "If they are better off not trying, don't you think the same goes for us?"

"I will not intercede for them with the Resistance," George barked.

"If you won't help them, I will."

George stood eye to eye with his son. "You won't, Captain. That's an order. None of us will. They've more guards, more dogs. They will not succeed. I will not be part of such a risk…will not condone it. We won't see them killed. Tell them I said no."

"I will not make their choices for them."

"Tell them, James…"

"No!"

Jamie stalked from the barracks, fuming; it was either that or strike him, and despite the anger and near-hatred he sometimes felt, George was still his father. Throwing a punch was out of the question. He made it as far as the center of the parade yard, making note of where the perimeter guards were before he stopped, hands clasped behind his head, to stare at the darkening sky.

Ray, seeing that no one was inclined to calm Jamie down, climbed out of his bunk and followed him.

Dusty grunted. "If we don't help them…if they do it anyways, without papers, maps, directions to the nearest safe house…any of them who do make it out are dead before they start. They're not soldiers. They're civilians."

"We'll be signing their death warrants by refusing to help," Bonny agreed.

Farmer, who had stopped his sit-ups the moment the father-son confrontation had begun, asked, "What could it hurt? Talk to…whoever it is you talk to…if they do this and fail, even with our help…at least we'll have a clear conscience."

"I sure as hell wouldn't want their failures on my back." Skip had enough on his back and shoulders.

"You should know…"

"Shut up, Vic," Leonard intervened, cutting the runner short.

"Fuck you," barked Vic, moving to his bunk with his winnings.

"Could at least try," Taffy said, standing shoulder to shoulder now with George, taking the stance of an equal and a friend instead of a submissive soldier. "What could it hurt?"

George was silent, staring out the door as he considered his men's' word. Most of them had retreated to their bunks, as it seemed the wisest place to be to give George his space. Only Taffy remained at his side. Dusty remained at the table, however, shuffling and reshuffling the battered deck of cards.

"I will talk to them…if I can…before they…" George muttered.

Taffy clasped the man's shoulder warmly. "You'll not regret it."

Skip, still in the doorway, started down the barrack's steps.

"Where do you think you're going?"

"Gonna give Jamie the news, Colonel…unless you want to do it?" When George shook his head, Skip disappeared into the night. He did not have far to go as Jamie, Ray, and Moretti stood less than twenty feet from the barracks door. It did not occur to Skip that he might not be the best person for this task, given how strained their relationship had been since Buckman's death, but Skip saw it as something he needed to do since no one else was volunteering.

Ray watched him approach but Jamie did not turn or otherwise acknowledge him. From the younger medic's expression, Skip gathered he had little success in calming Jamie down and wondered how much of the inside dialog the Italian might have heard.

"My father too," Moretti was saying quietly as Skip approached. "Sometimes there is no pleasing them…even when we do what they want." He shoved the lighter he had used to light Jamie's cigarette into his pocket with a sympathetic nod and added, "Good night, gentlemen."

"Goodnight," Ray replied. Jamie only grunted and nodded.

"We've talked sense into the old man," Skip started, waiting until Moretti had locked the camp gate and moved clear of the lamppost's glow before speaking. The scowl that had formed upon seeing Moretti there not faded.

He doubted Jamie had given away any intel to the Italian, but still, he worried.

Ray gave a defeated sigh. Skip rolled his eyes, guessing that Ray had not succeeded in calming Jamie because he had, instead, argued on the side of the elder Campbell's intentions before Moretti had joined them. "He's gonna talk to the Resistance?" Ray asked.

"Soon as he can…"

"Fuck off," hissed Jamie. Skip stopped and stepped beyond the reach of the man he was trying to help.

"Look, mate, I…"

"I don't want, or need, anyone's help." Moretti's commiserating words had done little to help. George was his father; that the man would listen to everyone but him insulted his already stinging ego.

"Hey…" Ray stepped between them, not wanting them to come to blows when Moretti might still be near enough to return. At the very least, they were within range of the rifles of those stationed in the watchtowers. A fight would ruin any chances for the upcoming celebration. The whistle blew for lights out, but Skip and Jamie continued to glower. "Come on…," Ray encouraged, hooking his hand around Jamie's arm, "unless you want to be shot…"

With a growl and a yank away from him, Jamie decided Ray was right, but his anger had not dwindled, only redirected itself temporarily on to Skip. That redirection lasted only until he reached the barracks steps where George waited, clearly, to Jamie, expecting a thank you for his change of heart. Instead, as he passed, Jamie threw him a seething glare but said nothing.

The second whistle blew.

George dragged his feet towards his bunk, wondering he would ever be able to make peace with his son.

❧*❦

When Captain Miller approached her before the noon meal, Marcella had been surprised. Such a thing never happened unless neither Zaline nor Clara were at the farmhouse. She doubted that any of the prisoners, even those who knew to speak to Zaline for help, knew of Marcella's marginal involvement with the Resistance. Given how she tried to avoid solitary conversation with the men, she never expected anyone to approach her for help.

Because she had the water pitcher in her hand when he came, she assumed the British officer wanted water. She was taken aback when he asked if she would be willing to help him and Skip in escaping.

There had been no hesitation. If the rest of the cell would not aide the two men, a fact she assumed to be true since Dusty had come to her as a last resort she imagined, she would gladly do her part, even though it meant she might never see Captain Henderson again. That mattered less, however, than his freedom and his life did. It was his need of her that compelled her to help. He needed to be free, to be safe and happy, and Marcella was willing to pay whatever price she must to fulfill that need. She wanted to give him something, anything to prove how much she admired and respected him. How much she loved him.

She could never tell him that, and after that fateful day when the Germans had come to Ste Marie, killing her fiancée, raping her, Marcella was not sure she could trust any man save her father...not even Skip. She feared him...but she loved him. She did not want to be afraid anymore.

Already this evening she had determined that the two motorbikes, left behind by the previous owners of the abandoned farmhouse she had made into her solitary home, were in working order. She acquired fuel for both, and as soon as it was dark, she intended to take them into the forest for Skip and Dusty to find. Earlier she had stolen two sets of forged papers from Sister Isabelle and hid them, along with what food she was able to collect, safely in her kitchen until the hour came. She was missing a pack of some sort, as well as water canteens and extra clothing. Where she could come up with the clothes, she did not know, but she knew there were drinking containers stored in her father's shed and burlap feed sacks from which she could fashion appropriate packs.

She would see it done even if she had to stay up all night.

She closed the door to the shed, one arm full of burlap and canteens, when the rumble of a truck engine grew loud behind her, its bright headlights illuminating her and the shed. Spinning to face the vehicle that now stopped, she worried about who it might be and what she would say to them. No one could know what she was doing. Miller had made that very clear.

But the figure that emerged from the small truck was one she was familiar with, the only man she had no reason to fear.

"Marca? What are you doing here at this hour?"

"Papa," she squeaked. Though she had no reason to fear him, it would have been easier to explain her actions here to the Germans than to her father. He would be more likely to tell if she was lying. "I was speaking with Sister Isabelle today…about the need for packs…for those who…I suggested I might be able to fashion something from burlap feed sacks…so I came to get some to work with…to try."

"You are welcome to them," Stasio said without thought, moving behind the truck and lowering the tailgate. "Is Clara here?"

"I think so…the lights are on, but I have not seen her."

Sensing her nervousness, attributing it to the darkness which might house Germans lying in ambush, he said, "Will you come in?"

"I must go…I promised the Sister I would do this for her tonight, but I must also prepare a dress for the party tomorrow…"

Recognizing the note of distress, Stasio set down the box he had just picked up and asked, "What party?"

With an awkward shuffle, Marcella murmured, "Oberfuhrer von Hausen is having a party for his wife's birthday…"

"What has this to…?"

"Sturmbannfuhrer Stetcher has demanded I attend with him," she said in a shaky, small voice. He was not one of the men who had violated her or who had killed her fiancée, but of the Germans she had met, he was the most frightening.

"Demanded…? You are not going." Forgetting the box in the truck, he slammed the tailgate closed.

"I must…"

"No, you must not. Not with that man…"

"I tried to refuse...to tell him I would not...but..." Her breath and voice caught in her throat. "He said if I do not, he will accuse me of harboring a radio...and will do what he must to be sure one is found with me..."

"Mon Dieu," Stasio swore, the knuckles of his hands that clutched the tailgate growing white with tension.

"It is only a party. Monsieur Porteur and Zaline will be there...they will watch over me...and..." She shifted the bundle she carried, carefully keeping the canteens hidden. "I will have to learn to take care of myself someday."

It would not be so simple, but she was determined. If accompanying Stetcher meant the man was distracted from Skip's attempted escape, it would be worth her effort to see to it.

Stasio did not know what to say. She was his baby, the child most like her mother. But she was, as she frequently reminded him, an adult now. She had remained stronger than expected after what she had endured at the hands of the Germans, and he knew that, when it came to those soldiers, no one in Ste Marie was safe. He wanted to protect her, keep the Germans from hurting her any more, but he could think of nothing to try that might not get them all killed.

It angered him that Stetcher had singled out his daughter for his attention, just as it angered him that the man had killed Etienne. But short of killing the Gestapo officer, what could Stasio do? What was there except to pray for his children's safety?

"Marca..." He hugged her awkwardly over the bundle she carried, enfolding her in his arms as though she was still the young child he often saw her to be. "Find some way...do not go..."

Pressing her cheek to his, she said, "If I can find a way out of it, you know I will. I cannot bear the thought of sitting beside him, eating...dancing with him...but better that than risk death."

"Oui...but please be careful..."

"I will...I promise." She freed herself from his embrace and set off across the field towards her home. It took great effort for Stasio to resist calling her back, to keep her near by demanding she sleep in her old room for the night, under his roof where he could protect her. But in the face of the evil that Anton Stetcher was capable of, Stasio knew that, even in her childhood home, Marcella might never be safe. No matter where they were, none of them were safe.

Stasio could not resist watching his child walk away.

He stared at the sky for some minutes, clenching his fists, until he heard the sound of her door closing across the field, a sound loud enough to suggest she was intentionally letting him know she had made it home safely. The harshness of the sound jarred him back to focus; leaving the supplies and goods in the bed of the truck, he went into his own house, seeking the reassurance of the woman within.

"I hate that man," he barked as he slammed the door behind him. Hurried footfalls rushed down the stairs and across the wooden floor as he crossed the kitchen. He met Clara in the doorway between rooms and without a sound drew her into his arms and kissed her, hoping it would erase the fear, anger, and desperation he was feeling.

It did not do that, but the fervor with which Clara returned the kiss did awaken other feelings to push those darker ones aside. Her hands played over his back, her body was pressed against his, creating a fierce desire to protect her too, to get her away from the madness of Ste Marie. That desire brought back the thoughts of his daughters, particularly Marcella tonight, and he reluctantly broke from the kiss long enough to stare into Clara's fevered eyes. Finally, he sighed and moved past her into the living room.

"What is it, Stas? Which man?" She followed, concerned for his anger and worried that he might do something regrettable. Stasio was not a man easily aroused to fury, but when he did get angry, she knew him to be capable of anything in defense of his family.

"Stetcher...von Hausen...the whole lot of them." He closed the curtains and stood with his back to her, the cloth of the drapes in his hand pulled tight against the rod that hung them. "It is demeaning enough that we must work to feed them, that they take so much from us...must we also dance for them and provide entertainment..."

"The party."

He released the curtains and turned to stare at her, surprised to hear that she already knew of it, but he realized quickly that Clara probably knew more about the situation than Marcella or anyone else except the von Hausens themselves.

"This morning...Louis told me; he and Philippe were both invited."

"How many more?"

Clara shrugged. "I don't know. No one else has mentioned it to me. It seems that the camp officers have been invited, some of the soldiers...a few prominent townsfolk. Philippe is not going..."

"A man with sense..."

"But Louis is, and so is Zaline." She said the last softly, knowing Stasio would be far from happy with that news, or the remainder left to give him. "Pensee was invited to attend, to keep Mila company. Zaline discussed the matter with me, and with Philippe, and decided that, with Louis as an escort, they should be safe enough."

"Pensee is a child. She doesn't belong mixed up in this." His clenched hands tried to uncurl. "What do you think? Is it a trap?"

Wrapping her hands around his, she replied, "I don't know. I don't think it is a trap; it wouldn't be Hans' style...Stetcher's either I suspect. And it is Jennifer's birthday; he's trying to win his wife back so I suspect it will be as pleasant an evening as possible, under the circumstances."

"But?" There was something she was not telling him. When Clara looked away, he touched his fingers to her chin and directed her face back towards him. "He has invited you."

Clara sighed. "He would not dare be so brazen. But Sturmbannfuhrer Moretti has asked me to accompany him, and I'm sure Hans put him up to it."

"You will go." He stepped away from her; she did not follow, perplexed about whether he was telling her to go or asking if she would.

"I have not accepted..."

"You will go. You must."

"Why?"

"Because Stetcher wants Marcella there...and if Zaline and Pensee are there as well...someone must look after them."

"Louis..."

"...is a coward. He would not even defend his son. With my daughters and granddaughter under that man's roof...within reach of Stetcher and Hirsch..." He shook his head. "Zaline can defend herself, I know...so long as Pensee is safe...but Marcella...after what she has been through...someone must look after them, Clara. You are the only one I trust to do that; the only one capable if I cannot be there..."

"Because I have a gun?"

He took a step closer, his eyes desperately searching hers. "Because you know how to use it, and because, as much as I hate it, von Hausen listens to you. Or is more likely to. If there is any sort of guarantee of their safety, you are it."

"But with all of us there...and you here..."

He did not fight as she closed the distance between them, slid her arms around his waist, and drew him close. "I will go mad with worry, it is true…but I shall not sleep until I know all of you are home safely, until you are back in my arms…"

"I don't know if I can…"

With his mouth moving from her ear to her throat, he whispered, "You must, Clara. For me. If anyone can…"

"And if I fail?"

There was the briefest of pauses as he brought his face to hers, his mouth inches away from her lips. "If you fail, then I will know that there was no way anyone else could have succeeded…and I will hate myself for allowing any of you to go."

She groaned. "I hope your faith in me is not misplaced." She tugged his shirt free of his trousers and slid her fingertips across his skin, feeling his body tense and shiver.

He kissed her, once more trying to lose his fear in the taste of her. When his wife had died, and for nearly fifteen years afterward, he had been certain that he would never know such unadulterated passion again. Despite the number of times he told himself he should let Clara go since she had come into his life, moments such as this, when she surrendered to him, served as a reminder that he could not have easily said goodbye to her then, or now.

"Besides," he crooned breathlessly between kisses, "you know you want to be there. How else are you to learn whatever Nazi secrets there might be to be had?"

She giggled as he nipped her chin and slid his fingers beneath the waistband of her skirt to fumble with the button that held it in place. "Keep this up and you know I will do anything you ask."

The button undone, the skirt slid to the floor and both arms crushed her to him. "Is that an invitation?" he murmured.

"No," she gasped. "It's an order."

He stepped away long enough to put out the living room lamp and then took her hand and pulled her towards the stairs. "Dites-moi ce que vous désirez, mon cher, je feran' importe quoi"

When Clara opened her eyes to darkness, her head was nestled against Stasio's throat and his arms were wrapped lightly around her body. She shivered and drew back to study his sleeping face. The distress he had felt earlier was gone, replaced by a peaceful, almost boy-like innocence. Almost, she thought, except for a small hint of a satisfied smile on his lips that was not innocent at all. The smile, and the memories it invoked, made her feel warm and giddy and tempted to wake him with kisses to initiate another bout of passionate lovemaking.

But waking in the dark like this usually prompted her to business-like thoughts, of the radio and London, and this night was no exception. Besides, if she did agree to attend this party, someone should know so that they would be prepared for further contact if she learned anything of use, or would know why she went silent if the party should go badly. So that they could replace her if something went wrong.

She settled for a kiss over his heart before prying from his embrace and getting out of bed. She picked up her robe and was wrapping it around herself when he shifted restlessly and muttered her name. She looked at him but he was still asleep and appeared to be dreaming.

She padded down the hall into the room that had once belonged to Zaline. Stasio had set it up for Clara when she had first come to Ste Marie, but she had only slept in it for four nights. The attraction between her and Stasio had been too powerful to ignore. After that, the room had been converted into something Pensee could use as she often spent nights here with her grandfather. But the child did not know about the panel in the ceiling, in which the all-important radio sometimes resided.

The radio hunters had not found that panel. The space behind had been empty during their visit, but finding the cubby would have laid deeper suspicion on them.

Clara lit one candle on the nightstand, its glow hidden from the world outside beyond the window by a metal shield Stasio had fabricated. She took down the radio, pieced it together and turned it on with practiced ease. As she waited for the system to warm up, she double checked the windows, this being the only room in the house overlooking both the front and rear of the structure. There was no sign of anything amiss. Hopefully, that meant she was safe and her conversation would be unheard by the enemy.

When the familiar static hum filled the silent night, she sat down, put the earpiece to her ear, and listened as she turned the dials, searching for the frequency her London contacts were using tonight. Before she could find it, however, she stumbled across another sound, darker and more sinister not just in tone but in the words themselves. Voices. German voices. Two of them. One nearby, judging by the strength of the signal and another, more distant that she had to struggle to hear through the static.

"Wir werden kommen."

"Wann?"

Clara went cold inside. That sounded like Stetcher's voice.

"Bald. Ein Tag oder zwei. Die Falle wird vorbereitet. Wir müssen wissen, daß alles bereit ist, ehe die Bombe geliefert wird."

"Wie...?"

"Wir erklären Ihnen den Zeitplan, wenn es notwendig wird, daß Sie mit dem Plan vertraut sind. Wir haben kein Interesse an Ihrem Tod. Stalag 31 ist unbedeutend. Es ist wichtig, daß von Hausen dort ist, wenn wir sie fallen lassen."

"Ja."

"Ich erwarte, dass Sie sich vergewissern, Herr Oberst."

Both radios went silent, and while Clara should have, perhaps, switched off hers, she sat bewildered by what she had heard. Surely it could not have been Stetcher, as the man was Sturmbannfuhrer in rank, not Oberst. But the voice sounded so much like him that she could not imagine it belonging to anyone else. Perhaps the radio static had distorted the words. Perhaps the other speaker had made an error in rank, or Stetcher had lied to him about his position, particularly since it sounded as if the other speaker had not been a native German. His use of the language and his accent were odd.

What Clara was sure of was that Hans, and indeed all of Stalag 31, was in some sort of peril. A bomb. And while a single bomb might not destroy the entire camp, it was clear that someone in German command, perhaps to keep the camp out of Allied hands, had plans for Ste Marie's camp.

And there was no possible way to warn Hans without giving away who and what she was.

"Merde."

The door of the room opened. It was Stasio, bare-chested and sleepy looking, but relieved to see her. "I should have known." He entered the room, noting the expression on her face. "What is it?"

She pressed her fingers to her lips as she once again moved the dials. When she found what she wanted, she made her own report. "Bonjour, mère. Il est moi, lune heureuse. Je suistrès bien mais fatigué. Ce soir j'assisterai à une celebration à la maison de mon oncle. Oui, oui. Et le grand-père dit qu'il a un present pour l'oncle et la Maria. Non, je ne sais pas. Y a-t-il desactualités au sujet de mes frères? Oui. Merci. Je t'aime aussi. Au revoir, mère"

As she spoke, Stasio stood behind her, his arms about her shoulders, holding her tenderly against his stomach as he listened. When she switched the radio off and dismantled it, he took the pieces and stashed them in their various hiding places, noting how Clara stared out the window, dazed and shaken. By now he understood enough of her coded phrases to know what she had said to the Englishman on the other end of the radio waves.

"A bomb?" he asked, squatting down beside her chair.

"I heard two Germans...or a German and a German speaker...they mentioned a bomb...of Hans needing to be here to receive it...of Stalag 31 being unimportant any longer..."

"Mon Dieu..." Those words could have meant anything from the intent to bomb the camp to von Hausen being given a bomb for some yet unspecified purpose. Stasio did not know, and at the moment did not want to know.

"Let's go back to bed...hold me..."

He held out his hand as he stood and helped her to her feet. The candle she had brought was picked up, and with her hand in his, he led her back to their room. As he toed the door open he asked, "No news about...?"

"I didn't ask. Maybe I have to accept that Paddy is..."

"Hush." He blew out the candle, set it upon the nightstand, and then, with steady hands, pushed her robe from her shoulders. It fell to the floor with a soft whoosh of air and fabric. "Do not say it, lest you jinx them. Have faith, Clara. Be strong for them...let me be strong for you." He pulled her into the bed beside him, but she sat instead of lying down, trying to still the voices rambling about within her skull. She thought she was succeeding until he lay a kiss on her stomach.

It was a gesture that brought up a mixture of guilt, sadness, and longing.

"I am not sure how much longer I can be strong," she admitted as she nestled beside him, accepting the arms and legs that wrapped around her. "Sometimes I feel so alone."

"But you aren't," he reminded her, though he understood why she felt that way. He did his best to help ease the burden of her duty, but in the end, it was hers alone. "I am always here for you, ma cherie."

She wept then, accepting his small kisses and light touches as she buried her face into the crook of his neck. So much she should say, so much she should tell him…and yet she could not find the courage or the words to try.

"I think something very bad is going to happen," she eventually whispered. The warmth of her breath upon the skin of his neck caused him to arch towards her. "And I don't think I can stop it."

"Then let us not think on those things now…but instead enjoy what we have. If it is meant to, a solution will come in time. It will be as God wills it."

With that, he rolled her onto her back and settled lightly atop her, his mouth meeting hers that welcomed him so fully.

Chapter 18
July 16, 1943

After morning appell, and having listened to Stetcher's acid-tongued list of admonitions about how the men were to behave this day if they wanted the arranged celebration that evening, Jamie gravitated towards the fence which separated Camps 1 and 2, hoping that one of the Frenchmen would notice him and come to talk before the guards shooed him away. Leonard brought him breakfast as he waited, and thus, standing with a plate of food left the guards in the watchtowers with the impression that the Camp 1 men were offering rations to the French, something they occasionally did. Not caring if the men went hungry because they were foolish enough to give their food away, they allowed Jamie to linger at the fence longer than they might have otherwise. And when a once bulky man ambled across the Camp 2 parade yard towards Jamie, the guards did little more than look at the two with jaded eyes.

"Here." Jamie shoved a bit of bread through the fence into the man's hand.

The fellow took the offering and quickly popped it into his mouth. "You have news?" he asked, his voice thick with his accent and chewing.

"Tell them to wait. We'll try to get what they need...but they have to wait."

"How long?"

Jamie glanced over his shoulder at his father. The elder Campbell was rarely selected for farm duty; the Germans usually kept him and Buckman inside the camp perimeter where they could keep an eye on them, as if they were high-risk threats. With Buckman's death, it left only Georg, who now sat on the steps of the GSH where he offered instruction to any man bored or interested enough to listen. He supposed George would delegate the contact with the Resistance to one of them.

Shrugging off his annoyance, Jamie was aware that not far away, Ray was speaking with one of the enlisted men. Or rather, the other fellow was speaking and Ray appeared to be looking past him at Jamie. When he saw the Canadian doctor looking at him, the young medic glanced away sheepishly and seemed to focus his attention more squarely upon his companion.

"I don't know," Jamie replied, lowering his voice. He did not think Ray was a threat, but something in the younger man's demeanor warranted caution. Jamie removed two cigarettes from his pocket and handed them through the fence. The Frenchman looked to be watching Ray as well. "He said we'd talk to them, but I don't know when that will be. And it will take time to get things together…provided they agree. I'll let you know."

Behind the Frenchman, Hirsch blew his whistle, summoning the Camp 2 men to their day's work. "I will tell them and hope they listen." If they did not, they could be embarking on a very short and futile journey.

❧*❧

After a morning spent doing the routine Camp duties and hastily devouring their lunch, the men in Camp 1 not assigned duties elsewhere had set to preparing for the evening's festivities. The GSH was cleaned more thoroughly than normal and its movable partitions pushed aside to create a single large room. Each barracks had pooled their daily rations to create an appropriate evening feast, understanding things would be lean in the days immediately afterward, and in the afternoon Wagner arrived with the news that some sort of pastry would be provided, courtesy of the Commandant in honor of his wife's birthday.

And ale. Half a barrel's worth, enough that each man might have a single small glass, also courtesy of the von Hausens.

The news was met with mixed reviews, as most of the prisoners thought of the woman whose birthday they were to 'honor', in less than friendly terms. Many, however, were willing to set prejudice aside if it meant partaking of a proper glass of beer rather than the vile brew that some of the barracks produced beneath their floorboards.

KC was chosen to be in charge of the phonograph player and had moved it near the GSH window so that it could be heard in the parade yard. He moved the small collection of recordings there as well, so he would have them on hand. The GSH tables and chairs were arranged to be best accessible to everyone, and some of the barracks chose to bring their tables and chairs outside. Now, as the Camp 1 residents awaited the return of the men who had worked the Arnaud fields that day, they were allowed the luxury of a shower. In the heat of mid-summer, no one objected to the cold water. Lined up to go in by barracks, they were only given minutes to bathe, but it was a treat equal in value in some ways to the party itself.

"Is she going?" Vic asked Sparks who stood beneath the running water, scrubbing his face until it was pink.

"What?" Swiping water and soap from his eyes, Sparks peered at him through barely parted lashes.

"Is your bird going?"

Sparks rubbed more water out of his eyes. Beyond the wiry runner, Dusty and Skip leaned against the water house wall, engrossed in quiet conversation that seemed more important than the upcoming shower. The gouges in Skip's back were healing, but the scars never would.

Ray, not far away, stared at the Aussie and his friend with a look that Sparks thought might be either annoyance or suspicions. Skip raised his head, looked directly at Ray, and gave him the finger.

As though surprised, perhaps not aware he had been staring, Ray blinked, scowled, and muttered, "If you're not going to shower, move out of line."

Dusty laughed. Skip, less forgiving, growled, "Fuck off," before charging under the most recently vacated showerhead. He was there long enough to saturate his hair and rub his hands over his wet body and then gave the water up to Dusty. He glared at Ray as he waited for his friend and they left the water house together.

"Wonder what that's about," Vic muttered, stepping out of the water's flow, allowing Ronny to replace him.

Sparks shrugged as he snatched up a thinning, grungy towel.

"So…is she coming or not?"

Annoyed that Vic would not let the subject of Clara drop, Sparks snapped him with the towel in between swipes over his wet skin. "How should I know? Like it matters. We won't be there…we'll be here. It'll be a party without the pleasure of female company this evening…"

"You'll have to settle for dancing with me…"

"You dance like an ox," Sparks laughed as he grabbed his trousers. "You're no substitute for the real thing."

"It's either me…or pretending."

"I'd rather pretend."

≈*≈

Nervous about the night's festivities, feeling out of his element and unsure of what he would do once in the home of Commandant von Hausen, Louis Porteur entered L'Oie de Vol, noting the excited group of familiar faces gathered around the bar. Over the creaking of the door, he did not hear what Isabelle said, but he did hear Philippe's excited response.

"You're sure? Let me see."

"Yes, look. Here it is. I compared the handwriting. It is his," the woman was saying. She handed him an envelope, from which he removed a neatly printed letter. Zaline, dressed in a pale blue dress that enhanced her eyes, peered over the innkeeper's shoulder, reading along with him.

"What is this?" asked Louis as he reached them.

"Good evening, Louis," the elder woman said with the widest smile he had seen in some time. "Good news! Sergeant O'Callaghan and Lieutenant Newton have made it safely to London."

Louis wondered if he looked as astonished as he felt. This was news he had given up on hearing. "That is good news…on a day when we need it." He wondered how much of the men's successful escape was due to his son's sacrifice and how much was due to the Irishman's survival instincts.

"We have to get word to Colonel Campbell. They should know about this," Philippe said, handing the letter back to his aunt.

Also smiling, Zaline picked up her purse from where it lay on the counter. "If there is opportunity, I will tell them tonight or in the morning. Let me fetch Pensee and we shall go." She hurried towards the back stairs; Philippe watched her, his excitement over the news melting into concern.

"You will keep her safe," he said to Louis without turning.

"Both of them. With Clara there, I pray we can head off trouble before it starts."

"I hope so…for all our sakes…"

"Oh pish," Isabelle said with a swat across her nephew's arm. "Let them have a little fun and stop trying to wish ill upon everyone. Clara assured me there is nothing amiss…"

Philippe scowled and crossed his arms, listening to the footsteps moving about above them. "I do not trust anything the Germans do, no matter what Clara says. Be careful, Louis. Bring them home safe.

"I will," the mayor promised, though the tension in his voice was heard by each of them.

❧*❧

Most of the guests had arrived, but Moretti remained on the porch, watching the deepening twilight, taking a slow drag on the cigarette held between his fingers. An interesting collection of attendees, he noted as one guest after another passed him, wondering what the attendance of each meant as he discreetly studied their faces. As expected, Dengler had come alone and was the second to arrive, the first having been Moretti himself. Dengler was followed not long after by Mayor Porteur, his daughter-in-law Zaline and his granddaughter Pensee. Moretti assumed that the youngster had been brought on Mila's behalf so she would have someone to spend her time with who was nearer her own age. An adult party would eventually bore the child, he imagined, even if it was on her mother's behalf. Hirsch had come with some young thing who Moretti did not recognize, someone he had likely brought with him from Guichen where he had been most of the day. There were a few other lower-ranking officers, a few dignitaries from Ste Marie's small population, but mostly they were faces he did not know.

Now with the arrival of Stetcher, a terrified-looking Marcella Arnaud upon his arm, the list of guests appeared to be nearly complete. Complete, that was, except for Clara Beton.

The Gestapo officer, dressed in his polished and pressed uniform, helped his red-clad date from the car, closed the door and approached the house.

"It appears you date has stood you up," Stetcher sneered as he mounted the steps, pulling Marcella behind him.

Moretti did not deign to respond since what he really wanted to do was punch the man in the face. Since the baiting failed, Stetcher went inside without speaking to the Italian further.

For that, Moretti was thankful.

The collection of guests made little sense. Not one of these people could be considered friends of Jennifer's. Other than the officers the Commandant felt compelled to invite, all of whom she seemed perpetually afraid of, the only other guests were French villagers, the dates of officers, or people of local import. Would the woman be pleased with this party by the end of the evening? Did she even want it? And what would she think if Clara arrived?

Dwelling on it again, Moretti hoped the woman had decided not to attend.

"Sturmbannfuhrer?"

It was Hans' voice. The Italian looked at his commander who was immaculately dressed though not in his uniform. Moretti imagined the man had spent many Berlin nights at business banquets and society parties which would demand such attire. He was thankful he had never been part of that world. Tonight von Hausen had specifically ordered the men not to wear their military uniform.

Stetcher, of course, had ignored that request. Moretti hoped that von Hausen would send the man packing due to his lack of obedience.

"Sir?"

"Is she…?"

"She did not say she would come…but I had hoped…"

The Oberfuhrer let out a long sigh which he tried to hide behind a shrug of indifference. "Well then…everyone else is here and drinks are served. Do come and join us."

"May I finish my cigarette first?"

Hans looked at the tiny stub in the Italian's fingers and nodded. "Of course…but come quickly."

"Yes, sir."

Hans retreated into the house where the sounds of music blocked out the noises of the outside world. Moretti's decision to finish his smoke was in his favor; as he took one last drag, the beat up truck belonging to Stasio Arnaud rattled up to the front of von Hausen's residence. The Italian watched the Frenchman circle the truck and open the door for its passenger. His offered hand drew Clara from the vehicle, before pulling her into a deep kiss with one hand possessively placed over the small of her back. She was dressed in off-white and gold, angelic colors that set off the golden red highlights in her hair. Though they could not make eye contact,

Moretti was certain the Frenchman was staring at him, daring him to attempt to lay claim to the woman in his arms.

Of course, Moretti had no intention of trying, but he was not so certain about von Hausen's intentions, particularly after the Oberfuhrer caught sight of her.

The kiss broke and Clara said something into Stasio's ear that Moretti could not hear. It did not matter. It was private and he was satisfied with that. When she started to walk to the steps, the Italian descended to greet her.

"I shall bring her directly home after the party," he called.

"I will hold you to that, monsieur," Stasio replied. He did not move until after Clara waved and blew him a kiss before passing into the house. Moretti bowed to him and followed her, bracing for von Hausen's first move of the night.

❧*❧

Entering the von Hausen home on Renzo Moretti's arm made her arrival slightly less awkward then it could have been, but Clara still felt the eyes upon her when she and her date entered the room, particularly those of Hirsch, Stetcher, and Hans himself. It was expected. Stetcher and Hirsch were leeches and would seek opportunities to corner her, slip her up, dance with her if she permitted. And Hans wanted her here, though he had not dared extend the invitation himself. She did her best to ignore his stare as she greeted Marcella, Zaline, and the only two youngsters here this evening. A hired pianist played in the corner, hors-d'oeuvres and a variety of finger foods were laid out on a side table, and the bar was arranged with a variety of beverages, most of them alcoholic. Clara declined when Renzo offered her one and chose to have water instead. As tempting as it was to drown the evening's discomfort, it was imperative to remain clear-headed. It was the only way to pick up any details of note and to stay ahead of every German predator in the room.

After minutes of uncomfortable and forced small-talk, heads turned again when Jennifer von Hausen floated down the stairs, her elegant red gown the sort she had likely worn to many operas but which there had been no cause to date to wear in Ste Marie.

Hans joined her at the foot of the stairs, hand out to her, an awed smile on his face. "Esteemed friends…may I introduce our guest of honor…our hostess…the Nightingale herself, my lovely wife Jennifer." There was a smattering of applause, the sort expected from guests whether they cared about the woman's arrival or not. It was enough to bring a genuine smile, a look of practiced poise learned from years upon the stage, to Jennifer's currently sober face.

Hans realized he should have made this effort sooner.

He forced himself to remain focused on his wife as she placed her hand in his, accepted the kiss upon her knuckles gracefully, and stepped nearer the perimeter of the crowd of guests. It was not as easy to do as he had hoped, no matter how beautiful Jennifer was and how much he adored her still. The first glimpse of Clara through the crowd caused his heart to thunder, his palms to sweat, and his groin to tighten in a way that frightened him. She was, next to his wife, the most beautiful woman in the room.

But the attention to Jennifer, his smile brightening as she continued to hold his hand, was as much for his sake as for hers. The guests, even those who did not know her, politely paid their respects and birthday wishes, and Clara, as soon as she could, withdrew deeper into the gathering to shield her attendance from Jennifer and not ruin the woman's grand entrance to her own party. Jennifer paused to accept her husband's kiss and the embrace of her daughter when the girl pushed forward to hug her.

It was during that mother-daughter embrace that Hans' eyes strayed again in search of Clara; she could feel it but she ignored him, even though his dashing figure in a well-fitted black suit made her heart beat faster. He loved his wife, she knew, but it was also obvious that whatever he felt for Clara was an addiction he could not stay away from.

She wondered again if she should not have come.

Led by her husband's hand at her elbow, Jennifer mingled, greeting those she did not know, and those whose faces she had seen in the streets of Ste Marie with the same degree of graciousness. As she rarely left the safety of the walls of this home, she did not actually know any of them. When introduced to Marcella, the frightened young woman cringing in Stetcher's uniformed shadow, she looked at the girl with pity and understanding and tried her best to pretend that uniform did not exist. She knew how it was to be forced to accompany horror in awkward situations and she knew every possible outcome the girl might face this night if she did not get away from Stetcher soon. If she could, Jennifer determined then to do whatever she could to make sure Marcella did not suffer the way she herself had once suffered. No woman deserved that fate.

When she reached the cluster of people in whom Clara had attempted to hide, with Renzo at her side, his arm about her waist possessively, protectively, it was the first moment Jennifer realized Clara was there. It did not surprise her since the woman was Mila's tutor and seemingly someone of import in Ste Marie, but seeing her made Jennifer pout and look at her husband with a pitiful expression. "Hans..." she whined softly, in a tone that begged 'how could you?'

Hans opened his mouth to reply, tearing his gaze from the angelic vision of Clara long enough to look at his wife and kiss her forehead, but Moretti was the one to speak. "Madame...may I wish you the happiest of birthdays? "You know my date..."

The Italian's date. So that was what she was. Jennifer's gaze traveled down to the man's hand on the woman's waist and disdain settled over her features as if to accuse Clara of getting around with the men...a crime Jennifer herself was guilty of. Her eyes swept over the simple cut of Clara's dress, it's pale, unspectacular color, and lifted her chin haughtily. To her, Clara was plain, unsophisticated, provincial. She looked about to say something as she snatched her first glass of brandy from a serving woman's tray, but something else more immediately threatening caught her attention.

Hirsch was speaking to Mila with a rapacious look that sickened Jennifer and brought up the protective mothering instinct.

"Excuse me..." she hissed, pulling free of Hans' grasp. The Oberfuhrer tried to take hold of her arm, attempted to stop her, but his hand came up empty as he saw what she was reacting to, and he too excused himself with a bow and a look into Clara's eyes that promised this would not be the last time their paths would cross.

He followed his wife, and by the time he caught up with her, Jennifer had already yanked Mila backward and put herself between both young girls and Hirsch. "Leave them alone," she snarled.

Hirsch looked offended, but his chuckle was one of amusement. "I was merely being sociable..."

"Go be sociable elsewhere."

"Harmless compliments, madam, nothing more..."

From the uncomfortable expressions on both Mila and Pensee's faces, as well as on the face of Hirsch's date, Hans doubted the compliments had been harmless, or appropriate, between a man Hirsch's age and the two not yet teen girls. "Stay away from them," the Commandant grunted. Perhaps if the order came from him, instead of his wife, Hirsch would obey and leave the girls alone.

"Yes, sir…apologies…"

The title was there, the apology as well, but Hans heard no respect in the man's voice and no true regret. Taking the girls safety into hand, as Jennifer now clung to a second glass of brandy, Hans said, "Why don't you two run along upstairs."

The girls looked relieved, Pensee perhaps more so than Mila, as they chirped, "Yes, sir," and "Yes, father," before scampering away. Hirsch was already laughing with his date and kissing her as if the episode had never happened.

◈*◈

The soulful strains of Nat King Cole crooning, "You're Nobody til Somebody Loves You," blared from the phonograph KC had placed on the GSH windowsill so that its music could be heard across the appell yard. Some men were dancing, others gathered in boisterous conversation. Tables of food had already been plundered, but men were scavenging for any morsels that had been missed. Beneath the open window, several men had gathered around Taffy as he sang along with the record; he could not be heard over the music or the laughter of the men around him but he was enjoying himself and those with him were as well.

The residents of Camp 1 were congregated in this portion of the appell yard, in front of the GSH and Barracks A, with most of the German searchlights pointed there to keep watch over the raucous captives. The lanterns' beams periodically swept the camp perimeter, illuminating the prisoners in Camp 2 who stood along the dividing fence, listening to the music and dancing amongst themselves though they were unable to participate in the party in any other fashion. Soon the whistle would send them to their barracks, but there was no doubt they would be listening for as long as the Germans allowed the Camp 1 party to continue.

And blow the whistle did, and Leonard watched from his perch on Barrack A's porch as the French captives shuffled away. He hummed with the music, but his expression was dispassionate as he drank from the tin cup of crude alcohol someone had supplied. When it was empty, someone behind him noted it and obligingly refilled it without his asking. He had not waited for the ale the Germans had promised. He intended to get drunk early and stay that way.

Jamie stood at the fence, his hands clasped behind his back, watching the von Hausen house where he had not long ago seen Zaline arrive and enter. His frown deepened as he watched members of the Ste Marie Resistance and the German camp officers collect under that one roof. That could spell trouble, he mused, even if it was intended to be a birthday party for the Commandant's wife.

Ray had joined him with a near identical expression of concern on his young face. Jamie wondered what he was thinking, if he was watching for someone in particular or merely watching out of curiosity. Clara, perhaps, or Marcella. Maybe even Zaline, though the thought made Jamie jealous. Stubbornly, he pushed the thought out of his head, refusing to believe the pacifist medic stood any sort of chance with the action-driven woman.

In the crowd of dancers near the GSH, Sparks and Vic were trying to teach Bonny a series of dance steps.

Skip sat on the GSH steps with Sparks' guitar on his knee, watching the three Celts. Though leaning in the doorway behind him, and thus unable to see the Aussie's face, Dusty knew the man's demeanor by the set of his shoulders. He wondered if his anger was directed at Vic, or if Skip disliked the song that must surely remind him of the girl at home he had lost. After watching Skip pluck soundlessly at the strings, Dusty squatted down behind him.

"You gonna sit there all night, or you gonna play that thing?"

"Not like anyone could bloody well hear over that racket," Skip muttered, gesturing over his shoulder towards Taffy and the turntable.

"So it's an audience you want," Dusty laughed with a smirk. He stood, whistled, waving his arms to get the men's attention. KC took the cue and stopped the record, but it took another piercing whistle and KC shouting, "Shut up!" before the rest of the men in camp directed their attention towards the GSH.

So did the Germans at the gate and in the watchtowers, in anticipation of trouble.

"How about some live entertainment?" Dusty called. The question brought favorable shouts, whistles, and catcalls, so Dusty bowed, gesturing to Skip, and stepped aside. The Aussie was momentarily flustered at the attention now on him after having been ostracized for so long, but he adjusted the guitar and gave his comrades his version of "Don't Fence Me In."

Many of the men joined in. Sparks found his way to the front of the crowd and Skip, knowing what was on the other man's mind, gave a crooked grinned and nodded.

At the fence, Jamie turned when Dusty whistled and smiled now to hear the Aussie singing. It had been some time since Skip had sung for them, quite a while since anyone in the camp had been willing to hear him. Maybe this was a good sign. He caught his father frowning and sighed. Tugging on Ray's arm, he grunted, "We should at least appear to be enjoying this…"

"But…" Ray started, reluctant to tear his eyes from where his beloved Jennifer was celebrating too.

"You don't want George coming down on your neck. Come on."

When that song ended, Skip handed the guitar to Sparks, who took it without hesitation and began a tune called "The Scottish Soldier". Vic and a few other Scots in the yard gathered to one side, arm in arm in a show of solidarity and sang along with their countryman. Even Dusty sang along, and many wondered once again at the man's affinity for the Scots.

Before the song was finished, however, Taffy put a hand on Spark's shoulder. "All well and good, Sparkie, but don't you think it's a tad somber for the occasion?"

Unperturbed by the interruption, Sparks shrugged and asked, "You got something livelier in mind?"

"Matter of fact," Skip replied, reaching for the guitar, "I think I do…one just for you, Sparks."

When he began a chorus of "Drunken Sailor," Sparks burst into laughter. He was one of the few naval officers in Stalag 31, but he appreciated the joke at his expense and took up the challenge of singing the responses of just what one did do with a drunken sailor. Their mutual mirth soon involved many of those men nearest them, until others were singing as well, making up verses as they went.

How many drinks had his wife had? Hans had lost count when she left his side to circle Stetcher and Marcella like a hawk, something he found disconcerting, inexplicable, and also irritating. It was not so irritating, however, that he tried to stop her. It would take several more drinks to incapacitate her, and her distraction gave him the opportunity to watch Clara whenever she happened to be near enough in her movement from one circle of guests to another to cross his path. Some couples danced, others stood around the perimeter talking about mundane matters or the war, some stood alone watching, or eating, or drinking without interacting. Dancing was what Hans had in mind, and if his wife would not oblige him, then he would seek out the one woman he was unable to stay away from, no matter how hard he tried.

Every time he attempted to approach her, however, she was found dancing in the arms of someone else, as if she was intentionally avoiding the host. It did not make him angry, for he knew that one dance with her tonight of all nights would ruin any chance he had of making peace with his wife. It was fortunate that Clara had more self-control then he had. If only his wife would stop stalking Stetcher, stop drinking, and come back to him.

Frustrated, Hans decided on one last effort to recapture his wife's attention, and if not hers, then he would have Clara's, Jennifer be damned. He smiled as he motioned the pianist away and took his place at the grand instrument. It had been a long time since he had played, and even longer since he had played for his wife, but he remembered the songs they once shared together. Though rusty, he managed to play through the opening bars of one of Jennifer's favorites, looking for her as he did so, hoping for her total attention.

His efforts worked, as the sound of the familiar beloved tune drew her away from Stetcher and Marcella and to the piano's side. She stared down at him with light dancing in her drink-glazed eyes and when he finished the song, she clapped with delight.

"Oh, Hansy…another one! Please," she begged. That he was playing for her was an inspiring birthday gift, the best she could imagine, since it meant that, for the moment, that he was not focusing on Clara. When he began a new song, she began to sing.

❧*❧

After many new verses were added to the Drunken Sailor, Vic succeeded in pushing his way to the GSH steps with his war-beaten bagpipes in hand. "You want lively?" he shouted, jumping onto the porch in a way that unseated Skip. The Aussie glared at him, tempted to drag him down and pummel him into the dirt. By now, however, the Scot was already playing, and Dusty had both hands on Skip's shoulders as if to remind him of what lay ahead that night.

"The Rogues of Scotland!" Sparks cried with delight at the choice of music and, wanting to divert tension away from a possible fight, swung the nearby Bonny around and attempted to draw him into a jig while Dusty pulled Skip out of the crowd.

Jamie shook his head. Sparks was succeeding with the jig steps, but Bonny was not. As Dusty and Skip disappeared into the GSH, he thought the two looked uneasy, or least disgruntled and off-put by Vic's lack of manners.

"Maybe we'll only have to hear one," Ray groaned in response to the bagpipe's wail. "Maybe it'll get it out of his system."

"He does like to be the center of attention," Jamie agreed.

Deeper in the crowd, a hand was waving above the heads of the other men. He thought it was Farmer, but he could not be sure. Still, if standing in the thick of the crowd would take his father's too-watchful eye off of him, Jamie decided it was worth a try. He pushed through the crowd, with Ray at his heels, but Ronny suddenly appeared there, grabbed Ray by the arm, and dragged the younger man away, leaving Jamie to continue alone.

Hans had no reason to think that his third musical offering, a song he and Jennifer had shared their first dance to on their wedding night, would send his wife fleeing to the porch, choking on tears. Was it the song, himself, he wondered, as he continued playing for the benefit of their guests, or was it the memories of better times it invoked. Or perhaps, he sighed, it was because for a split second he had looked up from the black and white keys and met Clara's gaze across the back of the piano and the gathering of guests around it. No, not that, he decided as he completed the song. Jennifer had not been looking at him then but had been once more watching Stetcher and Marcella. Some other reason then, and he was determined to find out what that was. He certainly had not meant to hurt her.

He stepped into the balmy darkness to find his wife nursing yet another glass of brandy, staring in the direction of the camp. The sound of men singing together could be heard over the music that resumed in the house behind them. It seemed her attention was riveted there rather than upon her own party.

Afraid to touch her lest he frighten her, Hans stopped at her side, wondering if she knew he was there. That question was answered when she eventually murmured, "Why, Hans?"

"Why?"

"Why did you do it? Play that…of all songs…?"

He sighed and reached for her glass; she moved it out of his reach. "I thought you would appreciate it…that it would…it is our song. I hoped it would help."

She said nothing, leaving him to wonder whether his efforts this evening had harmed their relationship more than helped it. He had been attentive to his wife when she allowed it, and had managed not to speak to Clara, despite his uncontrollable wandering eyes. He had done all of this for her…and she could not understand why?

That stung.

"What is wrong, Jenny Wren? Aren't you enjoying…?"

"Oh, yes…of course I am…it's just…" What was it? Hirsch and Stetcher and the hated Nazi uniforms? Clara Beton? Or something else she could not put her finger on? She shook her head in frustration and finished her drink. In the camp, another song \ began and she abruptly turned to her husband with a slightly wild-eyed, obviously intoxicated expression, to beg, "Please, Hans…let's go down there."

"Down there?" He scowled.

"There…let's share their party. All of this is too…stuffy…" She could not think of a better word, one that would not offend him, and she was not yet so inebriated that she would willingly risk making him angry. Not if she hoped to get what she wanted.

"Stuffy?" Was that what this party was? She had always thrived in such parties in the past, before his journey to the Eastern front. She had seemed to be enjoying herself…despite the presence of Stetcher and Hirsch. What was it about the camp party that seemed less stuffy…beyond the uninhibited laughter and singing that could be heard on the night air? Hans caught his breath. He understood. Those men, despite being prisoners, sounded like they were having fun. They were enjoying themselves in a way that the odd collection of people in the room behind them could not. The Germans had a façade to put on, and the locals were too wary to relax. There was too much tension between those who were prisoners of a different sort.

Wanting her to be happy, hoping that giving her what she desired would bring her back to him, he took the empty glass from her hand, put his arm around her, and turned her towards the house. "Yes…I think we can do that…for a little while." To hell with what Stetcher and Hirsch might think. Saving his marriage came first, and he believed there were enough precautions in place that she, and anyone else joining them, would be safe.

He paused inside the doorway and set the glass he carried upon a small table there. "Dear guests…Jennifer and I would like to thank all of you for joining us this evening…your wishes and company are greatly appreciated. For those interested in joining us, we are moving this celebration to Camp 1, to take advantage of…"

"Camp 1?" Stetcher exclaimed with an outraged hiss. "Sir…"

"To take advantage," Hans continued, "of a livelier set of music. Those who wish to remain here, to enjoy the food and drink, are welcomed to do so." He was not intending to be gone long from the house. He would give Jennifer a glimpse of how the prisoners partied, perhaps share a few dances, and then return to the house for the rest of the night. She was drunk enough now, after finishing another glass of brandy she had swiped from someone's hand as they came back inside, that he doubted she had any concept of time. Three minutes or three hours was going to be the same to her.

The guests looked at one another, some spoke in hushed voices about this unusual turn of events, and when Hans and Jennifer went out the door, a handful of guests followed. Hans glanced over his shoulder in the hopes that Clara was one of them.

There was no way she would miss this opportunity to get the news about Paddy and Newt's freedom to the men inside the camp. She met the Commandant's gaze and managed to smile.

He smiled brightly back, pleased to see she was coming.

Chapter 19
July 16, 1943

"**W**hy are we doing this?" Ray muttered, already feeling embarrassed though he, Ronny, and Dusty had not yet emerged from the GSH. Billie Holiday was singing, the song having just begun, so he knew there were a few more minutes to wait before their grand entrance. A few more minutes in which he could still back out of the craziness Ronny had somehow pressed he and Dusty into.

"It'll be fun," Dusty grinned, handing his partners each a long strip of cloth which Ray guessed had once been towels. He couldn't tell in the smoky light, and he did not really want to know. He either wanted out of this or wanted it over already.

Billie stopped singing. KC, with a grin on his face, looked at the trio as he changed the record and called, "Ladies and…er…gentlemen and gentlemen…" The men laughed. "May I present, direct from Barracks J, live for our entertainment…tonight only…the Andrew Sisters!"

He started the record.

Finding himself sandwiched between the other two men, Ray was prodded out of the GSH onto the porch with the fabric draped about him like a dress. He stood still for a few moments, his face pale as the opening notes began. He had agreed to an impersonation of the Andrew Sisters…but not to the Strip Polka! But Ronny and Dusty had already fallen into their roles, singing and dancing in their own 'dresses'. For him to stand there without joining in made him look even more like a fool.

When someone in the crowd shouted, "Take it off, Ray!" and someone else added, "Show us you got more going for you than those two tossers!" Ray found the nerve to step into line. He could not sing. He was not even going to try. But he could dance, and he quickly gave into the flow of the fun.

At the point of the song where he felt compelled to drop the cloth, however, as though in a real striptease, he turned to face the audience, dropped the fabric, and froze in horror.

The gate had opened; at the side of the crowd stood the von Hausens and some of their party guests. Jennifer was applauding loudly. How much had she seen, he gulped? Did she recognize him beneath the poor lighting? What must she think of him now?

The song's end was greeted with cheers and jeers from their audience, but Ray's expression, the delay in another record starting, and the fact the both Ronny and Dusty were now staring in the same direction caused a hush to fall over the camp as heads turned.

Jennifer, leaning seductively on Hans' arm, half purred, half whined into his ear. "Why did they stop, Hansy? I don't want them to stop."

Han shivered, partially because it had been too long since she had spoken to him in that tone, and partially because of the sudden fear that she would make a fool of him here amongst these men he was supposed to control. He was mentally kicking himself for giving in to her request, but they were here now, and leaving immediately would create more drama with Jennifer than he wanted to face.

"Please…it is my wife's wish to join in the celebration, to enjoy the music. Continue."

No one moved for several moments other than to look at one another with murmurs of surprise.

"You heard him," Stetcher bellowed, but Hans silenced him with a firm grip on his arm.

"No, this is not an order. They are not here to entertain us. No one is ordered to enjoy themselves, but…" His gaze swept across the men of Camp 1, "I do hope you will continue as if we are any other guests."

With an offended huff, Stetcher stalked towards the gate where he stopped, crossed his arms, and watched the Oberfuhrer coldly. Marcella was left beside her sister and Clara and visibly relaxed to be away from her 'date' at last. Other than Moretti and the von Hausens, the three women of the Resistance were the only ones to come here from the house party.

All three saw this as an opportunity, but all three also knew it could be a trap.

KC nodded and started another record. When Louis Armstrong began belting, "You Rascal," the prisoners began to break off into more party like activities. Many were especially willing to relax now that the promised small barrel of ale had been brought in and maneuvered onto a table in front of the GSH.

Moretti, sensing his date's eagerness to dance, especially since it would move her away from the immediate reach of Hans' eyes, whispered to her; she smiled and followed him further into the brightness of the searchlights.

It seemed, however, that nowhere was far enough away to keep the Commandant from watching her.

"Dance with me, Hansy," Jennifer purred. Hans tore his gaze from Clara to look at his wife. She had been speaking to him, but her eyes were thirstily eyeing the keg. Hoping to keep her away from the drink, hoping to distract himself from the vision of Clara dancing with someone else, he gave his wife the requested dance. But soon his gaze strayed again, now to the corner of the GSH hut where the Australian was hunkered down upon the ground with Dusty. The two men were deep in conversation, which meant that, for the moment, Skip was not paying attention to Jennifer. That gave Hans the relief he needed to release her from any obligation to him at the end of the dance. He would not be able to keep her from drinking, but he trusted her to be safe enough while the Aussie was otherwise occupied. Still, as his arms dropped and she took one shaky step towards the keg, he said, "Stay away from him."

Her expression looked both startled and confused but quickly went blank. She then smiled and said, "Of course, Hansy," before weaving her way towards the booze. Hans suspected she had no clue whom he had been speaking of.

"Now what?" Dusty asked. The arrival of von Hausen and his wife complicated their plans.

"How could she be here with that monster," Skip snarled, straightening his posture without rising to search the crowd, without moving.

"Because he's her husband?"

Skip's gaze narrowed, "Not her, wanker. Marcella…and Stetcher."

With a surprised intake of air, Dusty followed Skip's gaze to where Stetcher leaned against the fence. He had not been aware of any interest in Marcella Arnaud, but at least, he thought, if Skip was concerned with her, he might not cause trouble with the

Commandant's wife. But there were still other matters at hand that needed to be sorted.

"How should we proceed, Roo? We weren't expecting…"

"Won't matter. We'll manage. Probably better this way." He stood up and started forward without explaining.

"Where are you…?"

"Something I gotta do."

Dusty grunted as he rose as well and leaned against the corner of the building. "Like polish your libido." Arms folded across his chest, he decided to keep an eye on the von Hausens, the Italian, and Stetcher…and especially on his best friend.

Ray had not moved from the GSH porch; his 'dress' still lay at his feet as he watched, fixated on Jennifer as she danced with her husband and then freed herself to approach the GSH. Approach him, Ray told himself, though he did not know if it was true. His hope, however, was that she was coming for him. She had to be. At the fence, he had wished she could be with him tonight, wished for a single dance, to hold her and feel the press of her body against his. Now she was here. She had heard his wishes and granted them. Some part of his brain prompted him to move so that he reached the bottom step as she arrived, and when she stopped to stare at him, it took several seconds to convince his throat to cooperate.

"Hello, Jennifer…" He said her name softly, for fear that the other men would hear him talking with the enemy. It would not do to have them know he was on a first name basis with the Commandant's wife.

Jennifer, however, had no such scruples. "Hello, Ray," she said with an affectionate smile. "Such a lovely party."

"Thanks," he mumbled. "It's not really much…"

"Nonsense…it's perfect." Her voice trailed off as her gaze wandered again towards the keg.

"Let me get you a drink," he offered hastily, not considering that she might have had too much to drink already. He moved past her, his arm brushing across her breasts as he did so. He stopped to look at her, thinking he should apologize, but all she did was continue to smile and follow him towards the table. He could barely hold the partially full cup he picked up in his trembling hands, and when her fingers touched his hand as she took it, Ray almost dropped the cup.

He did not want to drink now. It would probably make him do something incredibly foolish.

She emptied it quickly. "Dance with me," Jennifer purred, setting the empty cup on the table and grabbing Ray's hand.

"Whoa…" cheered KC from the window, not realizing who the woman was. "Looks like Raymond's gonna be the man tonight!"

Ray blushed but did not reply. It took all of his willpower not to melt into an orgiastic puddle as Jennifer wrapped her arms around his neck, pressed herself against him, and began to sway to the rhythm of Moonlight Becomes Her.

Let them talk, he grumbled breathlessly. At the moment, Ray did not care

Marcella watched him draw closer, nervous and excited that the intensity of his eyes promised he was coming for her. Hypnotized, she took a few steps forward of her own, hesitant but exhilarated, until they met in the midst of the dancers.

"You wanna…?" Skip had not intended to ask her to dance. Every instinct screamed at him to stay away, to avoid the entanglement women could create. How could he trust her when experience told him that women were not to be trusted? And surely Bing Crosby crooning about moonlight, beauty, and dreams was the worst possible selection of music they could share. But now that he stood face to face with her, near enough to smell her, the words came out of his mouth unbidden. He thought by her expression that she might refuse, for if what Dusty said was true, she would know they would never see each other again after tonight. Still, she nodded, shivering as he put his arms around her, and began to sway.

The need to speak helped cover his awkwardness and lessen the draw he felt. "Dusty told me about…"

When he did not finish, assuming it was because he did not want anyone to overhear the conversation, she nodded and replied, "I hope it's everything; it wasn't easy, but I'd do anything…"

She felt him tense against her and stopped speaking; instead, she dropped her head and rested it against his chest. He was right, she knew. He did not want, or need, to hear that she would willingly do anything he asked of her. Likely he would think she meant to imply that she would even flee Ste Marie if he asked her to.

Which she would have.

He was grateful for her silence, grateful for the lack of words. Saying anything on his part had been foolish. Better to enjoy the moment and be done with her, for he would be gone soon enough.

But her sacrifice would not be forgotten. He murmured, "Thanks," and kissed the top of her head.

Marcella, eyes closed, knew at that moment that she loved this troublesome man more than she had ever loved anything or anyone in her life.

Only when the second song began and Vic had muscled his way into a dance with Clara, did Jamie dare to approach Zaline. As Vic pulled Clara further into the crowd, von Hausen was forced to step away from the two sisters, intent on his own quest and not particularly interested in the fact that the sisters were alone. Not truly alone, for Moretti left the dancing to stand where the Commandant had been and Marcella was drawn into the dancing by Skip.

"This is all very…peculiar," Jamie said as he stopped beside Zaline, grateful that it appeared the Italian was not interested in them or their conversation.

"Indeed. Frau von Hausen wanted to come here…and Marcella and I felt it better Clara not come alone. There is news we wanted to share tonight…" She brushed her fingers across Jamie's hand but stopped short of trying to hold it.

"News?"

Voice low, certain Moretti could not hear her, she replied, "Paddy and Newt are in London."

"How…when…?"

"We got the post today," she replied with a smile, glad to be the bearer of good news for once. "Little was said, though they suggested they'd had a rough go of it. Newt is being treated in hospital but Paddy believes he'll be fine."

"Thank God!" It was tempting to shout the news to everyone, but with Germans intermingling among them and surrounding them, a public announcement of that sort of news would be suicide for him as well as the women of the Resistance. "And especially you."

"Glad we could help…" Her sacrifice for their freedom was great, but Etienne would have wanted it this way.

Touched by the melancholy in her eyes, Jamie frowned and offered his hand. "Dance?"

She cocked her head to listen to the voice of Vera Lynn, her hand hovering above his but not yet taking it.

"Just one?" He did not want to pressure her but felt he owed her that much for all she had done.

A reluctant, hesitant smile broke to the surface. "Just one...then I must go. Father will be watching Pensee and will be beside himself with worry if I do not return at a reasonable hour." Louis had promised to take the girl to the farmhouse, getting her away from the von Hausen residence at his earliest convenience now that the party had relocated. She had only come to the camp to give Jamie this news. Zaline had no intention of staying.

Beyond them, Sparks was watching Clara like a schoolboy too nervous to ask for a dance as Ronny cut in on Vic and replaced him as Clara's partner. With Clara manipulating the dancing ever closer to the Scottish radio man, Jamie figured Sparks would get his chance soon. Skip's dance with Marcella had turned into a second one. Zaline smiled and took Jamie's hand at last.

"Just one it is," Jamie promised with his own smile.

"Don't you think you've had enough," Hans growled as Jennifer passed him with her dance partner. Ray, as though just realizing what he was doing and who he was with, turned crimson and stopped moving. Jennifer laughed and pulled him back into the dance.

"Just one more, Hansy...just one..."

By then she had moved out of range and would not have heard her husband's retort even if he had voiced it. He fumed silently, aware that Stetcher was watching, waiting for him to make some irreversible mistake in front of the prisoners. Likely, coming here had been a mistake in the Sturmbannfuhrer's eyes. Hans had not considered it to be one at first, wanting Jennifer to enjoy her birthday, wanting to prove he loved her, but as Clara crossed his line of sight, and Jennifer's drunken, raucous laughter could be heard from a different direction, Hans began to agree with his subordinate. Perhaps it was time to leave.

He did not believe his Commandant to be ill, but beneath the harsh lighting of the spotlights and the stationary perimeter lamps, Moretti could tell that Hans' face was flushed and haunted. The man was grinding his teeth, clenching his jaw and fists, and trying not to rock on his heels. The Italian watched the man's eyes flicker from his wife, who was draped over the young, dark-haired medic, to

Clara, who was dancing with her third partner of the evening, obviously losing herself to the enjoyment she could offer others. Moretti had to admit she was a fine dancer, his own dance with her had taught him that.

Likely the Oberfuhrer wanted his own dance but had yet to find an internal argument sufficient enough to allow himself the luxury. From his expression, Moretti suspected he would find the argument soon enough or would say to hell with it and make his move.

"Are you well, Oberfuhrer?" he asked, hoping to distract the man.

Startled, Hans looked at the man beside him. "No, I'm..." Jennifer's merriment wafted over the song now playing. With a stiffness that belied his words, the battle within lost, the Oberfuhrer marched around the fringes of the dancers, in the shadows, heading deliberately towards the GSH where Clara was also heading.

Moretti sighed and straightened his shoulders, wondering if he should act. The man was 'fine'…but for how much longer?

When KC came running from the latrine as the song ended, it provided enough of a pause between songs for Sparks to step up to Clara before anyone else had the chance to cut in on her again. He was pleased she appeared to have been waiting for him.

"You dance wonderfully," he said breathlessly as if he had been the one dancing.

"It has been awhile…but I guess it isn't something you forget."

"Nope," he agreed with a grin. "A drink?"

"A little of yours, perhaps." She did not resist as he took her hand and led her towards the table where the keg was. She was aware of Hans following on the periphery, but did her best to ignore him. She had not come here for trouble. She intended to dance, to share the good news, and forget for a short while that there was a war going on outside these barbed wire fences.

She and Sparks had not yet reached the table when KC started the next record. Sparks looked at her with a boyish grin, jumped onto the porch, and held his hand to her. "Forget the drink," he called over the opening notes of 'In the Mood'.

Clara happily obliged.

The change in song tempo had Jennifer dancing wildly with Ray, her mirth growing more boisterous as she lost herself in this uncommon sense of freedom. Seemingly unaware, she and Ray were dancing closer and closer to where Skip still danced with Marcella. His movements were not as free as others, the lashes still healing across his back, but for the moment he had forgotten his intent to share a single dance with the girl and no more. He was too caught up in the beauty of her dark eyes to notice anything else. Suddenly Jennifer spun out of Ray's arms, knocked Marcella aside to the ground, and found herself face to face with Skip, caught on his arm as he stared at her in shock.

Nonplussed, Jennifer smiled coyly. "Tom…" she purred, sliding her arms around his neck.

It took but a moment and the headiness of that purr for Skip's brain to register what had happened. Without thought, his hands encircled the woman's throat again, murder bleeding into his eyes in retaliation for the intrusion, for her treatment of Marcella, but mostly for the betrayal that had led to the death of Buckman. "Whore…" he swore. Then Dusty was there, having sworn to keep Skip out of trouble if they were to follow through with their plan. He and Marcella caught Skip's arms and pulled him away as the appalled Ray grasped Jennifer by the waist and pulled her free.

"Skip…it's time…" Dusty murmured into the man's ear, hoping his words would anchor the furious Australian back to earth. It was enough of a distraction for Ray to draw the teary-eyed, stunned woman into the center of the crowd, while Skip stared as if he had no idea who she was or what had almost happened.

Marcella lowered her hands, leaving Skip to Dusty's control. She had heard the blonde man's words, knew what he meant, and did not try to stop them as Dusty towed Skip towards Barrack J. Though he occasionally appeared to struggle against his friend, Marcella could not tell if he wanted to go after Jennifer or come back to her.

Stopping short of blowing him a kiss, she wiped her eyes and murmured, "Goodnight, Tom."

She stood alone, lost and afraid, but not for long. The new prisoner named Farmer, whom she had recently met, was beside her, his hand on her elbow, steering her away. "A lady should not be alone with all these heathens."

"I…should find my sister…" she sniffed. It was time to go home before Stetcher found her. With Skip she had felt safe. She no longer did.

"I'll take you to her."

It was to Marcella's credit that she resisted the temptation to look for Skip in the crowd. He would not want that from her, and she could not risk exposing them both.

"It'll be okay." Ray tried his best to console the woman, feeling that the eyes of every man in Camp 1 were on him now. He was still not sure what had happened, whether Jennifer had intended to find Tom or not, but he did believe that Skip would have killed her if not for the intervention. Despite his arms about her and his low, soothing words, Jennifer seemed immune to Ray's efforts, lost in her thoughts, until she suddenly straightened her shoulders and pulled away from him.

"I should be…Hans will be looking for me."

"But Jennifer…"

"It's okay." She kissed his cheek, the tears on her face rubbing off on his skin. "Thank you…for everything. I will see you soon…"

And she was gone.

Ray stared after her, wanting to call her back, feeling cold and empty without her nearness, but he could think of nothing to say or do that would not attract unwanted attention and make him appear as foolish as Skip had been.

He had witnessed firsthand what losing her had done to Skip.

"What was that about?"

The tone of George's voice made Ray feel even colder. "Trying to keep Skip from doing something stupid…" he began

George shook his head. "I mean that…"

The emphasis on the final word caused Ray to turn his head to look at Jennifer one more time but he could not find her retreating figure in the crowd. "Seemed the gentlemanly thing to do…"

"Hope that's all it was…"

From a nearby porch, Leonard's gaze was like icy daggers. The medic swallowed hard and decided he needed that drink now.

"You sure?" Jamie asked with a forlorn note in his voice. Marcella stood not far away, waiting for her sister with a miserable expression. Leave it to Skip to mess up what could have been a really good thing. Jamie did not yet know what part Jennifer von Hausen had in that messing up. Farmer stood at the young woman's side, intending to escort her and her sister to the gate.

Though in no rush to leave, Zaline sighed and nodded. "I've been here too long...I have to get her home...I'll see you soon..." With distance now between them, she felt awkward for what still seemed inappropriate attraction to her, but she was not going to deny it was there. She smiled, her heart fluttering as he took her hand and lay a lingering kiss upon her knuckles.

He wanted to do more than kiss her hand, but in these surroundings, those actions would not be appropriate. The other prisoners might not object, though some would be understandably jealous, but the Germans were another story.

"I'll get them safely out," Farmer promised with a nod.

"You'd better," Jamie called. He chose not to follow. If he stood with her at the gates, he would be tempted to do something that he would come to regret.

With Marlene Dietrich now belting out 'Boys in the Back' behind them, Dusty led Skip between E and F barracks and waited against the wall in the shadows as the spotlight did its sweep of the perimeter. There would be another five minutes before the next sweep of light, longer perhaps since the Germans in the watchtowers were singing now as well. Skip looked at Dusty. Dusty shrugged.

Skip studied the towers closest to them, and since the Germans' attention was elsewhere, he motioned Dusty forward. They had taken a single step when Skip grabbed his arm and pulled him abruptly back against the barracks' wall.

"What the...?"

Skip motioned for silence.

They waited.

Nothing happened.

"Thought I saw something..."

"Wanker...damn near gave me a heart attack," hissed Dusty.

The Aussie grinned and let him pass.

The Brit scooted towards the first fence on his hands and knees; when he reached it, he lay still for a few moments, listening to the sounds around him before cutting the wire enough that they could pass beneath it. Once it was cut, he slid into the area between the inner fence and the outer, gesturing to Skip to stay back while he focused on cutting the outer wire.

No point in both of them being caught so early in the game.

"Break it up, you two…you're making the rest of us jealous," Vic snorted as he climbed onto the GSH porch with his bagpipes under his arm.

"Don't like our dancing?" laughed Sparks as he jumped down and helped Clara down as well. His hands remained on her waist, unable to help himself. She looked, felt, and smelled beautiful.

"Would like it a whole lot more if you'd share," shouted KC from the window.

"Thought I should offer one more number before the Krauts pull the plug on our little party. This one's for you, Sparky."

As Vic began to play, Clara felt Sparks tense behind her. She turned her head enough to see him, her face mere inches from his. His eyes were misty and the corners of his mouth quivered.

"Robbie?"

He glanced at her, noting at once how near her mouth was to his. He had not thought she knew his name. "Over the Sea to Skye," he sang softly with the tune, in answer to her question, singing instead of kissing her as he wanted. "That's my home."

She smiled, nodded and looked back at Vic, relaxing against Sparks as he slid his arms around her waist. What harm could there be? She rested her head on his shoulder, aware of his arousal pressed against her. He did nothing more, however, except lower his head to sing against her ear, singing for her, but mostly for himself.

She felt safe, and for a few brief moments, she got her wish. The rest of the world ceased to exist.

Only after he had seen Dusty slide safely down the embankment outside the camp fence, and the spotlight had passed once more overhead, did Skip follow. His effort was easier, as he did not have to cut wire, but his heart thundered nonetheless. He scurried beneath the first wire, lay still to listen for trouble, and then pushed through the second fence as well. He rolled, rather than crawled, into the ditch as Vic's bagpipe began to wail.

"Thank God…they'll never hear us over that," Dusty grinned when Skip stopped beside him.

"Right. Stay low for a few hundred feet…then run like hell." Through the forest towards the double oak, just as Marcella had instructed…if she could be trusted. It was too late for second guesses. They waited in the gully until the spotlight passed overhead again. Both took a deep breath. Listened. Glanced behind. And ran.

It was one thing to tolerate his wife's boorish behavior in front of these men who were supposed to respect and obey him. It was another to endure Clara dancing with one partner after another, none of them being him. When Clara finally settled on her choice of partners and then relaxed into Sparks' embrace to listen to Vic's bagpipe serenade, it was the final straw.

Not that he had any claim on her, or any right to her. He knew he did not, any more than any of these men did. But he felt they shared a connection that no one else could, an understanding that made her his in a way that she could never belong to anyone else. In that small way, she was his, and he would be damned if he would let any of these dirty captives take advantage of her kind spirit.

He strode through the crowd of men, most of whom parted before him as though he was a scythe at harvest. When he stopped, prepared to raise some tirade against the ginger-bearded man, he found that all he could see was Clara. The way her head rested against the man's neck, the way her hands wrapped around his wrists as he held her.

Hans was not aware, at first, that everyone around him was expectantly awaiting trouble. He was not aware of the fury on his face or the fact that it had melted into something else entirely. He did not even notice that the music had stopped until both Sparks and Clara opened their eyes. She met his gaze evenly, though with an expression that, to Hans, reminded him painfully of a woman's face after a bout of passionate lovemaking.

His heart came to his throat.

"Clara…" He held out a hand to her.

"You don't have to…" started Sparks, not liking the way the Oberfuhrer was looking at her.

Clara reluctantly released Sparks' wrists and stepped away from him. There was no reason to fear Hans and every reason to protect Sparks. She could handle the Commandant, and if she refused his company, or allowed Sparks to interfere, there would be trouble. She did not want him hurt because of her. "It's okay, Robbie…"

But when Hans started away, pulling Clara behind him by the hand, Sparks decided not to let her go so easily. He was prevented from action, however, by two sets of hands. Bonnie and Jamie.

"Let me go."

"Don't do it," Jamie said.

Bonny nodded, echoing that sentiment. "She'll be okay…you heard her…"

"I don't…let go of me!"

The final sprint into the forest left both men breathless but they continued running, though slower, until they reached the great double oak, two trees fused into one by the passage of years.

"I'll be damned…" the Aussie muttered when the motorbikes and burlap knapsacks were discovered just where Marcella had said they would be. Dusty glanced at him smugly, pleased that the young woman had proven his friend wrong.

"Walk 'em till we're clear." If they continued north, they would reach the road a safe distance away, but they would have to hurry if they were to be clear of the Stalag before their absence was noted.

Skip grunted, tossed one of the packs at him, and began the tedious struggle of maneuvering the bike silently through the trees.

From the sounds of the music playing in camp, the first notes of Judy Garland's "Come on Get Happy, no one had yet noticed they were gone. Jennifer's interference had been excuse enough for Dusty to remove Skip from the heart of the party, enough of an excuse to stay with him to keep him out of trouble. No one was likely to question their absence until the whistle blew for lights out. Dusty followed Skip with the second bike but did not pause when the other man did. He glanced back to see Skip staring in the direction of the light through the tree boughs. Saying goodbye.

Skip grunted when the lyrics registered in his ears. "Let's go."

Dusty nodded, already well ahead of him.

"Hansy!" Jennifer called.

She was alone in the middle of a crowd of strange, potentially hostile men, and beginning to feel the first thread of panic now that she was unable to find either Hans or a way out of the crowd. Through the alcohol-induced cloud, all of the faces looked angry, leering, resentful, all reminders of a single face she was trying to forget and part of the reasons her husband now hated her.

She called his name again and in front of her, a man turned towards her. She gave a soft scream and might have fainted if not for the hands that steadied her.

"May I help you, Frau von Hausen?"

She only relaxed when she recognized the elegant Italian officer. She was not afraid of him as she was of so many others. With a pout, she wiped her cheeks and mumbled, "I'm looking for T...my husband...have you seen him?"

Ignoring that potentially awkward slip, Moretti said, "The last I saw him, he was this way...come, I will help you find him."

"You are so kind," she murmured, practically melting into his guiding arms. He shuddered distastefully, fearing what the Commandant would say when he saw them this way. But Moretti could not see leaving the woman, drunk or not, alone among the prisoners. They would be smart enough not to hurt her, he believed, but it seemed wisest not to take that chance. Besides, he had last seen the Commandant heading for Clara, and he hoped the man's wife would be enough to distract him from whatever course of action he was considering.

Clara said nothing as Hans turned into the empty alley between the GSH and the building that housed the solitary cells. Maybe she should have, maybe she should have fled, but too many things begun gnawed at her as she was pulled away from Sparks. The look in the Scot's eyes had cut into her soul.

What had she done?

"I thought you wanted to dance, Hans?"

Hans appeared not to hear her but he finally stopped and released her hand here in the relative privacy of the darkness. He began to pace, a furious movement of frustration that expressed tension too long contained. It had been a protracted struggle tonight, one he had grown weary of fighting. "I've tried, Clara...everything I do...everything I have done...has been for nothing..."

"I know, Hans," she breathed, feeling a glimmer of relief that what he wanted was someone to listen.

He again did not acknowledge her words. "Even tonight...I did all of this for her...came here for her...she asks, I give, she spurns me. Always drinking, throwing herself at one man or another, begging for attention, affection...but never mine. All I have wanted is to be good enough...but I cost her a child, or so she says, and now she no longer wants me. Am I so heinous? I need her...I need more than I get...but she persists in bedding everyone but me. I don't deserve this..."

"Of course you don't," Clara assured him, catching his arm as he passed.

He stopped moving. He looked at her hand upon his arm, trembling beneath her touch as the energy of pacing was restrained. "Then why? Why don't you want…?"

He was not sure if he had meant to say it, but both of them heard the shift nonetheless. This was no longer just about Jennifer. This was about Clara. Maybe most of it had not been about Jennifer. Coming to the camp, agreeing to be alone with him…mistakes made she could not now take back.

He stared into her eyes with a hunger and passion that went beyond anything she had ever seen there before. She had, in the past, been able to talk him down from his desires, but she realized she might not be able to do so tonight. There was panic, the fear of helplessness, the terror of knowing there was nothing she could do. Crying out would likely result in her execution or the execution of any man who came to her aid. Rather than fight, rather than putting energy into a useless struggle, she stood frozen like some small animal in the glare of oncoming headlights as his face drew closer.

The music in the background stopped abruptly as though someone had bumped the turntable. Loud annoyed shouts, but the music began again and the voices settled. Same song. Judy Garland. Come on, get happy.

Clara wondered how.

Then she blinked and found his mouth on hers, a greedy mouth seeking to devour every bit of her into himself in a search for peace. Her hands slid around his neck as though on marionette strings controlled by someone else. "Clara…" he groaned into her mouth as he put an arm around her waist and held her against him. With his other hand, he fumbled with the buttons at her neckline, and while part of her mind screamed that she should stop, there was no way to fight him. She was unable to do anything except give in to the inevitable nature of this moment.

She had always suspected it would come to this, hadn't she?

And when she did not stop him, did not try to hinder him, Hans found he had no desire or inclination to stop himself…

…until a shrill shriek at the edge of the building sliced through the haze of his desire.

He turned abruptly, shielding Clara from sight with his broad body. He did not need to turn to see who the cry had come from; he had already identified the voice.

Jennifer was a visual witness to the only act of indiscretion he had ever committed. No matter what else he said or did, she would never believe him again.

When she dropped in a faint, caught by Sturmbannfuhrer Moretti who stood behind her, all thoughts of Clara flew from his mind. "Jenny!" he cried, rushing to her side. He took her hand first, kissing it, trying to wake her, and then pulled her into an embrace. "Wake up, Jenny Wren…come back to me…"

Behind him, he was marginally aware that Clara had sunk down against the wall of the GSH but he did not look at her. He could not. What he had done to her, what he had been about to do, was inexcusable. He had lost her forever now, and after what Jennifer had witnessed, he knew he had lost his wife too.

"God, Jenny…wake up."

More footsteps came around the corner. Hans looked up, fearing it would be Stetcher. Instead, it was the Scot, Sparks, with Bonny and Taffy on his heels. "Clara!" Sparks cried, taking a step towards her. Once again he was stopped by their grips on his arm, and with that, he turned as if he would kick someone, preferably the Commandant if the man had been any closer.

Judging from the indescribable look on the German's face, and the way Clara huddled against the wall, Bonny thought it best to contain Sparks, who cursed him and Taffy and struggled to be free.

Hans ignored all of them, though what he felt inside was that he deserved every verbal slur and tirade the Scot wished to hurl at him. He might have even allowed the Scot to strike him with fists of hatred, but Jennifer was beginning to stir in his arms and Hans decided this was not the time for a confrontation with the Scot. He was still Oberfuhrer after all. He had to take command of this situation, however difficult or impossible it might be.

"Hans…" the woman whispered as her eyes fluttered open. "What…?"

"You fainted, my dear."

"Oh." She seemed to have forgotten what she had seen before the faint, and Hans was determined to keep it that way by keeping his body between the two women. He helped steady Jennifer on her feet, carefully angling Clara out of Jennifer's view.

"Sturmbannfuhrer Moretti...please escort her home..."

"Hans..."

"Ssh, Jenny Wren, it will be okay." He realized how his words to Moretti must have sounded to his wife. "I'll stay with you always..."

"Good," she slurred. "I want you with me."

Hans wanted to weep. This entire evening had been too much.

Moretti flinched upon hearing his name. He stared at Clara, certain that the Oberfuhrer had finally done what so many of the soldiers believed he had already done. "Yes, sir," he said quietly, moving slowly around the commandant who was guiding Jennifer away. The 'her' was not Jenny...but Clara. The French woman's hair was disheveled. The top three buttons of her dress were undone. She did not otherwise appear harmed but the shocked, vacant look in her eyes hurt Moretti the most. It was briefly tempting to let Sparks go after Hans, but instead, he buttoned the woman's dress, listening to the footsteps behind him.

The Oberfuhrer looked at Sparks as he passed. Perhaps earlier he had believed that this young man was intending to take advantage of Clara's good-hearted nature...the same as Hans had just tried to do. What he saw in the man's eyes now, however, was love, fury, despair and a touch of guilt. He thought he should say something, but every word that flashed through his mind sounded inappropriate. Finally, all Hans could say was, "I'm sorry."

It was insufficient and he knew it.

"I'll kill you," Sparks hissed as he twisted and nearly broke free of Bonny and Taffy's hold. Moretti coiled, ready to intervene if need be, or perhaps help.

Hans met the green eyes steadily and sighed. "I would not blame you if you did." Then he left the alley, guiding the silent Jennifer with his arm about her shoulders, stoically ignoring the deep ache for what he was leaving behind.

Clara watched the hands button her dress, her dispassionate eyes displaying none of the turmoil behind them. When Moretti pulled her up, she could not will her feet to move. It was as if she no longer had a will of her own. Hans had taken that away from her. Where she might have objected to Moretti's supporting arm, urging her to move, now she only did as he wished, seeing and sensing very little.

It was not until she heard his voice, that distressed plea of "Clara!" that she looked up from the ground and met Spark's eyes. So full of despair and...was that betrayal she thought she saw?

Had she betrayed him? Was this her fault? And God, what would Stasio say when he learned of this. Oh, how he would despise her!

Tears broke free. She held her hand out to him; he reached for it as she was led past, but he could not touch her and Bonny and Taffy refused to let him go. "I'm sorry…Robbie…" she mumbled.

Those words froze him. She disappeared around the corner and Sparks went slack in Bonny's grasp. "She thinks she is…that this…God, Bonny…if anyone is to blame, it's me…"

"If anyone's to blame, it's von Hausen," Taffy growled. "Come on."

"Just leave me…"

"You'll be okay?" Bonny did not know why he asked. By now, the Commandant was on his way to the house, and Moretti would soon have Clara to the gate. Sparks could not hurt any of them, but he could hurt himself, or take it out on someone else in Camp 1 if he was in the frame of mind for it.

Sparks shrugged. "Need a few minutes…"

Bonny and Taffy looked at one another, nodded, and then released him, leaving Sparks alone in the dark alley as he requested. Bonny clasped his shoulder lightly before departing.

Dear God, Clara," Spark's thought, banging his head against the wall of the GSH. No one would hear that sound over the music. He might not have done to her what the Oberfuhrer had, but he felt as though he had. He had led her to betray Stasio. It was with him she had let go of some of her inhibitions and betrayed the man she loved. Sparks felt he might as well have been the one to rape her for all of the damage he had done. She would never forgive him for that.

And he would never forgive himself.

Chapter 20
July 16, 1943

Hans grimaced as he half-supported, half-carried Jennifer in the direction of the gate under the eyes of everyone in Stalag 31. He would have to pass Stetcher to leave, and having felt the cold prick of the man's gaze from the moment he and Jennifer emerged from the dark side of the GSH, Hans knew the man was already suspicious. Had he seen him go there with Clara? Distrustful and always eager for tidbits that might feed his insatiable desire to quash his commander, it would not do for Hans to give Stetcher further ammunition against him.

How fitting then, the song that now seeped from the record player. 'Dirty, dirty, dirty,' the voice sang. Each repetition of the word made Hans cringe. Jennifer did not notice.

"Fifteen minutes," Hans barked to Stetcher. If he had to listen to any more of that music tonight, he was going to kill someone. He wanted it to stop. He wanted to forget.

With an air of clearly feigned ignorance, the Gestapo officer asked, "Sir?"

Hans looked at him sharply, angry that he should have to explain what would normally have been an obvious command. "This has gone on long enough. My wife has had too much excitement. I am taking her home. Fifteen minutes until lights out. No more. No less."

With a predatory leer, Stetcher replied in a bored tone, "Of course, Herr Oberfuhrer." He marched to the GSH, striking the turntable with his walking stick as he passed so that it skipped. Several men began to protest until they noted who the perpetrator was. The little Gestapo officer mounted the steps with as much fanfare as he could muster, tapping his stick as he went, and then blew upon his ever-present whistle.

"Can we go home, Hansy?"

Grumbling under his breath at his subordinate's behavior, Hans replied, "Yes, Jenny..." He caught sight of Moretti and Clara emerging from the side of the building and felt close to tears. "We're going home now."

"Fifteen minutes," roared Stetcher. When further protests erupted, he lashed out his walking stick and struck the nearest fellow across the shoulders. "You're wasting time. Those of you not on work detail tomorrow will attend to this mess you've created. To the barracks. All of you."

Disappointed to be so abruptly banished to their barracks but grateful for what they had been given that night, the men of Camp 1 did as they were commanded. It had been a good, if short, reprieve from routine. Fortunately, none of them knew what had brought about this sudden change. None, that was, except for Bonny and Taffy, who patiently waited for the third man to know the truth, Sparks, to join them from the shadows, the man looking as heartbroken as any man could.

☙*☙

Their pace with the bikes had slowed, but as they reached a portion of less dense forest, the two men took to a run. The longer they tarried, the closer they stayed to Ste Marie, the higher the chance of being caught. So they ran. They reached the north road. The road to freedom.

Dusty was the first on the bike; he kicked it into action and called over his shoulder, "Catch me if you can, tosser!"

Skip snorted, started his bike, and took off after the smaller man at full speed.

☙*☙

Leonard was the first to speak of the obvious as he climbed into his bunk. "Where's Dusty and Skip?"

Various sets of eyes turned towards the empty corner bunks. Others looked around the room at one another.

"Fuck if I know," Vic growled as he dropped his shoes on the floor. "I ain't their keeper."

"Haven't seen 'em since they took the guitar and..." KC started.

"I saw them..." Now the eyes turned to Ray, making him wish he had not spoken. His dances with the Commandant's wife had caused many to stare at him anyhow, as each wondered what the hell Ray was doing. He had not looked like a man forced into entertaining the woman against his will. "They came into the barracks after…" He shrugged his shoulders as he twisted in his bunk. Better he not mention that almost altercation. "I saw Dusty peer out the door a few times…haven't seen them since."

After Skip's confrontation with Jennifer von Hausen, George thought with a grunt. Most of the camp knew about that, even if Ray did not realize it. Farmer, being closest to the night latrine, climbed out of his bunk and banged on the door. "Skip? Dusty? Ya there?"

There was no response.

Jamie opened the barracks door and scanned the parade yard. With two buildings blocking his view, and the spotlights having returned to their normal, nighttime search pattern, he could not see much. "Don't see them. Maybe they passed out in one of the other barracks…"

"Or under one," giggled Ronny.

"You don't think they've…" Taffy looked at George. Farmer opened the latrine door, found no one there, and then peeked into the kitchen area.

"Skip? Dusty?" Farmer called.

Ronny's giggle became a low whistle. "I'll be damned…"

"Ronny," scolded Bonny. "Let's not jump to conclusions. They could well be in another barrack…or the GSH…"

"No one was there when I left," KC corrected. "I was last."

Jamie snorted. "They could have gone in after…or could be in the water house…or maybe they got slapped into the cooler." It was impossible to say. The only thing for certain was that they were not where they were supposed to be.

Adjusting his bedding so that he could lay on his stomach and stare out the window, Sparks muttered. "Face it, they've done a runner…"

"They wouldn't dare," growled George as the final whistle blew.

The last of the men scrambled into their bunks and Jamie pulled the light cord as Taffy said, "You know Skip…not like he had a reason to stay…"

"Or to stay alive," added Leonard.

"Fuck." The padre's profanity threw silence across the room.

After a long, pregnant pause, Ronny murmured, "I sure hope they made it."

And George, who still found the notion impossibly absurd, muttered, "If that's what they've done...so do I."

Jennifer resisted none of his efforts as Hans guided her into the house and up the stairs. She was warm and compliant against him, even when he began to remove her soiled dress. If she remembered what she had seen, she did not speak of it, nor did she recoil from his touch as she usually did. She sang soft and low, her arms around his neck, her expression lazy and worshipful as she murmured, "I love you, Hansy..."

Clara remained on the porch long after Moretti and Wagner had left her there. How long? Ten minutes? Twenty? She did not know. But the floodlights illuminating Stalag 31 had gone out and she had heard the second whistle, which meant that the prisoners were in their barracks now. It had taken some time just to walk from the camp to the house as her feet seemed unwilling to move without guidance. If the two men had not gently propelled her along, she likely would not have moved at all. When they reached her porch, they had been reluctant to leave her unattended, for she still bore the vacant, shell-shocked expression she had worn when Moretti had helped her to her feet. But she had managed to find her voice, to stay his hand when he had reached to knock on the door. He had said something to her, words she could not consciously recall, and she somehow assured them she would be okay without remembering the words she had spoken. They had left her here, on the porch, for what seemed like an eternity ago.

Alone. Alone with the chaos in her head, her heart, her soul. Alone with the questions that dogged her, demanded settlement, yet could have no answers. Alone with the child she carried.

As though her insides pained her, or perhaps to protect that within, she wrapped her arm around her stomach and slowly sank to her knees.

Though she should have heard the footsteps drawing near from within the house, she did not. When the door opened, she flinched but did nothing more. She did not look at him. She did not dare.

She should have realized he would be awake, would hear the cessation of music in the camp, would have seen the lights go out, would wait for what seemed an appropriate amount of time for her to return, and when she did not come in, he would look for her.

If she had wanted to hide from Stasio, this was not the way or the place to do it.

"Clara?"

He caught her up in his arms before she made it all the way to the ground and was appalled by how limp and compliant she was.

"Ma cherie…what is wrong?" That she would not speak, would not look at him, frightened him further. Picking her up, he brought her into the house and got as far as the staircase before she spoke.

"Zaline? Pensee? Marcella?"

"Ssh…they are fine. Zaline took Pensee home…and Marcella stopped in so I would not worry…"

"All safe." Her head rested against his naked shoulder. He was dressed for bed…and waiting for her.

Stasio was tempted to ask what she had needed to do to ensure their welfare, but he was afraid to know the truth. Whatever it had been had been less than pleasant, it seemed, and he was afraid of what he might do if she told him the truth.

"Yes," he assured her, kissing her forehead as they reached the top of the stairs.

Down the corridor they went, into the bedroom, where he felt her tense in his arms for the first time since he had met her. It was not enough to fight him, however, merely the sort of reaction one might have if they were uncertain about what might come next. That she might be afraid of him for any reason brought an unfamiliar ache in his chest. He sat her down carefully on the edge of the bed, brought the lamp to the bedside table, and studied her face.

There were no bruises, no damage, only a trace of tears. But when he knelt in front of her and brought his hands up to unfasten the buttons of her dress, the blank expression she wore quickly became one of panic. He stopped, one hand resting lightly near her throat. This was an expression he understood. A reaction he recalled from the day the Germans had come to Ste Marie and brutalized two young women…his Marcella and her fiancé's sister…because they had not followed the soldiers' instructions.

Rape? Clara?

"Cher Dieu…"

von Hausen.

Or was it? von Hausen had always treated her kindly, with respect and generosity. Rape did not seem his style. But what did Stasio really know of the man, save that he was German and that Clara trusted him? What did he know of any of them really? God knew there were many potential assailants…most specifically Hirsch or Stetcher. For any of them to have gotten the chance would have meant that she had been somewhere out of Moretti's…and von Hausen's reach. Which meant that, to Stasio, it was at least partially both of those men's fault.

Until she spoke about it, however, if she ever did, he would never know for certain what had happened.

Worse than it being the fault of the Germans, however, Stasio blamed himself. He had told her to go, urged it. Demanded it even, for the sake of his daughters and granddaughter. If he had not…

God how he hated himself for putting her in the path of danger.

His eyes traveled down the front of her dress, down her legs, then across her arms. Her dress did not appear dirty or torn, and other than bruises upon her arms that seemed to be of fingers, there was no visible sign of whatever had happened. No visible sign except for the rawness in her eyes.

"Do not be afraid, aimé…I will not hurt you."

He was surprised when she replied in a soft whisper, "I know."

Kissing her cheeks to clean them of tears, he asked, "Do you want to talk?"

"No…I only want…"

Something changed in her eyes, so swiftly that it caught him off guard. She slid from the bed and landed straddled across his lap, her arms and legs around him. There was no mistaking that smoldering gaze; the way she looked at him was enough to start his blood pounding in his veins.

But the change confused him, as it was the last thing he expected from her tonight.

"Aimé…are you sure?"

"I've never been more sure of anything," she rumbled, leaning forward to kiss below his ear. He angled his head, allowing the kiss to trail down his neck and around to the hollow at the base of his throat. He wanted to hesitate, to hold himself in check out of fear he would hurt or scare her, but the shivers produced by her nails that traced the contours of his back grew harder to ignore.

He would be careful...be prepared for her to change her mind and not be angry if she did...but if she wanted, or needed, this or him, Stasio would not deny her. He owed her too much.

❧*☙

Though he should have been in his bunk, Ray was restless, restless with longing for the woman he could not have, the woman he wanted despite every warning he had been given. No one paid him attention as he was not the first man to keep night vigil at the window. He stared at the house, wondering if she slept, if she dreamed of him, if she was well or if Hans had hurt her. The way he had carried the woman out of the camp, the bitter cold expression on the man's face, concerned Ray, as he was sure the Commandant would punish her for dancing with him, punish her for drinking, punish her for the confrontation with Skip. She had not even seen Ray as she passed, but it did not matter. He imagined her in that house, in her soft bed, dreaming of him, her nude body spread invitingly beneath the sheets, and as his imagination took hold, he rubbed one hand over the front of his trousers with a heavy groan.

❧*☙

In the bottom bunk, Vic had dropped off to sleep almost as soon as he hit the mattress, the alcohol in his system enough to knock him out once he allowed it to take hold. It had been so long since any of them had consumed a proper drink that Vic would not be the only one suffering a hangover come morning. Many of the others slept, but not all; some were worrying. Wondering. Praying.

But Spark's thoughts were not on the fates of Tom Henderson and Harry Miller.

They were on Clara and the way she had looked when led away.

With a grunt of annoyance, Sparks rolled onto his back and stared at the ceiling.

She had called his name though, he was sure of it, and in that parting word, Sparks believed that what he heard had not been blame or anger. If anything, he had heard a plea for forgiveness.

Which meant she was concerned about what he thought of her. If she was concerned, that might indicate that he meant more to her than just some passing fancy.

And if her dancing had been any indication, the way she had moved against him…

He thought back over the evening, reliving every detail of her he had noted. No, she had not danced with the others the way she had danced with him. The body contact had not been the same. Nor had the shared gazes…or her smile.

Remembering the sensations of her, his hands wandered across his chest, down his stomach, creating a trail of desire in their wake.

He closed his eyes and allowed the warm memories to fill him.

❧*❧

On the road north, the motorbikes' wheels hummed on through the darkness. Distance. Resolution. Escape.

❧*❧

Arms wrapped around herself, holding her shawl tight around her shoulders as she sat at the kitchen table, Marcella listened to the darkness, tears on her cheeks, imagining she could see Skip on the motorbike as he flew down the road towards freedom. Someday, she mused, she hoped he would appreciate what she had given up for him…and how much it had hurt her to do so.

❧*❧

It had been so long since he had heard those words spoken, particularly in that tone, that Hans could not stop himself. He crushed his mouth to Jennifer's, clinging to her like a starving animal, and when her hands began to work to divest him of his shirt, he released her long enough to struggle out of his trousers and shoes. She whimpered and moaned against him as they fell upon the bed together, rolling to and fro as they kissed hungrily, making up for years of lost passion.

❧*❧

Fingers wound in the hair at the back of his head, Clara eased Stasio backward, the kiss deep and strong, until he lay on the floor with her atop him. She stayed that way briefly, relishing his smoky taste, the smell of earth that never quite left him, the feel of work-hardened muscles, refusing to think of anything else except Stasio.

Not Hans. Not the Germans. Not Sparks. Only the man whose hands rubbed across her shoulders and caressed the skin at the nape of her neck. She adjusted her weight evenly across his hips and felt him stiffen and arch against her. But tonight, in this moment, she was going to be in control. She was going to regain what Hans had tried to take away.

She broke the kiss so she could sit up. Stasio watched her with heavy-lidded eyes, marveling at her hunger, and his own, waiting impatiently as she unfastened each of the buttons down the front of her dress. Not once did she break eye contact with him.

Only when the dress was tossed aside did he move; his hands worked up her sides, up beneath the camisole, raising it over her head. She shook her hair free, head back as his hands slid down over her breasts.

Her breath caught.

❧*❧

Lights in the distance through the racing trees, but they were far enough away from the road that no one would hear them or think twice if they did. Skip shrugged off the tendril of anxiety that sought to ensnare him and remained focused on the road in front of him and Dusty flying along behind.

❧*❧

With a wry smirk, Jamie listened to the sounds from the window near his bed. He could see Ray's silhouetted back, and though he could not see what the young man was doing, he did not need to. In this place, such things could not be hidden from others, and with no hopes of a woman to ease the longings, they each knew it was necessary to settle for their own hands whenever the need arose. Most of the time, the other men ignored it.

Though Zaline was the only thing on Jamie's mind, he did not feel any particular need to do more than enjoy the warm glow of the moments he had shared with the woman this evening. He was content to close his eyes, dream of her, and leave Ray to whatever fantasies he pursued.

Across town, with her finger tracing his name on the window glass, Zaline looked in the direction of Stalag 31 and wondered if

Jamie was thinking of her…and wondered if Etienne, wherever he was, would mind that she was thinking of another so soon.

He had thought it would be enough to simply remember. To recall the dancing, imagine the feel of her in his arms. But the remembrance created a longing for something he could not have. Trying to be as quiet as possible, Sparks eased himself out of the bunk and staggered in the darkness to the night latrine. Most men did this without any real concern for their bunkmates or the notice of the rest of the barracks' residents. Ray did not even notice him as he passed.

But Sparks was not about to risk embarrassment or teasing from Vic should the man wake up to a shuddering bed.

Closing the door behind him, he leaned against it and unbuttoned his trousers, moaning softly at the jolt the touch of his hand brought. He squeezed his eyes tight and sucked in on his bottom lip.

She had to relinquish her position so that Stasio could undress, but when he had wiggled back far enough to be rid of his pants, she stopped him and chose to remove them herself. He laughed a little at the tickle of her fingers, but that sensation was quickly forgotten beneath the path of caresses and kisses that wound first down one leg and then the other. There was something different tonight, something he did not understand, something creating a more heightened response from him. He bit his lip as she slid back up his body, her breasts and then stomach rubbing over him. He groaned, and when she stopped, he used his hands to grasp her arms and gently urge her up to where he could wrap his arms around her and drown once more in her kiss.

And while she accepted the direction, she resisted his attempts to work his hips between her thighs. He trembled, understanding that she would remain in control until this night was over, and he tried his best not to direct her further. He needed absolution in her eyes, forgiveness for sending her into that monster's den. He would do anything for her. Anything at all.

⮑*⮐

Around the bend in the road, wary of a suspected roadblock. It was not there. "Thank God," muttered Dusty but the words were lost to the rush of air as he picked up speed to keep up with Skip.

With Jennifer on her back, writhing beneath him, Hans used one hand to draw a long, slender leg up around his hip with the hope of finally claiming his wife the way he had longed to do for so long. When she did not fight him off as he slid home, actually arched up to welcome him, he almost spent himself at once.

"God I've missed you, Jenny…"

Hand moving faster inside of his loose trousers, Ray imagined her beneath him and mouthed her name to the night. "Jenny…"

Beneath his kisses and her hands, he was completely at her mercy. The movement of his hips, the near-delirious glow on his face and the quickness of his breathing told her everything she needed to know. There came a moment when he was no longer able to passively participate, and when she sat back to brush her hair from her face, he pulled her knees up further to where he could work one hand up each leg, his fingers in search of the heat which embraced him. This was a luxury Clara chose to allow, as it was a talent of his she had never been able to resist.

And she knew Stasio was a giver. No matter how much she gave, he would find their lovemaking incomplete without the opportunity to reciprocate.

But tonight, she found that his touch made her cry; it reached something deeper within than it normally did. His actions were those of desperation, a plea, and though it took time to understand, she eventually realized he felt guilty for having urged her to attend that party to begin with.

But to her, she had so much more that needed to be forgiven, and did not feel he was to blame for anything.

She let her head fall back, hoping to hide the tears, not thinking he would understand.

For she did not fully understand it herself.

❧*❧

Somewhere to their left, towards the distant river, far back in the bushes, a dog barked. If it was the motorbikes that disturbed it, the animal chose not to pursue. Faster. They needed more speed if they were to reach the city before daylight. They had not looked in the packs to see what they contained and Skip prayed that, when they reached their first destination, there would be some form of documentation to protect them.

❧*❧

She was too close. Any closer and she would cross over before she was ready. With one hand she stilled his efforts, and with a single, well-practiced move, held him deep within. Caught off guard by the suddenness of that intimate embrace and the ecstasy of having her once more, Stasio bucked up to meet her, sitting up and drawing her body against his with a moan. He felt the sob run through her, felt the tears on her cheeks as her face pressed against his.

"Clara…"

She tightened her arms around his neck, weeping against his shoulder, and he understood then that these were not tears of pain or sadness.

He kissed her face, her neck, her hair, holding her tenderly, rocking with her in the night.

❧*❧

Jennifer did not open her eyes to the lovemaking, kept them closed as if drowning in the bliss of something long lost. Without thinking, his words echoed in her ears and drew a response. "I've missed you too, Tom…"

❧*❧

His body was wet with sweat. His heart thundered in his ears. He leaned forward, one arm propping him up against the opposite wall and his head rested on his arm. Though it was his own pleasuring hand upon his flesh, all he could see, could hear, could feel, was Clara Beton. When his imagination brought him back to the feel of her back pressed against his torso, her head against his neck and shoulder, such that he could breathe in the scent of her soft hair, his body gave in to the stimulation.

His head dropped back. Mouth open, gasping for air, as the adrenalin peaked and then ebbed, he groaned.

And then, with a little whimper of disappointment that her presence had only been a fantasy, and with the overwhelming sadness of how the evening had ended overtaking him, he whispered, "Clara…"

❧*❦

The sound of tires as they clattered across the wooden planked bridge sounded too loud to Dusty. And Skip was getting further ahead. He glanced into the black river below and wondered briefly if he should ditch the bike and swim. He was holding Skip back. But it was too late, as the rubber tires once more met the packed dirt of the roadway. Head bent into the wind, he tried to milk more speed from the bike. He had to keep up. He could not let Skip down.

❧*❦

Hans froze mid-thrust and stared at his wife with disbelief, disbelief blossoming into anger when she stared at him with innocent blue eyes seemingly unaware of what she had said. He jerked back, pulling free of her, and she pouted as he lurched off the bed.

"Hansy…?"

But it was too late for words. Hans retreated into the bathroom and locked the door before he did something he would forever regret.

❧*❦

The way she shook in his embrace told Stasio more than words could. Yet she continued to hold back, denying herself completion, either basking in the journey or else punishing herself by disallowing what she sought.

Then she looked into his eyes, nose to nose, lips inches from his, one arm around his neck, the other hand at the back of his head.

"Tell me you love me."

There was desperation in that request.

His pause was brief. There had been some unspoken agreement between them for so long that those words need never be said. That their actions alone would suffice to express their affection. But tonight, something had changed, something that now demanded words that he had never shared with her.

In that pause, her hips began to push against his, drawing from him his ability to maintain control of his impulses. He growled, gasped, and moaned as she pulled his physical response in the direction she desired to go. And after the quickening of her movements and the tiny shriek that began working its way up from the pit of her being, he ceased holding back as well.

At the moment when she bucked and tensed, clinging to him, he gave her what she wanted. His own completion and the words she needed to hear.

"I do love you, ma cherie…"

∾*∾

Far ahead of them, a glow approached from around another corner. Skip waved his arm, motioning for Dusty to get off the road, hide in the trees. The Aussie's bike was already leaving the well-worn, rutted dirt lane by the time Dusty noticed. The glow of headlights, for that was the only thing it could be, was brighter, closer. Dusty turned the bike towards the trees.

But when the front tire hit the softer dirt and loose gravel at the roadside, it slid out from under him, pulling the back tire around and pitching Dusty off the bike onto the ground while it slid several feet and came to a halt with the engine roaring its defense.

∾*∾

He splashed cold water on his face, dampening the initial surge of anger and the heat of arousal. As drunk as she was, could he truly be angry with her? She was too inebriated to know who she was with, or where she was; he knew her drunken states well by now. Better that he found out now that she had been thinking of someone else than afterward …right? He should talk to her…try again…

But when he came back into the room, it was to find Jennifer curled up on her side, snoring gently, sound asleep. Hans groaned, wiped his face and then grabbed his clothes from where they had fallen upon the floor. When he left the bedroom that night, he did not expect he would ever sleep there again.

⮜*⮞

Having collapsed into a tangled heap on the floor, not feeling any desire to move from the comfort of each other's arms, Stasio pulled the sheet from the bed and the nearest pillow as well. Now they lay together, sweating, panting, lounging in the afterglow of spent passion. Clara lay against his chest, curled like a child, cherishing his arms around her and the sensation of his breath against her forehead, in her hair.

He had not moved in many minutes. The candle on the table spluttered as the flame neared the end of its life. Thinking him asleep now, Clara murmured, "I love you too."

And Stasio, not to startle her, allowed himself a small, unseen smile and tears of joy as he nuzzled his face into her hair.

⮜*⮞

Over the hammering of his heart and the rumble of the bikes, Skip heard the pop of Dusty's tires when they hit the gravel and spun sideways out from under him. Skip looked back to see the worst of it.

The bike was sliding off the pavement.

Dusty was thrown clear to land in the middle of the road, landing on his left shoulder, his head impacting with the hardened surface, into the path of the headlights that were drawing ever nearer and would soon come around the nearest corner to reach them.

"Dusty!" Skip waved his hands frantically for his friend to crawl to the side of the road. It appeared that Dusty looked at him, but he did not obey the command.

For the Brit understood that, if the Aussie was to make it to freedom, he had to leave Dusty behind. His shoulder and head pained him too much, and even if he succeeded in crawling off the road before the car reached them, the rumbling, abandoned bike at the side would attract attention and a search. They could not count on the driver being friendly.

"Go," Dusty called, the effort filling his head with splitting pain.

Skip, as usual, listened to no one but himself. He dropped his bike and raced up the embankment to his friend's side.

"Go," Dusty barked when the Australian reached him. Skip tried to get his hands under Dusty's shoulders to drag him off the road. "Fuck!" the Brit howled, "I can't, Roo…you gotta go without me."

"No…you can do this…"

The headlights rounded the corner and were covering the last several hundred yards at a steady pace.

"Don't let me be the one you blame later…I'll only hold you back…now go."

"I'm not leaving you."

"Then we go back…or die."

Skip hesitated, feeling the impact of Dusty's words. He did not want to return to the Stalag. Did not want to face the possibility of death for another attempted escape. Nor was he sure he wanted to face Marcella after everything she had done to help him be free. But his code of honor would not allow him to abandon his friend and fallen soldier any more than Jamie's had allowed him to leave the fallen Frenchman…or to allow Buck to abandon Jamie. Skip finally understood.

Dusty's eyes rolled back into his head. Skip slapped his face to wake him and grunted, "We go back," his mind made up in favor of saving his friend. It might be a short-lived saving, but the possibility of life was worth the shot.

If they were fortunate, the driver or passengers in the oncoming car would be friendly.

There was no other choice. As the lights drew closer, the vehicle slowed. Skip left Dusty's side long enough to shove the second bike into the ditch, hoping that, over the particularly loud throbbing of the car's engine, the occupant would not hear the bikes or find the burlap packs. He squatted next to Dusty again.

"Gonna pick you up…"

Dusty's head lolled to one side. "Roo…I don't feel so…" His head fell limply upon his chest.

"Don't you die on me, wanker," Skip growled, standing with his burden, staring into the now stationary headlights. Not one, but four figures emerged from the vehicle, and from the bearing of the silhouettes, Skip knew they were in deep trouble.

Fuck.

"What have we here?" one of the heavily accented Germans said as he moved forward cautiously.

Any sudden moves and the Germans would shoot. Skip would not be able to outrun a bullet, with or without Dusty in his arms. But he had to speak carefully if they were to avoid being killed outright. Maybe they would not even be recognized as prisoners or soldiers, though Skip did not speak enough French to pass as a local either.

"He needs help," Skip replied, knowing his accent damned them both.

"Does he?" The speaker drew close enough for Skip to see his older, well-worked face, and the Oberstgruppenfuhrer stripes upon his jacket.

"Yeah...he does. We're on our way to Ste Marie..." The last words were said with a touch of a growl, revealing his frustration at his predicament.

"Not German," said one of the others with the stripes of a major, "and not French..."

Another with dark hair, who had emerged from the driver's seat, chortled. "One of Oberfuhrer von Hausen's mistakes, no doubt."

Skip did not understand the German dialogue, but he understood von Hausen, and the way the man laughed and the pitying look of regret upon the Oberstgruppenfuhrer's face, he knew that whatever they were discussing could not be good.

Behind him, a second car, an open-topped Jeep, had now caught up to the first car. A blonde man, lean and hollow of face, stood to see what was happening.

"I suspect so," the Oberstgruppenfuhrer said in English as he circled Skip, studying both men with all of the curiosity of a butcher studying a carcass.

The attention made Skip edgy and angry. "Well?"

"Are you in a hurry to get back?" the man asked with a dry laugh.

"Not particularly," he admitted, "but I don't want him to die."

"One of you more or less...you English are too concerned with your comrades..."

"Australian."

The man stopped his circle. "Pardon?

"Australian...not English."

"Australian, English, all the same." He turned to one of the other men. "Sturmbannfuhrer Ulrich, take these men to the Jeep; you and Untersturmfuhrer Bannon will take them where they belong."

Waving a pistol and shoving Skip forward, Ulrich growled, "Come on."

Skip neither argued nor resisted, as his concern for Dusty was too great. The escape had been well planned, hadn't it? It should have worked. No one could have foreseen the road conditions or this turn of events. It made him no less angry about failure, however, and as he climbed into the Jeep, careful of Dusty's head and shoulder, he kept asking himself what he had done wrong. How had he failed?

"Couple of wayward guests of Stalag 31, Ulrich was saying to the one called Bannon who had stayed with the Jeep.

The blond shook his head as he started the vehicle moving again. Over his shoulder, to the passengers in the rear, he said, "You don't realize how big of a mistake you have made."

It was nearly enough for Skip to strike him. Those words were a threat, but it seemed that more was implied in those words than what he deduced on the surface.

The hairs on the back of his neck stood up. He felt cold.

The Jeep bounced along, following the officer's car, and still Dusty did not wake. By the time they reached the Stalag, Skip was afraid it had been too long. Dusty was going to die and he could find no flaw in their planning or executions, except, perhaps, for driving too fast. He could not blame anyone for ratting them out this time. There were no easy culprits to blame except for the hand of fate.

Chapter 21
July 17, 1943

S parks emerged from the night latrine and returned to his bunk but he could not sleep. It would be dawn within a few hours, and thus time to rise and work, and he would undoubtedly regret not sleeping then, but it could not be helped. Every nerve in his body seemed too alive, too sensitive, and so he lay staring out the window at the few stars he could see.

With Ray returned to his bunk and asleep, Sparks was the first, other than the guards at the gate, to see the two vehicles arrive. They passed through the gates and stopped near the infirmary. The driver of the elegant sedan in front jumped out and banged on the infirmary door. They were undoubtedly German officers.

Sparks propped himself up on his elbows to see better.

From the Jeep, two shadows emerged and then someone carrying another. Even at this distance, Sparks recognized Skip's gate.

"Holy shite…"

"What?"

Jamie sat up on his bunk, having awakened to the sound of the vehicles' arrivals and having seen Spark's reaction to whatever was happening outside.

By now, Dengler had opened the infirmary door. "Skip…Dusty, I wager…a handful of Germans.

Jamie reached the window in time to see Skip carry Dusty through the infirmary door. All of the Germans save one followed. One stopped at the top of the stairs, spoke briefly to Dengler, and as both went inside, one of Dengler's assistants ran past them, down the stairs, in the direction of the officers' barracks.

"Doesn't look like they got very far," Jamie muttered, looking over his shoulder to see if anyone else had awakened. No one had.

"Damn lucky they weren't shot on sight," snorted Sparks.

Jamie nodded his agreement. But the night was still young. Plenty of time for shooting remained.

Shortly thereafter, Stetcher, Hirsch, and three others came into view, Stetcher's stick thrashing violently as he walked. The two within the barracks could make out shouting from inside the infirmary, but the words were unintelligible. Before long, two of the soldiers crashed out of the infirmary with Skip half dragged between them, heading into Camp 1 towards the Cooler. There was no sign of Dusty. Or of Dengler, Stetcher, or the visiting Germans.

Sparks looked at Jamie but neither said a word. They knew that, whatever was happening, the result was not going to be good.

☙*❧

The sounds of vehicles passing at such an odd hour of the night brought Hans to the sitting room window to watch, and when he saw the pair pull through the Stalag gates, instinct told him their arrival was no accident. No one came for him, however, as he hurriedly finished dressing, which set off alarms in his head. As Commandant, he should have been the first person to know of any scheduled, or unscheduled, ranking visitors or guests. By the time he stormed to the front door and threw it open, he was fuming again and nearly ran headlong into Wagner and a man he had not seen in a very long time. Oberstgruppenfuhrer Volheim.

"Sir," he stammered, the man's unexpected appearance there taking some of the bluster out of his fury.

"My apologies, Hans, for the ungodly hour. I've endured so many delays on my journey…I hoped to be here for dinner, to share Jennifer's birthday…"

Volheim did not wait for, or ask, for an invitation, but rather pushed into the house with an arrogant air. Hans stepped aside to allow passage, surprised that the man remembered Jennifer's birthday and flustered at his rude behavior. The Oberstgruppenfuhrer was as thin and gangly as ever, almost skeletal, and when he smiled it filled the room with the same eerie creepiness as a dead man's smiling skull would have. The two had known each other for so long, traveled in the same social circles for longer than Hans could remember, that Hans rarely made note of the man's disturbing aura, but tonight he noticed, especially when Volheim removed his gloves, tucked them under his arm, and gave him that death's head smile.

That smile made Hans grateful that the man had not arrived earlier as he had planned. With the way the evening had gone, the General's presence would have made things even more disastrous.

Hans gestured to Wagner to close the door, and after doing so, the young soldier waited there for further instructions. Volheim had asked him to come, and so he did not think leaving without being dismissed would be a good choice.

"What may I do for you, sir? I didn't know you were coming…"

"No, you wouldn't have. I'm doing a tour of our facilities and offices…inspections, you know." The man smiled smoothly, looking around the room with eyes that scrutinized everything. Hans knew he should have expected an inspection after his meeting with Ulrich, but something about this visit did not sit well with him. "Hirsch is seeing to our accommodations; I hope you do not object to a few more bodies in your barracks…"

What Hans heard in the man's tone was the hopes that Hans would instead invite him and his men to stay in his home. There was but a single extra bedroom, however, and given Jennifer's behavior of late, Hans wanted Volheim nowhere near her. "No…of course I don't mind…" he said, feigning ignorance of the attempted hint. He felt little better about the man staying in camp, however, and on second thought decided it was better if Volheim was here, under his roof and watchful eye. "But there is room for you here if you would prefer…" The man had lied to him, to his wife, before. Hans wanted him where he could watch him.

"Why thank you, Hans," the man started, his smile wider.

Quite footfalls on the stairs, unsteady and slow, announced Jennifer's descent. She clung to the railing, the only way to avoid tumbling down the stairs, and her eyes were glazed and sleep-filled. "Hansy? Who are you…?"

Her eyes locked onto Volheim across the several feet separating them, but he might as well have been standing next to her for the horror she expressed. She had not seen the object of her nightmares for a long time, and she had tried desperately to believe that here, in France, she would be safe from the man who had repeatedly raped and lied to her behind her husband's back. Yet here he was, far from Berlin, standing in her home to torment her all over again. Hans barely reached her in time to keep her from hitting her head on the stone stairs as her face drained of color and she fainted with a soft, choking sound.

"I say..." Volheim took a step nearer. He seemed less concerned for her welfare than curious, and Hans wished he would leave.

"She has not been well," he quickly explained, making excuses both for her appearance and her fainting. "She is not supposed to be out of bed." Her heart was fluttering violently against his chest, her breathing quick and shallow, and Hans knew without a doubt that she was terrified. It further suggested that something more than lies stood between him and his commanding officer. The notion made his skin crawl.

The man looked her over with what Hans considered to be a leer and said, coolly, "Then by all means...see to your lovely wife, Oberfuhrer. I am not here to be an imposition." Hans had a feeling that being an imposition was exactly why Volheim had come. "I think it best I quarter in the barracks...in case her condition is contagious...but I do expect a tour of your facilities in the morning."

"Yes, sir," Hans replied.

Wagner opened the door as Volheim neared. The man stopped there, glanced back with a haughty lift of his chin as he put his gloves back on, and said, "By the way...I brought two of your guests back. You might want to see to their proper...care."

Hans blinked. Two of his men? Not knowing about Skip and Dusty's escape attempt, as that would not have become obvious until morning appell, Hans' at first assumed the two men to either be soldiers on leave or else the pair of prisoners who had disappeared some weeks back. He was curious as to how they had come to be in Volheim's custody but decided it was a matter best dealt with after putting Jennifer to bed...and seeing the two escapees himself. "I will, sir. Right away."

Volheim nodded with a grunt and went out without looking back. Wagner, however, did meet Hans' gaze for a moment, long enough for Hans to realize that he was not the only one with misgivings about the Oberstgruppenfuhrer's visit. Knowing he was not alone in suspicion and fear was not so reassuring this time.

☙*❧

Clara awoke on the floor to the first feeble rays of dawn upon her face, and though she had hoped to find Stasio beside her, she was alone. That was no surprise, as a lifetime of farming had instilled in him the need to rise with the sun. She wished, however, that just once he would sleep in beside her.

A loud pounding echoed through the floorboards and she realized that the sound was what had roused her. It seemed too early for anyone to be knocking, but given the events of the previous evening, perhaps it should not surprise her. She stood, dressed hastily, and made it as far as the upper landing of the staircase as Stasio, shirtless and disheveled, came from the kitchen to start up the stairs. He waited for her to come down, his hand outstretched with a troubled expression on his face.

"What...?"

He enfolded her against his chest, an action meant to be soothing, but from his agitation, she presumed it was done more to soothe himself. "Did they wake you?"

"Something did. Who was...?"

"Sturmbannfuhrer Moretti...and the day's work crew."

She looked into his face. "So early?"

"I'd say nearly double the workers too...and there is someone else with him...a young SS officer I have never seen before."

She frowned. From his trembling, she knew there was more that he was not telling her. Rather, he held her head against his shoulder, stroking her hair. Dusting her lips across his skin, she asked, "What did they say? Why are they...?"

"This...Ulrich, I think Moretti called him...he wants to search the house, the premises...some sort of inspection of the Stalag and all facilities the prisoners have access to. I told them to search the outer buildings if he wishes, but that the prisoners never come into the house beyond the kitchen...and that my family was asleep. I threatened that von Hausen would hear about it if you were disturbed after whatever happened last night. Moretti went ghostly," he paused, "and relayed the message, or some version of it. This Ulrich looked amused, contemptuous, but he agreed...though I suspect they will insist on looking soon enough..."

"It's safe..."

"Mon Dieu, Clara, is it? For how much longer? You are so certain you are untouchable..."

"As long as Hans..."

"He cannot protect you forever, particularly if there is a threat against him as you believe. There have been too many close calls...they are growing suspicious and you know it."

Clara drew back enough that she was no longer in his embrace, but his hands remained upon her. "What am I to do? I cannot stop...not now..."

"Then what? When is it too late? Can't you stop for a little while, until suspicion fades?"

"Let us go away from here then, a few weeks...you and I..."

"To where? Who will tend the farm...?"

"Marcella can..."

"Who will mind her? She is a child..."

Now Clara removed herself from his contact, anger and hurt coloring her face. "Is that what I am then? A child? One that you would send into the wolf's den and yet you would shelter Marcella?"

Stasio looked stung by her pain and the words he had not anticipated. Whatever had happened last night, she blamed him. He took a step backward. "What happened last night, ma cherie...?"

"Nothing," she muttered, moving past him into the kitchen. Through the open screen door and window, she could see men already at work in the field. She grimaced, feeling in Stasio's silence the bite of her words upon him. There had been no secrets between them before, no hiding anything. Lately, however, the secrets had begun to pile up, and that she was refusing to speak freely hurt him. She stopped at the door, noting that, while there were familiar faces among the workers, none of them were Sparks.

Thank God for that, she thought as she wrapped her arms around herself.

In the awkward silence, Stasio stood still for many moments and then went upstairs without pursuing her. For some reason, Clara found that more painful than an argument would have been, and by the time he returned, fully dressed, she was crying softly. She heard him pause in the kitchen doorway before approaching her and hesitantly putting his arms around her.

It took considerable willpower not to collapse against him.

"I should not have asked you to...should never have sent you, aimé. I wanted to believe, as you did, that you would be safe..."

"I danced," she said quietly. "More than I should have, perhaps..."

"So Zaline said; I am happy you had the chance to enjoy..."

"There was an incident...with Hans and his wife...he tried to...he kissed me...and she saw it." Now she did move as though to shrink into him completely, lose herself in his embrace and strength. "I should not have let him…"

"Let him? How could you have stopped him?" There was a fine line, he knew, in the game she played with von Hausen, keeping him on the hook and interested, keeping his trust and protection, without giving too much of herself. A kiss was a small price to pay.

"I don't know…"

"And he has kissed you before…hasn't he?"

She sobbed, aching to realize what he must think of her, what he must believe she had done in the past with the Oberfuhrer to gain so much favor and influence with him. "No…not like that. Never like that. I made it clear to him when we first…that it would not be allowed…that I couldn't…that I'm yours…but last night…I should not have…but he was so…and I think he meant to…"

"Rape you? Did he?"

She shook her head with a deep breath. "No. But he…perhaps he would have. I did not try to stop him…I was afraid and I almost…betrayed you…"

Stasio tightened his embrace, closing his eyes as he listened. The sense of betrayal she felt for a kiss, and whatever von Hausen had tried to force upon her, supported his belief that she had remained faithful to him in all of those hours and days she spent in the Oberfuhrer's company. Her loyalty increased the love he felt for her.

"I sent you," he murmured. "You were reluctant to go but I…and I am deeply sorry, ma cherie. You did what you had to do…for me…my family…the war…and it has caused you great pain. I cannot apologize for that, nor atone enough, but don't you think…if he did these things…how much longer can you be safe here?"

She did not answer but he did not expect her to. All she did was bury her face against his neck. If he was the man she believed he was, Hans would be more protective of her now, as restitution for his mistakes. If he was not, then she would soon be lost.

Finally, Stasio said. "I am sorry, Clara. If you will…be careful with the radio…for a few more weeks…once the last planting is done, you and I shall go away from here. Brest, perhaps. It is the best I can offer in repayment."

Now she looked at him with a tear stained face and swollen red eyes. "You do not hate me for…?"

"Hate you? Mon Dieu…what for? Something you could not control? Something forced upon you by…? Never, ma cherie. I could never hate you. And I thank God he did not hurt you."

No more than I have hurt myself, she thought, reveling in her relief at his love and devotion. "I should make sure it is…I should prepare a proper…"

"Allow me…"

"You do not need…"

He tilted her face up to his and kissed her soft mouth. "I know. That is why I will. In the meantime, see to the other business, before Ulrich comes knocking again."

"Yes." She returned his kiss with a tiny smile and retreated upstairs, glad that she had come clean about Hans, but wondering if she should have said anything about Sparks.

And she regretted again that she had not yet mentioned the child.

Chapter 22
July 17-23, 1943

As fortune had it, Sister Isabelle came to the house that day and smuggled the radio off the premises before Sturmbannfuhrer Ulrich conducted his search without his noticing her visit. It was a more thorough search than the previous two Germans had conducted. The Italian followed, answering questions but not participating or hindering the search. Clara followed as well, doing her best to appear nothing more than a housewife concerned with the invasion of her home. Neither Moretti nor Ulrich suspected anything and found nothing unusual, not even finding her hiding places, which was a great relief to both Clara and Stasio.

Ulrich also failed to notice that Clara understood every word spoken between him and the Italian. Moretti translated for her, for those things he thought she needed to know or questions that were meant for her to answer, but the rest of the conversation remained in German between the two, intentionally attempting to leave her out.

This unique opportunity afforded her information she would not otherwise have gained. The four-man delegation from Berlin had come to France to inspect all of the Reich's interests and they seemed particularly interested in the operations of Stalag 31. Ulrich was evasive and answered few of Moretti's questions directly, such that by the time the two left the farmhouse with their henchmen in tow, Clara knew she was not the only one suspicious and uncomfortable in Ulrich's company. His behavior brought to mind the intercepted radio transmission, but it had not been Ulrich's voice she had heard that night. Of that she was certain.

More importantly, however, she concluded that their main purpose in being in Ste Marie was to investigate Commandant von Hausen, and the real purpose in invading Stasio's home was to learn more about his connections to Clara, to figure out what, if anything, he was hiding about his relationship with the Frenchwoman. Every mention of the Commandant in the conversation was met with contempt from Ulrich. He might be dangerous himself, but she was sure he was the spearhead of something much more unpleasant and Hans was likely to bear the brunt of it.

It was Mila, on the one day that week that she came to the farmhouse, who gave concrete weight to Clara's suspicions. Mila reported how each of the four officers was given multiple tours of the camp, of the town, and even of the von Hausen home since none were staying there. Each spent a considerable amount of time interviewing the Stalag staff, particularly Hans. They dined at the von Hausen table every evening, and although Jennifer was pardoned from attending due to the illness Hans claimed she had, Mila was compelled to endure every meal with her father and the strangers. She was rarely spoken to, mostly ignored, but the time spent allowed her to describe each of the four men to Clara in detail.

Three of the four were men Hans knew, if not well then at least by reputation. The fourth spoke little. Of those three, Hans only seemed comfortable around the young Untersturmfuhrer Bannon. Mila remembered Volheim from her early childhood in Berlin; he was a man she feared, a man who caused her mother great upset. He was also a man her father seemed especially leery of.

Mila reported that both of her parents were moodier than usual. Not knowing about the late night events during her mother's party, she assumed the tension was caused by the officers, and by a conversation she had overheard when eavesdropping on the men smoking below her bedroom window; there was the possibility that the family would be relocated out of Ste Marie. They might be moving back to Berlin. It was a move she did not want, preferring to remain in the country, with Clara who gave her life some small measure of stability. She also expressed the wish to stay with Clara and Stasio for as long as Volheim was in Ste Marie, but it was a wish Mila knew her mother would never allow.

To her young eyes, neither of her parents seemed keen on returning to Berlin, despite her father's praise of the city and her mother's frequent complaints that there was no 'society' in Ste Marie. They had talked about returning to Berlin after the war, now both seemed afraid of the idea. The only upside to Volheim's visit was that her father was more attentive to Jennifer. It was the first time in a long time she had not heard daily fighting between her parents.

Clara could imagine why Hans might not want to return to Berlin. If the feeling she got from him was any indicator, there was trouble brewing, and a summons to Berlin could mean a death sentence…for him, his wife, and his child. She did not see him at all that week, except for brief glimpses across the field and through the Stalag fence. It was just as well, for her presence would likely have caused him nothing but difficulties. Besides she was not looking forward to their next meeting. This time separated from him was for the best. Everything was changing, in the camp, between her and Stasio, between Hans and his wife if what Mila said was correct, and most certainly between Hans and Clara.

Without the Commandant to cater to, or his daughter to tutor, and no feasible means to attempt a radio dispatch to London about this turn of events, Clara funneled her energy into Stasio, the farm, and the Resistance, which was forced to operate more cautiously than usual with the presence of the Oberstgruppenfuhrer so near.

And though Sparks worked the farm three days that week, Clara resisted approaching him. She could barely bring herself to look at him without remembering his arms about her. It meant she had not seen his longing, his disappointment, his concern for her. She could not even get the rest of the parts for his radio to him as the Germans had severely limited all prisoner contact with the villagers.

That was a condition that Stetcher, no doubt, found late in coming. The Gestapo officer was at the farm only one day with Oberstgruppenfuhrer Volheim, a man Clara disliked on sight as he leered and sneered at her his entire stay. Likely he thought that if she was Hans' mistress, as so many believed, she would accommodate him as well. Fortunately, she did not have the need to find out, since he left the farm after only a few hours and did not return. But more than once during that time, Stetcher would point at her, speaking quiet words she could not hear; by the time they left, Clara had no doubt that the layer of suspicion about her had grown thicker.

Perhaps they could not wait for the planting to be done. Perhaps it was best if she and Stasio left now.

She could not wait much longer. From the deepening concern in Stasio's eyes as the week waned, she knew he knew it too.

He could encourage her to go away without him, but she refused to leave him…not now. Not ever.

❧*❦

In the camp itself, it was the nearest to a week in hell that any of the men had yet to experience there. As Stetcher had threatened so many times, they were summoned to work an hour earlier, rising while the sky was still dark. Mealtimes were shortened and they were ordered into their barracks as soon as the evening meal was over. Lights out came an hour earlier, before the sun had fully set. More men were put to work each day, even if it was only for something as tedious as raking dirt from one place to another. They were discouraged from fraternizing while working, not allowed to speak with those who ran the farm except to ask for water, and that was only permitted once before lunch and once after. They were prevented from speaking with their jailers unless it was in response to a direct question or it was about their work.

When Moretti commented that an officer's camp should not be run like the camps in the east, Stetcher hit him so hard across the face with his walking stick that he lost a tooth and required stitches across his cheek. He was kept off duty for two days because of it. Volheim had watched without expression. The Italian was sure he was not the only one hoping that the representatives of the Red Cross or some other such organization would turn up for their own surprise inspection and set matters right.

Jamie was witness to that episode of brutality and had been the one to tend to Moretti until Dengler had come. The incident left a bitter taste in his mouth and stomach. Such issues were beyond his ability to affect; it was a matter for von Hausen to address, but if the Commandant did anything, it was impossible to tell. Since nothing changed after Moretti returned to duty, it appeared that no words had been spoken, either to Volheim or to Stetcher. Or perhaps Volheim's command trumped von Hausen's.

The Commandant was rarely seen by the prisoners that week, which left them at the mercy of Stetcher and Hirsch. When he was seen, it was always in the company of one or more of the SS officers, usually Volheim or Ulrich. Vic described the Oberstgruppenfuhrer as a gargoyle, an epitaph which stuck, as he was always watching, leering, saying little but always wearing a deadly air of danger and disdain. He would cross the parade yard or stand at the gate, watching, occasionally speaking quiet words to von Hausen, but mostly he watched as the gargoyles watched from a church's rafters.

There was an air of discomfort surrounding the Commandant in those times; everyone in Camp 1 noticed. Many felt sorry for the man though few would admit it. The Oberfuhrer's efforts to provide some degree of humane treatment for his charges were met with hostility, ridicule, and disdain by his superiors. The men in both camps began to realize how good life had been compared to what it could be. They each knew the opinions and influence of Volheim on von Hausen did not bode well for the future of the Stalag inmates.

It was Sparks' theory that the camp was being prepared for new leadership...potentially Stetcher...which was a possibility they feared. That the von Hausens might be subjected to whatever fate awaited officers who failed to meet the Reich's expectations was sobering. For those like Jennifer and Mila, who simply did not belong, a shining future could not be expected.

The men in Camp 1 worked. They slept. They did not risk their weekly Flight Meeting and limited their poker games to brief, non-betting ones. Even Vic did not have the heart for them. Ray never spoke, only stared from time to time at the von Hausen home through the barrack's window. It was clear to the others that he had fallen under the spell of the Commandant's wife, though just how far under he had fallen no one knew. They shared words of warning meant to steer him clear of vice without them knowing it was too late for that.

Sparks, steeped in melancholia, was obsessed with making his radio work without being caught, giving him no chance for solitary contemplation. Clara had made mention of a bomb she believed was meant for von Hausen, either to be delivered for his use or to be used against him, but Sparks was unable to access his radio to confirm the rumor. Nothing in the camp suggested an answer either way.

And in the Cooler, Skip paced, oblivious to the outer world's goings-on, except for the daily notes that Bonny managed to slip to him when the Padre delivered his meals. He was angry again. Angry that the escape had failed, angry that the failure had brought so much misery to the camp, though he was reasonably certain that he was not responsible for the SS officers coming here. He was also angry that he could not place blame anywhere except, unacceptably, on fate.

But at least he had not yet been executed, a fate he was sure was coming. He was relieved Dusty had only suffered a dislocated shoulder and minor concussion, relieved that Dengler insisted on keeping Dusty in the infirmary for the week to monitor his condition so that the Brit could not be pushed into labor beneath the hot, late July sun.

And for once Skip was thankful for the week in the miserable Cooler, as it kept him from conflict with the four visiting SS officers, conflict that would undoubtedly result in a hasty death.

He did not, however, have any idea what lay in store when he was released at the week's end. If he lived that long.

Chapter 23
July 24, 1943

After one of the worst weeks he had ever endured, Hans was relieved to watch the four SS officers prepare for departure. He hoped his relief was not evident upon his face, nor his puzzlement and disappointment.

He supposed he was not surprised by this turn of events, the decision to close Stalag 31. Compared to many camps, it was small and did not produce anything of value to contribute to the war effort. Indeed, though they provided their own food with the help of the Arnaud farm, their needs for munitions, uniforms, other materials and even manpower, were a drain the Reich could not afford at this stage in the war. With the Allies advancing around them, the Reich had either to close the camp and move its prisoners elsewhere, or risk having the soldiers stationed there captured and the prisoners freed. Closing the camp was, Hans agreed, possibly the wisest thing to do.

But he was unhappy about the thought of leaving Ste Marie, for he understood well enough, without any words being spoken, that not only would he be leaving this post, he would be leaving behind a great deal more. Particularly Clara, whom he had been forced to push aside in his mind all week as he appeased the SS officers and struggled to appear to be the loving, doting husband of an ailing wife who obviously did not want his company.

A third vehicle, an armored transport, had arrived yesterday to extract the first of the officers and staff from Stalag 31. A total of seven men. As far as Hans knew, he was the only one to have been told of the upcoming closure; the explanation for removing the soldiers was that men were needed at the front and thus all camps were enduring staff reductions. He did not think any of his subordinates believed the story, but he had been instructed to make sure that his officers supported the official explanation until it was deemed time to make the official announcement.

At the moment, near the front of the string of vehicles, Volheim was involved in conversation with Dengler, who looked displeased with whatever he was being told. At the rear, on the steps of the officers' quarters, Stetcher appeared to be in a heated discussion with Ulrich, but that was one conversation Hans did not want to hear or be involved in. Haupsturmfuhrer Heinrich was sitting in the front car, looking bored as he waited for Volheim to get into the vehicle.

Untersturmfuhrer Bannon finished loading the last of the luggage into the Jeep, nearest where Hans waited for whatever would be required next.

"That's all, sir," Bannon called. Volheim waved to indicate he had heard and would be along shortly. Alone with the Commandant, Bannon half turned to Hans and said, "It has been good to see you again, Oberfuhrer."

"Likewise." He shook the younger man's hand. He liked the youngster well enough when they had first met in Berlin, found him to be intelligent, trustworthy, and dependable, but the thought of finding someone like that in Volheim's company was disconcerting. "How did you fall into his orbit?" he murmured in a low voice.

Bannon shrugged as he lit a cigarette. "I go where they send me." He emphasized the word they, and it occurred to Hans that Bannon might be on some assignment unrelated to whatever Volheim was doing. "They wanted me to deliver a message."

Hans felt the hairs on the back of his neck prickle to attention. He wanted to glance towards Ulrich, but settled for side-eying Volheim. It was Bannon who cast a quick look over his shoulder at Ulrich who had descended the steps but was still conversing with Stetcher.

"Be careful."

"I always am."

Bannon scowled wryly. "Not careful enough. Something's brewing back home. I don't know what…they don't either," he tilted his head towards Volheim. "Whatever it is, you're at the heart of it."

"Sturmbannfuhrer Ulrich! Let's go!" Volheim shouted. He cast Hans a cold look that undermined the years of perceived friendship Hans had believed they shared. It looked more and more that Jennifer's tale of Volheim's lies and betrayal might not be false. Caught between that look and Bannon's words, Hans felt frozen, inside and out. He had not needed the warning; he had guessed long ago, as Stetcher began to be called away on frequent business trips, that something was happening. The news of the camp's impending closure set off further alarms in his head. Bannon's words were merely confirmation of his suspicions.

"Oberfuhrer," Volheim said, close enough now to offer his hand. "Your hospitality and generosity have been appreciated. Please tell your wife that seeing her again has been the highlight of this dreary tour of business and I hope she recovers soon."

Hans bristled internally but hid his annoyance. Volheim's tone of voice was familiar in more ways than one. "Yes," was all he said as he shook the offered hand. Volheim might miss seeing her, but Hans knew his wife would not miss him. He still did not know precisely what had passed between them, but he knew enough to recognize that she was violently afraid of the man. It made him ache to think about what the man he had positioned to protect her might have done. If he had been the man to rape her, as Hans now suspected, he prayed the man would never again have a peaceful night's rest and would meet an untimely, and excruciating, death.

Volheim gave a short laugh. "Now Hans, no hard feelings about the camp."

"Oh no," Hans said with a shake of his head, relieved to hear the closing of the truck door behind him as Ulrich took the driver's seat of the transport vehicle. Hans stepped aside to allow Bannon into the driver's side of the Jeep. "I understand the strategic and economic necessity. The Reich needs to best allocate its resources."

"I'm glad you understand. I'll make my report to headquarters and be in touch. With luck, we shall meet in Berlin soon."

"With luck," Hans replied, wishing that his luck would keep him and his family far away from Volheim and Berlin.

The Oberstgruppenfuhrer got into the front car, closed the door, and rolled down the window. "Good day, Oberfuhrer."

To which Hans replied, "Have a good trip."

Nearby, Stetcher stood with arms crossed, his walking stick crooked into the crease of his arm, as he rocked back and forth on his heels. Dengler remained where he was, displeasure still on his face. As the cars began to roll, Bannon caught Hans' eye and gestured to him as though in salute but in what Hans' was sure was a reminder.

And on the porch of the von Hausen residence, Jennifer appeared, clinging to the doorframe, to watch the cars drive east. She thought she saw Volheim looking at her and she squeezed her eyes shut to block the image from her memory.

Volheim, in turn, smiled smugly and rolled up his window against the dry summer dust.

"I hope you're right about this," Ronny muttered as he shoved another bunch of dirt behind him to Ollie. Ollie, in turn, sent the dirt to the guy behind him and so on until it was scattered back some fifteen feet. There were six of them together, six men trying to tunnel from Barracks C, under the fence, and up into the bushes that separated Stalag 31 from the farm. They had been working on the tunnel for so long that some of them had begun to believe it would never be finished or that they would be caught before that day came.

And Ronny, for one, could not shake the feeling that something was wrong with their efforts. They were on the uphill slope now, and it was late. They had been digging for most of the night, believing that this was their last night of it. Soon they would reach the end, and once they did, they would be free. It was stifling in the tunnel, the men's body heat and breath filling the tight space, and with only two lanterns to aid them, it was perpetually dim, giving them no clear sense of the passage of time.

"Time?" Ronny asked.

"Forget time," snorted Ollie, the architect of this project. "By my calculations, we should be there. Just keep digging."

Hans glanced at Moretti from the corner of his eye. The Italian was unusually quiet this morning, but then again, Hans was as well. For the Commandant, it stemmed from the fact that as soon as she had known Volheim was gone, Jennifer had fallen to drink more heavily than ever, rendering herself incapacitated much of the previous day. He had been proud of her for staying sober for the entire week, had hoped that, as the sickness of withdrawal passed she would have given up drink for good. But such was not the case and she seemed now to be worse than ever.

"Stetcher was not very pleased with your decision, Oberfuhrer?"

Hans did not make the reply that first came to mind. Instead, he kept walking, the two of them headed to the Cooler to release Skip at last. "Henderson's week of punishment is up. So is Camp One's. He said a week, and a week it will be. It is time to return to a normal routine."

"I agree," the Italian said with a nod. Normal, he knew, was not going to last much longer.

"I'm pleased I'm not the only man here with sense." Hans wondered, if it were not for the war, if he and this Italian would have found it possible to be friends.

They stopped in front of the Cooler as Moretti fumbled with the keys at his waist in search of the right one. Hans rapped once upon the metal door.

"What?" barked the voice with sleepy annoyance.

"It is time to rejoin the others," Hans grunted, irritated at speaking with one of the men who had bedded his wife.

"About fucking time…"

❧*❧

Ronny wiped his brow again, eager for a breath of fresh air. What he wouldn't do for Dusty's mining expertise. They should have consulted that man before even starting.

"Feels like we're nearly through," he said over his shoulder.

❧*❧

Hans pulled the door open as soon as it was unlocked. He looked Henderson over; in spite of needing a shave and being wet with dirty sweat, the Aussie did not seem any worse for wear. Skip was putting his shoes back on, which caused Hans to frown, as usually such items as laces were disallowed when prisoners were confined, lest they tried to hang themselves with them. He wondered at Stetcher's failure, or if the Gestapo officer had hoped Skip would do just that. It would have rid the camp of a troublemaker that Hans continued to tolerate. If Skip had hung himself, Hans was willing to bet that Stetcher would have found a way to blame him.

Hans had heard Volheim's version of finding the two escapees, was surprised the man had not killed them instead of bringing them back to Stalag 31, but he was mostly curious as to how the two had pulled off the escape. Someone had repaired the cut fencing before it could be found, and Dusty had refused to reveal their secret. If any of the Germans had learned anything, about the fence, about the bikes and packs which had been scavenged by locals before the Germans could retrieve them, they had not shared the information with the Oberfuhrer. The how of it no longer mattered, since soon the Aussie would be sent elsewhere and would no longer be his problem.

"Bit early, isn't it?" Skip grunted.

Hans shrugged, too weary to be baited today. "I'm a busy man, Henderson."

"So why'd you come when your goons...?"

"I wanted to tell you in person that it is in your best interest not to attempt this again. I applaud your ingenuity...but for once, I think you should add wisdom to the list of attributes you possess and practice."

"What...?"

❧*❧

"Yes!" hissed Ronny happily as his fingers broke through the surface. "We're through!"

❧*❧

"There have been changes this past week, changes you will be apprised of in due course. If you think Stetcher has been hard on you, you will not like the results of any further..."

He noted a peculiar look on the Australian's face as the man tried not to stare at the ground some five feet beyond Hans. The Oberfuhrer turned to see what was of interest and Moretti stepped sideways to do likewise.

All three watched in the beginning light of dawn as first one hand broke through the surface, then a second. Skip started to speak, wanting to warn whoever was tunneling into their presence, but a raised hand from the Oberfuhrer kept him silent. Before long, the hole was wide enough for Ronny's broad shoulders to fit through.

He popped up and took a quick assessment of his surroundings, instantly realizing they had emerged within the camp's perimeter, having dug too far north instead of east. Just as quickly, he realized he was being watched by Skip, Moretti, and Oberfuhrer von Hausen, all staring with confusion, astonishment, and amusement.

"Shit..." he said, trying to laugh instead of panic. He pulled himself up through the hole and sat on its edge with his feet dangling within. "It's a damn good thing I'm not a miner," he quipped.

The others within the tunnel, realizing that something was wrong, began to scuttle backward.

"Helluva miscalculation," Skip scoffed. Ronny was not going to get away with this, for all of the joking. "Easier ways to get into the Cooler..." He hoped to make it sound like the tunnel had been planned to break him out, which might lessen the pilot's punishment.

Ronny shrugged. "Faulty intelligence, you know..."

"Yeah...I know how that is." Skip knew that feeling and failure all too well.

"Captain." Hans motioned to the still open Cooler door.

Groaning, Ronny got to his feet. "Must I?"

"It is either this or I leave your punishment to Sturmbannfuhrer Stetcher."

"No...I wouldn't want that. How long?"

"Full week, the standard for prisoners caught attempting..."

"A week?" he whined. "It's not like we..."

"We? Who else is in there?" He squatted down to take a look but could see nothing in the darkness.

Ronny shook his head. "No one...just me...me and my intelligence sources..."

Hans stood and cleared his throat, cutting Ronny off. "Sturmbannfuhrer, search the barracks and find where this tunnel originated. Every man in that barracks will be enlisted to fill it, whether he helped dig it or not."

"Yes, sir," Moretti said with a salute. Ronny was prodded into the tiny room Skip had just vacated; Skip clasped him on the shoulder with sympathy and Ronny shrugged sheepishly, still laughing at himself. The door closed as the usual morning ritual of Stetcher blasting the German National Anthem over the speakers began to rouse the entire Stalag.

Skip was surprised to note that he was not the only one to bristle at the sound. From Moretti, it was expected, as it had never been a secret that the Italian had little love for his German superiors. No one had ever quite figured out why the Italian was serving in the German ranks except that it had something to do with living up to his father's expectations. But just for a moment, before the dispassionate mask fell once more over von Hausen's face, Skip caught a hint of loathing there. Skip almost scowled, almost asked what it meant, but instead kept silent and followed the officers into the appell yard where he joined the other men from his barracks.

Most gave him a wide berth, even George, or they chose to ignore him. But Ray did not shrink away when he passed, Bonny smiled, and Jamie nodded in greeting. Sparks murmured, "Hey." Four friendly parties, or at least four non-hostile ones, was more than Skip had expected. His actions had not gotten anyone killed thus far, but he had left without sharing the plan with others, without giving them a chance as well, and that was commonly treated as taboo within the officers' barracks. What pleased Skip most, however, was seeing Dusty in his usual place, his arm in a sling but looking no worse for his ordeal. The Brit grinned and Skip relaxed.

Stetcher was reading off the day's work assignments, glaring to the side of the yard where Hans watched. The man was annoyed about leniency being restored to the camp routine, and from the sounds of the assignments, Stetcher had not been the one to make the day's duty roster. Sparks was assigned milking, a duty which clearly gave him mixed feelings. Though Farmer and KC were included in the farming today, and Bonny sent to the Commandant's garden in Ronny's place, the rest of the officers were not employed. From George's expression, and from the looks on some of the other men's faces as they glanced at one another, it was clear they understood that something unusual was transpiring.

Not as unusual, however, as the number of Camp 1 men who were sent to work in the various labor sheds in place of Camp 2 workers.

"What's up?" Vic shouted to Stetcher, ignoring the man's penchant for hating interruptions. The Gestapo officer, touchier than usual this morning, had his pistol pointed at the Scot before he finished speaking.

"Sturmbannfuhrer!" demanded Hans.

Stetcher hesitated, startled, as though he had forgotten von Hausen's presence or had not expected his intervention. He did not apologize, merely holstered his pistol before replying, "There is something else they are required to do today."

It was more of an explanation than expected, and a look passed between the two Campbells, both wondering if word of the Camp 2 plans had fallen into German hands. There had been no further exchange of information with the French yet, no arrangements made with the Resistance, but that did not mean planning had not continued. Stetcher's tone hinted at something malicious, and from

Camp 2, Hirsch could be heard barking orders though most men in Camp 1 could not understand what was being said.

Voice low, Jamie muttered, "They're being sent to repair the bridge…"

"What the fuck for?" snorted Vic. "That thing has been down as long as I've been here…"

"Longer than that," corrected Sparks.

Bonny rubbed his eyes. "Must be planning to use it."

"Maybe," said Jamie with a scowl. Ray was staring straight ahead at attention, facing Stetcher, as though the rest of the dialogue did not interest him, with an expression that concerned Jamie.

"Where's Ronny?" asked Taffy.

"In the Cooler," Skip replied. Some heads turned as though he had spoken out of turn and Skip shrugged. "Let's just say his excavation attempt did not go as planned either."

"Damn it," barked George. "Doesn't anyone ever listen to me?"

Jamie refused to look at him as he replied, "Apparently not."

Chapter 24
July 24, 1943

When Stasio came into the barn, approaching him for the first time in memory, Sparks thought there would be harsh words spoken over the intimate dances shared with Clara. Instead, the older man set down an empty pail beside him and picked up the full one, in the exchange depositing a small parcel onto Sparks' lap. Surprised, he looked into Stasio's face.

"She'll be going there soon...to see him..." Stasio grunted before leaving the barn with the pail of milk.

Whether he told Sparks because he knew she and the Scot were friendly or something more, Sparks did not know but he hurried through the milking so he could return to the barracks with his bundle as quickly as possible. He had barely passed through the gates when he saw her arrive, dressed in the white of surrender, expression determined and sad. His heart went out to her, a woman caught, it seemed, between the pull of three men. One of whom she loved, one of whom held power over her life, and the third...

Sparks did not know precisely what he was to her, but at the moment it did not matter. What mattered was her safety, and he did not believe she would find that in the Commandant's office.

Alone in Hans' office, Clara debated sitting but she did not. The thought of being seated when he arrived, of feeling him tower over her, was a frightening one today. Nor did she remove her hat as she usually did when here. It would have been a signal of comfort that she did not feel. It was safer to stand, to be ready to fight, or run, though if she did either she might be met with a bullet. The thought that he might kill her was a sad one.

She paced instead, but as that only made her feel more on edge, she stopped to study the various pictures upon his wall, particularly the one of Hans and the Fuhrer. Hans' smile in that photo looked forced, rather like it had been added as an afterthought once the photo had been developed. The two men were shaking hands as if closing an agreement. Also in the photo were Oberstgruppenfuhrer Volheim and a much younger Untersturmfuhrer Bannon. The gargoyle nature of the older man as he sneered in Hans' direction was more evident than ever there.

Beside it was a picture of a much younger Hans standing on a beach Clara recognized. Marseilles. The thought of that beach brought up the many long conversations she had shared with the German Commandant. That, in turn, brought tears to her eyes.

Lost. All of it was lost.

She looked away from that photo, that handsome young man who had been untainted by the worries of war and an unfaithful wife, and instead looked to the one on the other side of the Hitler one. Hans and his family, taken when Mila was little more than four or five. Mila sat atop a small horse, wearing the grin of a child on top of the world. Hans and Jennifer stood arm in arm, beaming proudly, and from the looks of it, the woman had been with child when the photo had been taken. In the rear, a large structure loomed, one that Clara presumed was Hans' Bavarian estate though he had never identified it as such. The love between husband and wife was evident. Now that was lost as well.

That one, too, was difficult to look at, so she found herself gravitating back to the photo on the beach, fingers touching the image of Hans just as the man entered through the door beside her. She did not look at him, not wanting him to see the tears she quickly blinked away. He closed the door and stopped behind her, near enough that she could feel the heat and solidity of his form without the need for physical contact.

Hidden in the back stall of the latrine, where Vic happened to be on duty and thus could warn him of approaching Germans, Sparks worked busily to get his radio working. Assembly had been easy with the parts Stasio had given him, but finding a decipherable frequency was more tedious, particularly over Vic's loud, off-tune singing meant to mask any sound the radio might make.

He found several, gave each a brief listen for keywords of interest, but heard nothing particularly noteworthy until he came across a gruff German speaker. Scribbling down what he was hearing with his charcoal stick onto the back of someone's envelope from home, he muttered, "Shite," as a cold knot formed within. How this fit in with what Clara had told him of a bomb, he did not know, but he was certain that it did.

❧*❧

"Marseilles?" she asked softly for something to fill the awkwardness between them.

"I was barely nineteen then." She listened to the rustle of fabric as his arm came up then felt his fingers in her hair. She closed her eyes and did not move, memories of fear intermixed with those of the savored kiss, and she wondered how conflicting remembrances could cause such turmoil. But his hand dropped after a moment and he moved away, pulling his chair around to the front of his desk so that it was beside the other. "Please. Sit…Clara."

There was no command in his tone, which made doing as he asked easier. He noticed the tears at the corners of her eyes, and the way she behaved, more restrained in his presence than she had been at any other time since their first meeting. He had done this; there was no one else to blame, and now he had to try to set things right.

"I wanted to tell you…" He leaned his elbows on his knees and steepled his hands beneath his chin. "This is difficult to say; I do not quite know how…"

"Just say it, Hans. You've never been afraid to talk to me before."

There was a catch in her quavering voice. He rubbed his thumbs across his eyes. "I know…and you were never afraid either…but that was before I acted so stupidly…"

"Don't…"

He stopped her with a hand upon her knee. He both felt and saw her body tense at the contact, but he did not remove his hand, nor do anything other than leave it there. "It was wrong of me…and I have no excuse other than I was selfish and out of control. I have hurt Jennifer…again…though she does not seem to remember that night…and I have hurt the one person I have trusted most in the last few years. Thank God it went no further. I owe you more than an apology, but I am afraid there is little I can offer."

Clara stared at his hand upon her leg. "I know."

"No…I don't really think you do. How can you…when I don't?" He got up and went around the desk as if to pour himself a drink, but his hand stopped on the decanter and did not pick it up. "I cannot…continue this, Clara. I cannot continue to hurt those people dearest to me. Mila…Jennifer…you. I promised myself I would not see you again."

"Then why am I…?"

"Because I wanted to tell you to your face. One final time, so that you can understand and…lord help me…because I am too weak to do this alone. I do not know how I shall avoid you when your scent lingers in these walls…"

Now he did pour a drink and swallowed it quickly. "But I have to do it…for your sake as much as Jennifer's. I love her…and I think I have hurt her enough with my choices…but you…after what I have done…and there is talk…the Gestapo is suspicious of you."

"I know," she admitted.

He studied her long and hard. "I suspect you do. After having your home searched twice…you are a very perceptive woman. You miss few details. Every time I bring you here, it places us both, but especially you, in danger. I thought I could protect you from that…but I am no longer certain I can protect myself."

Clara kept the alarm at bay. "What do you mean? Are you in danger?"

With a scoffing chuckle, Hans set his glass down and returned to the chair. "Everyone in the Reich is in danger, constantly, especially those in positions of power. With an organization run by paranoia, greed, and personal ambition, it is impossible not to be. Someone always wants what you have. It has been made clear of late that my superiors are more untrustworthy than anyone else I know, and that any amount of protection I thought I could offer is a myth. Keeping away from you is in your best interest."

Though inside she was swearing over the loss of information, she had always known this outcome was a possibility. "How will we…will I…when I must obey any summons you make of me…?"

With a groaning sigh, Hans leaned backward, his head dropping back, and covered his face with his intertwined fingers. "That shall be a small problem, but one that will not exist much longer, I'm afraid." He looked at her, his hands now behind his head. He had not shared his news with most of the officers or the guards yet, but he felt he had to tell her. He trusted her...and she needed to know. "Stalag 31 is to be decommissioned...and I and my family are returning to Berlin."

It did not take words for Clara to understand the possible implications of both the decommissioning and the return to Berlin, given what she had overheard on the radio. "Do you think they will...?"

Trying to sound reassuring, Hans leaned forward enough to pat her leg. "Oh, I'll be fine, I am sure..."

"Hans." Now she took his hand, her fear for him offsetting any fear of him. He did not seem to know about a bomb, although maybe it had not been a real bomb but rather the sort that came as unexpected news dropped into one's lap. But if he was afraid of returning to Berlin, there was a reason for it. "It's me, Hans."

Quaking, he kissed the back of her hand. "I fear not so much for myself as I do for my family. I have...done things that...hell...I was even part of a plot to..." His eyes flickered to the photo of Hitler, but he did not finish the sentence. "They were bound to catch us sooner or later. And despite the uniform, I am not what they consider quality SS material. But Jennifer and Mila...I do not know how I can protect them. Taking Jennifer to Berlin is sentencing her to death."

"Go to London."

He appeared startled at her suggestion, as though he had never considered flight. And she realized he probably had not. Other people fled. Not Hans von Hausen. Not the German army, if they could help it. Like a bulldog, Hans would tenaciously hold on until he could no longer do so, even if it was a foolish thing to do.

"Or send Jennifer and Mila. She is a British citizen; it should be a simple enough thing to..."

"Despite what she thinks of me now, she would never leave."

"To protect her daughter, Hans? There are ways, people who can help...who will help..." She cut herself short, realizing how close she was to giving away both the Ste Marie cell and her position in it. There was no duplicity in Hans, no sense that he was trying to trap her, but for all she knew, Stetcher was standing with his ear to the door or an adjacent wall. "You must know people who could help you," she finished, turning the suggestion back onto him.

Freeing his hand, Hans stood again, and with his back to her, looked at the trio of pictures on the wall. "We both have too much history..." Clara had the sense he was not speaking of shared history but rather something much bigger. "If you are ever in Marseilles, look for me."

"Yes," she whispered, feeling a door closing within her. This was more than merely the end of their acquaintance and friendship.

"And if it comes to it...Jennifer may never let you...but if you can...protect my daughter, Clara."

Their eyes met with a fire that drew Clara out of her chair. She came to stand beside him. "I shall do what I can, Hans, but...?"

"I don't know how," he finished for her, "but I believe you can do it. In exchange...I can only promise you that, whatever happens, I will do my best to protect you until I can no longer do so."

"And I will do what I can...if I can...to be certain that Berlin will never harm you on my account."

With a small smile, he touched the side of her face. "I do not know how you can prevent that, geliebte, but I appreciate the sentiment. I do not deserve such loyalty after what I have done."

"There is nothing to forgive, Hans."

And she realized as she said it, that the words were true. He may have kissed her, and he might have done more if the opportunity had been there, but he had not meant to harm her. If anything, she was the one who should apologize for using him, for not being what he believed her to be. But she could not. It was safer for them both if he never knew the truth. And now that it was over, there was no need for him to know. She did not need to take that last illusion away.

"I shall call a car for you..."

"I would rather walk."

He nodded. "I understand. You know..." He looked from her face to the picture of Marseilles. "It is a pity thing can't be different."

"It would never be different...war or no. You have a wife you love, in spite of everything. See to it she knows." She paused and then kissed him, a soft lingering touch of her mouth to his, no more. "Please be careful. And take care of them. Take care of yourself."

Though he wanted to embrace her, he did not move. He left the moment as it was in his memory, sweet, innocent, and entirely reminiscent of everything Clara was to him. But he did follow her into the corridor and to the front door of the officers' building.

"Clara," he started, calling to her as she reached the bottom step. She looked at him, seeing the heady emotional conflict in his eyes.

"Don't, Hans…"

He looked about to say something but his words were cut off by the echoing of machine gun fire from the direction of the river. Forget what he had promised, he thought, grabbing Clara's arm and pulling her along behind him. She was here and he would protect her from whatever was happening, no matter what Jennifer might think.

The machine gun fire was loud enough that every man on the Arnaud farm and in Stalag 31 heard it. In the field, KC and farmer looked at one another and then at Stasio who worked near them. The Frenchman dropped the tool from his hand and looked at the camp instead of in the direction of the shots. Every man there had stopped working despite their overseers' efforts to push them back to it. Stasio, however, took off towards the house in a panicked run.

Bonny started from his weeding, staring in the direction of the sound, and quickly dropped his head in prayer. He was in the midst of genuflecting when he heard an upstairs window of the house open. Young Mila leaned out, terror on her face as she strained to see into the distance. At another window, Jennifer wrung her hands, her expression more horrified and panic-stricken than her daughter's.

Most of the men in Camp 1 gathered along the back fence, hoping to see something, wanting to know what had happened, who was shooting at whom. Not likely other soldiers, although the rumor was, from Sparks, that the Allied soldiers were drawing closer every day. There had been a single volley of shots, without return fire nothing that indicated a firefight even though there were occasional pops of gunfire moving west along the river.

Jamie's thoughts turned immediately to the escape the French prisoners had planned. He had prayed they would not attempt it today, despite the seemingly perfect timing and opportunity the work at the bridge presented. Something in Stetcher's voice that morning had been akin to a dare, tinged with a knowing note that suggested to Jamie the Germans had gotten wind of the plans and decided to give the Camp 2 men an opportunity to hang themselves, to be slapped down with a show of force that smelled strongly of Stetcher's sadistic nature.

Jamie was mending one of his shirts when the shots came, and he and his father shared a glance over whatever George was reading. They stared at one another, both avoiding an argument yet clearly wondering which of them was wrong and which was right. When the racket of men leaving their barracks interrupted, they both went out to witness what was happening. From the direction of the latrine, Sparks and Vic came running, both stuffing items into pockets and trousers as they came. Sparks, however, did not follow the majority of the crowd towards the back fence; instead, he went to the fence near the Camp 1 entrance and stared down the row of German-occupied buildings. Jamie wondered what he was doing, but that question was shortly answered when von Hausen appeared pulling Clara along behind him.

"Clara!" Sparks called. He did not care what von Hausen thought. He had to know she was alright.

"Je suis très bien," she called back, knowing that Hans could understand her and Sparks as well, but many others would not.

She and Hans stopped in front of the infirmary, where Dengler stood on the porch, his arms folded across his chest with a grim expression. There was no sign of Stetcher, so Hans concluded he must have joined Hirsch in overseeing the French work detail. The Commandant's face darkened with anger. From the corner, Moretti came running, his revolver drawn, looking for the source of the disturbance. Now everyone stood quiet, anxiously waiting.

In the distance, to the south, in the direction of the forest and river, several German soldiers herded the nearly two dozen Frenchmen back towards Stalag 31. The prisoners had their heads down, their hands upon their head as though they had just been captured, but there were still some fifteen or more men missing by Jamie's count. He presumed this was not the renegade bunch that had tried to escape, rather those who had been stubborn enough, or smart enough, to remain behind, but what had become of the others?

Hirsch and Stetcher were not with the group.

"I bloody well hope Stetcher is face down in the river with a bullet up his arse," Vic spat.

Despite the crudeness of the sentiment, the men clustered around him agreed. Leonard looked to be suffering a flashback of bad memories and clung to the fence with George's steadying arm around his shoulders. Ray's expression was unreadable, a mixture of what might have been guilt, discomfort, fear or disgust twisting his face with each step the returning French took. Taffy, on George's other side, whispered something to George, but Jamie could not hear it or read the lip movements because Skip and Dusty stood in the way. Both men's hands gripped the barbed wire as they wondered if any of the French had succeeded where they had not.

"Stay here," Hans grunted to Clara. He gestured to Moretti and the two hurried towards the main gate to greet the arriving men. When the gates opened and the prisoners passed through, most with a look of defeat, one of the German guards was pulled aside for interrogation by the Commandant. Clara's stomach twisted and her jaw clenched. Even without knowing the details, she guessed that some sort of escape had been attempted by the more tightly guarded men from Camp 2. She wondered what impact this would have on Ste Marie, the men in Camp 1 and Hans himself.

They did not have to wait long for Hirsch, Stetcher, and the last remaining German soldiers to emerge from the forest surrounding eight of the French prisoners Jamie hoped to see. The Frenchman Jamie knew best, the man whose leg he had tended only days ago, was one of the eight still alive, the severity of his limp likely having contributed to his recapture. Those eight carried three bodies with them, but that still left others unaccounted for, more blemishes upon Hans' shaky record, if they had escaped rather than having been shot and lost into the river. If they had escaped, Stetcher had made no effort, spared no men, to go after them.

Clara gritted her teeth, praying the others were dead and in the river, beyond retrieval, not because she wished them ill, but because today she wanted none of Stetcher's efforts to prove Hans' incompetence to be successful. If she had brought a gun, she might have killed the Gestapo officer then and there.

They too entered through the main gate, and while Stetcher stopped to speak with Hans, Hirsch led the rest into Camp 2. The younger officer looked overly smug as he instructed them to lay their dead near the gate and then to line up against the fence beside them, away from the others who had been forced into appell formation in the parade yard. Moretti, likewise, went into Camp 1 to summon the men to line up so that they could see into Camp 2 without difficulty. Hans and Stetcher were arguing in low voices as the men from the fields were brought back into camp, as was Bonny. Whatever would happen was something the Germans intended everyone to witness.

Finally, with a look of annoyance and defeat, Hans went back to the infirmary step, while Stetcher walked briskly to Camp 2. He summoned Hirsch to the fence, spoke to him briefly, and then climbed the wooden rungs into the guard tower that stood at the internal junction of the three sections of Stalag 31. Someone climbed up after him and presented him with a bullhorn.

In Camp 2, three 7.63 millimeter tripod mounted machine guns had been placed in direct line of sight for those eight unfortunate men, one of whom Jamie could not believe had been trying to escape, not with his injured leg. The setup had a dramatic effect upon every prisoner, as never before had execution on this scale been the consequence of a failed escape attempt in Stalag 31.

"You should go," Hans said as he rejoined Clara. He looked pale and trapped and she hated what this was doing to him. "You should not see this...and I wish very much that this not be your last memory of me."

Clara cast a quick glance into Camp 2, knowing what was about to happen without anyone saying it. Hans was right; she did not want to watch this. In Hans' favor, however, she blamed no one but Stetcher. She nodded in acceptance of his command.

"Josef...escort her to the gate, please. Let no one harm her."

The doctor, taken aback by being addressed by his first name, inhaled sharply but said, "Yes, sir." He guided Clara away with a hand low on her back as Stetcher brought the bullhorn to his mouth.

"By order of the high command, in the name of the Fuhrer, all Stalag officers throughout the Reich have been given authority to execute any man trying to escape custody. There shall be no further attempts from this camp. No man shall be excused. To impress upon you the serious nature of such efforts, and to show you that none are immune to the actions of others..." He paused, looking lost without his walking stick to tap with and wave about. He cleared his throat and started again. "Fifteen men tried to escape today. Eight lived to be recaptured. They should have died with their comrades. You eight shall die indeed, but for each man who escaped this punishment today, Haupsturmfuhrer Hirsch will select another."

Clara stopped at the gate, barely believing she had heard Stetcher correctly. But the slump of Hans' shoulders proved that she had and that he was powerless to prevent it without putting himself at risk, as long as Stetcher was alive. She wondered if there was more to the

Oberstgruppenfuhrer visit that Hans had not revealed. Perhaps he was already stripped of command. That thought made her feel numb.

"You fucking kidding me?" Dusty shouted. Skip managed to keep his friend from saying more, as the soldiers in the watchtower where Stetcher stood aimed their guns at the mouthy Brit. But Stetcher himself ignored Dusty, having more interesting pursuits to entertain. Nor did he hear further words when Dusty hissed, "Like being killed isn't punishment enough..."

"Shut your trap unless you want to get us all killed," Vic snarled.

"You'd think he's the one in charge..." Taffy murmured. Watching the Commandant, it certainly looked as if the man felt he no longer controlled this camp.

In Camp 2, Hirsch walked through the ranks of Frenchmen and gypsies and selected the seven he wanted. He lingered here and there, and then continued on, making his selections with no apparent reasoning until fifteen men stood against the back fence, some facing the guns alone while others embraced or clasped hands in farewell.

"Watch," Stetcher charged the men in both camps, "or you too will die. The choice is yours." Some sort of visual exchange occurred between Stetcher and von Hausen, rather like Stetcher asking for permission and daring the Commandant to deny it. Instead, the Oberfuhrer turned his head and looked away, pretending the man did not exist. Stetcher paused for effect and then gestured to Hirsch.

The Haupsturmfuhrer barked, "Mark!" to the men with the guns.

Pause.

"Fire!"

There was a short eruption of noise, the acrid smell of spent munitions, and then silence.

Bodies lay twisted and deflated at the rear of Camp 2. Compared to the faces of the living, their faces were calm, albeit frightened, as they faced death with dignity. For the others, there was shock, remorse, terror, and anger.

For Hans von Hausen, there was the deafening sense that he too would soon face that wall of gunfire.

And that it would be Stetcher pulling the trigger.

At the gate, Clara waited just long enough for it to be opened, and then she ran. Hans regretted with all his heart that her final glimpse of him would be one of his failure as a leader.

With a wicked smile, Stetcher climbed from the watchtower, crossed to the infirmary, and handed the bullhorn to Hans.

"It would be fitting, don't you think, that you shared the news?" needled the little man.

Fitting, thought Hans, and humiliating. He should have guessed that Stetcher knew the orders as well, which meant that Hirsch likely did too. His hand gripped white-knuckled around the handle as he made a slow glance across the faces of his charges. Head high, he walked to the fenced intersection of the three camp sections, hoping that the inflicted carnage would be enough to appease Stetcher today, that the man would now disappear behind his desk to file whatever reports or paperwork he needed to on these events. But Stetcher appeared, for the moment, to be determined to watch Hans fall.

And Hans was equally determined to remain dignified. There was no logical reason he had to share this news…except out of respect for the ranks they bore, and respect for each of them as men.

"Some of you will be relieved to know that you will have to endure Stalag 31 only a short while longer. It has been decided that the resources required to sustain this facility are best distributed elsewhere." Not to mention, he thought, it was stupid in the face of the rumored encroaching allied forces.

"What's he…?" started Vic.

Dusty elbowed him in the ribs.

Hans continued. "You will be moved to other facilities." He paused long enough to allow the stunned murmur to run its course through the ranks, aware that even his own men were looking at one another with surprise and consternation. "The removal will be in stages, as soon as it is determined what facilities you will be sent to."

"Death camps most likely," Skip blurted. Death camps were a rumor; none of the men in Stalag 31 had actually seen one, seen evidence of one, or had known anyone who had. But where else would troublesome men, extra mouths to feed, be sent?

von Hausen met his gaze. "It is up to the Reich where you will find yourselves, but I assure you, Captain, none of you are to be sent anywhere except to similar facilities…unless you persist in causing trouble before your departure or while you are in transit." It was not a guarantee he could make, but by the time he might be proven wrong, he imagined he would be far beyond the reach of any man here. "My staff and I will work out the transfer schedules as details come in. Once all of you have been removed from this facility, those of us with talents fit for the Reich to use will be reassigned."

He walked back to his office since he was in no mood to face his wife now. As he passed them, he could hear the tension in his men, their disbelief and above all their fears. Life here in Ste Marie had been good. Reassignment meant the possibility of being sent to the war front with a high likelihood of dying for a cause that Hans himself did not believe in, in a war that, despite the propaganda, Hans believed they were losing.

He had no means to assuage their fears. He could no more assure his men of the futures then he could promise that the prisoners would live out the war…or even the month. It was wholly out of his hands.

❧*❧

After hearing the initial gunfire, Stasio hoped to find Clara already home from her visit to the camp upon his retreat to the house, hoping for proof that the shots fired had nothing to do with her. If von Hausen killed her, or allowed her to be killed, Stasio intended to be the one to kill him in return without any thought to his own welfare.

He did not think he could live without Clara.

During one of his passes near the kitchen door, he witnessed the return of the farm workers to the camp, and then a few minutes later the line of men being escorted from the river was seen. Knowing that the shots had been somehow prisoner related brought only a small amount of relief, but not until Clara was at his side would he know peace, for if she was still at the camp there was the continued potential for her death.

He paced from back door to front, looking for her, and not seeing her was beginning to tear a gaping maw in his stomach. His heart had succumbed to it long ago. Should his mind do so as well, he would go mad.

Back and forth several more times, wondering if he should go out, watch what was happening, or go to the camp and bring Clara home himself.

The second burst of gunfire, closer than the first, came as he reached the front door again. His heart leaped into his throat. He took a few stumbling steps backward and collapsed onto the arm of the sofa, hanging his head, certain that Clara had been at the receiving end of that barrage.

How could he continue on alone?

He was still sitting there when the clatter of heels upon the porch echoed through the open screen. He looked up as the door was thrown open and stood in time to catch Clara, mid-run, in his arms. He stroked her hair, kissed her face, her head, her mouth. The despair of losing her was replaced with the knowledge that she was alive and safe and brought forth tears. She was the nearest he had ever seen to hysterical, but in his arms, she grew calmer as he did.

Clara muttered into his kisses, into his neck and shoulder, "Camp 2...new decree...any trying to escape will be executed. Stetcher says...fifteen...he killed seven more to prove he could...and Hans cannot stop him. The camp is to be closed; he will go back to Berlin...where he and his family will probably face execution...and Stasio...Mon Dieu! There is nothing I can do. Over...all over."

He could say nothing, only hold her and let her weep. Over. Without von Hausen to shield her, Clara might no longer be safe in Ste Marie, which left Stasio with a difficult decision to make. He did not know if he was capable of it, but there was little choice. Clara was running out of time.

Chapter 25
July 24, 1943

B y the time Hans entered his home, there was only one thing on his mind. How could he save his family? Perhaps Jennifer would be stubborn about leaving him, but it was the only way. The only way to protect their daughter. For all of her parents' faults, Mila von Hausen did not deserve to suffer.

Jennifer was in the music room, plunking at the keyboard, drinking again as Hans barreled past, heading for the stairs. She did not notice, which gave him time to pack a small bag for himself without her questions. But any hope he had of slipping away unnoticed was dashed when he came downstairs, intending to go through his desk for the necessary papers. Jennifer saw him, saw the bag in his hand, and the fear that she was being abandoned brought her from the music room wailing his name.

He sighed, defeated. "Yes, Jennifer?" There was no point in endearments. He had accepted that she stayed with him out of fear of being alone, knowing she would not survive on her own, but in truth, their marriage was over. He loved her still but there was no point in pretending anymore.

"You're leaving?" she screeched. "Now?"

Another sigh. "For a few days. There is business that needs tending…urgent business…"

"But what if he comes back?"

He being Volheim. She did not need to say his name for Hans to know whom she meant. "He won't. He's washed his hands of Ste Marie." And of me.

"Take me with you." She crossed the room, for once ignoring the uniform, and hung her arms about his shoulders. "Please."

"You need to stay with Mila…"

"She can come too. We can make a family outing…maybe a show…have a picnic…"

Hans shook his head. He wanted to believe she wanted to be a family again, but fear was her only sincere emotion. "As much as I would like those things, there will be no time for that on this trip. It will be urgent, boring business that should not have a child hanging around while I conduct it. I will be back soon, and then we shall go away together, make a day of it." He continued to busy himself as he spoke, finding birth records, passports, their marriage certificate, and any sort of important documents he thought he might need. He also gathered together every bit of money he could find. Hans was taking no chances of failure.

"Please," she begged.

He looked down at her hands tugging at his arm and wondered if she had any inkling of what lay ahead for them. No doubt, she understood the risks of returning to Berlin, which was why she was interested in staying away from that city, but did she know what he was intending to do now?

In no mood for whining, unwilling to change his mind, he yanked away from her so that he could stuff his briefcase and slam it closed. "No, Jennifer...not this time," he said, his voice thick and rough with what she would likely hear as anger, but which was actually fear for her safety. "Watch Mila; I'm leaving Moretti to see to your care. I will be back soon."

Thinking he had made his point since she did not follow him to the sitting room door, he felt both relief and sadness. Sadness because he knew that, all too soon, he might never see her again. Relief that he did not have to fight with her. The thought of never seeing her made him look back, and when he did, she threw her arms around his neck and kissed him deep and passionate.

"I love you, Hans..." she whispered. "Hurry home."

Eyes brimming with tears at those unexpected words, he replied, "I know, Jennifer," before releasing her and going out. This time, he did not look back.

❧*❧

It was with amazement that Bonny was allowed to oversee the burial of the executed Frenchmen instead of dumping them into a pit or leaving their corpses exposed as a rotting reminder. The duty left the gardening open. Not having been to the house since that afternoon spent in Jennifer's bed, Ray was deliriously happy to be chosen to replace the padre. The thought of potentially being alone with her was enough to obliterate the thoughts of the executions. He was there, hard at work, when Hans returned to the house, there when Hans left with a briefcase and suitcase not long after, and there when the wail went up within the house that sounded to him like the shattering of an already broken heart. One of the two guards rushed inside, certain that the Commandant's wife was being harmed, but when he returned a few short moments later he grunted, "She needs your help to move furniture," to the truly concerned Ray. The man thought the reason for the shout dubious, given the Commandant's recent departure, but he allowed Ray to go inside.

Ray bounded up the porch steps two or three at a time and in his haste did not bother to knock before entering. He found the woman in the study, seated on a divan with her head between her knees as if she had fainted or was trying not to, and Mila at the foot of the stairs peering into the room with fright. She looked at him when his footsteps stopped, saw her daughter there, and quickly wiped her face of tears. "It's alright, darling. I had a fright. You know how I dislike insects. Go back to your studies…"

Mila looked at her mother and the medic dubiously, sighed, and said, "Yes, mother." Her studying had ceased with the sound of machine gun fire. She would rather not be alone, but she would do as her mother asked.

When she was gone, Ray plopped down on the divan beside her; she threw her arms around him and gave in to the weeping she had hidden from her child. "He's gone, Ray…I know it," she croaked.

"Gone?" He guessed she meant her husband, but he did not want to appear either excited by that news or eager to take advantage of it.

"He says it's business…that he'll be back in a few days…but I know he's lying…I know he's left me…"

Ray swallowed back a dozen different things he wanted to say, before finally deciding on, "He's got responsibilities, Jenny…he'll be back." He did not personally know the Commandant, but from what he had seen, if he said he was going to do something, he did it…at least it seemed so to Ray.

He held her, stroking her hair, kissing the top of her head as she sobbed. "My fault…he's gone…I'm never going to see him again."

Ray could only hope that was true.

৯*৯

"We need a foolproof plan," George started, now that everyone due to attend the impromptu Flight Meeting had arrived. "If we aren't careful, we'll all be shot…"

"And a lot of others will be too," Taffy reminded him.

"Your fault," Vic growled, glaring at Skip and Dusty. "You and your sneaking off without…"

Skip growled too, the sound defensive and annoyed. "What about Ronny and his…?"

"This new rule came into place before he was caught…you know it, even if von Hausen spared him by shoving him into the Cooler before Stetcher found out," Leonard muttered. "If it wasn't for you, all of those people would be…"

"It wasn't them." Ray stood up, speaking in Skip's defense for the first time. "It is not their fault…"

The Aussie, however, did not appreciate the help. He spun on Ray and threw a punch, hitting the younger man squarely in the nose. "I can smell her on you, traitor…"

Vic, ever one for a fight, jumped at Skip, and Bonny and Jamie scrambled to pull them apart as George barked, "She who?" What in the hell was Skip on about?

"Shut up," hissed Sparks from his bunk, ear glued to the radio as usual. The fight might have continued if not for him; the need to hear the radio, especially tonight, was the one thing every man in the barracks agreed upon. The German on the radio was crackly and distorted, but there were words that were clear enough and understood by those who spoke the language.

Bomb. Ste Marie.

"Looks like she was right," Sparks swore.

"Who?" snarled Skip, wary about the possibility of trusting any woman other than Marcella. She had done right by him. There was no reason not to trust her.

"Clara." His own ears had confirmed what Clara claimed, what Stasio had hinted at. Some sort of trouble was headed their way.

"Well, I'm not going to wait here and be a target."

Taffy nodded. "I'm with Dusty. If there's a high chance of dying either way…shouldn't we take the risk that might at least buy us freedom?"

"Not just some of us…all of us," insisted Jamie.

"The whole camp?" scowled George.

"Why the hell not?"

"We'd never…"

Vic interrupted after tossing his playing cards on the table. "There's the woods…if we scatter, there's a better chance that some of us will make it."

"How do we know for sure we are in danger?" Ray asked. "I mean…if they're decommissioning the place, it makes sense they would destroy it afterward, keep it out of…"

"You want to take your chances being sent east, suit yourself," shrugged Vic.

"Or risk being here when it's leveled," Bonny reminded Ray.

"We don't even know if they'll get to that part of the wood pile," George continued, redirecting the conversation back to the original plan being discussed and away from the moral arguments.

Bonny, sitting in the doorway on watch for the Germans, said, "We move it to the top…soon as we're ready…or we light it ourselves so it coincides with a delivery…"

"The gates will be open long enough for everyone to make a run," continued Dusty.

"Every man for himself," snorted Skip. He was all for the basic plan, no matter how suicidal it might be. The chances of a bombing reduced the likelihood of survival, and he was not going to take chances. If no one else acted, he certainly would.

The whistle blew. The men looked at each other. There was no solid plan yet, but they had the base of one, and that was good enough for tonight. No one knew, however, how long they had left in Ste Marie. They had to work fast.

George rose from the table with that thought in mind. "Same time and place, tomorrow night. Be careful what you say to who, and no one," he threw a heated glance at Ray, "does anything stupid."

"Anything that gives us a chance to survive isn't stupid," muttered Skip. "I'd say its bloody brilliant."

అSuspicion's Gate

Chapter 26
July 25, 1943

S unday morning's appell was accompanied by the usual weekly distribution of letters, parcels and Red Cross packets. Though the Red Cross supplies were no different than before, the volume of mail seemed particularly light. Light enough that even Skip, who had not received mail at all in recent weeks, took notice. Seated upon the barracks' porch, he mused aloud as to whether the skimpy amount of mail had anything to do with the camp being closed or if a mail delivery somewhere had been delayed. He also mused about the likelihood that, if they were moved, whether mail would ever find them again. Dusty shrugged and continued to polish his shoes, choosing not to dwell on dark thoughts today. Others were perusing their letters, digging through parcels, or standing around chatting as they waited for Bonny's weekly service, perhaps the last ever in Ste Marie, to begin. Only Jamie remained alone. The Canadian was seated with his back to the barracks' outer wall, writing something in a notebook he had received that day.

Skip wondered if his writings had anything to do with Zaline.

Leave Stalag 31. Leave Ste Marie. As much as he hated it here, as much as they all hated it, many of the men had come here from other camps, harsher facilities, more restrictive, less tolerant. As much as he longed to be free, it was, in a strange way, home, and like everyone else here, he had no desire to be sent to a less certain fate.

But he had yet to come up with a logical, feasible way to get the majority of men out of the camp.

If only some made the attempt, what of those left behind? Would Stetcher butcher them all in reprisal? Skip winced at the thought.

Within the barracks, Farmer and Ray were cleaning up the morning meal, which was fortunate for Ray because it kept him away from the others. At the moment, most refused to speak to the young medic because of his near-certain, involvement with Jennifer.

Having himself been branded a traitor for falling under her spell, perhaps Skip should feel pity for the idealistic younger man.

But he did not. All he felt was anger at the perceived betrayal of both of them. Ray should have known better, should have learned from Skip's mistakes, and Jennifer...she had sworn she loved him, and after betraying him to her husband, now turned to corrupting a man too naïve to resist, using a fine youngster, however principled he was, whom she would never be loyal to. The notion of strangling her resurfaced, strong enough that he hoped he would not be picked for garden duty any time soon. His back was healing from the flogging he had received. If he tried to kill her again, succeed or fail, he would be executed.

Now that there was a glimmer of hope for freedom, Skip chose to live.

Italian obscenities erupted in the German quarter of the camp, followed by the slamming of a door and what sounded like someone kicking, or being thrown against, the side of an automobile. "You can't do this!" Moretti shouted. "You have no right!" The outraged cry was followed by Stetcher's cold, bitter, laughter.

Skip and Dusty rose from the porch to see what was happening and others followed, gathering at the fence for the best view. Dengler opened the infirmary door but did not step outside. From the direction of the officer's quarters, Stetcher, Hirsch, and three other soldiers were propelling the Italian towards Camp 1. The Italian was not in uniform; rather it appeared as though he had been in the process of dressing when Stetcher barged in on him.

The group of soldiers and officers paused long enough for the Camp 1 gate to be opened, then they passed through it, none speaking, not even Moretti any longer. Now, with so many eyes upon him, the Italian was trying to maintain the most dignified composure he could under the circumstances.

He was barely succeeding.

George waved his men back and took a step towards the Germans, a brazen move that might gain him injury or death if Stetcher took offense. "What is this about?" he asked, not expecting an answer. Had Moretti's charities to the men under his watch been put to a halt? The first guess many of the prisoners made was that the Italian had defied the Germans one too many time, or else had been impolite in some manner that had particularly irritated Stetcher. Since von Hausen had not been seen since his departure from the camp the day before, it left Stetcher in charge and free to do as he wished to anyone who displeased him or got in his way.

The Gestapo officer stopped but waved his subordinates and Moretti towards the Cooler. Vic and Sparks looked at each other, Sparks with a deep frown on his bearded face. "The Italians are no longer allies of the Reich," Stetcher responded almost gleefully. "Mr. Moretti is relieved of his duties and his command. He will be held until the transports come to remove the French." He tapped his walking stick furiously upon the end of his boot, visibly satisfied to have the 'soft' Italian out of his hair.

"As you can see, Colonel," he sneered at George, "all of our enemies fall before us. Soon there will be no one left to challenge the Reich and you will understand the meaning of domination."

Hirsch and the soldiers were already returning without Moretti. Hirsch shook Stetcher's hand in a congratulatory fashion and they left Camp 1 together, Stetcher seemingly having forgotten that he had been in a one-sided conversation.

Once they were gone, George shook his head as if to clear it of his disbelief. He glanced at Sparks and Vic and motioned for them to follow as he returned to where the rest of the men J had gathered. By the time George reached the steps, most of the officers were inside waiting for him.

"Sounds to me like rats fleeing a sinking ship then enemies falling before them," snorted Taffy as all except Ray gathered around George at the table. Ray remained in the doorway, looking like a scolded puppy.

"We need to talk…"

"Sir?"

"Padre?"

Bonny stood just inside the doorway; it was as far as he had gotten. "The men will be expecting me…"

George contemplated the matter briefly before nodding. "Go on." There was no need to disrupt camp routine any further, or raise concerns until the officers reached some sort of decision. "We'll update you later."

"Thank you, sir."

"Any of you wish to join him, feel free…" But no one else moved. Bonny did not feel slighted, as there was clearly something important afoot and the officers needed to deal with the issue promptly. George waited for a few heartbeats, until Bonny's steps had left the wooden porch, before speaking again. "Seems the Italians have switched sides in this war…"

"No shit," whistled Dusty.

"You sure?" Skip asked, his gaze drifting to Sparks for confirmation. Neither he nor Dusty had been near enough to hear what Stetcher had said.

"Haven't had the chance for a listen," the bearded Scot started.

George continued, "Stetcher just put Moretti in the Cooler…"

"We heard the words straight from Stetcher's mouth…though he made it sound like a grand German victory," added Vic.

"We all know how reliable Stetcher…" Skip snorted.

"I wouldn't trust my life in his hands," agreed George, "but this time I think there's truth to his claim…either that or he's taking advantage of von Hausen's absence to clean house."

Leonard kicked the leg of the bed nearest him. "How long before he cleans us?"

That was a question no one wanted to answer. Taffy changed the subject by tapping on the table. "Ronny can put his time in the Cooler to use and get the story from Moretti…I can get a message to him at lunch…maybe we'll know something by evening appell."

"Good idea," George grunted with a nod.

Jumping up onto Dusty's bunk, careful not to hit or kick Skip in the process, KC asked, "What does this do to us getting out of here?"

George shrugged and leaned his elbows on the table. "Nothing. Moretti's got nothing to do with…"

"Unless he'd be willing to help us." Jamie patted his pocket for a cigarette and pulled the newly arrived pack from his shirt.

He and Skip exchanged glances, the Aussie prepared to remark about the insanity of such a suggestion but it quickly occurred to him that it might not be such a bad idea…if they could trust the Italian. If it was true, if the Germans and Italians were now enemies, what could Moretti have to lose by allying with them?

"Odds are he wants out of this hellhole as badly as we do…can you imagine the fate awaiting him wherever he's sent?" Dusty said in a low voice.

"If Stetcher doesn't kill him first," reminded Leonard.

Sparks crossed his arms. "He knows everything…routines, duty rosters, maybe even some of the dates for the transports."

Determined to have his say, the sheepish sounding Ray said, "This could be a trap; maybe Stetcher wants us to trust Moretti…"

"I'm not sure Renz would..." began Taffy.

"Maybe not, but we should consider the possibility."

The men knew that George was right. There was a pause as the notion was measured before Sparks spoke again. "What we do know is that it seems likely there are bombs headed our way...if that doesn't kill us, we'll be shipped off to the far corners of Europe..."

"...or else shot and left as carrion for French scavengers," Farmer sighed.

Leaning against the bedpost, Skip cleared his throat. "Leaves one question...do we risk trusting Moretti or not?"

The men looked at one another in silence, not even George willing to speak first until he gauged each man's mood and expression. Finally, he nodded at the consensus that he saw and said what each man was thinking. "Yes."

"I'm in," said Sparks and Dusty at the same time.

Vic shot Sparks a nasty look over his shoulder before asking, "Who put you in charge, Henderson? You're the one who thought we should trust the bitch..."

Bristling Skip shot back, "I asked a question...that does not put me in charge."

"An important, necessary question," George remarked, putting his words between the two and hoping it was enough to prevent them from coming to blows. "One I've ruled on. There will be no fighting about it." For once, most of the men were willing to abide by his decision, but for George, it was significant because he and his son agreed on something.

"Taffy...talk to Ronny...and to Moretti if you can, otherwise get Ronny to do it. Whatever you learn, bring it to me right away and we'll see if we can use it to..."

"Count me out of this insanity," growled Vic.

"Stay and die for all I care," Skip snarled back.

"Son of a bitch..."

Though Vic tried to lunge at the Aussie, Sparks held his arm and Dusty jumped in front of Skip as George got up to stand between them. "Enough. We need each other's expertise if we are to get out of here alive. We can't afford more of you in the Cooler..." the Colonel barked

"Or under Stetcher's firing squad," Sparks reminded them.

"Especially," said Dusty with a grin, tousling Skip's hair, "since we're due for inspection and your bed looks like shit, Roo."

"I'll show you shit, wanker." With that, Skip's annoyance with Vic was swiftly converted into playfully pushing Dusty into the wall.

"Right," George continued. "We clean the barracks and go about routine as usual. Don't give the Germans any reason to suspect anything or give them any reason to punish you. Dusty, watch the door while Sparks tries to get us some news about the Italians. The rest of us will cover your duties…and Ronny's."

"Yes, sir." Sparks, having anticipated the cue, was already heading for the hidden bits of radio.

"When we come together for lunch, we'll talk again." They had to work fast. They could feel time slipping away each second they loitered undecided.

Looking at his father as though seeing him for the first time, Jamie nodded his agreement and acceptance. There just might be hope for them as father and son yet.

~*~

Pounding his fists upon the cell only caused pain, and if any of the men he had once worked beside were still within earshot, they ignored his string of Italian obscenities and pleas. Being ignored only made Moretti angrier.

He did not understand the politics that had gotten him here. In fact, until Stetcher had burst into his room while he had been dressing, the Italian had known nothing of his homeland's change in political position. Personally he was pleased that his country had finally abandoned Hitler's cause, had finally chosen a path of their own, but this sudden shift in allegiance had left others such as himself, those who had been sent for a variety of reasons to serve the Reich outside of Italy, in a position of being labeled traitors and enemies. They would suffer the same consequences as Moretti without warning.

It was logical, he imagined, for his superiors to want to isolate him, as he carried information they might want to control, but had he not already proven his loyalties? What would he have done if they had simply dismissed him? There was nowhere to go, no way to get home without traveling through hostile territory at great risk to himself. Moretti was in a no-win position and he hated it.

"Moretti? That you?"

The voice speaking directly to him startled Moretti until he recalled that Major Zane was in the adjoining room. The walls were timber and their thinness and the tiny ventilation duct at floor level provided some amount of communication if prisoners desired it. From the sound of the voice, Moretti deduced that Zane was speaking near the duct, possibly lying on the filthy floor.

He scowled, debating whether to talk to the American pilot or not. They were technically no longer enemies, both imprisoned by the same men, a position that Zane had considerably more experience with at the prisoner end of things. Moretti decided there was no harm in speaking to the other man, and so sat down on the floor to speak into the vent in reply.

"Si…it is."

"What in God's name are you doing in here?"

Moretti had expected amusement from the jokester, but instead, all he heard was confusion and concern. The lack of ridicule helped put the Italian at ease.

"My country has turned from the German cause…I suppose that makes me one of you."

"Helluva position to put you in," Ronny whispered. "Taffy told me last night…the camp is being shut down? What gives? What will happen to us?"

Shrugging, though Zane could not see him, Moretti replied, "You will be…we will all be…taken elsewhere. I do not know where. I think perhaps only Oberfuhrer knows…and maybe not even him. It is all very secretive, and not well received by the men."

"They ain't the only ones who don't like it…but if Georgie has anything to say about it, no one is taking us anywhere."

"What?"

Ronny's tone of voice became evasive and defensive. "Nothin'…just not our style to sit around and be herded like sheep."

"Nor mine, Major Zane," Moretti said after many minutes of silence. "I do not blame you for thinking me a spy…and I have no proof to offer, but believe me, I am not here willingly."

There was a long pause on the other side of the wall, and though Moretti had not heard any movement, he presumed Ronny had given up the conversation. Eventually, however, the barnstormer muttered, "No…I imagine not. If only there was a way we could help each other outta here…"

"If there's anything I can do, Major…"

"It's Ronny," the pilot replied. "Might as well drop the formalities. Maybe if we put our heads together, we can come up with a plan…let's see what you've got."

≈*≈

Jennifer stood in the open doorway, watching the men working in her flowerbeds, sipping brandy as she oversaw the few minutes she had allowed her daughter to enjoy in the sunshine on the porch. Jennifer would have preferred to keep the girl indoors; with her husband's departure, she felt even less safe than before, but she could not keep the girl locked up forever. Hans would be back soon, everyone said so, and then things would be fine. In the meantime, she supposed there was no harm in allowing her daughter to read on the porch.

No harm, she believed, until she saw Hirsch slithering his way towards her home like a python on the hunt. He was coming straight towards the two guards posted there to oversee the working prisoners, but his eyes were on Jennifer and her daughter as he drew ever closer. Jennifer moved defensively towards Mila and wrapped her arms around the girl, causing Mila to look up from her book. Ever since the party, Jennifer had endeavored to keep her daughter clear of every German soldier in this place. Now, however, it appeared that Hirsch had come to them, and even as he conducted his business with the guards, his eyes never left the women. Mila noticed it too and closed her book as she retreated behind her mother.

Just in time, she felt, for Hirsch came to the bottom porch step to leer at them. "Good day, Frau von Hausen," he said in a voice that may have been meant to sound cordial but felt to be something much different. "When do you expect your husband home?"

Believing he would know more about her husband's comings and goings then she did, but not wanting to give him the satisfaction of knowing that, she replied coolly, "Soon. Very soon. He should be back any time."

"Hmmph." Hirsch looked over his shoulder towards the main road as if expecting to see the man in questions approaching the house. "Well, I do not hope too soon. The three of us are due for a nice long evening together…don't you think so?"

Mila's grip on her mother's skirt tightened, expecting the woman to protect her. But this time, without her husband's strength to bolster her, Jennifer blanched and backed away, unable to be defiant in the face of this man in a uniform that represented everything in life she feared.

"Get into the house, Mila," she squeaked. The girl quickly obeyed, and Jennifer, afraid to turn her back to Hirsch lest he grab her unseen, backed hastily away. She could not relax when the door was slammed shut between them, for outside, Hirsch laughed darkly. Through the window, she watched him saunter towards camp; only when she could no longer see him did she dare believe she and her daughter were safe.

❧*❦

"Gypsies and French are being shipped out Tuesday," Taffy reported with his cigarette dangling from his mouth. "Should be eight Krauts sent with them…"

George rubbed his chin. "That'll leave…twenty-seven to staff the camp…not including von Hausen of course…"

The officers were again seated around the table, as close to one another as they could get. Farmer had brought lunch but it sat untouched; no one seemed particularly interested in eating. Only Sparks, Ray, and Vic sat apart. Ray was seated in the doorway once more, ostensibly to keep an eye out for the Germans, but mostly attempting to stay away from the others. And, Skip thought, the young man seemed to be staring at the von Hausen home, mourning the fact that soon he would never see Jennifer again.

For Skip, that day could not come soon enough.

Vic was not sitting with the group, still unconvinced to be part of the plan, but he stayed close enough to listen, and to interject his opinions when he had the chance. Sparks' separation was due to the radio he continued to toy with on his bunk, where he had been all morning attempting to confirm Stetcher's claims about the collapse of German-Italian alliance. The news had finally come; it was true. The Italians were no longer their enemies. But still Sparks' listened, taking advantage of as much time with the receiver as he could get in the hopes of learning something they could use.

Skip frowned pensively at the Welshman's words, but said, "Hardly enough to keep an eye on all of us…"

"Which likely means our own transports won't be long behind," Leonard sighed.

"Or else we're done for," snorted Vic.

Dusty was not the only one to give him a sour look. "Must you be so damned pessimistic?"

"But we should assume Vic's right," George said grimly.

"Particularly," Jamie nodded, "since Moretti claims no idea when the next transport will be…we don't know how long we have."

"Maybe he doesn't know because there isn't one," Dusty grunted.

"Good news is that…"

"There's good news?" Vic interrupted with a bitter chuckle.

"Could be," continued Taffy undaunted. "Seems there's a fair amount of dissension among the Germans. Those boys got it good here; most don't want to be sent to the front any more than we want to be sent east. Moretti thinks there may be a few of them willing to help us…if it means avoiding that fate…maybe an exchange of sanctuary in England if they're lucky."

Skip choked on his water. "Germans? Helping us?"

"In exchange for a way out of this war…a way off the continent? Maybe."

"They're not all pricks and assholes," Jamie interjected. "They've got a job to do…and not all have treated us like Stetcher."

"Like Wagner," Sparks agreed without looking up.

"Exactly," Jamie said with a nod.

Taffy stretched. "He's the one Moretti suggested we approach. He's due to be shipped out on Tuesday with the others…poor kid even went so far as to approach Moretti and Dengler about obtaining some sort of medical discharge to avoid being sent to the front. He'll know who the others are that are being sent out…and who else might be able to work with us."

"You're all looking to be strung up, aren't you," muttered Ray.

George snapped, "No one asked you, Corporal. If you have nothing useful to add, keep your negativity to yourself."

"Fine." Ray crossed his arms over his chest and stared across the appell yard with a huff.

"Bonny?"

The Padre looked up from his sermon notebook, a book that contained information beyond just sermons. "Sir?"

"You've talked to Wagner; he knows you speak German?"

"Yes, he does."

"Talk to him. Don't give us away…but see what you can learn…especially whether you think he'll be willing to help us.

You'll have to do it before dinner. Whoever has farm duty tomorrow…and I pray at least one of us does…must get a message to the Cell. Maybe they already know about the camp closure, but we cannot assume that. We do know they know about the potential bombing, so they know we may need their help sooner."

Farmer scowled, "You're not seriously going to try to get all of us out at once, are you? There's no way they could help with that…"

Taffy stubbed out his cigarette. "Kid's got a point…if we all go, no one will be here to look after the enlisted men…"

"I will not assign anyone to certain death," George said with a shake of his head.

Dusty gestured for some paper from Bonny's notebook. "Don't assign…we draw lots. Some of us stay to organize the others…some of us go…maybe break us into three or four groups…"

"Either we all go, or I'm not going," snorted Ray.

Skip shrugged. "Good…gives us one less man to worry about."

"By Tuesday," Leonard added, "Ronny's still going to be in the cooler if we can't find a way to spring him."

"Bad timing on his part," Jamie said grimly. "Still think we should all try to get out…"

George gave the matter consideration, how the odds were stacked against them and how best to look after the men in the camp. With an impending bombing and no idea what lay ahead after Tuesday's transports, it seemed unfair to leave anyone in the camp to that unknown. "We're drawing lots. Ones, twos, and threes. Five ones, four of the others. I'll draw for Ronny. We'll make some plans for each group…how to proceed…and each group of officers will be responsible for their assigned enlisted units. We're gonna do our best to get everyone out of here…be it one group at a time or all at once. I'm not condemning any man to stay here and die."

Everyone watched as Dusty tore slips of paper, wrote upon them, and folded them in half. Farmer brought a clean, dry pot, into which the papers were dropped, and after a good shaking about, it was presented first to George.

The colonel paused before reaching into the pot. He looked at Ray, and then beyond him into the parade yard. "Even you'll have a number, Corporal. It is fair. If you don't like the position you draw and someone is willing to trade, fine. Otherwise, you go when chosen. If you won't select, I will do it for you."

Ray pretended not to listen, though his face went pale nonetheless. He did not want to be in charge of any man's life but his own. His plan, once he was free, was to get Jennifer to safety, though he did not know how.

Soon, all hands had reached into the pot, except for Sparks who still sat with the radio. Jamie drew a number and took it to him.

With his notepad ready, Bonny asked, "Ones?"

Hands went up. Dusty and Skip, who both seemed immensely relieved with their luck, Jamie who was surprised at his, and lastly George and Taffy, who glanced at one another before both senior officers looked at the others in the room.

Bonny did not notice the visual dialogue as he wrote down the names. Leonard, Ray, Farmer, and Sparks. Ray tossed his paper in KC's direction with a growl. "I told you, I am not going."

"Bonny," Taffy said, "Scratch my name off the ones…"

"Sir?" Bonny started as George grunted, "Ray…"

"Simple, George. You and me and Ronny are the senior officers. Ronny's gonna hold out to the bitter end, just as he's always done…assuming we can get him out of the Cooler…but one of us, you or I, should go with the second…"

"It should be me…"

"No," Jamie said emphatically, refusing to be separated from his father. Taffy smiled at the younger Campbell before nodding.

"Listen to your son, George…stick with your family. This way…if we end up breaking this into separate attempts…at least we keep a ranking officer in each group…and a medic. Robbie?"

Sparks looked up from his transcription, surprised to be called by name. Taffy got up and went to the man's bunk. "You've been in this place longer than any of us. You get to be the first one out…"

"But sir…the radio…"

Taffy clasped the younger man's knee. "Not going to be needing it much longer, son. If it comes down to it, we'll manage a few days without. Take the chance and get outta here. Go home. You've done your duty long enough."

With a trembling hand, Sparks traded slips of paper with the Welshman "Thank you, sir."

George stood, avoiding Jamie's eyes and the notion of family that had been thrust upon him. "It's settled. We work on Wagner…and how to get Ronny and Moretti out. Let the Cell know we're working on a plan...see if they can help. We meet again tonight to discuss it more. Any questions?"

There were none, at least none that were voiced, and the group broke up to go their separate ways, some of them taking a plate of food as they went but most not bothering to eat. They spoke in hushed tones or pondered alone ways they might be able to empty the Stalag of its men before it was too late.

And no doubt, some were thinking about those they would be leaving behind. Sparks thought of Clara and sighed painfully. What could he do? As long as she could help the Cell, fight the war in her way, help von Hausen, she was not likely to go anywhere. And Sparks knew that, no matter what, if anything, she felt for him, she would not leave Stasio.

That did not matter, he decided. He gritted his teeth as he dismantled the radio. He would not let her stay in Ste Marie to die. He would find some way to get her away, even if he had to bring Stasio to be sure she was safe. Better she be safe and alive with Stasio then here, in Ste Marie, facing certain death. Sparks could tolerate her loving another man, so long as she was safe.

Chapter 27
July 26, 1943

S parks was not expecting anyone to be in the barn when he arrived for the morning milking. Caught in thoughts of the future, of tomorrow and what it might bring, caught in wondering whether he would live past the morning, he paid little attention to his surroundings. When he entered the normally empty structure, silent except for the lowing of the cows at the far end, he went about his business as usual. He picked up the empty pails from their normal place and approached the cows, only to stop in surprise when he found Clara there, sitting upon a bale of hay, fondling the animal's ear as she stared, lost in thought. Whether it was the clanking of the metal pails or his arrival, she jolted, surprised, and looked at him with troubled green eyes.

Sparks could not identify the expression that crossed her face, but very little of it seemed positive. She seemed sad, lost, confused and worried, all of which were reasonable given what lay ahead. There looked to be a plethora of other emotions as well, but he could not identify them. When their gazes met, he thought he recognized panic, but it was there only for a moment and then it was gone. He thought she might get up and leave, but she did not stand or otherwise move, only continued to look at him.

He could not help thinking that she was waiting for him, a silly notion that he quickly dismissed as she had no way of knowing who would be assigned this duty for the day. It also struck him as silly because if she had been expecting, or hoping for, his arrival, there should have been no reason for that moment of panic. He concluded she had only come here to be alone and he had intruded upon her solitude, surprising her so that she felt guilty at being caught or afraid he had been a German soldier.

"I'm sorry if I…"

She shook her head. He wished she would say something, even if it was a request to be left alone, but she said nothing.

"You know about the camp?" he managed to stutter, feeling the need to speak in response to her gaze, to fill the awkward silence. He set the pails down, went for the milking stool, and found that she had not moved by the time he returned.

If anything, she seemed sadder than when he had first found her. She sighed as he sat. "Hans told me."

"Oh." He should have realized that. Most likely, the thought of what awaited the Commandant wherever he was being sent next was doing little to ease her mood. "They're wasting no time with the rest of us. First transport trucks are coming tomorrow…taking the French…and Moretti…did you hear about the Italians."

"Only briefly…in town. I have not dared…"

Sparks felt foolish for the third time in those few minutes. He wondered why all he could do this morning was say stupid, obvious things to her. "I can't believe…you've had too many close calls as it is…they'll catch one or the other of us before long…"

"I know." Judging by the slump of her shoulders, he decided that her position in Ste Marie, with the Germans, without Hans to protect her, was weighing heavily upon her. Forgetting the milking for the moment, he sat beside her upon the bale. The least he could do was offer a friendly ear to make amends for his ill-thought words.

She smelled good, like fresh flowers and the warm aromas of a cooking kitchen. He quickly realized that sitting so near her was another bad move, but he could not tear himself away now without looking rude. "What are you going to do?"

In the following silence, she thought about how best to answer that question, her eyes filling with tears as she struggled for an answer. He wanted to hold her, to make things better, but he did not know how. His frustration at his own helplessness was growing to the point where he was considering leaving the barn until she did so, before he did something stupid, but she stopped him with a whisper, "I don't know, Robbie."

There was another awkward silence as he covered the thrill of hearing his name on her lips with rubbing his foot in the straw on the floor. His next words came out abruptly, with little thought, an impulsive gesture he would never be able to take back once made. "Come with me."

She stared with surprise and question, wondering if he meant what she believed he meant, noting that he appeared just as surprised to have voiced that plea as she was to hear it. Before she could respond, he continued, speaking hastily in a hushed tone. He had already done more than his share of stupid today, why, he scolded himself as he spoke, should he stop now?

"Some of us…maybe all of us…are going to try to use the transport tomorrow for cover. I don't know how yet, but it's either try or wait for them to kill us. Few of us believe we're gonna be relocated…that would be too expensive. Cheaper, easier, to waste a few bullets. So come tomorrow…we'll be free…somehow…and you can come with us."

She stiffened and he thought she would rise and leave. But she did not. "I can't," she murmured, but to Sparks, it sounded as though she found the idea tempting.

"Clara…"

She shook her head. "There is work here. Things I must…"

"It is too dangerous now; you bloody well know it. I can see it in your eyes."

"I shall have to face…"

Without a thought, he kissed her. Kissed her to silence the protests, kissed her to convince her that leaving with him was her best chance for survival. She did not resist, rather surrendered into his kiss, far too easily, too completely, for a woman who belonged to another man.

And with that thought, and the taste of her thick and sweet upon his tongue, he drew back, again berating himself. No matter what came next, he doubted he could do anything more foolish than what he had just done. She did not look ashamed of what had happened; her cheeks were flushed and her eyes were bright with fire. With a pang of regret, he realized he could have her then, if he was willing to pursue her, willing to risk being caught. But he had seen what Hans had done to her, seen the effect it had, and he refused to hurt her in the same way.

For once he wished he was not so damn noble.

He drew his tongue across his lips as he calmed his breathing and tried to arrange his thoughts into some sort of speaking order.

"Clara…you know how I feel. I can't bear the thought of you being here when the bomb…"

"If," she corrected, though she too believed it was a matter of when it came, not if.

"If they come," Sparks conceded. "Nor can I bear the thought of the Germans using you for target practice if they catch you…you must come…"

Now she did stand, a look of weary defeat on her face. "I can't. You do not want…"

"But I do, Clara, more than I have ever…"

"I am carrying Stasio's child," she said without looking at him. "I know how men feel about such things…and I cannot leave him. Not now…not ever."

Sparks' breath caught as he leaned against the barn wall. Of all the arguments she could have used to remain in Ste Marie, pregnancy was not the one he had expected. He saw no reason to think she was fabricating the story to be rid of him. And he knew she expected the fact of her condition to make a difference. But it took only a few moments of consideration before he spoke again. "Doesn't the bairn deserve a chance to grow up, to live, somewhere safe and far away from this bloody war? Doesn't it deserve the chance to grow up with a mother and a father and…"

"I will not leave Stasio."

She was decided. Determined. He could see it, and feel it, and he had known it to be her answer all along. But still, it did not matter. "Then bring him." She looked at him skeptically. He stood and grasped her hands. "Both of you…come with us…away from here."

"You would…?"

"Aye…it will be hell…but it would be a greater hell to leave you here…and I'm not so much a rogue as all that. If I were, I would've…" He shrugged. "I'd rather you be away from here, happy with him, then come back here someday and find your marker in Ste Marie because you wouldn't…"

"I don't know…I don't think he will…"

"Not even for his child?"

"He doesn't…"

She stopped, but Sparks heard the last word of the sentence without it being said. He did not ask why she had not told Stasio. Perhaps she had just learned of it herself and that was why she had seemed so forlorn when he found her in the barn. Besides, the reasons for it was none of Sparks' business.

"Tell him. Convince him that leaving is for the best. If he won't go without his family, bring them too. There must be a way out…for all of you."

Clara tugged at the ends of her hair and chewed her lip as she gave his words consideration. "I will…see what can be done…but if he chooses to stay…"

Sparks could hear in her voice that she believed Stasio would choose to remain in his childhood home and that she would stay as well if that was the case. As she turned to leave the stall, he swallowed down the cold acid taste in the back of his throat. He watched until she reached the barn door where she stopped and looked back with large eyes full of immense sadness. "If I don't see you before…good luck and…goodbye, Robbie."

She was gone.

He was left knowing he might never see her again, and he prayed that the tears burning his eyes would blind his sight forever, for he did not think he could stand a world without her in it.

❧*❦

Bonny found it fortunate that he had not been assigned any work detail when Monday morning came, as Obersturmfuhrer Wagner happened to be on Camp 1 duty that morning, weaving through the barracks to make certain they, the latrines, and the grounds were tidy. Not that it mattered any longer, with the impending closure of the Stalag on the horizon. But Stetcher demanded order, insisted that routine was maintained, and so Wagner was tasked with making sure things were done correctly. With his Bible in hand, and thus under the guise of planning a religious discussion with the German soldier, which he had done in the past, Bonny approached Wagner and fell into step beside him.

"Good morning."

The other man smiled wanly. "I apologize for the abruptness with which I was forced to end our discussion last night."

Bonny smiled too, pleased that Wagner had neither forgotten the dialogue nor seemed reluctant to resume it. "I understand. Duty often interferes. You seemed willing to…"

Lowering his voice, Wagner cut him off. "Willing? Nien…eager. I was a business student before my father bid my brother and I enlist. I am no soldier, Padre. I do not wish to be here…and I certainly do not wish to go to the east. My brother has already died there. I have spoken to others…those who will remain behind when the transports go tomorrow…and those who are due to leave with the transports…"

"Do you think…?" Bonny opened his Bible as they stopped walking and the guards in the watchtowers stared. He pointed at a random passage and continued speaking quietly. "It has been discussed that we might use the transports to our advantage…maybe get several of us out in those vehicles…"

"It is possible. There will be three trucks and two Jeeps, sometime early in the morning…but how…?"

"I don't know. The Colonel is still working on the details. Knowing there'll be at least five of you to help…it might give him something to use."

Wagner nodded as he, too, side-eyed the watchtowers and tried to appear calm. "I think this…is enough for one moment, Padre. Give him what I said, and let me know if there is more I can do. I will try to make my tour of the camp this morning as long as I can, in case you need to speak with me again."

The Padre genuflected, touched the man's head as if in blessing, and then ambled away, careful not to go to the barracks where George was waiting so the guards would be less likely to suspect anything. Wagner continued his tour, confident he was doing the right thing but feeling very little assurance about it at the same time.

Zaline paused as she filled the bucket of drinking water and caught Jamie's eye when the Canadian doctor passed by. She already knew, having spoken with Clara, that a massive escape effort was afoot. With such notice, members of the cell were scrambling to find ways to help while going about their daily routines. No one wanted to raise suspicion. It was why she did her best to flash Jamie the calmest smile she could muster, even though she felt anything but calm. When he reached her and took the cup of water, their hands brushed and she tried to prolong that contact as long as she could.

"Be careful," she whispered. "Stay safe." She wanted to say more, but with German soldiers nearby, and other men waiting for water, she did not have the chance.

"You too," Jamie whispered gravely. He stepped away, wiping his mouth on his sleeve, and thought grimly that this was one hell of a depressing goodbye.

❧*❧

The china cup shattered when it hit the floor.

"Bloody shit-headed pig!"

To Wagner's perception, Stetcher was yelling the insult before the cup fell. He and the soldier beside him, Sturmann Gerde, must have perceived the same thing as both took almost imperceptible steps backward away from Stetcher. The third soldier, the one they had followed from the mess hall who was bringing Stetcher breakfast, was too stunned to react or respond in time. It was for that failure, more than the fumbled cup of coffee, that he paid.

"There will be changes!" the Gestapo officer continued to rail.

The ever-present stick came down…and then again…striking the man repeatedly across the side of the head with a violent crack of wood and bone. Again and again, even after the man had fallen and ceased struggling and the walking stick had splintered in two.

Wagner and Gerde could do no more than watch in horrified silence.

Gradually, the warped fury on Stetcher's face was replaced by a deceptive calm, and then by a benign shade of apathy, which to Wagner gave the impression that the man had no idea what he had just done.

Perhaps, he mused, Stetcher was truly as mad as so many men in Stalag 31 believed.

But the precision of care with which the man cleaned blood from the fractured stick before tossing it aside indicated that he knew precisely what had happened. If Stetcher was mad, it was the most dangerous sort of madness of all.

"You had better see your comrade to the infirmary," Stetcher grunted in a disgustingly bored tone.

Wagner looked at Gerde, wondering how best to move a man so badly injured, perhaps not even alive, and wondering if there was anything Dengler would be able to do for him if he were alive.

And Stetcher, with his back towards them as he stared towards the von Hausen residence, added, "See to it that someone cleans up this mess. The Oberfuhrer will not be coming back, so it would behoove everyone to understand the penalties for sloth and carelessness."

Wagner swallowed the lump in his throat and the sick feeling in his stomach. von Hausen…not coming back? Was it true? If so, it did not bode well for any of them, including the Oberfuhrer's wife and daughter. He wondered if they were aware of what was taking place around them.

❧*❦

They were discussing plans for some sort of large-scale escape, that much Marcella knew as she paused out of sight of the gathering of friends and family to listen to them discussing meeting points along the river, at secret groves in the woods and further along the roads out of Ste Marie in all directions. This was going to be the largest effort the Cell had ever attempted from the sounds of it, and Marcella guessed that it meant only one thing.

The prisoners of Stalag 31 were planning something massive.

In the past she had been willing, marginally at least, to hang in the shadows, to let Skip leave without her. But after the last failed attempt, the last time she had bid him goodbye, she knew she could not do that again. She might be able to help him, if nothing else, and with some of Ste Marie's population beginning to vacate the village in preparation for some sort of bombing, Marcella had no intention of remaining here to die. She would help the men, help Skip, regardless of her sister or her father's wishes.

❧*❦

Ray hesitantly, but with merry eyes, stepped into the doorway of the von Hausen home, glancing around furtively with his hat in his hands as Jennifer stepped out of the drawing room as if headed for the staircase. "You wanted to see me, ma'am," he asked formally, only because there were German soldiers within earshot. Jennifer smiled, a welcoming sight despite the pain in her eyes and face, grasped him by the arm, and tugged him into the music room.

"I want your help with something, Corporal," she said for the benefit of those soldiers, who seemed not to care when she closed the door. As soon as the doors closed, whether they could hear her or not, she gasped and threw her arms around him. "Oh Ray…I'm afraid," she whimpered. "There are tigers coming…I heard them say so…and Hans isn't due back until tomorrow I've been told. What am I supposed to do?"

Tigers. Tanks? Were those the bombs Sparks had referred to, not falling from the sky but shot from tanks? Ray shivered. "You'll be okay," he promised. Surely the Germans were not planning on attacking the Commandant's home.

"But what if Hans is not here? I'm not German! They won't care about me...or Mila!"

He embraced her more tightly, stroking her hair, her back, barely resisting the urge to take more of her than this. "Nothing will happen to you...I'll make sure of it," he murmured into her ear as he nuzzled her hair. Whether it was his touch, his embrace, or his words, Jennifer began to calm.

It did not ease the fear on her face, however, as she drew back to look him in the eye. "How? You can't..."

"I'll find a way, Jennifer. I swear it...just...arrange for us to meet again...and I'll come up with something. I will protect you."

"You swear?" she murmured, sounding dazed.

"Yes...I swear."

❧*❧

"No shit," whistled Ronny as he took the lunch Taffy offered in exchange for the strip of cloth he had written on. Taffy had informed him of the incident in Stetcher's office, and Sturmann Gerde was there to confirm it, being the soldier assigned to monitor the meal exchange that day. The young German was clearly angry, despite his efforts to hide it. He had allowed the Welshman to relay the story, but now he closed and locked the door with a gruff, "We've been here too long." Taffy did not argue, as the soldier had every reason to be nervous after what he had seen. Stetcher had killed one man for spilling a cup of coffee. What would he do to someone caught dallying with prisoners?

Muffled voices in the cell, Ronny and Moretti discussing what had happened as the two men outside walked away. Taffy stuffed the message into his pocket and grunted, "Blame it on me if you need to. They had to know the state of things. If Stetcher can beat a man to death over coffee, who knows what he will do to the two of them if he stops to consider them at all."

"News will travel quickly, as will the rumor about Oberfuhrer von Hausen. We know what he's like...have seen the things he does…and Maurice was well-liked. I wager once others learn of this, you'll have all the help you need."

"They may be too terrified for that…"

Looking deeply offended, Gerde growled, "We may be slow to act on occasion, Sturmbannfuhrer, and we may not want to face the Russian front, but we are not cowards. I do not know what has become of the Oberfuhrer that Stetcher believes he will not return, but this man is a tyrant of the worst sort and will see us all dead if he is not stopped. And he'll be stopped, I assure you."

Taffy, like the others, had not been sure they could trust Gerde. He was not a familiar face, having spent most of his hours in Camp 2. They knew, however, that he was often in the company of Wagner when not on duty, and Wagner had sworn to Bonny that Gerde was on their side, one of those not due to be shipped out with tomorrow's transports. He would thus be able to help with any proposed escape attempts, even though he had rarely spoken with the Camp 1 inmates and seemed uneasy about dealing with them.

His outrage at the unnecessary and brutal death doled out by Stetcher was honest, however, hence the Allied soldiers in Stalag 31 were willing to risk trusting him.

They paused as they reached the edge of the appell yard. "How do you plan to…?"

Gerde stopped long enough to look at Taffy and shake his head. "That is not your concern, Sturmbannfuhrer. Concentrate on freedom and what you must do to achieve it. We will take care of our own."

❧*❧

Stetcher dropped the receiver back in its cradle as his other hand tapped furiously on his desk. von Hausen's desk, actually, that the Gestapo officer had commandeered as soon as the Oberfuhrer left Ste Marie. Convinced that the man would not return, he was unafraid of being ejected from this room. Seated across from him, nursing a cup of coffee, Hirsch noted the scowl, having heard one half of the dialogue, and muttered, "I thought you said he wasn't coming back."

"He isn't." The Oberfuhrer was supposed to have been taken care of already, but someone had clearly botched the job. "If he shows…well, he won't be here long." Stetcher felt no compunction about doing the deed himself, but he had hoped for a less messy transfer of power. If von Hausen showed himself in Ste Marie again, it was only going to make the men around him suspicious. Maybe even afraid.

He smiled. Fear was a good thing. He liked the stench of fear. It made him feel alive.

"It will be a minor setback, nothing to worry about. We'll take advantage of the transports…and von Hausen will be out of our way for good."

❧*❧

The phone shook in his trembling hand as Hans waited for his wife to answer. It felt as if he had been away from Ste Marie, from her, for a lifetime, and though he was eager to get back to his family, to perhaps see Clara one last time, he would have been just as happy to turn his back on that life, on what awaited him there, and forget that there had ever been a great war. But his daughter needed him, and it was for his daughter's sake he was calling now.

"Hello?" said the small, terrified voice on the other end of the line when someone finally answered.

"Jennifer? Is that you?" He believed it was, but her voice was so strained he could not be sure.

"Hansy! Thank God! Where are you? They said you were dead! That you're not coming back…" she shrieked.

"I'm not dead," he replied, suppressing his annoyance. Not yet, at least, he thought with an uncomfortable shiver. "Are you alright? And Mila?"

"Mila is fine…but we're scared, Hans. There are tigers! Stetcher said so…" She did not mention Hirsch. After what she had endured in Berlin so many years ago, she was convinced Hans would blame her for Hirsch's attention, accuse her of deserving what she got. At least, Hirsch had convinced her it was so without saying a word.

Tigers? Hans scowled but kept his voice calm. "They will just be passing through, Jennifer; they are nothing for you to worry about." He wished he knew that to be true.

Jennifer wanted so badly to believe him as she quickly downed a glass of brandy, that she murmured, "Are you sure? Will you be home soon?"

Ste Marie was not home. Nowhere was home any longer. But he knew what Jennifer meant and he wanted to soothe her, keep her calm. The only way she was going to be able to function, to follow his next instructions, was to be calm.

"I'm sure, Jennifer. I have word from Command myself. But Jennifer, you must listen to me now. I want you to pack a bag for yourself and one for Mila. Not too much, you understand, just the necessities. I will be there tomorrow and then the three of us are going on that trip I promised. I have made all the arrangements…"

"But the camp…?" Jennifer had no idea how the conditions of the camp were under Stetcher, as she made it a point, most of the time, of pretending the place did not exist. Even when the men came to her gardens, she pretended they were simple gardeners like she had employed in Berlin. Staying behind drawn drapes, locked in the relative safety of the house, was the only way she could cope with the world. But she knew that the camp had been Hans' life since coming to Ste Marie. She could barely imagine him deserting his post during these last days of its existence.

Hans looked down at the train tickets in his hand. He did not want to lie to her, but he did not trust her enough in her drunkenness with something this important. Instead, he continued the lie about a proposed vacation and prayed she would believe him. "Stetcher can manage it for a few days. They don't need me to get the men transferred, and we'll be back in time for the end."

A car horn blew behind him. It was not his car, but she did not have to know that. "Jennifer, I have to go. Remember, one bag for each of you…and be ready when I get there, alright?"

Sensing the strain in his voice, but not attributing it to anything more than work and duty, she said, "We'll be ready, Hans."

"Good." He had not said it when he left the house, but he said it now. "I love you. You know that, right?" Another car horn. "I've got to go.

"I love you too, Hansy…"

He leaned against the wall as he put the phone in the receiver, only barely catching her parting words. He did not want to hear her say what might well be a lie. He only wanted to remember her as she had been long ago. The woman he was risking everything to save.

Wagner watched Clara Beton approach the camp on foot and thought it curious since he believed that she must surely know that the Commandant was not here, that with Stetcher in charge it was more dangerous for her here than ever. She stopped at the gates and an argument ensued as the guards did not understand her French and she did not speak their German. The Commandant's name and rank seemed to be the only bit of dialogue either side understood. Curiosity drew him closer, and when she met his gaze, she squared her shoulders and said in English, "Obersturmfuhrer Wagner. Please, will you assist me?"

It was no secret that both spoke English, so the guards did not question hearing it. But Wagner was surprised she dared speak to him in front of witnesses and so he approached cautiously, a wary expression on his face.

"These louts do not understand my French," she said crossly when he was near enough for an unstrained conversation.

"Nor should they, mademoiselle…"

"And English? Do they not…?"

"Even fewer of us have learned that. If you are looking for the Oberfuhrer, you must know he is not here."

"I know…but I want to return these." Two books were placed in his hands, one in French, one in English. The French one was a child's book with Mila's name printed neatly inside the cover, and so he assumed the books were intended to go to von Hausen. The other, however, written in English, had a maple leaf imprinted on the cover but no name inside. "If you would be so kind as to deliver them to the Colonel for me…"

It was, he realized, intended for an entirely different colonel. He looked at her with surprise that she would so boldly come to the camp, try to pass information through him, or anyone at all. There was no mistaking the understanding that went across his young face. Taffy had told him to expect contact from an outside source, from someone intending to assist the escapees from the outside. He had not been surprised to learn that the prisoners had access to such resources, even in such a small town as Ste Marie.

What did surprise him was that the one woman to have had the most constant access to Stalag 31 and its Commandant would be one of those resources. Then again, he mused, perhaps it should not surprise him at all. It would, however, surprise and dismay von Hausen when he learned of it. If he learned of it. Just what was her role? How long had she been at this ruse? Clara was taking an immense risk revealing herself to any member of the German staff, a bigger risk than she had taken at any other time, and Wagner suddenly felt a great new respect for her, even though she technically was the enemy.

"It is all here. I don't think I've forgotten anything. If there are more left behind, he is welcome to come for them."

Wagner did not know what her words meant, but he was quick enough to latch on to the fact that the colonel would. "I can deliver these, and your message, to the Colonel and to Mila," he said with a nod, gesturing to the books, knowing the guards at least understood the word Colonel and would assume she wished to leave the books for the Commandant. Having been the girl's tutor and knowing the von Hausens were due to leave Ste Marie, it made sense to return any borrowed books now.

"I knew he would want them...before he leaves."

In other words, Wagner decided, he was to get the message contained within the bigger book to Colonel Campbell as soon as possible.

"I'll see that he gets it. Anything more?"

"No." Her tone was dark with melancholy. She turned, took a few steps, and then looked back. "Wait...yes...please tell the colonel...I will miss him when he is gone."

Then she walked quickly away, trying to hide the break in her voice, leaving Wagner to wonder if that final message was meant for Colonel Campbell...or for Oberfuhrer von Hausen.

The expressions around the table that night were nearly as grim as they had been the night after Buckman's death. Tigers rolling into Ste Marie, even if only passing through to some other more significant destination, could not be a good thing.

"I haven't heard anything about tanks," Sparks said. "If they're moving, there's been no mention of them."

"So we have no way of knowing when they're likely to push through." Jamie rubbed the back of his neck. "This puts a wrench in things."

"It only means we'll have to be quick, and careful, in whatever we do," said George in a reassuring low voice.

Dusty glanced at Skip and then agreed. "Doesn't need to stop us...doesn't change anything..."

"Unless they get here before the transports and shell the hell out of this place." Taffy's words were the one contingency they could not anticipate.

"Considering the source, can we even believe it?" growled Skip, leering sourly at Ray.

"Normally, I'd say no," George sighed, "but Wagner believes the report to be accurate…and I believe him."

"So we keep our eyes and ears open and hope for the best?" Leonard asked. Only the fact that Wagner and his German friends had some sort of plan for dealing with Hirsch and Stetcher made Leonard relax about those men being left behind in this initial escape attempt. He still intended to get everyone out on the first run if he could manage it.

"And I'd say be ready to run like blazes."

Heads bobbed in agreement with Vic as the lights out whistle sounded. Come morning, for some of those in this room, this nightmare would be over, one way or another. Most of those men intended to see to it that it ended well for others too…even at the risk of their own lives.

☙*☙

After having stood on the front porch, gazing across the small scatter of lights that made up Ste Marie, thinking back over the memories of her years in this place and trying to decide upon a course of action, the only thing Clara could decide upon was that tonight, no matter what, she had to tell Stasio about the baby. Without that vital bit of information, he could not make an informed decision about their future.

Nor could she.

The only decision made was one that she had made long ago. She would not leave Ste Marie, would not leave France, without Stasio Arnaud.

Most of the lights in the house had gone off except for the oil lamp in the living room and two rooms upstairs. Because of the chaos of cell business today, of which Stasio knew very little, Pensee had been brought to the farmhouse to spend the night. Zaline had thought it was the best place for her child to be. Clara had not been pleased with the decision, as she felt they were too close to the camp to afford anyone safety. She had also felt that the child's presence

☙339☙

would detract from her ability to talk openly with Stasio, but because of his neutrality and lack of information, Clara had to agree that Pensee might be safest here. And the look on Stasio's face as he had catered to his granddaughter all evening had been worth whatever inconvenience it might cause Clara.

Besides, how could any of them possibly have known of the things she had to discuss with him?

She left the porch, closing the door and locking it behind her, and then took the lamp from the desk so that she could find her way upstairs. At the foot of them, she paused to look around the room. Something ominous hung in the air. She did not know what it was, but the sense of impending ruin seemed to seep from the walls to cling to her. It tried to leech her resolve, but she shook the melancholy free and padded softly up the stairs.

At the top, she blew out the lamp. Enough light spilled into the corridor from the two open rooms that she did not need the lamp to find her way. But it was the voice from the first open doorway that held her still for a few moments and then pulled her to the door.

With his back to Clara, Stasio sat on the edge of Pensee's bed, adjusting the sheets over his granddaughter who looked at him with adoration as he sang.

His voice was low, sweet, and warm. Comforting, soothing...and above all, safe.

A lullaby. The one he always sang to Pensee. The one he sometimes sang to Clara to calm her racing mind. The one he had sung to his own children when they had been young enough to appreciate his efforts to scare away the evils of the night.

Clara listened. It brought tears to her eyes to hear the loving ministrations this man lavished upon the child. That she had held the news of her pregnancy from him for so long and had continued to place her life, and the babe's, in peril, suddenly seemed selfish and foolish. The dam of tears was ruptured by the sob that escaped her chest. With wetness on her cheeks, she retreated, but not without first seeing that Stasio had turned to look at her.

He finished his song, struggling to keep his voice steady behind the strain of worry. He did not know of the events about to wash over Ste Marie, but he did know that danger was upon them. The cell's efforts that day made that obvious. When the final note of his song drifted into stillness, he bent to kiss the girl goodnight.

"Is Tante Clara alright?" Pensee murmured sleepily.

He smiled at her. "I'm sure she is. She has had a long busy day and is very tired…just like you. Sleep now."

"Yes, Grand-pére." She kissed his bearded chin and settle further into her pillows as he adjusted her sheets again.

Stasio blew out the lamp and watched her from the doorway for several minutes before turning his focus to Clara. He followed the faded echo of her footsteps and sobs, worried about what he would find when he reached her.

"Clara?"

He entered the bedroom, apprehensive about her state of mind. She was standing in her nightgown, her back to him, staring out the window, her arms wrapped around herself. It was a stance he recognized, one that begged comfort, shielding, and refuge, and so he obliged by putting his arms around her.

"It has been a long day, ma cherie."

She lay her head against his shoulder, finding comfort in his nearness. "Yes."

"Are you okay?"

"No." There was no reason to lie to him. "I don't know if that will ever again be possible."

"Come." He tried to turn her towards the bed; when she resisted, he did not try again. He kept his arms enfolded around her and though she nestled against him once more, she did not relax."

"You know that the Stalag is going to be…"

"Oui…so you said…"

"It seems that…Hans may not make it to Berlin. He may not be coming back to Ste Marie…and his family…"

Stasio kissed the side of her head. Perhaps she had not been in love with the Commandant, but she had clearly grown to care deeply for him, and he knew she cared about Mila. The implications of the man not returning to Ste Marie, of his likely death and what that meant for the Stalag went much further than that. It came down to the matter of her safety, to the safety of Ste Marie and everyone in it, the men of Stalag 31 and the villagers. Stasio understood this. He held her tighter as his thoughts began again to circle the matter of how best to keep her safe.

"Tomorrow, the French prisoners are being transferred elsewhere…and several of the others are planning to use that…"

"…for the escape the cell is helping to organize?"

For a man who seemed to know so little, who strove to stay away from Cell business, he knew more than Clara expected. "Yes," she sighed, "assuming they're not killed instead of actually transferred. They're convinced that most will never be transported, that it was never intended…that if Stetcher does not kill them, they will die in the bombing…"

"Has it been confirmed then?"

"As much as anything can be these days. I've told Louis and Isabelle, hoping they will take precautions…get people out of Ste Marie to safety…but so many are determined to stay."

"This is their home," he murmured against her ear. "Most have lived here for generations. They would rather die than…"

"And you?" She looked up at him beseechingly. "Would you sooner die than leave here, with me and…?"

He brushed her cheeks with his lips. "Ma cherie…"

"Sparks…Lieutenant McKenzie…is part of the escape planned for tomorrow. He asked me to go with him, to not stay here to die…"

Holding her head against his shoulder, Stasio fought the lump in his throat that cut off the flow of air. He knew that her leaving Ste Marie was the only answer to protecting her, but he had never anticipated that the idea might come to her from another man. After struggling with the tumble of thoughts and emotions, he murmured, "You should go, ma cherie."

She pulled free of his arms and stared at him, shocked and hurt. He had expected a negative response, but not the depth of pain he saw in her eyes. Regretting speaking, he continued in an attempt to clarify his position. "Whether there is a bombing or not, without von Hausen to protect you…you are in too much danger here. Stetcher will kill you at the first opportunity he finds…or creates…perhaps merely for crossing the street. You can stay here no longer. If McKenzie can protect you…and I believe that he cares for you as much as I do…if he can keep you safe and see you away from here…then you should go with him."

"I cannot."

"Clara. I need you to be safe…and you are not. Not here. Not anymore…if indeed you ever were."

"I will not go unless you come with me," she sniffed stubbornly.

"I cannot." He kissed her mouth gently. "I cannot stand in the way of your future, and I believe that if God wills it you will find your way back to me when this war is over…"

"What of our future, Stasio? Yours and mine and…" She stared out the window again. There had been more that she had intended to say, but before he could ask her what that was, she looked back at him with an unusual, uncertain fear in her eyes and asked, "Doesn't your child deserve to know its father?"

"My child…?" Frozen, he stared at her. Though he questioned what his ears had heard, he understood now. Everything. Her moods, her behavior, her fears. "You are…?" He inched closer.

"Near two months…I think…" She lowered her gaze in embarrassment.

"And you did not…?"

"How could I? I just learned of it myself. Your daughters are grown. You have a granddaughter. You made it clear early that…the sort of commitment a family entailed was not what you wanted of me. And…there was always a chance you would think it was his…that you'd be angry…"

"His? von Hausen's? Mon Dieu…I know you better than that. And just because I…because Zaline and Marcella are…"

He fumbled for words, flustered by the notion of fatherhood, and by the rush of love and adoration he felt for this woman who had given to him so selflessly, who was willing to remain in harm's way and risk death for him. The woman who carried his child.

"That is all the more reason for you to…"

She shook her head. "I will not leave Ste Marie without you. This is your home, your history, your life. You are my…our…future. If you stay, so do we…unless you demand I go and…"

"I could never send you anywhere. It would kill me to do that. You are right. I did not want a new family…but I love you too much…and you are family whether I have said it or not. As such, I cannot let you, either of you, stay and face death on my behalf."

She tiled her fact towards his, so sweet and innocent and beguiling that he kissed her. The innocence of the kiss was lost quickly as she pulled his shirt free and slid her hands up his back. That was the beginning, the return of fire, of the woman he loved. She took a step, making him back up until they tumbled onto the bed. Holding her, he pulled her with him as he fell.

Stasio freed himself long enough to complete the process of undressing. "I will speak to Zaline in the morning and have her make the necessary preparations; we shall be gone from here as soon as it can be arranged. There is only one thing I ask."

She stared at him, knowing what he wanted. Chewing her lip as he settled her weight upon him, she weighed the question only briefly. If he were willing to give up the only life he had ever known for her, for their child, then she could surely give up the single most dangerous aspect of hers.

"Just one more...I will update them in the morning about upcoming events...tell them it is no longer safe for me to..."

Kissing the hollow of her throat as his hands moved down her sides to find the hem of her nightgown, he said softly, "Fair enough."

"I love you, Stasio."

In her voice he recognized the sound of crying in the darkness, reading the pleading expression upon her face without being able to see it clearly, waiting for him to say what she wanted to hear. This time, however, she did not need to ask for it.

With his mouth near hers, he murmured, "I love you, ma cherie."

He kissed her and held her tight, intending to never let her go.

Chapter 28
July 27, 1943

I t was not yet dawn when the two soldiers came off duty. Wagner could hear the barracks door open, hear their heavy boots on the wooden floor as he shoved the tiny vial into the stuffing of his pillow. By the time the two reached him, he was stirring cups of coffee on a tray. There were three, and as the men shared a corner of the bunkroom and often brought coffee for one another, neither thought it unusual when he offered a cup to each. They stripped as they drank, none speaking, and before either finished their drink, they were staggering as if drunk and were helped to bed by their accommodating companion. Wagner made each comfortable, gathered up the uniforms, and put all three cups into the latrine sink. He needed the uniforms, and he needed these two particular men out of the way. Knowing they would hinder his cause if they could, it made more sense to let them sleep through today's duty...even though their names had been on the roster for departure. Let Stetcher figure out the mix up later. By the time someone learned of the problem, Wagner intended to be far away from Stalag 31.

❧*❧

The dialogue with her British contacts had gone much smoother than anticipated. With the closing of Stalag 31, and the potential bombing of the camp, the village, or both, in the offing, it made sense to all that she ceased communications indefinitely. Clara had been prepared to fight, to struggle to make her case, and that it had not been necessary was both troubling and reassuring. How vital had her work been to London and to the Resistance and to the war effort at large? She had saved lives, she knew, and aided in dealing several crippling blows to the local German movements, but the thought that she might have been less important than she wanted to be left a sour taste in her mouth. That was tempered, however, with the gratitude that someone just might see her life as valuable enough to be saved while it was still possible to do so.

In truth, however, neither mattered now. All of that was a thing of her past, a life she intended to leave behind. She was going back to Stasio, steering the wagon through the early morning dawn, bouncing over the dirt road as quickly as the single horse could pull her along. She would get home, and by then Stasio would have spoken to Zaline and, with any luck, they would leave Ste Marie before noon, nightfall at the latest.

There had been no available information from London about the impending bombing or the relocation of Stalag 31 staff or prisoners. Perhaps they deemed it unimportant to tell her, since she was ceasing contact, or wisest not to tell her so that she would have no further intel weighing her down. It was also possible that, given the lack of details she had picked up recently, there was nothing to share. From here on out, she was on her own.

A loud crack and snapping of wood shattered the early morning tranquility as a wheel hit a rut in the road and the back corner of the wagon dropped with a crash. Clara hung on to the reins and the wooden frame in front of her, barely avoiding being thrown from the seat to the ground.

"Merde," she muttered, climbing out of the wagon. She took her hat from her head and laid it upon the seat. Fortunately, there was a spare wheel kept within the wagon, and the tools required to replace the broken one, but this was a delay she did not want or need today. All she wanted was to be with Stasio, whom she had left standing in the kitchen doorway waving with a satisfied, peaceful expression. Everything was going to be alright.

How could she have guessed that the conception of a child would mean so much, have such a profound impact on his outlook?

Her struggle with the wagon wheel was interrupted by the sound of an approaching automobile on the road behind her. Anyone else traveling at such an early hour was surprising, and that surprise urged her to look up, to make note of the sort of vehicle it might be. German, she assumed, before spotting it, which brought her heart throbbing into her throat. She could not afford to be caught here, now. Not like this.

Even at this distance, however, she recognized the sleek grey car, and when she did, her trembling hands dropped the spare wheel.

She stared, straightened, trying to appear calm, even grateful, when the car came to a stop behind the wagon. Unconsciously, however, she backed away from the man as he got out of the car.

"Clara?"

Hans. Alive. Not dead as Stetcher claimed, as she had feared…or maybe even hoped for. Alive. How could this be?

Though he seemed pleased to see her, as well as surprised and confused by it, his whole demeanor was too dull with worry and surrender to brighten as much as it normally did upon seeing her. Still, he managed a smile as he came closer. "What are you doing out here so early?"

She stepped away from him, realizing as she did so that the action might be perceived as fear, and so she covered the movement by picking up the dropped spare wheel. "I'm on my way home from Larrey. I was there yesterday on business, but it was too late to leave by the time I finished my errands."

"Yes…a woman traveling alone at night now is not safe." He scowled a little, reminded of his promise to his wife and his previous promise to Clara. He meant nothing in approaching her, only wanting to offer friendly assistance, but she seemed determined to keep distance between them, lest he forget those promises and do something they would both later regret. He sighed, realizing there was little time for regret now. He could take what he wanted, if he wished, but he respected and loved Clara too much for that. He had made that mistake with her once. "You must have left early to get this far…"

"I want to be home," she replied. From his slightly downturned gaze, she knew that Hans interpreted her words to mean that she wanted to be with Stasio; it was the truth, but not all of it.

He glanced at the wagon. "Seems you've had a bit of trouble. I could give you a ride back to Ste Marie…"

"I can't leave the wagon and horse here. It will only take me a few minutes to…"

"True…someone might steal them. Well then, let me help…"

"That's not necessary, Hans."

"Don't be silly, Clara. I am here. I might as well help. A little manual labor won't kill me." It meant putting off his return to Stalag 31, a brief blessing he wanted to take advantage of. "Let me help you get back on your way."

He waited while Clara got the broken wheel off, holding up the back end of the wagon as she did so, and then continued to hold it while she slid the replacement into place. He watched her every move, awed that such a dainty thing could do such difficult work on her own. There was the scraping of wood against wood as she pulled a box of tools from beneath the wagon's seat and began to rummage through it.

Heart hammering so loudly she believed he had to hear it, she tried her best to maneuver the radio out of sight while looking for the tools she needed. She had not taken the time to dismantle it before starting home, in her haste she had taken the risk that she could make it home without incident. If Hans found it, she did not know what he would do.

"I can manage now, Hans," she stammered. "The wagon's weight will keep the wheel in place while I fasten it," so long as there were no jarring side to side movements to dislodge it. "You must have better things to do than…" She wanted him to leave before something went horribly wrong.

"Actually…I don't…"

Clara met his gaze. Both knew what awaited him when he returned to the Stalag, and she could not blame him for not wanting to face it. She did not want him to face that humiliating end either; her knotted stomach began to sink within her, crawling slowly down to her knees. He let the wagon's weight settle on the not yet fastened wheel and asked, "Has anything interesting happened in Ste Marie while I have been away?" as he started around the other side of the wagon, intent on helping find the needed tools. Panic-stricken, Clara drew the revolver that she had kept with her during this trip and hid it behind her back with one hand as she tried to push the radio under the seat with the other.

"More than you want to know about, I'm afraid," she replied shakily. He sighed with understanding and disappointment.

The radio caught on the uneven floorboards.

"I'm afraid with my return, things will get worse if I'm caught…"

"Hans…"

He reached beneath the wagon seat without looking and pulled out the first thing his hand came in contact with, expecting it to be a box of more tools. When he looked down, recognizing the object at once, there was a distinctly familiar click from the other side of the wagon. His head slowly lifted, sweat forming on his brow, and he found himself staring into the barrel of a revolver…held by Clara Beton.

For several long moments, they stared at one another.

Without looking at the radio again, or touching it further, Hans carefully backed away from the wagon. He understood now. Understood all of those tiny signals she had been sending since the first day they met. Signals telling him not to trust her, not to open up to her, not to be her friend. Because as he looked at her now, he understood how painfully duplicitous her life had been. There were grief and torment in her eyes; she had come to think of him as a friend, an almost lover, when he was supposed to be nothing more than a job. Even now, duty and emotion warred powerfully within her, causing her hands to shake.

Watching him, Clara reached her own level of understanding as well. To let him walk away from this moment was death to herself and to Stasio, as well as to Jennifer, Mila, and even Hans himself. They both knew he was destined to die; if he did not know about the bombing, he certainly knew that death awaited him in Berlin, unless it found him in Stalag 31 at Stetcher's hands, for the man would not welcome him back with open arms. So long as he lived, his family was condemned to death, for Jennifer, for all of her faults, would never leave him.

For Hans von Hausen, death was the only future that awaited.

For Clara, the choices and options were not so clear-cut. Both recalled their parting words, the last time they had spoken. There was no way, regardless of his intentions and desires, that Hans could protect her, particularly now that he knew the truth. And Clara had promised to protect him from the powers in Berlin if she could.

Her gaze flickered to the radio and back to Hans' face.

If he had been on the same side of the wagon, he could have rushed her. He was stronger; he could have taken the gun. But for what? She could protect him, as promised, and they both knew it. He sighed heavily and then looked at her with pleading in his eyes, pushing the host of 'what ifs' from his mind. This was peculiarly, perversely, poetic, and he found a degree of peace in that moment that he knew he would never feel staring down a firing squad or down the barrel of Stetcher's gun. She had to be the one to do it. It had to be Clara. She had to do what needed to be done.

But why, she begged with her own pleading eyes as tears slid down her cheeks and his, did it have to be her?

"Make sure Jennifer and Mila are safe," he begged, "and please…save yourself…"

He tried to smile, to thank her, and closed his eyes in acceptance of the inevitable. There was no need to make this harder for her. No need to make this harder for either of them.

She squeezed hers shut too…and squeezed the trigger.

The shot in the morning air was like thunder, and Hans slumped to the ground with an expression of relief, reaching for her as the red stain of life spread upon his white dress shirt.

She did not move. For what felt like an eternity, Clara stood with the gun pointing at the spot where Hans had stood, even though she could no longer see him. It was the sound of coughing, the gurgle of drowning, that made her feet move and brought her around the wagon to where the blonde man lay in an ever-widening pool of blood. He reached for her and the gun lowered.

She wondered what she should do. The spark in his blue eyes was dimming, blood beginning to seep from the corner of his mouth. She had done this. She had been the one to shoot him, to kill him, and those realizations made her drop to her knees and clutch his hand as she pulled his head onto her lap. Whatever else the man may have done, might be, she did not believe he deserved to die alone. For what she had done, giving in to the inevitable to save them both, she owed him this last act of kindness. He had offered his life to save his family…and to save hers. A heroic act she would never forget.

"I'm sorry, Hans…" she whispered tearfully.

His grip tightened on her hand. "Don't be…I'm glad…if it had to be anyone…it is you. Now you are safe, my Clara…" He gave her one last weak, fading smile.

His hand went limp and the light left his eyes.

She stared, letting tears fall, thankful there was no one nearby to see this. She felt nothing except pain, shock, and a rawness gnawing in her belly that screamed she had just killed a man.

How ironic, she thought, that the first man, the only man, she had killed in this bloody war had been a German. A Nazi. And a beloved friend.

She looked at the car, and then the wagon. She dared not take the car to Ste Marie, for it was an SS vehicle and one that would mark her as some sort of threat to anyone who saw her. And, she realized with a sinking sensation, that she should not return to Ste Marie at all. Hans' blood was on her hands, literally, on her lap as well, and by the time she could reach the farmhouse with the wagon, or even on horseback, someone was likely to have found the car, and the body, and she and Stasio would never make it out of Ste Marie.

If she left the wagon, if it was identified, Stasio would be in grave danger. It seemed wiser, as she sorted through her options, that she turn and travel the remaining distance to Larrey, phone Stasio from there, and have him come for her in the truck.

Now that practicality had set in, she slid Hans' head gently from her lap, fighting the impulse to cry, and hastened to finish attaching the wagon wheel. No one else came as she worked, for which she was grateful. She climbed into the wagon, turned it east, but stopped before she could start her final journey away from Ste Marie.

She looked at Hans' body on the road.

It seemed wrong to leave him this way. Lord knew what would become of his corpse, or how long it would lie there before he was found. She was not strong enough to get him back into the car, however, and she respected him too much to drag him into the bushes where he would never be found. Groaning, she climbed from the wagon, returned to his side, and knelt near him again. Was there something she should take, something to send to his daughter someday, if she could, to serve as a reminder of the father she had just lost. Doing so would implicate Clara in a death she wanted no responsibility for...ever...even though she was to blame.

Maybe it would be better for Mila to never learn the truth.

But Clara needed something for herself, something to remember Hans by. Something more painful and permanent than the blood-stained clothing she wore. She pulled his rank pins from his lapel, shoved them into her pocket and then, as an afterthought, pulled his wedding ring from his finger and felt in his trouser pockets for his wallet. From it she withdrew what money there was, hoping that would make his death appear to be a robbery, and hesitated when she found a tiny picture of Hans and his family, the same one he always carried, the proof to his errant wife that he loved her more than she would ever know.

With a trembling hand, she pulled the photo free and took his revolver from his holster. She bent low, laid a kiss on Hans' forehead before closing his blue eyes forever, getting back into the wagon without noticing the pair of bloody train tickets she was leaving behind.

East.

Away from Hans and what she had done.

Chapter 29
July 27, 1943

Morning appell was over and the men from Camp 1 were sent their separate ways for the day's work. The camp might be facing imminent closure, but Stetcher was determined to keep every prisoner working until the end. Idle hands would only result in trouble. George and Jamie were sent to the repair shed as Wagner had previously told them they would be. The only unanticipated change was that Ray was sent with Leonard to work in the von Hausen's garden when Ray had been meant to serve in the fields, a development that made the Allied officers nervous. They watched Ray saunter off with a bounce in his step and worried that he might not have learned from Skip's past mistakes. If there was a chance for any betrayal of their plans, it was going to come from Ray…unless Leonard could stop him.

❧*❦

"Everything you'll need is either in the mattress, in the ceiling, or with Leonard," Sparks explained breathlessly as he hurriedly dried himself. Farmer stood in the water house doorway, keeping lookout though he was supposed to be sharing latrine cleaning duties with Sparks. It was a duty both had volunteered for. As promised, Wagner had left two German uniforms hidden there, intended for both Sparks and Jamie, two of the most fluent German speakers in the camp. Unable to fathom wearing such a uniform smelling like a dirty latrine, the Scot opted for a quick but discreet washing as Farmer stood guard.

Now, with his body still slightly damp, the Scot was trying to pull on a uniform that was sticking to his skin. A uniform that made him feel dirty despite the shower.

"I'll find it," Farmer assured him.

"And you remember how to…?"

"I tinkered a bit with them back home. I'll manage…and if it doesn't work, it'll only be a few more days at most for the rest of us…provided Stetcher doesn't…"

Sparks looked at him with remorse. "I'm really sorry about that…"

"Don't be." Farmer looked outside to continue his lookout, but mainly to steady his voice. "We all took our chances coming into this war…things happen…besides…if things go well today, maybe we'll all get out of here." He knew Sparks did not know what he meant, but he was not going to elaborate. Sparks had enough to worry about. "You've got the letters for…?"

Sparks patted the bundle of envelopes that lay beside the uniform jacket. "I'll make sure they get out if I can…and they'll know you'll be home soon."

"Thanks."

Sparks wanted to say more, thought he should say more, but both knew the odds today, and in the days that followed, were stacked against them. Regardless of whether the escape failed or succeed, men were going to die.

Some of the men from Stalag 31 would never make it home.

Farmer whistled over his shoulder. "Jamie's coming." Sparks threw on the jacket just as the Canadian medic entered the water house, ostensibly to use the latrine.

"Here." Sparks tossed the remaining uniform in Jamie's direction.

"Why do you get the shower?" grumbled Jamie as he peeled out of his unwashed clothing to exchange it for a German uniform.

"I got here first…" He rubbed his smooth chin. "And I had to get rid of this." Not many German officers he had seen wore beards. It had to go.

Farmer tapped on the wall. "It's clear…and…" They could hear the rumble of trucks. "Convoy's here."

"Showtime." Sparks emerged from the latrine, adjusting his hat, and looked into the distance, speaking as if scolding Farmer until he was joined by the nearby Wagner. Barely getting his uniform on as the trucks rolled through the gates a few minutes ahead of schedule, Jamie yanked on the polished boots and stumbled out to join them.

❧*❧

Anton Stetcher tapped his newly fashioned metal walking stick on the toe of his boot, scanning the road in all directions as the transport convoy pulled through the gates. Three trucks and two Jeeps, just as he had been told. Everything was as it should be.

Except for von Hausen.

Not that he wanted the Oberfuhrer here. He had believed it when the Oberfuhrer had told him he had been called away, and he had believed that the man was being taken care of elsewhere. The phone call from von Hausen yesterday, announcing that he would return to the Stalag this morning before the arrival of the transport, was definitely a glitch. Yet the news also satisfied his sadistic streak, for if von Hausen did arrive, not before the convoy's arrival but perhaps before its departure, it would give Stetcher the joy of killing the Oberfuhrer himself, preferably in front of his family and every man in the camp, something he had wanted to do for a very long time.

But the sun was up, moments ticked past, and now the convoy was here without a sign of von Hausen. It was possible he had finally been eliminated elsewhere, but Stetcher needed to know. He did not want surprises. Knowing was infinitely better than wondering how or when the Oberfuhrer would arrive to interfere in events controlled by outside, untouchable forces.

Within the perimeter of Camp 2, Hirsch had kept the men at parade stance since appell, refusing to allow them either a bathroom break or breakfast. He saw no reason to waste food on people who would shortly no longer be his problem. He stood now near the gate, watching, awaiting orders. The men behind him looked at the ground, or each other, or furtively around with the expressions of men leaving a beloved home. Stalag 31 had been unpleasant, but an uncertain future was worse. Stetcher, smirking at the irony of these men wanting to stay despite the way he had treated them, straightened his uniform and tapped his stick on the wooden planks.

He stepped off the infirmary porch, stick tapping as he walked, and approached the officer who emerged from the front Jeep.

"Haupsturmfuhrer," he grunted to the roundish little man who saluted him.

If the man noticed the condescension in the Gestapo's voice, he gave no sign of it. "Sturmbannfuhrer. We are ready." The fellow produced a fistful of documents. "You will find everything in order."

Stetcher took his time leafing through the pages, looking for all necessary signatures, every detail, though he did not care about any of it. He just wanted these men gone. He wondered, after he tucked the bundle under his arm, how much this Haupsturmfuhrer knew about what lay in store today.

Wagner wiped his brow as he looked at the men beside him. McKenzie was adjusting his collar, appearing hot and uncomfortable in the unfamiliar uniform and naked without his beard. Trying to escape was stressful enough. Doing it in a German uniform was almost unbearable. "We should get closer; he'll want to load soon. Do what you're told, keep your head down, don't speak if you can avoid it, and whatever you do, stay away from Stetcher." Wagner did not know if Stetcher knew each German soldier by face or by name, but he would definitely recognize the familiar Camp 1 faces.

Staring straight ahead, head bobbing once, Sparks muttered, "Easier said than done."

Satisfied with the formality of documents and feeling they had waited long enough, Stetcher waved his hand. "Let's get this over with."

"Load up," the Haupsturmfuhrer shouted. The few soldiers and drivers standing at attention near their vehicles hurried to obey, opening the tailgates of the trucks while the guards stationed outside Camp 2 unlocked and opened the gates.

Stetcher pointed the prisoners into three lines, each to be led to one of the trucks. The conditions would be crowded, stifling, unbearable, but they had no choice but to comply. "Behave yourselves and this will be painless and quick."

The few men who understood his German looked at each other as if to say, 'sounds like a death sentence to me'.

No one had thought it necessary to tell the mail service what was to transpire in Ste Marie. The little truck bounced along the dirt road, its driver whistling to himself, oblivious to the chaos he was about to stumble into. He had passed a woman in a wagon some time ago, but such sights were common and he had thought nothing of it. Unarmed and a peaceful man by nature, a man sent to deliver letters, nothing more, he was not looking for trouble.

He was not looking, but it found him.

The parked sedan on the side of the road did not immediately attract attention. Could be someone was lost, or was taking a break, or had even parked the car to catch up on sleep. It was not until he eased his mail truck to the other side of the road to pass that he saw the body. That drew his attention. He frowned, stopped the truck, and eased out, looking around for signs of trouble. Peering through the open sedan window revealed an empty car and he saw no evidence of anyone else in the vicinity. The officer, a German officer, was clearly dead, judging by the pool of blood in which he lay and that was spread across his chest. The mail driver looked around again, this time in panic. What was he supposed to do?

❧*❦

The German soldier at the gate of Camp 1 allowed Wagner, Sparks, and Jamie to pass without asking questions or giving them a second look. Neither knew whether this was because he was one of Wagner's men or because he did not recognize them or suspect trouble. Wagner had said not to worry about such things, and thus far the German had been as good as his word. It was best to ignore coincidences, focus on the task at hand…and pray.

The men from Camp 2 were now filing through the gate towards the transports.

"Wagner!" shouted someone near the front Jeep. "Help me load. You…" he pointed at Jamie, "wait there and help those that need assistance into the truck."

"You…" Two soldiers, including Gerde, approached Sparks from the rear of the convoy. "Come with us. We must retrieve Moretti."

Sparks opened his mouth to speak, the words almost in English, but caught himself before the mistake was made and said, "Yes, sir," in German. As he followed, he glanced at Jamie and Wagner with some concern. Jamie too appeared uneasy, left alone to load prisoners with no one for back up should the Germans recognize him. But there was nothing they could do to change things. Sparks instead focused forward, aware that some within Camp 1 were staring with an intensity of interest that he hoped would not blow his cover. Then again, he reminded himself, the Germans were often stared at when they entered the camps. And they were heading towards the Cooler, where they knew Moretti to be. The interest in their activities should appear, to the Germans, entirely normal.

Vic rose from the Barracks J porch, scowling, to join the cluster of men gathered along the gate fence. The rabble, led by Ollie, was clutching the wire, yelling obscenities at the Germans and throwing rocks at the vehicles, while also shouting words of encouragement to the men from Camp 2. The Germans seemed to have better things to do today than shoot at them to make them behave. In their midst, Dusty and Skip were biding their time, waiting for their cue to act, watching the proceedings for signs of trouble.

Dusty was mainly watching the porch of the tool repair shed where George had come out alone. He was sharpening an ax blade as he watched the loading, making a show of not shirking responsibility. Skip's gaze aimed further away, at the tiny form that was Ray who watched from the von Hausen's garden, hoe in hand. Beside him, Leonard toyed with a spade, his stance suggesting that, should Ray do anything questionable, he would not hesitate to stop him, even if it meant killing him.

⊱*⊰

The Camp 2 prisoners were brought to the trucks and instructed to wait.

"Search them," Stetcher ordered from the porch. Jamie glanced questioningly at Wagner, who waited beside the third truck. It seemed that Stetcher, for whatever reason, found it distasteful to walk amongst the Camp 2 prisoners, and Hirsch had gone to the porch to stand with him. It left the soldiers to the loading duties. It would, Jamie hoped, give them more freedom to begin the searching as he started with the first of the men to climb into the second truck.

Prepared for what would happen later, the French had done as instructed, hiding knives, sharpened sticks, and strips of wood with nails in them within their clothing. Wagner had his men at each of the trucks so that they carried their makeshift weapons with them into the back of each vehicle.

⊱*⊰

"It's going to get crazy," muttered the Italian under his breath as they released him from confinement. He wished they could release Ronny as well, but doing so would attract attention and they could not afford that. The key to the lock, however, was left inside the empty solitary cell, with others from Barracks J knowing it was there so that they could release the barnstormer as soon as it seemed safe to do so. Moretti walked in the midst of the tiny group of soldiers, with Gerde in the front and Sparks in the rear. The Scot scanned the crowd along the fence, and the truck beyond, wondering exactly what these men had planned. For he could tell their actions were calculated, even though whatever they were plotting had not been initiated, arranged, or planned by George.

When the group reached the gate, the soldier there unlocked it and slipped the key to Gerde as he and the other soldier held back the crowd long enough for Sparks to escort the Italian through the gate.

Moretti pretended not to notice any peculiarity in their behavior.

With the gate unlocked and opened, the two passed through just moments before Skip and Dusty charged. The surge of men was too much for Gerde and his fellow officers and they were pushed beyond those inner gates as prisoners surged forward, shouting prearranged insults at the Italian traitor.

Vic was there also, less to help than to take advantage of the chaos, to do something he had wanted to do for weeks. "Gonna get us fucking killed!" he shouted, catching Skip's arm, spinning him around, and landing a fist squarely across the Aussie's jaw.

"What in God's name...?" Dusty swore.

Forgetting the plan for a moment, Skip rushed headfirst into Vic's stomach, knocking the Scot backward with a roar.

Before he fell, Vic managed to bring one knee up to catch Skip in the lower abdomen, a blow low enough that it caused Skip to yelp and sink to his knees.

"Oh no you don't." Dusty yanked Skip to his unsteady feet.

The Germans in the surrounding towers were barking orders, hesitant to shoot into the melee where German soldiers were caught. Gerde and his companions continued to try to hold the men back as he shouted, "Don't worry about us! Get him into the truck."

Sparks propelled Moretti along more roughly than he liked, flinching with the crack of a rifle behind him.

"Don't let them see that it bothers you," Moretti hissed.

Sparks snorted and kept moving.

In the midst of the melee, as the swarm of prisoners filled the vacuum between Skip and Vic, Dusty shouted at the Scot, "I hope the Nazis blow your damn head off!"

"In your dreams!"

Some of the men had, by now, maneuvered their way out of the Camp 1 gate, Ollie included. Other soldiers from around the Stalag were rushing to put down the impending riot, including Hirsch, who had wisely fled Stetcher's side to appease the red-faced Gestapo officer rather than risk the wrath of the walking stick.

"Hurry up!" Stetcher yelled. "Get them in the trucks!"

There was so much commotion in the Stalag now that the Germans did not notice that Dusty had successfully pulled Skip outside of the gate and slipped into the line of Camp 2 prisoners being herded into the third truck. Vic's blow had been enough to hamper Skip's walking, but he made it with Dusty's aid until Wagner hustled them into the vehicle before Hirsch got close enough to notice. The French, aware of what was happening, showed no indication that anything was unusual.

In their haste to comply with Stetcher's demands, the Germans were no longer counting the men as they loaded the trucks. From where Stetcher stood on the infirmary porch, he was unable to see any of the commotion clearly.

As the swarm of German soldiers came, the count too short as those Wagner had drugged continued to sleep, George slipped off of the porch and into the rushing mass of bodies. From his garden vantage point, Ray began to call out, although to who was unclear. Leonard elbowed him sharply in the ribs, silencing the young man. Out of Stetcher's line of sight, George peeled out of the running mass and slipped into the line of prisoners being loaded into the middle truck. Jamie saw his father coming and assisted him up without a proper search. George still carried the ax blade in the pocket of his officer's jacket.

❧*❧

The rusted out mail truck bounced to a halt well away from the camp gates and the convoy of men the driver could see being loaded. He had parked closer to the von Hausen home to avoid the camp chaos, and after getting out of the truck, he stood beside it, his hat in his hands, staring from the ground to the camp gates. Not a brave man, he did not look forward to the notion of approaching the commanding officer with this particular delivery.

Jennifer, having watched the morning's events from the window, came onto the porch when the truck stopped, hoping for some form of good news or a distracting bit of mail…or even her husband if he had been forced to use some other form of transportation. She cast a cursory glance at Ray, barely seeing him, before shooing her daughter indoors. One of the guards overseeing Ray and Leonard's work approached the mail truck.

Stetcher, seeing a protracted argument erupt between two of his soldiers and the mousy mail driver, snarled under his breath. Leaving the loading under Hirsch's command, he left the porch and marched through the gates towards the von Hausen's house. His anger fueled his pace so that he was quickly upon the arguing men; when he reached them he banged his metal stick on the side of the truck and shouted, "Enough!"

Despite his best efforts, the dirt road had caused his payload to shift. When the mail driver opened the rear of the truck, the body he had dutifully brought with him, against every gut instinct, tumbled onto the hard-packed earth.

She recognized him, recognized that hated uniform, even across the distance between them. Jennifer screamed, "Hansy!" and started to run to him. Ray, afraid for her safety, shouted, "Jennifer," and went after her, grabbing for her arm to pull her back.

Maybe he was aiming at Jennifer. Maybe not. The bark of Stetcher's firearm stopped everyone, prisoners and soldiers alike, in their tracks.

Within the Stalag, Jamie could not move. Almost could not breathe with the short, quick gasps that involuntarily erupted felt like swallowing fire into his lungs. He paid no attention to the Camp 2 prisoners still climbing into the truck as he watched Ray fly backward and land with a crack against the house steps.

"Get in the house!" Stetcher snarled at Jennifer, the fury in his voice shifting targets now as the gun aimed at her. The second soldier who had been inches away from Ray looked ghostly white as he pulled the screeching woman by the arm towards her front door.

From the doorway, Mila was screaming as well, as Jennifer continued to try to reach her husband's lifeless body.

"Mama!"

As they started up the steps, unable to fight the man dragging her, Jennifer stumbled over the body sprawled there. She looked down; the sight of Ray with a gaping red hole in his head made her realize what had just happened and she wailed even louder. This time, without aid from the soldier, she ran inside of her own accord into the open arms of her daughter.

Ray. Dead.

Jamie's doctoring instincts told him to run to where the young medic had fallen as soon as the shot's echo died, but his father's hand upon his arm staid him. There was nothing they could do and he knew it. To make a move now was to expose himself and endanger everything they were trying to accomplish. Instead, he watched Dengler and Hirsch join Stetcher beside von Hausen's body and shivered with dread. Stetcher withdrew something from the Commandant's pocket and then stood with a sneer on his face. There was no doubt the Oberfuhrer was dead. Stetcher now had free reign. If they did not get out of the camp soon, they were all doomed.

Only a miracle could save them, and no one in Stalag 31 believed in miracles anymore.

Bonny was not even sure he did, despite his religious calling.

The two soldiers picked up the Commandant's body and carried it towards the camp infirmary. Dengler and Leonard followed with Ray slung over Leonard's shoulder. Words were spoken between Stetcher and Hirsch, whatever Stetcher held in his hand was given to the other man, and then Hirsch went up to the house while Stetcher spoke to the mail driver. Jamie wondered what Stetcher had ordered, or was permitting, Hirsch to do, what he had given him. After all, with the Oberfuhrer dead, there was no protection for the English woman and her daughter any longer. There was no one to stand in the way of Stetcher's thirst for blood.

Muttering curses, Dengler slammed the infirmary door closed.

Fortunately, the Gestapo officer could not hear him. Callously, he shot the mail driver in the head before shouting back into the camp, his finger pointed at Wagner. "Oversee the loading. I've got business to attend." He laid eyes upon Gerde, who had peeled himself away from the Camp 1 melee once the gunshot had brought them under control. "You, come with me."

Looks were exchanged, of confusion and worry, as Stetcher climbed into the mail truck, the vehicle closest at hand, and waited just long enough for Gerde to reach him at a run and jump into the other side. Two others leaped into the open back end of the truck, spilling more mail onto the ground. It took moments to deduce where the Gestapo officer was headed.

The farmhouse.

Sparks reached for the gun Wagner had supplied. Moretti stopped him with a hissed, "Don't."

"But Clara…"

"There is nothing you can do for her."

Sparks knew it was true. A shot at Stetcher taken at this distance would miss and get him killed. He should call her, warn her, but with such a short distance to the farmhouse, he would not have time to reach a telephone, even the one in the nearby infirmary. He could only hope that the gunshot, the morning's commotion, and the knowledge of what was happening today, had been enough to get Clara and Stasio out of that house and far away from danger.

Wagner, now in charge of the transport organization, barked orders to bring some of the prisoners from Camp 1 and cram them into the trucks as well. For whatever reason, no one chose to countermand the order. He doubted Stetcher would notice, and if, as most of the men believed, those in the trucks were bound for execution, the convoy drivers did not care if they had extra passengers. For all they knew, this had all been planned.

"You think you can escape me!" Hirsch roared as he entered the von Hausen home.

Panic-stricken, Jennifer's first thought was to run for the telephone, but her hands were shaking too much to dial, even if she had known who to call, and she could not stop gasping, moaning, and screaming which precluded any sort of dialog if she had made a call. When the front door burst open and the first heavy boot fall came, she knew who it was before he spoke. Grabbing her daughter by the arm, she raced for the back door. She was surprised to find it already open, but she did not question why. It was enough of a chance that she shouted, "Run, Mila!" as she let the girl go. Saving her daughter was the only thing that mattered. When a female figure, a woman Mila recognized as Marcella Arnaud, emerged from the shadows of the dark kitchen, she screamed and almost stopped running, but then the first gunshot came and she shrieked.

Firing back, a haphazard shot that went wide, Marcella shoved a piece of paper into Jennifer's hand. "Take this; follow the river. Go."

"Bitch!" shouted Hirsch.

Jennifer did not ask why or how Marcella was there. There was no time. More gunfire was exchanged and she and Mila ran. She did not see Hirsch jerk sideways, go down and not move again.

Chapter 30
July 26, 1943

I t took longer to reach Larrey and to be rid of the wagon and her bloody clothes than Clara had hoped. There was a sick feeling in her stomach as she rushed from one public establishment to another, hoping to find a telephone, a means to reach Stasio. Every minute of delay was one that pulled them further apart, making her feel more and more helpless.

She entered the fourth establishment, some sort of medical office it appeared as there were people in the waiting room in various degrees of poor health. A dowdy older woman sat behind the desk, typing, and near her elbow was the telephone Clara sought. She rushed to the desk; with her hat long ago lost along the roadside, her hair was disheveled and the dress she wore was ill-fitting and damp as she had pulled it from a clothesline in her haste. The woman behind the desk looked her over and scowled.

"Veuillez m'aider," Clara said breathlessly. "Est-ce que je peux utilizer le téléphone? C'est important."

The woman seemed disinclined to be of assistance, so Clara rummaged through her handbag and drew out most of the money she had taken from Hans. She had hoped to use it for other things, like safe passage out of France, but reaching Stasio was more important.

"Je peux payer. Ma famille est en danger. Puis-je utilise le téléphone s'il vous plaî?"

It was not the money that gained her the use of the phone, for the woman shoved Clara's hand away as though it was dangerous to show that much German currency in a public place...unless you were a German soldier. Rather, the mention of her family, or perhaps the desperation upon Clara's face was convincing enough that the woman turned the phone so Clara could dial.

❧*❧

"Where is she?"

Stasio had not moved from the kitchen table for some time. The arrangements were made. Philippe and Sister Isabelle had done whatever was necessary to secure safe passage out of France for Stasio, Clara, and the unborn child…but they had to leave today.

He expected Clara to be home when he returned, but she was not. She had not come back as he waited with his head bowed in prayer, their packed bags waiting upstairs until she came for them. She had not come back after he had taken the time to feed the animals for good measure, to hold them over until Louis came to see to them that evening. There were few reasons he could think of for her delay, and none of those that came to mind were good. Now Stasio was berating himself as the image of her lying dead, a bullet through her head, dogged his thoughts. He had waited too long to get her away from Ste Marie. It was too late. She was likely dead and the child with her. He would have given anything then to secure their freedom, their lives…anything at all. But they had waited too long.

Though the sound of the front door being kicked open startled him, Stasio was not surprised to find Stetcher and three soldiers bursting into his home. With Clara missing, it seemed reasonable to assume that Stetcher had a hand in her absence. Stasio stood up from the table calmly, as Stetcher crossed the living room and entered the kitchen.

"Qui…"

Stetcher's walking stick caught Stasio across the upper arm, knocking him sideways against the table.

"English!" he barked. Stasio almost smiled. Stetcher knew Stasio spoke no German, and had himself never bothered to learn French. English, the language of the enemy, was the only language in which they could communicate. "The whore? Where is she?"

"There are no whores here…"

The stick flailed again, bringing with it another painful blow to his arm. "Miss Beton!"

Stasio, rubbing his arm, did not speak.

"Überall suchen," Stetcher snapped to the soldiers with him. One went outside towards the barn, one of the few places she could hide. Another went upstairs, and Gerde, hoping to run what interference he could, began to search downstairs.

"She's not here." He would never reveal where she was, even if he knew, and he hoped the packed bags upstairs would not bring retribution.

"Quiet!" He swung the stick again, but this time Stasio was able to avoid being struck. Doing so, however, angered Stetcher, and he took a few stalking steps forward like a big cat on the hunt. He expected Stasio to back away; when the Frenchman did not, and Stetcher stopped inches away, he found he had to look up to see eye to eye with the farmer. He did not like looking up to anyone.

"We know about the radio." In truth, he did not, but he decided to throw that on the table for good measure, a threat too good not to use. Stasio's jaw twitched but he did not otherwise react. "And we know she killed Oberfuhrer von Hausen..." Again he had no evidence, but the mail currier's description of the only person he had seen on the road into Ste Marie had matched hers enough for Stetcher to willingly use that against her as well.

"Killed...von...?" It was willpower that kept Stasio standing when his legs threatened to buckle. Deciding this was a bluff, he squared his shoulders. "That is not possible. He has been away from Ste Marie for many days..."

"I assure you, Monsieur, it is very possible. There is a witness. I have seen his body." All that the witness, now dead, had seen was a woman in a wagon many miles from the scene of the crime and the dead man's body, but Stetcher did not care.

"You cannot prove..."

"I don't need to prove anything. She shot and killed..."

"She does not own a..."

Stasio's mind was racing. It was possible that Hans had somehow caught her with the radio, although how seemed far-fetched and a question he did not want to think about. The possibility of her being caught had fueled his prayers for her each morning. But given her fondness for the commandant, he could not imagine that she could be responsible for his death under any circumstances. To Stasio, her killing von Hausen was as unlikely as the chances were of Stetcher walking out of his house now and allowing him to live.

That realization was sobering, a thought that brought a lump to his throat and tears to his eyes. He would die here, he had no doubt, but if Stetcher was looking for Clara, then that meant there was a chance she was still alive...that Stasio might still be able to protect her and the child.

The telephone in the living room began to ring.

Stasio took a step to answer it, but Stetcher stopped him with the wave of his walking stick and a heated, vile glance.

❧*❧

The woman was watching her. Three rings. Four.

"Il pourrait être dans le jardin," Clara mumbled to her, more to reassure herself that there was an innocent reason why Stasio was not answering the phone. He had to be outside.

But the sick feeling she had carried all morning quickly began to transform into one of terror.

She should have gone back to Ste Marie. Should have gone to him. Should not have left without him.

Five rings. Six.

❧*❧

"Herr Sturmbannfuhrer, there is no one up here," called the soldier at the top of the stairs.

The telephone continued to ring. Six. Seven times.

Stasio knew in his gut it was Clara. He wanted to answer it, to warn her away from Ste Marie, to give her the chance to save herself.

"Would you silence that thing?" Stetcher shouted into the living room. He turned to face that doorway as Gerde, who had finished his search of downstairs, was coming into the kitchen to give his report. He lifted the receiver and set it on the table, knowing that whoever was on the other end would be able to hear what was happening here. Perhaps it would serve to warn that someone away.

It was the only chance Stasio had. From the kitchen counter behind him, he picked up the sharp knife left lying upon the cutting board from cutting ham at breakfast. Stetcher did not have the chance to register the movement behind him, before the Frenchman lunged, plunging the knife deep between the Gestapo officer's ribs.

Stetcher turned with his pistol drawn.

Stasio kept hold of the knife long enough for it to gnaw through more flesh as the man turned, then he released it and stepped back, his ears faintly catching Clara speaking his name from somewhere far away.

Double gunshots. Fire in his breast and a look of shock and surprise as he slumped back against the counter. Stetcher falling with him. Behind Stetcher, Gerde stood with his pistol aimed at the spot where Stetcher had stood. His eyes were narrowed, cold and purposeful. His shot had been more accurate than Stetcher's had been. The Gestapo officer was dead from that shot and the knife sunk deep into a lung.

The voice still called in the distance, more tentative now.

Stasio clung to life. "Clara…run!" he gasped as loud as he could, stretching his hand towards the phone he could not see.

Gerde turned towards the phone, only to be met with a bullet in his stomach as the soldier who had been searching upstairs sought to avenge Stetcher's death. He had been aiming at Stasio, but Gerde's movement put him directly into the line of fire. Gerde dropped.

The phone had gone silent…shortly to be followed by the off the hook buzzing tone.

"Clara…"

The tears on his cheeks were Stasio's final message to the woman he loved so dearly.

❧*❧

The phone clattered from her hand.

She did not try to retrieve it.

A cold gust filled her as the sound of gunshots burst through the receiver, followed by his voice, shouting her name one last time. And then all was silent.

Stasio.

"Madame?" The woman at the desk put the receiver back into its cradle with a look of concern.

Clara did not answer; she turned her head to gaze out the front window, wondering what she should do next.

Across the street, two uniformed Germans entered a building. Others, including the one in which she stood, began to tremble and shake, and the people within began to scream and run into the street in a panic.

Four German Tiger tanks crawled their way through the narrow street, heading west.

Heading towards Ste Marie.

Remembering the man she had killed, and the one she had just lost, Clara ran around the desk, down the corridor behind it, and was fortunate enough to find a rear-exiting door.

"Madame!" shouted the woman at the desk.

The two revolvers in her purse felt heavier now, but Clara clutched the bag tightly. Survival was all that mattered.

Unaware of what had transpired either in the von Hausen's home or in the Arnaud farmhouse, beyond a series of gunshots in each which unbeknownst to them left the soldiers in Stalag 31 leaderless, Wagner was the last man into the Jeep while other uniformed officers closed the tailgates. The convoy began to move as the tiny mail truck tore into the yard at breakneck speed and the soldier who hopped out of it began shouting for the unseen Dengler, telling him to come quick, that Stetcher needed him.

The Allied officers in the trucks looked at the others around them, and back to their friends and comrades being left behind, the expressions blank save for the haunted tension in their eyes and the regrets that they could not do more.

In Camp 1, Leonard caught KC and Farmer's gaze over the heads of those crowded around the gate, still trying to push past the soldiers. Something had happened to Stetcher, and Hirsch was preoccupied with Frau von Hausen. This was the break they needed.

Chapter 31
July 27, 1943

J amie glanced at the watch Wagner had given him as part of the German disguise he now wore. They had been outside of the gates for nearly thirty-five minutes, with no sign of trouble. He made a quick glance at those around him. Each truck of prisoners carried two uniformed soldiers in the front, to take turns as drivers, and two in the back to guard the prisoners although there was one extra German in the first truck where Moretti was bound. Of those in the back, Jamie and Sparks were not German, of course, and Wagner, in the third truck, was an ally, and of the six riding in the front of the trucks, four were also allies. If luck was with them, this escape would go off as planned. The Germans in the accompanying Jeeps would be a problem, however, since only one was known to be friendly.

The officers were eager for this to be over. The warning about Tigers, though unconfirmed, still rang in their ears. Tanks would make their efforts more dangerous, and Jamie knew he was not the only one considering upping their timetable.

But it was not yet time. Not until Dusty, Skip, and Wagner made it clear of the last truck, in the vicinity of the river landing they were to use to get safely away.

Jamie was not sure Skip and Dusty were in any condition to run or fight.

In the rear truck, Skip looked at Dusty at last and nodded. His insides hurt from the blow Vic had given, a pain worse than his still-healing back, but neither was enough to keep him from the undertaking before them. His condition would make what he had in mind more convincing, so he decided to take advantage of it now that the time had come.

He slumped across Dusty's lap as if in a faint. Wagner jumped, startled, and after seeming to check the man's condition, he banged on the rear wall of the driver compartment in his own vehicle before leaning over the tailgate to motion to the Jeep behind them.

"Wir müssen anhalten," he called, trying to shout over the rumbling clatter of engines and tires. "Dem Mann geht's gar nicht gut."

"Was?" the Jeep driver shouted back, his hand cupped to his ear to indicate he could not hear well.

Hoping that the Jeep and the rest of the convoy would stop as expected, and that he would not be questioned for caring about the condition of their prisoners, Wagner called back, "er ist am sterben," as he unlatched the tailgate.

In the front truck, it had been easier than expected to slip Moretti the key to his cuffs when the man was escorted into it. But the gun on Sparks' hip, which he had been instructed to get into the Italian's possession, was something Sparks would not give up. The gunshots heard from the Arnaud farmhouse still echoed in his head and left the Scot with a powerful desire to kill someone, preferably someone German and in command.

He eyed the string of vehicles behind them as though bored as the convoy ambled towards whatever fate the Germans had planned for them. At the rear, the Jeep was now driving incredibly close to the truck in front of it. Sparks wondered what was up. It was up to Skip, Dusty, and Wagner to overpower the Germans in the rear and gain control of the vehicles to signal the others to make the next move. Not knowing how they planned to accomplish this feat, maybe that was what was transpiring now.

Nerves on edge as he continued to watch out of the corner of his eyes, Sparks spun around with the revolver drawn when he heard the clatter of metal upon the floorboards behind him. One of the two Germans threw Moretti against the sidewall, a gun to his head, as the other reached for the fallen key.

"Nein!" Sparks barked, pointing his revolver at the soldier about to shoot Moretti. With a big fist, one of the Camp 2 prisoners hit the third soldier across the temple, causing him to slump against the prisoners nearest him. Several more men grabbed the first and dragging him off of the Italian. As hands scrambled to get the key to Moretti's cuffs, the German wrenched himself free and in the ensuing skirmish, managed to produce a knife. The blade sliced across the Italian's thigh, but the action went unfinished as it was met with a solid crack of a bullet into the guard's skull.

"Was?" The Jeep in the rear moved closer until its bumper was nearly banging into the truck.

"Er stirbt," Wagner shouted again.

The Jeep's driver looked confused, not entirely sure what he should do. He looked at the man beside him, who shrugged. In the truck, Skip had been carefully moved so that, by the time the Jeep actually bumped the truck, he was able to leap onto the hood.

Timing right, he jumped, ignoring the pain lancing through his body as he landed on the Jeep's hood.

The car swerved as the driver reacted to the unexpected action. Skip was unable to find a handhold, and after the leap, slid off onto the roadside. The driver of the truck saw this through his side mirror, blew his horn to signal the rest of the convoy, which brought the other three trucks to a halt. Now that those vehicles were stopped, with the Jeep's driver standing on the seat with his machine gun pointed at Skip, Wagner leaped over the partially lowered tailgate with his own gun pointed at the driver.

"Halt!" he commanded.

The driver of the last truck, assuming that Wagner was yelling at prisoners who were attempting to escape, opened the door to lend a hand when his co-driver drew a gun on him… as a gunshot blasted the air from the first truck in the convoy. It drew enough attention that Wagner was able to quickly disarm and subdue the Jeep's driver.

All of the vehicles had now stopped.

"Goddammit…" George swore as the truck's abrupt stop threw his weight into Jamie, who in turn slammed hard enough into the tailgate that it fell open. The two Canadians, one in German dress, tumbled out of the truck onto the ground.

Others jumped out and crouched around them. Someone started to speak, to ask what was happening, but George frantically gestured him to silence as their driver got out and came into view. The Colonel having rolled to his feet, felled him with a blow to the side of his neck with the ax blade he carried and then dropped back to safety when a second shot barked.

"Jamie!" He motioned in the direction he wanted his son to go.

Jamie hesitated briefly, surprised to hear his father not use the name James for the first time, but he did as ordered, circling to the other side of the vehicle while one of the French helped other men from the truck.

Jamie could see Sparks, revolver in hand, aiming at the drivers of the first truck and Jeep. One body, a German, was already face down on the ground where he had landed when kicked out of the truck, and another Frenchman was disarming the Germans whilst Moretti helped prisoners to freedom.

Behind the last truck, the Germans were already subdued and were now being bound and loaded into the back.

"What…?" started Moretti, hearing a growling sound that did not belong in this countryside.

Jamie waved his hand for silence, but most of the men were no longer speaking or moving, only Sparks who continued yelling in German at the dead soldier at his feet, waving the gun in his hand furiously. Only Moretti's hand upon Sparks' arm stilled his fury and the need for revenge long enough for them to notice something new.

The rumble was faint, distant, but it was noticeable enough that the air and ground had begun to shake with it.

"Tigers," Dusty barked, assuming it to be true.

"Bitch was right," groaned Skip, voicing what he knew others were thinking.

The sound was drawing closer and seemed to be headed to just one destination…Ste Marie and Stalag 31. Fury peaking, Sparks shouted, "Nazi bastards! You're gonna kill them all!" as he shot one of the living Germans in the back of the head out of spite.

Dusty was already in motion. "Roo…the gas cans! We'll build 'em a nice little surprise…"

There were enough men available that each of the fully loaded gas cans from each vehicle was loaded into the first truck in a matter of minutes. By the time they were finished, Dusty shouted, "You guys get outta here…"

"Like hell I'm gonna let you do this alone," Skip growled stubbornly.

One of the Frenchmen put his hand on Skip's arm. "He won't be alone, Captain. This is our fight, not yours. Plan was for you to go your ways and we take the truck and go ours. We've got families here…homes to protect…this is our place…our fight…"

"Against Tigers?" Jamie started. That was suicide…but maybe it was what was needed to stop the tanks. The rumble grew louder but the tanks could not yet be seen.

"We either die fighting or as prisoners. We choose to fight…and you have a boat to catch."

"Get outta here, Roo," Dusty encouraged. "I'll stick around long enough to get this little present delivered; I'll be right behind you."

"Let me…"

"It won't take the two of us to drive this thing…"

George, who had gotten their directional bearings in the clearing, shouted. "That's an order, Henderson. River's this way. Let's go." When Wagner stopped to retrieve a machine gun, George added, "Leave it…they'll need it more than we will."

Not wanting to be unarmed, however, Skip hesitated long enough to accept a knife from a Frenchman's hand. The handful of defecting German soldiers had shed their uniforms; some sided with the French, remaining to take a stand against the encroaching tanks, while others fled. Only Wagner remained, and he and the Allied soldiers, along with the Italian, began to run. They had not made the tree line when the Tigers rolled into sight. One of them turned its turret in the direction of the fleeing men and fired.

Dirt, shrapnel, and smoke filled the air. Sparks hit the ground, dropping instinctively to avoid flying debris. Beside him, Moretti did likewise with an expression that told Sparks that, despite his rank, the Italian had never been in combat. He motioned for Moretti to follow and began crawling quickly towards the trees.

"Dad!" shouted Jamie. He had seen his father go down in front of him and nearly tripped over the man, propelled by the blast from the tank's turret. Now he crawled to his father's side to find the man face down in the dirt with a large piece of something, metal or stone Jamie was not sure, protruding from his back. Right through his spinal column, the doctor recognized without further examination. No matter what he did, his father would not walk again, would likely not even live judging by the amount of blood, but Jamie could not just leave the man there, whatever their differences.

He turned the man's head to the side. "Dad! Talk to me!"

Behind them, Skip crouched, acting as a shield between them and the tanks.

There were two Tigers; one of them was turning its gun to the other side of the clearing where Dusty and one of the Frenchmen drove their truck way from the tanks, luring them away from the escaping men. Others, French and German, had jumped into other vehicles and were driving them madly around the clearing in an effort to confuse the tank drivers. The first Tiger seemed determined to drive over the first Jeep, even though it was obviously one of their own, and a handful of men not involved with the vehicles were rushing the tank, jumping onto it, climbing towards the hatch in hopes of gaining access to the men inside. The tank came to a halt.

The other tank stopped behind and to the right of the first. It had been the one to fire at the fleeing men and now that its occupants could not see any men running any longer, they turned their rotating gun to take aim at the stationary truck.

The one the bound, captured Germans soldiers were in.

If they hit it, it would destroy not only that truck but the Jeep nearest it as well, which two of the Frenchman were having difficulty starting.

"Dad!" Jamie continued trying to revive his father. The man was breathing, but they were labored gasps. From the growing red stain, Jamie knew it was a losing battle; there was no way to staunch the flow.

"Gotta go," Skip said, pulling at Jamie's arm as he started to rise.

"I will not leave him!"

"You think he'd want you to die here? You got family back home, right? Jamie opened his mouth but Skip continued. "They're gonna blow up the whole fucking convoy…none of us, German or Allies…are meant to get out of this. He bloody well wouldn't want you to…"

"He's my father!"

"Then act like the man he wants you to be! Get your ass moving and live to fight!"

"I will not…"

"Suit yourself." Skip stood just as the rear Tiger fired upon the stationary truck. The shell fell short but the force of the explosion launched the truck into the air, causing the bound Germans inside to tumble out, screaming in terror as debris flew in all directions.

"Jamie…"

"Dad…" Jamie brushed dirt from his father's face.

"See to your sister."

"I will not…"

"You will…because I never did. In my pocket…take it…go."

Jamie fished in the man's pocket and pulled out a tarnished watch he had given the man many years ago. Skip yanked Jamie to his feet.

"Make the man proud, will ya?" the Aussie growled.

"Jamie…the ax…"

Jamie pulled away from Skip's grasp and pried the blade from the man's twitching fingers. "Dad…"

"Always been proud of you, son…don't believe any different. Now go."

The clang of metal reverberated around the clearing as the hatch of the second tank opened. A German soldier with a machine gun opened fire on the parasites swarming over her sister tank. Some of the men fell, others returned fire.

The eruption of machine gun fire set Skip into motion and he ran towards the trees, dragging Jamie unwillingly behind him. From the other side of the clearing, near the opposite tree line, Dusty began to bellow like a wild beast.

The German truck loaded with spare gasoline cans was beginning to lurch towards the side of the second tank like an injured bear picking up determined steam. If Dusty's aim was true, and the truck hit where he intended, there would be a fireball unlike anything he had ever seen.

"Die you bastards!" Dusty shouted in between his bull-like bellows.

"We're not gonna want to be anywhere near here when that thing goes," Skip shouted to Jamie, trying not to think about Dusty. The trees were nearer now. Sparks and Wagner had already disappeared into them, and Moretti, having lost sight of him, was crouched in the brush, waiting for Skip and Jamie to catch up so that he would know where he was supposed to go.

"The river!" Skip yelled at the Italian. "Go til you find it!"

"Let go of me!" snarled Jamie, running on his own now to flee the smatter of gunfire that may or may not have been aimed at them.

Each step further from his father tore more of his heart away but also steeled his resolve to go on. He had to survive for his father.

In the tank, the Germans saw the truck preparing to broadside them, though they did not know it was full of gasoline. The collision alone would damage the track, however, and possibly injure those above, so they ducked inside for the protection they expected the tank's metal walls to afford. The French scurried in all directions, abandoning their efforts to get inside.

Skip, Jamie, and Moretti reached the cover of the forest, listening to the spray of back and forth machine gun fire.
Then a rapturous eruption lit the mid-day sky.
At least one of the Tigers was no longer a threat.

Running. Had to keep running.

Smacking branches whipped their faces. The sounds of the firefight faded and swelled in a rhythmic cacophony of terror as men in the glade shot at each other, tried to avoid the burning material showering the clearing, and in the case of some of them, Allies and Germans alike, trying to catch the men fleeing towards the river.
Those sounds fell further and further away. Skip refused to dwell on Dusty's fate. Dusty was a good soldier. Skip had to trust him to do what was best for the unit, and survive.
"Found it!"
That was Sparks' voice, and Skip presumed he meant the river. They followed the voice until they broke through the trees to find themselves at the river's edge. A small dirt trail, barely wide enough for a wagon, followed the water from the east and stopped near the first of two small buildings, just as they had been told. One was a dwelling, little more than a shack, the other smaller, like a shed. Parked there was a small car that none of them recognized.
Still a distance away from them, Jamie suddenly spun and shoved the Aussie into a nearby tree.
"You killed my father, you son of a bitch!"
"Jamie..." Skip tried to grab his arm but Jamie eluded him and started towards the shelters.
"Touch me and I swear to God I'll kill you!" he growled over his shoulder, not caring if he was being irrational. Now that the surge of

adrenalin had ebbed just a little, the need for flight lessening momentarily, the loss of his father, what he had been forced to do, erupted to the surface.

Better to blame Skip then to blame himself for leaving his father behind.

Pistol at the ready, Sparks circled the vehicle with caution, his hand upon the hood when the others caught up to him. "Still warm."

Skip, refusing to hold a grudge when tensions were so high, pushed Jamie's words out of his mind and squatted beside the vehicle. "They may still be here. Renz…watch the dock. Our boat should be here soon…."

"Assuming this fucker did not take it," Jamie hissed.

Skip shot him a scathing look, a warning to be quiet, and peeled off towards the building he was closest to.

"Sparks, check the perimeter…signal if you find anything…or if you see the boat."

The Scot nodded, leaving Wagner to stand watch and Jamie to scout the remaining building alone.

≈Suspicion's Gate≈

Chapter 32
July 27, 1943

K nife in hand, Skip crept into the small hovel, not sure what to expect. It was a single room with a sleeping loft, its furnishings upended and other goods, pots, pans, plates and a few articles of clothing scattered about as if it had been ransacked. Right inside the doorway were the four bundles that had been left for them, packs containing clothes, food, travel documents and any other last minutes provisions the Ste Marie cell had managed to put together. There were few places a person could hide in this place. The most likely place was the loft, and so he approached it with caution, alert for sounds of danger inside the building or outside. The car had belonged to someone. They could not have gone far unless they had confiscated the boat. In the distance, the sounds of machine gun fire and shouting were drawing nearer. There was a chance, he thought, that Dusty would make it after all.

One hand was on the wooden rungs that would take him into the loft, the other clutching the confiscated knife, when a skitter of wood on wood and the creak of floorboards sounded to his right. Skip did not think, only reacted to the sound. He spun and threw the knife at the same moment the sounds ceased. There was something else…

…an unexpected plea of fear, "Tom…!"

It was too late. Skip's training and her drunken staggering as she got to her feet were to Jennifer's detriment, the knife caught her square in the throat. For a long moment the two locked eyes before she dropped, her hands clutching at the blade as her daughter, crouching behind the turned over table, screamed, "Mama!"

"Bloody hell," Skip swore, angry at her and at himself for killing a civilian. Not that long ago, he had wanted her dead…but not like this. He tried to rush to her side, tripped over a broken stool, and only just reached her as Jamie burst into the room. She reached for her daughter, but Mila would not move.

"Goddamn it, Skip," the Canadian cried, pulling Mila behind him so that she would not have to continue staring at her mother who was rapidly losing blood.

"I didn't know!" Skip snapped. This was not the way this should have played out. He knelt beside her as she tried to speak, tried to say her daughter's name, but only managed a drowning bubbling sound. It seemed in that moment that, whatever had passed between them before was forgiven as Skip tried to slow the blood loss, hold off the inevitable. "Get her out of here," he snorted at Jamie. There was no use in Mila watching her mother's final moments.

Outside, the Italian cried, "Boat!" simultaneous to a long burst of machine gun fire that was nearer than ever, the sounds interrupting Skip's wasted efforts to save Jennifer's life. Jamie backed out the door, but Skip could only stare at the woman he had tried to love, the woman who had betrayed him…had betrayed all of them.

"Jamie! Skip!" Sparks cried, "Come on."

Jennifer squeezed Tom's arm. "I'm sorry…" she whispered. "Tell Mila…Hansy…" Her strength gave out and her hand fell away. "Thank you."

Skip stared as her warmth and regret bled into cold emptiness.

With two of the four bundles slung over his shoulder, and Mila huddled against his side with her face buried in his shirt, Jamie emerged from the house, expecting to see a barge of some sort pulled up to the dock. The girl was crying, understandably in shock, but she did not resist his efforts to herd her along. Who else did she have to trust in this world of insanity if her mother and father were gone?

Instead of a barge, Moretti and Sparks had pulled a small, motorized boat from the reeds at the side of the river. They had both heard a child's scream and looked to see Mila at Jamie's side. "Shite," Sparks muttered under his breath. They were not prepared for a child, but he was not going to turn the girl away. "No one else is around, but the fighting's closer. We gotta go."

Skip made it as far as the doorway of the house, his steps slow and automatic. He was both numb and furious at once. Through the open door, he could see the boat being maneuvered to the dock. Small. Unwieldy. Certainly not meant for more than maybe six passengers, and not equipped to offer them cover should they take fire from the shore. Somewhere back there, his best friend was still in the middle of the war, and to get into that boat, with the others, might only cause further problems for those already climbing into it.

He looked at his red-stained hands, now clutching the instrument of murder, and back into the room. He paused only long enough to look at Jennifer von Hausen one last time and swore.

Tossing the two bundles onto the boat before helping Mila on board, Jamie grunted, "How can we all…?"

"We will bloody well fit," Sparks said, voice clipped.

"What about Miller?" asked Wagner as he pulled Mila down between him and Moretti. If she was afraid of them, it did not show.

Sparks shrugged, eyeing the forest with a hint of sadness. "I don't think he's coming…and if he is, he can get the next boat." There were scheduled to be more to take whoever found their way here from Stalag 31. It might take a few hours, or a few days, but someone would come for them.

"It is foolish to wait longer," Moretti agreed. The nearing gunfire supported his assertion.

"I'll get Skip and the other packs…"

"You can't leave him here?" Mila's eyes implored as she pouted. After what had happened, Jamie could not blame her for being afraid of the man who had, accidentally or not, killed her mother.

"No, sweetheart, I'm afraid we can't. We need his help." Jamie ran back to the shack. "Skip! Let's go!"

As he grabbed the remaining two packs, there was no one inside to be seen except Jennifer's twisted, deflated form. He shuddered at the sight of her. It was not the death itself that troubled him; it was something else. Something he had seen in Jennifer's eyes as her life had slipped away. Something that spoke of deep regret and loneliness. In the end, despite her efforts to draw men into her life, the forlorn woman had died alone, without even the one man who truly loved her at her side.

"Skip!"

But there was no one there. No way could the Aussie have gone out the front door without one of them seeing him. Jamie kicked over a pile of debris, reached to shove aside the fractured armoire, and then noticed a hole in the planks of the back wall of the house, a hole large enough for a man to have wiggled through…even a man as large as Skip. On the end of one sharp, protruding plank edge, a small shred of military green fabric fluttered in the breeze. Jamie squatted, peered through the opening into the forest, but saw nothing. There was no sign of Tom Henderson.

If the man had gone his way, it must have been many moments ago. He would be long gone by now, likely in the direction of combat. Back to Dusty.

Gunfire erupted nearby.

"Come on," Wagner shouted.

Jamie shouldered the packs and scurried back to the river bank, where Sparks held the boat steady near the shore. The packs were tossed inside.

"Drop!"

As Jamie floundered his way into the boat, staying low to be pulled in by Wagner and Moretti, the Scot fired into the trees. Someone gave a shout of pain."

"That could have been Skip!" Jamie shouted, appalled at the thought.

Sparks' face went pale. "What the...bloody hell..." With the others in the boat, Sparks pushed away from the shore with a leap that landed him safely within it as well.

"That was not Henderson," Wagner said, confident that the voice he had heard had been foe, not friend.

Pants wet up to his knees, Sparks situated himself on the seat next to Wagner, who had moved to let Jamie sit with Mila, and huffed, "Then they won't be troubling us. Where's...?"

"Gone back for Dusty, I imagine," Jamie replied as he wrapped an arm around the girl and kissed the top of her head to comfort himself as much as her. He too had been orphaned this day, and like Mila, there had been no opportunity or means to change it.

"Then I wish him luck," Wagner murmured, offering his jacket to the girl who shook her head in refusal. She did not want a German jacket. She did not want the reminder of her father's death. Moretti began sorting through the packs, distributing clothing so they could each ditch the uniforms they wore. A boat full of men in German uniforms was just as exposed as a group of men in prison attire. Best they looked like the local population. "They'll need it."

❧*❧

Skip doubled back through the forest, listening to the sounds of gunfire, letting it draw him towards his objective. As long as the sound continued, the back and forth exchange of bullets, he had hope that Dusty was alive, and he was determined to reach his friend. He made it to the edge of the dirt road, the one Jennifer had probably driven on to get to the cottage, and though the shooting was close, he could not see anyone, friend or foe. He certainly did not want to shoot errantly and risk killing his best friend.

He had already mistakenly killed one person today.

Crouched low, he crept through the brush, listening to the pounding of his heart in his ears, trying to ignore it so he could better analyze the fighting nearby. He could now hear a vehicle drawing near and wondered who in their right mind was driving through the middle of a combat zone. One of the French in one of the trucks or Jeeps, perhaps, or maybe Dusty had commandeered one of them. Hoping it was so, Skip peered through the foliage in time to recognize the driver, who was now taking fire from a sniper on the other side of the trail. She ducked and swerved, barely avoiding being hit, and Skip, suddenly furious at her, at Dusty, at himself, at the shooter, stood with a roar and fired two shots from the rifle he had snatched from one of the Germans earlier. The first shot went wild. The second resulted in a distant scream and a cessation of return fire, but not before he felt fire tear through his side, a fire which dropped him to the ground in agony.

"Get out of here!" he shouted to Marcella, waving her on, assuming she was heading for the boat landing.

She should have been there already. The skirmish with Hirsch, and then the need to skirt around the tanks in the clearing had slowed her progress. She might be too late for this first boat, but there would be others. Either way, she was not going to leave Skip behind. Marcella would rather die than do that.

With the motor still running, she leaped from the car and ran to the fallen man. There was a lot of blood, but not being a physician, she had no idea how bad the injury really was. "Come…into the car," she insisted, trying to lift his bulky form off the ground.

"You should go…I've got to help Dusty…" But Skip's legs kept bucking, and he knew he was not going to be running after anyone.

"You saved my life, Captain," she insisted, throwing open the passenger side door and helping him inside. "I am saving yours." The jarring movement, the pain in his side and in his back, meant that he passed out before the door was closed, leaving him unable to protest. With no further incoming gunfire, the sound of it farther away through the forest to her right, possibly between her and the boat landing, she sped towards her secondary destination, praying as she cast glances at the man beside her that he was not going to die.

The boat she expected was just coming into view when she reached the secondary landing, but there was no sign of anyone else, Allies or Germans. She whistled and waved as she jumped from the still running vehicle, and soon one of the three men from the boat came to assist her with Skip.

"Where are…?"

"I don't know," she said over the engine's rumble and another closer volley of shots. The man shouldered Skip's weight and got him into the boat. "I should…"

"We can't stay, mademoiselle…they are too close."

Marcella looked in the direction of the gunfire as one of the others in the boat opened fire on two German soldiers who emerged from the trees. She screamed and dove into the boat. One of the three men screamed too and dropped down beside her, clutching the side of his now bloody face. Having never seen anything so terrifyingly gruesome at that range, Marcella fainted as the boatmen pushed away from land, leaving the shore littered with the bodies of two German soldiers…and leaving behind Dusty Miller and anyone else who might have been due to utilize this means of escape.

Chapter 33
July 27, 1943

When their tiny boat motored past the vicinity of Stalag 31 and the picturesque village of Ste Marie, it took both Wagner and Moretti to keep Sparks from going over the side and swimming to shore. Everything on the northern shore was silent, however, no sounds of shouting or machine gun fire, and so it was apparently business as usual for the villagers and the camp.

Or else, Jamie thought with a shudder, it was the silence of death. At least he felt confident that they had stopped the tanks.

In the packs the Resistance had left, they had found the papers necessary to travel within France and to get out of the country, along with the clothing they now wore. Jamie wondered, as he shed the German uniform, if they should have left one of the packs for Skip and Dusty, or left some of the contents at least, as they would have need of the papers too. But he suspected those two men were never leaving France. He doubted he would ever see either of them again.

Despite the part Skip had in Jennifer's death, and the fact that Skip had pushed him to leave George behind, Jamie did not think the man deserved to die. In war, when tensions were taut, anything could happen. If not for Skip and Dusty, those in the boat with him, Mila included, might never have gotten this far. The two had bought them time, and for that alone, Jamie would hold the Aussie in esteem.

They eased down the river, east towards the rendezvous point in Larrey, untroubled by anyone on the shore. The few villagers they passed either gave a friendly wave or did no more than glance curiously in their direction. Boat traffic to Larrey was common. There was no reason for them to seem out of place, so long as none of them spoke.

Yet they did not relax, especially Sparks who, though he had pocketed the gun to remove it from Mila's sight, still fingered it within his jacket. It did not escape Jamie that the Scot had already killed at least twice today and was itching to kill more. He was agitated enough that the Canadian briefly considered taking the gun away before Sparks did something stupid or unfortunate. He decided against it. There seemed little good in upsetting the Scot more, and if possessing the gun was keeping him together, so be it. Besides, they needed someone on alert, someone prepared to fight back at a moment's notice. Today, Sparks was that man.

The rumble of tanks on the northern shore came again, quite loud though out of sight of the river, and it was impossible to tell if the tanks had come from the north or east, and whether they were headed in the direction of Larrey or Ste Marie. Instinct and intuition, however, suggested the war machines were lumbering towards Stalag 31, just as the previous two had been. Heads bowed in prayer, as Wagner clenched the tiller more tightly and willed the boat to move faster. Sparks in turn crouched, gun drawn, and kept it aimed at the shore, his hands steady and his eyes focused.

He might be emotionally strung out, but so far, Sparks was in control.

The sounds of the tanks gradually drifted away.

The signs of inhabitation grew more frequent and Sparks was once more forced to hide the handgun. More houses appeared along the shore, and with them, more people. Other boats were tied to their moorings or also easing their way towards Larrey. Sparks' agitation continued to grow, and the Italian began to look ill. Jamie scowled, knowing the hardest part of the escape lay ahead of them, and joined the others in scanning the shore as Mila dozed against his shoulder.

"We can't take this thing all the way," Sparks said to the unspoken question he could read on Wagner's face. "Too much traffic…bigger boats…we might look suspicious."

"So where?" asked Jamie, making careful note of each dock they neared. The sound of his voice roused Mila, who grew wide-eyed with panic when she realized they were approaching civilization. Jamie stroked her shoulder and kissed the side of her head.

"And what do we do after?" Moretti muttered, aware that his features and accent were going to target him as a foreigner. The locals might not be suspect of an Italian in their midst, but any Germans in the area likely would be.

"There," hissed Sparks, pointing at the shore, too busy seeking landfall to answer the Italian's question.

As Wagner turned the boat in the direction Sparks indicated, Jamie said, "We walk…to the boat. Robbie and I as brothers…" With the IDs provided, they could pull that off. "We know enough French between us to get by."

"I don't," Moretti reminded them.

Nosing the boat ashore, Wagner added, "Nor do I."

Jamie shrugged. "So don't talk."

"What about me?"

He glanced at Mila. None of their plans had included a child, and he wondered again how Mila and Jennifer had come to be in that boathouse. "We'll say you're my daughter; you don't need to say anything."

"I know French; Mademoiselle Beton taught me…"

"Christ!" Sparks swore as the boat bumped the dock. It was enough of a lurch to toss everyone off balance, but whether the profanity was due to that or to the mention of Clara, none were sure. Wagner quickly cut the engine as Sparks jumped out of the boat and began to tie her off.

"Ssh," Jamie said as he helped the girl to her feet. Sparks offered his hand to help others ashore, the boat held steady by the rope that kept her moored. There was angry misery in the Scot's eyes, and Jamie prayed he could hold himself together a little longer. It would help if they could limit the reminders of Clara, and so to Mila he whispered, "I have little doubt you can…but we don't want to take any chance of anyone recognizing you as German…" Or as British. He did not think either was likely, but he did not want to risk her life.

The packs were tossed onto the dock and each man grabbed one as they came ashore. The small case Mila had been carrying was tucked under Jamie's arm. They looked at the boat, debating setting her adrift or not. Once they did there was no going back.

It was a choice that Sparks made for them. The boat was untied and sent down the river with a kick to her side. The tension in his shoulders gave way to the slight shudder of weeping, though his face remained mostly neutral. Jamie wished he could say or do something to make this easier on the man. He knew how it felt to leave someone behind, but at least he had every reason to believe that Zaline was still alive and would make it out of Ste Marie before the tanks arrived. Sparks had none of that hope.

One hand on Sparks' arm, Jamie murmured, "Let's go."

From the twitch in his shoulder, Jamie thought Sparks would shrug him away, or perhaps draw the pistol on him, but instead the Scot made a gesture to the little boat, some sort of farewell perhaps as it drifted away, and then he turned and followed Jamie up the embankment to where the others waited.

Larrey was larger than Ste Marie. There were more small structures, homes, businesses, and warehouses, many connected to the business of the river and of the rail line that passed through on its way south. It seemed logical to Jamie that they should walk east along the river until they reached the Vilaine. That proved impossible, however, as it would entail crossing through yards and businesses. Necessity forced them to drift through the streets and alleys, weaving east and south at a slow, careful pace. They stopped frequently while Sparks tried to keep his bearings fixed on the two rivers, the Canut to the north and the Vilaine to the south. They sought the place where the rivers met, but without a city map, and not being a naval man by any stretch, Jamie had no idea where to go.

It appeared that Sparks did, or rather, Jamie hoped he did, since the Scot had taken to leading and seemed confident enough in where he was going that the others followed.

More frightening than the uncertainty of their location and route, however, was the increasing number of German soldiers they saw, trucks parked here and there, some idling, some silent, pointed west, as if passing through Larrey. Pointed towards Ste Marie. Jamie wondered if the others shared his trepidation. Were the knots in their stomachs and throats as large and heavy? Twice they had to change routes because of milling soldiers or military vehicles blocking their route, but Sparks did not let their presence slow or deter him. He knew where they needed to go and he was determined to get there.

Having come up through an empty alley, avoiding half a dozen Germans loitering in the street he intended to use, when Sparks stopped abruptly once again it was no surprise. They had endured so many stops and starts in their efforts to cross the town, each wondered if they would ever reach their destination in time. The look on Sparks' face, however, when he glanced at Jamie, read of a deeper concern than before.

"Convoy."

Pulling the trembling, dazed girl against him, Jamie grunted, "How many?" As near as he guessed they were to the Vilaine dock, he guessed there were fewer paths available to them now.

Sparks peered around the corner. "Five I can see...they go around the block...no idea how many men that might mean..."

"Too many," Wagner replied, "depending on the vehicle and its purpose."

"Fuck."

After a long pause, waiting for Sparks to suggest something, Jamie asked, "We double back?" It seemed a waste of time since the routes they had passed had all been blocked, funneling them here like lab rats to an unsatisfying end.

Sparks glanced back down the alley but shook his head. "Don't think that would help." He swept his hair from his face with one hand. "We should be nearly there...can't be too many more streets between us and the Vilaine. If we make it across the street, up that alley," he pointed directly across from their position, "without being noticed...turn right again..."

"Five of us coming out of the alley together would look..."

Suspicious. Sparks agreed with the Italian's assessment.

It was Wagner, however, who made the obvious suggestion. "We split. You three can blend into a group of people as they pass... continue up the street until you can get around the convoy."

"Keep our heads down," Sparks nodded, "we should blend in."

Jamie looked less convinced. "What about...?"

Wagner patted his hip beneath the long shirt he wore. I've got this...and I'm one of them...at least on the surface. Renz and I will watch until your safely by, then we'll cross for the alley, either meeting you there or at the boat."

"You don't know..."

"We'll find it..."

Shaking his head, Sparks grunted, "You go...I'll cover you."

"We're not leaving you here," Jamie hissed.

"I'll be fine. Someone needs to cover the rest of you." What went unsaid was that he felt he had less of a reason to live then he believed the others did, and he had hopes of killing a few more Nazis before his day ended.

Knowing that arguing would be useless and neither wanting to attract attention or waste time, Jamie clutched Mila's hand and said to the Scot, "No talking to anyone if you can help it," and sauntered into the street into the middle of a passing group of workmen who appeared to be headed towards the docks. Jamie did not look back and kept his hand tightly around Mila's, trying his best to be nothing more than a loving father out with his daughter, planning a day's outing with a backpack and her small case. With the number of Germans in town, a man choosing to vacate his home was hardly suspicious. Mila forced a smile as she chattered about an imaginary friend as if the conversation between them was the most natural thing in the world.

Sparks watched them go. He watched the Germans he could see, men who appeared to be loading up as several soldiers came from a variety of directions and began climbing into the trucks or heading in the direction of those he believed were parked around the corner. The day was hot, the air dusty and putrid with a distant tang of old fish and wet rope. It was those smells as much as his sense of direction which had guided Sparks this far, but he did not think that smell was going to be of use much longer. Not until he dispatched the German blockade.

Gun heavy in his hand but still in his coat pocket, he toyed with the trigger, swallowing away the constriction in his throat every time one of the soldiers glanced into the passing crowd. No one stopped Jamie and Mila, and when the two paused as if to browse in a store window, Mila pointing to something with feigned excitement, Jamie's glance back towards the alley gave nothing away. Sparks could not be seen.

But Sparks could see him and took that as his signal to propel the other two on their way. "Go," he muttered to Wagner and Moretti as Jamie and Mila began to walk again, the girl's hand still held tightly.

The Italian, less confident about blending in, followed slightly behind Wagner, trying to appear casual despite his quick pace, his heart beating so hard in his breast that he wondered why no one heard it. When they had to pause at the curb to allow a wagon to pass, however, instead of keeping his eyes forward, he glanced back.

Sparks motioned him on with a worried expression, a look that puzzled the Italian until the horse and carriage were past and he noticed an older man in German uniform across the street, looking at him and Wagner, then into the dark alley, and then at the pair again.

Wagner ignored the older fellow and Moretti, swallowing his fear, continued to walk beside him, even though each step as they avoided horses and carriages in the road brought them closer to the wary soldier. To do anything else, to veer suddenly away, would have been suspicious and could not be risked.

The soldier, distrustful enough, had shortened the distance between them by stepping off of the opposite curb. "Halt," he barked before they reached the side of the road.

Moretti wondered if he should run or simply proceed as though he had not heard or understood the order. Wagner, however, resisting a look towards the alley, had already stopped, carefully out of the path of the majority of Larrey traffic. Choosing to assume that the man had been speaking to Wagner, resisting the temptation to look at Sparks for orders or down the street towards Jamie and Mila, the Italian took another step forward and reached the footpath, appearing as though he would continue about his business.

The soldier repeated his command as Wagner caught the Italian's arm. Moretti looked surprised. He hoped that, by doing as the soldier asked, it would be enough of a distraction for Sparks to make his own escape into the street.

If he was lucky, the soldier might only harass them to see their papers and would let them go.

"Wie lautet dein Name?"

Moretti looked at the man as though he did not understand while Wagner dug into his pocket.

"Tourist," Wagner said, shoving his papers in the soldier's direction. The man did not even look at them.

Instead, he barked again, "Namen? Wie <u>heißen</u> Sie?"

With a frown, Moretti tried to indicate that he did not understand, but the soldier grabbed him by the arm and shoved him against a lamppost.

In the alley, Sparks readied his pistol, shifting its weight in his hand, half hoping he would not be forced to use it, to give away his position, half hoping for an excuse to kill another German soldier. Further down the street, Jamie glanced back, but the convoy trucks blocked his view.

Moretti, gesturing madly, fumbled within his pack, planning to produce his papers to provide his alias, hoping to prove he was a different man than the one they seemed to be seeking. Wagner, however, stopped him, believing he was intending something else, something foolish. The German must have thought the same thing, for the revolver he carried was now aimed at the Italian's head. Wagner took a startled step back.

There was a single gunshot, barely heard over the now clanging church bells. Eyes squeezed shut, Moretti wondered why he could hear the peeling, the screams when he had to be dead. What was that heavy weight now sliding down his body?

"Vada," shouted Wagner. Moretti opened his eyes to find German blood smeared down his clothing as the soldier slid to the ground. Wagner pulled him into the alley they were aiming for as Sparks, across the street, emerged from the alley and shot another two Germans in the moment it took the Italian to realize what was happening. He ran, no longer needing Wagner's motivation.

The exchange of gunfire created panic in the streets and villagers ran for the cover of the nearest buildings. Horses jolted, screaming, and veered wildly from their paths. Germans tumbled from the trucks in search of the enemy. Mila, hearing the shots, began to scream, though Jamie was not sure if it was in fright or if it was a ruse, an act that those around them might expect from a frightened girl. Without a gun of his own, having to keep the girl safe, there was nothing Jamie could do for his comrades. He continued to pull Mila along, seeking the Vilaine. The fact that they were running meant nothing to the Germans, as the townsfolk around them also scattered and ran.

Jamie did not know what had happened, why Sparks had opened fire or stepped into the open, but that action gave him and Mila the chance to run for the transport. He took the opportunity without looking back. Mila could not keep up, however, a fact he found maddening, and since he could not leave her, he did the only thing he could. As the second and then third shot rang out, and Mila again screamed, he scooped her into his arms and continued running.

On the next street over, Wagner and Moretti found themselves separated by a cluster of panicking villagers, all pushing and running in directions other than the one the two men were trying to go. Their efforts to fight against the tide was futile and then, both thinking it might be wiser to move with the crowd rather than against it, gave in to the jostling. As the mob carried them along, they worked towards one another, and when they reunited on the opposite side of the street, they slipped out of the crowd and into another passage between buildings without much effort. Neither paused to rest, or to see if they were being followed, but instead resumed their run hoping the next street over would be clearer of panicking townsfolk, dodging crates, debris, and people as they ran.

Once there, they both turned in the direction they believed the Vilaine should be and ran faster.

When the third German soldier fell, Sparks withdrew into the alley followed by a volley of shots, swearing, and shouted commands, as well as a dozen or more Nazis. He was aware that the cluster of soldiers they had passed would likely join their comrades, drawn by the sound of gunshots, unless he was lucky enough that the bells had contained the sound of most of his shots to the immediate vicinity of that street where he had stood.

As fortune would have it, when he broke into the next lane, there were no soldiers in sight. Perhaps those he had seen before were part of the same group loading into the convoy. That might mean his threats were all behind him. Unable to continue east or south towards the Vilaine as the way was blocked by those looking for him, he ran west, fighting off despair with the need for survival. He would never make it to the transport; they would be forced to leave without him. At least, he thought, he was giving the others a better than fighting chance to get away and live.

If he did not die today, perhaps he would be able to get back to Ste Marie in time to help the others …get back to Clara.

He snorted, admitting as he ducked into an open doorway that the odds were he would die in Larrey. The German presence was too thick and he had few bullets in his gun. Without another gun, fighting back would be futile…and he had no intention of crawling in a hole to hide indefinitely. He would find a good vantage point to make his last stand, if he could not reach the transport, and he would buy the others as much time as he could.

The warehouse was dark, illuminated only by a source on the southern wall. It provided light enough for him to realize he had stumbled into a storage, full of carriages, autos, and farm equipment, large machines and vehicles that provided good cover as he slid quietly between them. Hopefully, it would be enough cover to throw the Germans off. He doubted anyone had seen him come in, but if the soldiers did flow through the street he had just left and failed to find him, they would search the buildings, if they had time enough before their transport was due to leave. Hopefully, they would be recalled to the trucks. Hopefully, he was not putting other people in danger by hiding.

Gradually, as he crept between shielding obstacles, he found the source of illumination, a doorframe no longer containing a door. It was wide, likely used to get the vehicles in and out of the building. The missing door made the building open to the street and he scowled as he pressed himself against the framing, out of sight of any in the street, still in the shadows while he assessed the situation.

Swallowing hard, he peered out. The street seemed empty, though he could hear distant shouting and running footsteps, sounds that bounced and echoed between buildings, making it difficult to be sure where they originated. The soldiers might be closer behind him than he hoped. So far, however, they had not entered the building where he was hidden.

He glanced at the gun in his hand. Five shots. He had used five shots, already, hadn't he? Or had it been six? He was not sure. And though he knew it was a Luger and should, therefore, house at most ten bullets, he had not bothered to check it when Wagner had given it to him. He did not know if the clip had been full or if there had already been one round chambered, which might have given him eleven shots at best. Nor could he recall now if there had been other clips on the uniform belt, but as he had ditched the jacket and belt as they traveled down the river, wondering was of no use. Whatever rounds were left in the gun were all he had. This was not the time to berate himself for shortsightedness.

He opted to hide the gun, shoving the warm metal into the waistband of his trousers and pulling his untucked shirt down over it and adjusting his light jacket to conceal the bulge further. With luck, he would pass as a local as he backtracked towards the Vilaine. One more glance in all directions, and then he left the safety of the building to stroll calmly across the street. With no soldiers in sight, it proved easy to do, allowing him to turn east towards the confluence, in the direction of safety and an escape from France. There might be a chance to live. It was more than Clara had gotten.

Chapter 34
July 27, 1943

Pausing to catch his breath, Moretti strained to hear anything that would give him a clue where he was and what had happened to the others. Wagner stopped beside him to do likewise. Neither had expected to be allies in this escape, but it had turned out they had no one to trust but each other. There had been no further gunshots, but they did not know what that meant. And as it felt as if they had run for hours, both wondered if they were heading in the right direction or were now hopelessly lost.

He looked at the sun and studied the direction of the falling shadows. It was late afternoon, nearing dusk, thus he knew the sun should be lowest behind them if they were heading in the right direction. To his relief, it was. All they had to do, therefore, was continue east and sooner or later they would find the place where the Canut met the Vilaine. They had not crossed it, had seen no trace of a river, so they concluded it had to be somewhere ahead of them still.

With a nod of silent agreement from Wagner, and a deep intake of air, the pair ran again.

❧*❧

"Jàmie!"

The surprised cry inadvertently escaped Zaline's lips at the sight of the Canadian. It had been a difficult decision to come here, to choose to leave Ste Marie with her daughter. But because her father and sister had chosen to leave as well, Zaline had felt no reason to stay. Her husband was dead and any sort of future would have to be found somewhere away from his memory and the war. When she arrived in Larrey, it was to find no trace of her sister, her father, or even Clara. There was no sign of anyone she knew. She had guessed that Marcella, stubborn girl that she was, had opted to go to the first rendezvous point after warning Frau von Hausen and her daughter, choosing to go where Skip would most likely be. But why her father and Clara were not yet here, she hated to think about.

She had been in Larrey long enough to make note of the westbound soldiers. To see the Tigers and make a call to Ste Marie, to the inn, providing them the only warning they might otherwise have. No one answered the phone. Clara's assessment that Stalag 31 would fall under attack was disconcerting, and the fear that Ste Marie might not be spared caused Zaline worry for her father's safety. Such an attack on the largely helpless, unarmed villagers was a terrifying thought.

She and Pensee waited in a nearby café, watching the boats, waiting for the one they were to use to leave this place forever. They sipped tea, shared sweets, and talked about the adventure they hoped to have in their new home. Soon after the boat docked, they boarded, and after she made sure that Pensee was safely stowed in their room, out of sight and shooting range of any Germans on the shore, Zaline paced the deck, waiting, watching, hoping. Praying for her father and sister, praying for the men who were supposed to make use of this vessel with her.

The longer the delay in their arrival, the more likely they were not coming at all. Time was slipping away. The boat was bound to leave at dusk, whether any of the other passengers arrived or not.

She heard the gunshots earlier and stood clutching the rail until her white-knuckled hands hurt, staring into the streets, wondering what was happening, afraid to learn the truth. Seeing Jamie now, sweaty, dirty, and wild-eyed, with Mila in his arms, was a surprising relief. She could not help but call out to him.

Jamie hastened across the plank towards her, meeting Zaline on deck with his own overwhelming relief. Zaline, assuming that the shots had been directed at Jamie, was intent on ushering the two below to safety, though what she wanted most was to embrace him.

"The others?" she asked as Jamie set Mila down and encouraged her down the steps into the bowels of the boat.

"Skip and Dusty…" He shrugged, carefully choosing words. "They missed the boat. Dad didn't…" He choked before looking over his shoulder at the docks. "Sparks, Moretti, and Wagner are here somewhere…"

The hitch in his voice told her that his father had not made it out alive. She clasped his hands tenderly. "Mila?" It was easier to ask that than for news about her father.

"Long story...but the others should be..."

"They've got a little time." She met the ship captain's gaze and the man nodded, agreeing to wait though he looked both worried and displeased about a delay. He had agreed to this venture, so he was not about to make an early departure if he could help it. Men's lives were at stake; he would wait a little longer.

"Should we go below?" Jamie would rather wait for the others, but he did not want to take any more risks. Before descending the stairs, however, he took one last look across the horizon in the hopes of some sign of his friends.

There was none.

❧*❧

His feet came to an abrupt halt as he and Wagner broke from the maze of streets and alleys upon the collection of sailing vessels moored before them. They had reached the docks at last, but which boat did they want? The Italian had not been given that information, and it seemed that Wagner was likewise uninformed, leaving them at a loss for what to do next. As a man unfamiliar with the sea, all of the vessels looked more or less the same to Moretti, particularly in the gathering twilight. He was sure they had arrived in time, but would they find the boat they wanted before it left without them.

There was a shrill whistle. He turned his head as Wagner tugged on his arm.

Upon the deck of a dinghy fishing vessel, he recognized Jamie Campbell and the lithe figure of Zaline Porteur. Somehow, the knowledge that she was here, was a part of this, did not surprise him. The recent death of her husband seemed to have put into motion so many of this past month's events and after much of what he had seen and experienced today, he believed little would surprise him now.

He paused long enough to straighten his bloody, rumpled clothing and to smooth down his hair before he and the German officer beside him casually crossed the empty expanse between them and the boat. They hoped they appeared to belong here, despite the blood on Moretti's clothes.

No one stopped them. No one they passed said a word.

When he made it onto the deck of the boat, it was all Moretti could do to keep from falling into Jamie's arms, laughing or weeping with relief.

☙*☙

Having made it across another street without incident, Sparks steadily pushed east. It seemed that the Germans had lost his scent, or else had given up looking for him as he had not seen or heard any sign of them for many minutes. He was near enough to the rendezvous point now that he could hear the long-unheard, but familiar sounds that always accompanied boats. The slapping of water against the hulls. The creak and gran of straining ropes, wood, and metal as vessels tugged to be free of the docks. The echo of footsteps and the sounds of objects moving across hollow decks.

Reminders of home.

He did not hear the crack of the bullet until the fire of it ripped through his calf. He went down with a sharp cry, pulled the Luger from his waistband as he dropped, then rolled to return fire.

But the second gunshot came from somewhere ahead and to the left of him, rather than from the gun he held.

It was a shot that took his German assailant by surprise. It caught him in the neck; he fell where he stood and did not move.

"Get below!" Jamie yanked Moretti's arm, pulling him into the belly of the boat as he himself flew up onto the deck.

"Jamie" cried Zaline.

"That's Sparks!" He would recognize that cry anywhere.

The captain, already beginning to fire his engines now that the sound of gunfire had gotten too close for his liking, shouted, "We're not waiting!"

"I'm not leaving him! Go...I will find you!"

Both the captain and Zaline started to shout after him, but Jamie was already across the platform and back on land before either could utter a word. The captain growled. He would wait, despite his words, but he was not going to wait very long.

"Must've died..." Sparks mumbled as a familiar, beautiful face moved into his line of vision. He could never recall seeing anything, anyone lovelier than she was to him at that moment. Her hair was disheveled, her face red and splotchy and her expression was grim, but it was Clara, and that made her beautiful. She was with him now. What angels had sent her back from the dead to save him?

But the gun in her hand and the fire in his leg as she struggled to help him to his feet told him that this was no heaven, no afterlife that he could envision. Hell, perhaps, but not heaven, despite Clara's presence.

"What the...?"

"Ssh," she hissed, not looking at him directly. It almost seemed that she did not recognize him, or did not care who he was, that her only concern was reaching safety. This was not the Clara he knew. This woman, who hobbled beside him and in the course of moving closer to the boats swore several times, was hard, cold, and efficient. A killer without remorse. There seemed to be none of the familiar tenderness in her. That she had killed a man and had not reacted to it in the fashion most women might, with no more concern than if she had butchered a farm animal or a pesky rodent, said a great deal. Sparks grimaced in pain and consternation, wondering just how much about her he did not know, or what had happened to her today to draw this protective shield over her. For now, however, his energy was focused on moving, on staying upright, on reaching the boat to freedom. It gave him no chance for deep pondering. It took too much effort to ignore the pain in his leg and keep moving for serious thought.

More gunshots erupted behind them, but none found their target.

"Merde," she grumbled. She had heard the earlier gunshots, had followed the Germans movements across town hoping to find that it was Stasio they were chasing, whom they were shooting at, though she knew that to be an illogical wish. She had not expected to find any of the men from Stalag 31.

Indeed, she had been so caught in her own hell that she had forgotten about their plans to attempt escape.

But it meant that somewhere there was a boat waiting. She, however, had no plans to be on it. Not without Stasio.

She and Sparks left the cover of the buildings, cutting across the open space towards the moored boats; when Jamie saw them, he ran in their direction, intending to help.

"Good to see you," Sparks grunted.

"You too, Sparky. Here, let me." He shifted Sparks' weight off of Clara so that she could readjust her blouse and push her hair out of her face. "Boat's ready..."

"You go," Clara murmured, voice flat and cool. "I'll cover you."

Jamie took her words as the logical thing to do. She was armed, he was not, and Sparks was in no condition to be an effective soldier. The men would need cover if they were to reach shelter before the shouting Germans reached them.

Sparks, on the other hand, understood what Clara meant without her saying it. "Clara…"

"Go, Robbie. Now."

"You must…"

"I'm not leaving without…"

"He's gone, Clara!"

Now Jamie stopped too, realizing what was happening, and that, more than likely, Zaline did not know about her father either. Or rather, she had not, but standing on the prow of the boat, she had to hear them now.

"No…"

"Stetcher went looking for you…"

"No."

Jamie groaned. "There were two gunshots…we all thought…"

Six Germans broke onto the docks to their left. Jamie hurriedly pulled Sparks towards the boat, where Moretti and Wagner had now emerged and were trying to assist, both as cover and as strength. Clara had not moved.

"Clara!"

"No!" She turned without warning. One shot. Cleanly through one soldier's chest.

A second shot and another clutched his abdomen and fell to the ground. A third and a soldier tripped over coiled ropes and landed face first on wet planking.

She could hear Robbie's sobbing grow fainter as he was pulled away. She dodged behind a collection of crates, barely missing the next bullet meant for her.

Stasio.

Burst out from behind the crates. A fourth shot brought down a soldier with a bullet to his head. Back to safety as a shot shattered wood and embedded into whatever the crates held.

Stasio.

The men on the boat watched with amazement at the accuracy with which the woman they thought they knew dispatched one German soldier after another. Sparks did not want to leave her behind, but how could he force her to follow if she did not want to go? He did not have the strength to drag her against her will.

With as much of that strength as he could manage, before he was steered across the plank onto the boat, he shouted her name one more time and sent the Luger he had carried skittering across the ground in her direction. He did not know how many shots it held, but any shots were better than none.

At the sound of his voice, Clara looked at him. The Luger stopped not far from her feet. She noted in that instant of eye contact his despair, but also his understanding. If she were to survive, she needed another gun, for she was, by now, nearly out of ammunition in her own and she had no idea how much ammunition Hans' weapon in her pack contained. If she stayed, he would, despite his heart's desire, provide her with a fighting chance to survive.

She lunged from the crates, the next shot she took going wild, but the sound of it was enough to cause the last two Germans to drop, seeking cover. Clara came up with the Luger in her hand, waited, and when one of the two popped up into her line of sight, she fired again. The last German thought to finish her while she was occupied with his companion.

But a shot from the boat ended his life, and Wagner slowly lowered his gun. He had killed enough of his own today that there was no returning to Germany.

The immediate threat was gone.

But so was Stasio.

She had already known it to be true, from the moment the phone receiver dropped from her hand. The sounds of gunfire echoing over the line continued to buzz in her head. The coldness of knowing had strangled her since that moment, but it had been her refusal to accept it that kept her going, her efforts to hope that he might have made it out alive that had allowed her to persevere. Robbie was not being selfish in telling her; he and Jamie had honestly believed she did not know and intended only to spare her life.

Still behind the crates, she watched Wagner assist Jamie in getting Sparks settled and tending his wound. Zaline was already there, but there was no sign that she could see of Skip, Dusty, George, or even Marcella and Pensee. Perhaps they were below deck. Perhaps they were all safe and she had done well. If Zaline was here, then Pensee lived…and so did Clara and her unborn child. The last bit of Stasio to survive.

There was only one logical choice, made all the easier by another trio of Germans coming into the open and firing on her position. She ran. Firing the Luger over her shoulder, one German fell...then another. At the plank, Wagner grabbed her and pulled her to safety as the boat broke away from the dock. The Luger fell from her hand as she stumbled and fell to the deck. Their Italian ally picked it up and fired. The last German soldier dropped.

"I've wanted to do that for a very long time," Moretti muttered.

As the boat pushed away, a droning roar echoed from the horizon. Breaths caught and held as eyes turned to the sky.

Three German bombers passed overhead...flying in the direction of Stalag 31.

Chapter 35
July 27, 1943

"**W**hat the fuck…?"
Hearing the sound of planes, Skip awoke with a start and tried to scramble to his feet, looking for a gun that was not within his reach. The effort was aborted when the gunshot he had sustained shot fire through his torso, along with the unsteadiness of the craft they were in, brought him crashing across Marcella's lap. He looked up at her, startled to see her there, as the three German planes passed their position along the north shore of the river.

Marcella, stroking his hair, watched the plane too. Clara had said that the Stalag was to be bombed…and that now looked to be true, despite the destruction of the tanks. She shivered and crossed herself when she realized she might never see her home again…and that many men left in that place were about to die.

The skipper of their boat pushed the vessel to go faster.

๛*๛

There had been a tense sort of silence over the Stalag as the German soldiers left behind tried to make out what was to be done. The deaths of von Hausen, Stetcher, and Hirsch all within such a short time had left Dengler in charge, although he was trying his best to get out of the responsibility. The phone lines were down, and with only a handful of soldiers at his disposal, half of those on duty and the other half of them now sharing dinner within the mess hall, he was grateful for only a single camp to run.

A camp of men who had broken the Camp 1 gate, and then broke into Camp 2 in spite of the Germans efforts to contain them. Dengler had insisted on no more killing, but that left little means of control for the handful of Germans left behind. With no commands forthcoming, and no knowledge of when the next transport convoy was due, Dengler, standing behind what had been von Hausen's desk to stare from the window at the darkening sky, was left with his hands tied, with no idea what lay in store.

The pot of coffee percolated upon the woodstove of the mess hall as weary, confused, and demoralized soldiers gathered around it, waiting to fill their cups. It had been a troubling day, and at the moment, with no true leadership in place for the Germans who remained, their future was filled with uncertainty. Few wanted to be sent to the front. Few wanted to die so far from their families. Most wanted one simple thing.

To go home.

One of the men squatted in front of the stove, opened it, and poked through the ashes. "More wood," he said. Someone grabbed two slabs and gave them to him. He placed them into the stove, stirred the ashes again to help the new wood catch fire, and closed the stove door. Wiping his hands on his trousers, he got to his feet, reached for the coffee pot to begin serving the others. Heads turned and some of the men started for the doors as the sounds of war machines rumbled through the outside air.

A massive explosion rocked the whole of Stalag 31.

Dengler was putting the earpiece of the radio down when a drone and rumble first reached his ears. He was staring out the window still, but as it drew closer, he stepped outside to see that he was not the only one to come to see who, or what, was coming. With the gun that he had never used drawn, his heart pounding in his throat, he put one foot onto the steps to begin his descent when an explosion came from beyond the infirmary, from the mess hall. The men in Camp 1 cheered, but Dengler attributed that to the now recognizable sound of tanks at the far end of town and the aircraft overhead. After all, he was aware of the reports that the Allied forces were encroaching on the German lines in France. He would have cheered too if he had been a prisoner and believed deliverance was at hand.

There was screaming within the mess hall, soldiers scattering, some pouring out of the building with their clothing ablaze. Those Germans not in the watchtowers came to put out the fire and help their fellows, leaving the prisoners unattended. Their cheers now turned to shouts of panic when they, along with the soldiers in the watchtowers, spotted the incoming planes. Not Allied planes, but German ones. Everyone watched as the planes dropped lower, closer…and began to pepper the Stalag with bullets and bombs.

Men scattered in every direction, seeking shelter in buildings that crumbled or erupted into flames. Dengler knew at once what was happening; he yanked the keys from his belt and ran to open the main gate into the Stalag, inviting every man who could to flee to safety. Such a mass slaughter as this was going to be destroyed the last shred of loyalty he had to the Reich's cause. German command be damned. If they were going to target their own soldiers, then he was going to make sure that even the prisoners had a chance at freedom and life.

❧*❧

Philippe, on the porch of the inn, was the first in Ste Marie to hear, and then see, the planes flying overhead, the German tanks that appeared in the village streets. There was no need to sound an alarm as the noise was enough to draw every citizen from their homes and businesses. The Germans within the tanks and planes were prepared to ignore the villagers, as their orders only indicated destroying the Stalag, but as the last tank came into sight, those soldiers discovered how well armed the citizens of Ste Marie were…and how determined they were to protect not just themselves but the prisoners within Stalag 31 as well.

At the confluence of the Vilaine and Canut, all eyes turned west, and as ears strained to hear the inevitable, billows of smoke began to rise above the distant treetops.

As the key slipped into the lock at the gate between the German section of the camp and the rest of Stalag 31, the planes turned for their second pass.

"Come on, damn it!" Vic shouted as he and other men pushed and rattled at the main gate, trying to strain the metal to the point of breaking. "Open the goddamn gate!" Dengler had made it through the first entry and was trying to push his way through the crowd to the main postern. Leonard grabbed his arm and yanked him along, shoved Vic aside, and held the Scot back so that the doctor could unlock this lock as well. The key slid in, but as he began to turn it, bullets from above ripped through the crowd of pushing men, biting through Dengler's chest cleanly through into Leonard behind him. The doctor slumped toward the gate, the lock still in his hand, while Leonard was thrown backward into the men crowded around him, some who also fell under the assault. Others ran. Vic, however, his life saved when Leonard pushed him aside, scrambled to his feet and struggled to get the lock and key out of Dengler's hand. He turned it, and with one kick the gate swung open.

"Come on!" he cried, leading the charge out of Camp 1, ignoring the Germans who were now too intent on saving their own lives to care about the escaping prisoners.

The ferocious bite of the tank smashed into the wall behind Philippe, pitching him forward beneath the rubble and dust, knocking the gun from his hand. More than one building now bore the brunt of the tank assault. Across the street, Louis yelled in rage and led a charge of men straight at the offending metal monster. Its hatch opened and one of its occupants popped out to spray machine gun fire into the crowd on Philippe's side of the street. That distraction gave Louis and his handful of followers the chance to reach the tank and drop sparking dynamite into the hatch. It was the bravest thing he had done to date, followed rapidly by thrusting a knife into the side of the soldier with the machine gun. "This is for my son!" he cried...as the soldier, shocked by the pain, spun around, his finger locked on the trigger so that bullets sprayed in every direction.

Knocked back by the explosion within and the bullets that ripped across his chest and throat, Louis fell backward to the ground, amidst the other Ste Marie wounded and dead. Behind where he fell, Sister Isabelle took a single shot with the hunting rifle Philippe kept in the inn, and caught the German in the head so that he slumped over the side of the smoking, stationary tank. The only other tank still in Ste Marie's streets turned its turret in her direction...and fired.

Bonny and KC were right behind Vic, running for their lives, surrounded by others from Stalag 31 who had managed to reach the gate. Their steps faltered, however, as they came face to face with two tanks. Not the Allied tanks they had hoped for, but German Tigers. Sparks and Clara had been right. The threat of bombing was intended to totally eradicate Stalag 31. As the first turret began to turn towards them, someone shouted, "Run!" and men scattered.

Farmer grabbed Taffy's hand, the older man struggling to keep up, and pulled him along, shouting encouragement as they ran.

The air bellowed. The earth shook. Debris pelted Farmer and he looked back. There was only an arm in his hand now; Taffy was nowhere to be seen. KC had fallen beside Bonny, but the Padre kept running as the planes came around again. Everyone was too afraid to look behind them now.

Ordinance rained from the sky. Whatever its intended target, the first bomb landed squarely upon the German tank, but there was no one there to see it, or to witness the collapse of building after building of the tiny, ancient village. Any survivors in Ste Marie were either buried in rubble or had taken cover. As the bombs continued to fall, only the proud church that stood apart from the town remained untouched...

"Let me out!" shouted Ronny again, banging on the Cooler door. Farmer had unlocked the door earlier, though Ronny had chosen to remain within, to not rouse German suspicion, until the time came for escape or the night whistle called. Now, however, the shifting of the structure due to the barrage the camp was taking had caused the door to jam so that he could not force it open. Through the tiny window, he could see little of what was happening, but he could hear it, and feel it. "Someone...!"

"I'm trying, damn it," shouted Ollie, trying to use Dengler's keys and his strength, in addition to Ronny's to force open the door.

The explosions were getting nearer.

"Hurry up, damn you..."

Shrapnel and debris from a mortar shell ripped through the Cooler walls, burying Ronny and Ollie where they stood as the entire building collapsed,

...and soon enough, even the ancient church towers succumbed to the power of the German air assault.

❧Suspicion's Gate❧

Chapter 36
July 27, 1943

"**G**od help them…" murmured Moretti as he and the others stood at the rear of the boat, watching the world fall away behind them. Wagner's head was bowed, but his eyes were upturned to the horizon to watch, while Jamie stood with his arms around the weeping Zaline as the distant smoke turn to flames. Beside her, Clara watched with a cold, blank expression, even though Sparks stood nearby to offer comfort if she wanted it. But there was no comfort to be had as they watched the cloud over Ste Marie grow thicker, darker. Each imagined they could hear, over the sounds of explosions and mortar fire, the screaming of the wounded, the dying, and the clatter of metal to earth as the great church bell, which had rung time and again as the concussions in the air rocked her in place, fell from its tower to be forever silenced.

"God help them all."

≈Suspicion's Gate≈

Epilogue

R obbie looked at Clara as he held open the van door for Zaline to get into the vehicle. Pensee and Mila were already inside. Though Pensee had visited the memorials and her father's grave near the ruined church, Mila remained in the van with her daughter the entire time they had been in the vicinity of what had once been the village of Ste Marie sur Canut. He could not blame her for that; most of the memories this place held for her were not pleasant ones. Her mother and father's names had been placed on the the memorial erected here, but she had not gone to see it. She was not yet ready for such reminders. Perhaps she would never be ready. He was not sure why she had come, except perhaps because Zaline and Jamie had asked her to. She certainly had no desire to go to their next destination but it seemed she preferred the car ride over the possibility of remaining here for a while longer with Clara.

He hated leaving Clara behind, squatting near the marker upon which the names of Ste Marie's dead were inscribed. Stasio Arnaud's name, however, was not there. His grave was marked separately, as Clara wished it, and because she was partially funding these memorials, her wishes had been respected. It was at his grave that she knelt now, her hands brushing away dust and debris from the stone with care, her shoulders trembling with the unresolved grief that came from never having had the chance to say goodbye.

It still touched Robbie that Philippe had chosen to honor her wish and collaborated with her to construct these memorials. It was indicative of how special and important Clara had been to the people of Ste Marie.

Behind her, Stasio Junior, barely ten years old, stood quietly, his small hands clasping a bouquet of flowers, watching his mother cry over his father's grave. Of course, he had never met the man; Robbie was the only father he had ever known. But Robbie had made it a point, as Clara wished, of teaching the boy just how vital his father had been to so many people during the war. Little Stasio knew the stories of the man so well that it was as if he had known the man he had never seen. All he had was a handful of pictures Zaline had managed to save.

These visits to Ste Marie were as important to him as they were to his mother.

"Robbie?"

He responded to Jamie's voice by getting into the van, noting as he did so that Philippe Cuvier was lumbering across the empty field to join Clara at the graveside. That she would not be alone there made Robbie feel better, so he started the engine, backed the van out of the grove, and turned it towards the road. He would be back for Clara and Stasio later.

Philippe waved at them.

Jamie waved back.

Robbie kept his eyes on the road.

❧*❧

"Eleven years…" the Canadian muttered, watching the ruins of Ste Marie and the field where Stalag 31 had once stood pass outside his window.

There had been little left of the village, little the handful of survivors had felt worth rebuilding and little most of the living could afford to rebuild. Other than the ruined hulks of stone structures that had endured the ravages of time, only the three memorials stood upon the line that had been the border between Stalag 31 and the Arnaud farm. Philippe had the farm now, the only one Clara and Zaline had felt worthy of claiming it after the war. He was one of the few people around for miles.

"You've done good here, Robbie" Zaline murmured, squeezing Jamie's hand.

"It was all her doing…her and Philippe. I only offered support and finances…"

"Mighty generous of you. My father would have appreciated it," added Jamie.

Robbie shrugged after a glance in the rearview mirror. "It was worth it. Each year it gets a little better for her, now that this is here. Maybe…in time…"

"She'll be fine," Pensee said quietly, clasping Robbie's shoulder.

Robbie only nodded.

The silence was awkward as the van bumped down the now mostly unused road along the river. They finally reached pavement, and as they traveled, the young Jennifer, only two years old, sang softly to herself. Mila watched out the window, her expression dour. Jamie, who sat in the front alongside Robbie, looked back at his wife; Zaline shrugged and sighed. They had done their best to provide a home for Mila, to raise her and provide for her the things her parents would have wanted, but sometimes it seemed that the young woman was somewhere far away.

With the car now on smoother terrain, Zaline leaned forward between the two men and asked, "How are the kids?"

Robbie smiled in spite of himself. "Robert's doing exceptionally well in school; he and Marcus can't seem to stay out of mischief though. Fortunately, they adore Lizzie. It makes it easier to handle them all."

"You certainly have your hands full," she chuckled.

Jamie turned sideways. "And the others? You've kept in touch?"

"Yeah…I keep hoping to get all of us together, but it's proving harder than I'd hoped." He was quiet for several moments as he waited at a stop sign to turn right towards the river. "Newt's the same…still running real estate in Sydney. Haven't heard from Paddy in a while, but last I knew he and Bonny were doing missionary work in Africa, so they're not easy to reach. Renz's law practice is thriving, and he's due to be a grandfather any time now. Conrad's a grocer of all things…and doing quite the business as I hear it. Ronny's still flying, Vic's still coaching and Farmer's a U.S. senator…elected last month."

"I'll be damned." Breathed Jamie. He had not seen any of those men since leaving Ste Marie, and he was still surprised at how many of those faces he had lived side by side with in those dark days were alive. He had not seen Robbie before today either, but he had kept in touch because of the relationship their wives shared and through Robbie, he could keep track of those he had lived and bled beside in those long months of captivity.

If only his father was one of them.

"And Dusty?" Zaline asked, knowing that Jamie would not speak the man's name though he wanted to know.

Robbie sighed. "Still nothing. We're looking…but so far…" His raw voice trailed into silence and it took considerable effort to will his white knuckles on the steering wheel to relax. Why the missing

Brit caused him so much pain, he was not sure. Maybe it was because in his gut he continued to cling to the hope that the man was alive. Maybe it was because, out of all the residents of Barracks J, Harry Miller was the one man unaccounted for.

The only loose end that refused to be tied off.

The spring farm country began to give way to thickening forest, the pave road turning to dirt again that grew rougher with each passing landmark. Jamie, in the stillness of the bouncing van, finally asked the question he had put off all day. He did not think he would get through what lay ahead if he did not ask. "How is he?"

Robbie sighed. "Not good. As I said when I called, whatever's eating at him has got him by the throat. All he does is sit in that chair. Marcella can't even reach him anymore..."

Jamie squinted as he watched the road. A series of images passed through his head, many of them negative. All of the errors in judgment that Skip could possibly be kicking himself for, things that made him want to give up...including Dusty's loss and the choice to leave George Campbell behind. That matter, however, was one that Jamie had long ago concluded had not been an error in judgment. If not for Skip's perseverance, and George urging his son to go on, Jamie might be dead too.

"I mean...what's he like? As a man? Has he changed?"

The corners of Robbie's lips tried to tug into a smile. "Not so much...until recently. He can still be the same pompous bastard he was...though I think he's gonna be pleased to see you. He's talked about you a lot lately...I think he's given up living and is searching for something to hold on to."

Jamie looked at Zaline as the Scot stopped talking lest the emotion in his voice spill over into tears.

Zaline asked, "You see them a lot then?"

In the seat beside her, little Jenny asked, "We almost there?"

"Hush, Jenny...you're interrupting your grandmother," Mila scolded. It was the only time she had turned away from the window, although Jamie judged by her haunted expression that she had been listening to their conversation.

It was the first time Robbie had heard her speak since the initial greeting that morning.

"Tired of riding, mummy..."

Zaline looked at Mila as if to suggest that she should have allowed the child to get out of the vehicle when they stopped in Ste

Marie. All she said, however, was directed at the little blonde girl. "We will be there soon, darling."

Mila looked away without blinking.

The van slowed as the road narrowed and the forest thickened. Jamie stopped toying with his sleeve and spoke again. "You've seen him recently?" It had been years since Zaline had been able to see her sister, but they had kept in touch through Clara. Jamie, on the other hand, had not kept in touch with Skip. Their parting had been awkward and painful, and Jamie could never decide what he should say if he spoke to Skip again.

Now, however, he felt the time had come to put the past to rest.

"Just after Christmas. We bring the kids down every chance we get...he really gets on well with them, surprisingly." Given the Aussie's overall gruff demeanor, that was, Jamie admitted, surprising indeed. "And we call a lot."

The melancholy in his voice brought a long silent pause and then the van turned up another rutty road. Jamie clutched the dashboard, his knuckles paling, but soon the vehicle bumped to a stop.

"We're here."

Jamie exhaled as if he had been sucker punched.

Beyond the trees at the end of the uneven drive was a small, well-kept home. Wood and whitewash, faded in places but still neat and clean, with well-groomed flowers in the window boxes and a white rocker upon the porch. There were stairs there, white and strong, but also a ramp, whose railings had not been painted and were dark with weather. Upon the porch was a small table with its matching wicker chair, and it was there the woman sat, peeling potatoes in the afternoon sun.

Though it had been eleven years, Zaline knew her sister at once, and Marcella, having expected their arrival, stood from the table after pushing the potatoes aside, and ran down the steps with her arms open in greeting.

Before Robbie turned the engine off, Zaline had the van door thrown open and raced to tearfully embrace her long lost little sister. Until Robbie and Clara had found the two still living in France, Zaline had feared her sister to be dead, and Marcella had no way of knowing what had become of her sister, or their father, or Clara.

Jamie waited for the engine to still before stepping out after his wife. He opened the door for Mila, scooped little Jenny into his arms, and then set her down on the grass to help her mother from the van. From behind the house, a dog barked. Mila emphatically shook her head, refusing to leave the safety of the van. At the sight of the thick-coated brown and white dog that loped into view, barking though its tail wagged in a friendly manner. Jenny squealed with delight and ran after the animal.

"Jenny!" Mila cried, her child running away being enough to bring her out.

Her call came at the same moment as a gruffer, grumpier voice shouted, "Belle…shut up!" Jamie and Robbie, standing side by side, looked at one another. Eleven years may have passed, but there was no mistaking that tone or voice. Jamie's eyes clouded with tears.

In response to her master's voice, the dog turned and scurried back to where it had come. Little Jenny followed.

"Jennifer!" Now Mila was not only fearful of the strange dog, but even more so of the voice that had summoned it.

The child darted around the corner of the small house and stopped abruptly, having heard the voice but not expecting to find anyone here until she saw him. Near the back corner of the house, seated in a wheelchair but still bent over a broken rake he was trying to repair, was a scruffy, frumpy man. The dog stopped beside the wheelchair and he reached absently to scratch the animal's ear when the little girl first saw him.

She stared with a child's curiosity, uncertain but not truly frightened.

Skip lifted his head, staring back at her as if seeing a ghost. He knew his eyesight was deteriorating, but this still could not be.

"Mila?"

That was impossible. That had been too many years ago, and Mila had been older than this the last time he had seen her. She would be a grown woman by now if she had lived.

The child took a step, drawn by the dog's wagging tail, but her progress was halted by her mother's arms suddenly wrapped around her. Jenny looked up at her mother, not understanding the flashes of emotion that bled from one to another on the woman's face.

Skip stared.

She was dead.

Dead at his hand.

Mila did not look at her daughter. She could not tear her eyes away from the man who, in her memory, had once tried to kill her mother…and had, the second time, succeeded.

Skip's gaze traveled from mother to daughter and back again.

Dead at his hand. Or was she?

He had not actually examined the woman after he removed the knife blade, but had assumed, from the placement of the injury and the blood loss he had seen, that she had died. But maybe Jamie had saved her. Maybe Jennifer von Hausen had lived.

During the long years since that dreadful day, Skip had clung to the belief that her death could have been avoided, despite the fact that everything he had seen in her eyes that day had said differently. It was something that, as far as he knew, no one else had seen. No one would ever believe that Jennifer had wanted to die, least of all her daughter.

He began to tremble. He blinked. He tried to swallow the fear, the anger, and the shame. He coughed anxiously.

The rake dropped from his lap.

More footsteps brought his wife and her sister and another young woman around the corner of the house; Skip felt ambushed, trapped. Something began to wiggle in his gut. Sparks appeared, a familiar, calm, reassuring face, and he remembered the visit scheduled today. But he had not expected these women…or the face of a man he had thought never to see again.

Jamie Campbell.

The Canadian's gaze was all-encompassing, taking in both the man's medical condition as well as his apparent mental and emotional frame of mind. Finally, he met the man's gaze.

Skip's mouth trembled.

Jamie was drawn forward by what he saw in the other man's eyes. Too many burdens that the Aussie had always tried, or been made, to carry alone. Too many questions and unresolved issues that had been left between them. Too much stubbornness and bitterness and the solitude that would not allow him to move on with his life and find peace.

But in Jamie's eyes, shame and guilt for things done in wartime had no place here. No place in their lives any longer.

Mila saw it too and admitted to herself the one truth she had resisted accepting over the years. Skip had not intended to kill her mother. Jennifer von Hausen had chosen to step into the line of fire, had chosen to remain in Ste Marie, to die with her husband, just as she had always promised Hans she would do. Despite her faults, and his, Jennifer had loved her husband and had refused to leave France without him. She had not known how to live without him beside her. She had not had the fortitude to carry on, not even for her daughter's sake. Mila had never truly understood her mother's actions, her choices, but she realized now that she no longer needed to understand. It was time to respect the decisions the woman had made and the sacrifices that had gone along with them. It was time to let her mother go.

For the moment, the women were forgotten. Hesitantly, Jamie reached for Skip's hand. They had been comrades once, friends, until so much about that poisoned place had come between them. Had all of that been lost behind the gates of suspicion where they had lived?

Skip just as reluctantly accepted the offered hand, and found himself pulled into Jamie's tight embrace. There was no shame in it, or in the tears that both men shed upon the other's strong shoulders. Eyes closed, both men wept.

Release.

When Skip opened his eyes again, he looked directly at Mila and offered his hand.

And when little Jennifer tugged free of her mother's grasp and went to the wheelchair to take that hand, Mila did not attempt to stop her. She followed, her mouth trembling, and clasped both hands between hers.

It was time to let the past go.

All of it.

The End

About the Author

Unsatisfied with 'how the story ends' as a young reader, Tamara took on the challenge of crafting endings to the tales of others to better suit her vision of the world. That desire to mold reality into how she imagined it should be gave birth to a life-long fascination with the written word, and its capacity, particularly through realms of fantasy and science fiction, to foster an understanding of the people, events, thoughts and emotions that make us who we are.

A long-time resident of Clearlake, California, after a life that took her back and forth across the country, Tamara is owned by a pack of papillions, a pride of cats, and an eclectic arsenal of films she enjoys in her off-moments.

Suspicion's Gate is Tamara's third novel.

Lightning Source UK Ltd.
Milton Keynes UK
UKHW02f1847210918
329323UK00014B/1075/P